★

If a middle-aged, out-of-condition, overweight P.I. picks up an eight-stone woman and tries to run along a narrow burning beam in dense smoke that reduces visibility to nil and breathing to less, how does someone explain to his pet cat, Whitey, why he never came home again?

Answer: not applicable. Man would have to be mad to try it.

Such was the verdict of rational thought. But Joe was a slow thinker and he'd been up and running before good old rational thought had even got out of its blocks. The woman was in his arms. He hit the slope of the roof at the point where he'd already removed the slates to make a breathing hole, erupted into the cold Welsh night like a comet, went straight over the edge, crash-landed on the lean-to roof, bounced twice, caught the edge of the water butt with his heels, twisted in the air to give the woman the soft landing, and found himself lying on the blessed ground, looking up at a sky so packed with stars, he felt he was trembling on the brink of eternity.

★

"...one of today's best British mystery writers."

—Booklist

Previously published Worldwide Mystery titles by
REGINALD HILL

BLOOD SYMPATHY
BORN GUILTY
KILLING THE LAWYERS

REGINALD HILL

SINGING THE SADNESS

WORLDWIDE®

TORONTO • NEW YORK • LONDON
AMSTERDAM • PARIS • SYDNEY • HAMBURG
STOCKHOLM • ATHENS • TOKYO • MILAN
MADRID • WARSAW • BUDAPEST • AUCKLAND

SINGING THE SADNESS

A Worldwide Mystery/January 2001

First published by St. Martin's Press, Incorporated.

ISBN 0-373-26371-6

Printed In U.S.A.

For
POLLY
without whose contribution
this book would have been finished
a great deal sooner

ONE

THE BOYLING CORNER Chapel Choir sped across the heart of England like a nest of singing birds and as they crossed the Welsh border there was a spontaneous outburst of 'We'll Keep a Welcome in the Hillsides'. Not even when the coach ground to a halt half an hour or so later in a puff of smoke dark enough to hide a demon king did their spirits sink.

Not at first anyway.

'No sweat,' assured their driver, Merv Golightly, whose broad smile and cheerful manner had been honed at the wheel of a Luton taxi. 'We're only half an hour away and I'll fix this in a jiffy.'

Several jiffies later, Joe Sixsmith got out and strolled round to join Merv at the open bonnet. The two of them had been workmates at Robco Engineering of Luton till the economic miracle workers of the sick eighties had told them to take up their P45s and walk. Joe's years of working at a lathe and on a much-loved, much-regretted Morris Oxford, had left him with a high degree of mechanical expertise, but Merv's years of driving a fork-lift truck had never taken him beyond the bang-it-with-a-spanner school of repair.

The spanner was in Merv's hand now, the same outsize length of metal nicknamed Percy which he kept beneath his taxi seat for those situations which neither his cheerful manner nor broad smile could defuse.

'Hand about, Merv,' said Joe, seeing the spanner poised menacingly. 'Let the dog see the rabbit.'

It didn't take long and it wasn't a rabbit but a dead donkey.

'Oil pump's gone,' he said. 'Merv, where'd you buy this heap of junk? At a Transport Museum boot sale?'

'Hey, I've got all the safety certs and such, you seen them,' said Merv, hurt.

This was true. Joe had insisted on seeing them soon as he heard Merv had not only extended his personal transport service to include coach hire but had put in the lowest bid for the Boyling

Corner expedition to Wales. It was Rev. Pot, pastor and choir-master, who made the final choice, but many of the choristers, led by Joe's Aunt Mirabelle, were convinced Joe had put in a fix.

'Can you patch it up?' asked Merv hopefully.

His hope was mirrored on the faces of Rev. Pot and others who'd also congregated round the bonnet.

'No way,' said Joe dolefully. 'Needs a new pump. At least. Which means it needs a garage.'

All eyes turned to the empty road ahead. There were fewer signs of life there than in Westminster on a Friday, and they'd passed no human habitation for at least ten miles.

Then Joe, with a politician's timing, let a broad smile dawn on his face and said, 'So, no problem. I'll just call up help,' and produced his mobile phone.

The effect was slightly spoilt when he couldn't get it to work till Beryl Boddington took it gently out of his hand and switched it on.

Five minutes later he was able to announce that a mechanic was on the way with the necessary part.

Aunt Mirabelle gave him a don't-think-that's-going-to-change-my-mind glower. She still regarded his post-lathe career in private investigation as a symptom of stress-induced brain fever which marriage to a good woman, plus regular attendance at chapel and the job centre, would soon cure. She'd reacted to the news that Joe had bought a mobile like a Sally Army captain catching a reformed drunk coming out of an off-licence with a brown paper parcel.

'What you need that thing for?' she'd demanded.

'For my work,' Joe explained.

'For your work? For the devil's work, you mean!'

'No, Auntie,' Joe had retorted with a rare flash of open rebellion. 'So's I can keep in touch with my clients. Not everyone in our family's got such big ears they can hear other folks' private business twenty miles off just by flapping them!'

But now she confined herself to the glower, then set about distributing the sandwiches which she'd packed, on the grounds that when you visited a foreign country, there was no telling how long before you'd be able to find something a Christian soul could eat.

It was a mild late-spring afternoon and soon the choristers were sprawled out along the rock-strewn banks of the fast-flowing stream which ran parallel to the road. Joe lay next to Beryl Boddington, who was high among the runners in his aunt's nuptial stakes. But Joe had long since come to realize that Beryl ran under no colours but her own, and now it came into his mind how very much he was enjoying his present situation. Only way it could be improved was by beaming the rest of the choir out of sight somewhere. Or failing that, moving himself and Beryl somewhere a little more private.

He sat upright and said casually, 'Thought I might take a little stroll and stretch my legs. You fancy a bit of exercise?'

She didn't answer but lay there looking up at him and smiling broadly.

'What?' he said.

'Joe Sixsmith,' she said. 'I recall you telling me you were a through and through city boy, couldn't get on with country life. Now I see why.'

'Yeah? Why?'

'It's all this fresh air, turns you into some kind of wild animal. Like a werewolf.'

'Shoot, all I said was, let's take a walk.'

'And that's all you want, Joe? A walk?'

She pouted as if disappointed and, emboldened, he said, 'That'll do for starters. So, what you say?'

'Well, I'm tempted, Joe. Only...'

'Yeah?'

'Hadn't you better be around when the breakdown truck arrives to see Merv don't get ripped off?'

Joe followed her gaze. About a mile ahead along the road a van was approaching. Who'd have thought they'd be so quick out here in the sticks? Then he glanced at his watch and saw that more than an hour had passed since he rang. He'd never make a Don Juan. A real operator would have got to work at least forty-five minutes ago.

On the other hand, a real operator probably wouldn't have enjoyed simply lying alongside Beryl in the warm sunshine the way he did.

He smiled at her and she smiled back.

'We've got all this countryside for the next three days, Joe. Plenty of time to be stretching our muscles.'

That sounded like a promise. Jauntily he made his way back to the coach.

The van bore the single word BREAKDOWN like a command, and its engine coughed asthmatically as if eager to obey.

Merv scowled and said. 'Listen to that. And *he's* coming to mend *my* machine.'

'Not to worry,' said Joe. 'Best barbers always have the worst haircuts.'

'Oh yeah?' said Merv. 'Well, if he draws in his breath sharply when he sees my engine, I'm going to hit him with Percy.'

'You'll need to aim low,' said Joe as the van halted and the driver slid out.

He was square-shaped, about five by five, with no visible neck, so that his head sat on his shoulders like a traitor's displayed on a city wall. Joe was reminded of Starbright Jones, another Welshman he'd met on a recent case, who'd been carved out of the same rough granite. The memory made him smile—he'd grown quite fond of Starbright—and the smile won an indifferent nod, or maybe it was directed at Merv's scowl, and without other greeting the man went straight to the bonnet.

There was no sharp intake of breath but there was a note of incredulity as he said, 'Just the oil pump you want me to sort out, is it?' like the Good Samaritan told that half an aspirin and a Band-aid would do.

Percy twitched and Joe said quickly, 'What else you got in mind?'

The man said, 'In alphabetical order...' and listed half a dozen areas of trouble or potential trouble. His alphabet was erratic but his diagnosis confirmed many of Joe's own fears.

'Better take a look then,' he said, interposing his body between Merv and the Welshman. 'Want a hand?'

He got a pro sneer in reply, which might have annoyed a more self-regarding man, but Joe took it in his stride and after ten minutes, when his assistance had demonstrated he was no know-it-all amateur, the man thawed a little and let it be known his name was Nye.

'Nye Garage they call me, from the job, see? Round here knowing what people do is important.'

This might have been a lure but Joe ignored it. Professionally he'd spent a lot of time experimenting with subtle techniques for getting people to talk and the sum total of his wisdom was, if a man wants to know something, best way usually is to ask.

Eventually Nye got round to it.

'Trippers, is it?' he said, glancing at the lounging choristers. 'Going to the seaside?'

'Look like trippers, do we?' said Joe grinning.

'Don't look like mountain climbers,' said Nye.

There was no gainsaying this, and Joe replied, 'We're singers. A choir. We're on our way to the Llanffugiol Choral Festival.'

He spoke with modest pride, confident of making some kind of impression. After all, this was the land of song where a good voice vied with the ability to run very fast with a pointed ball as the gift most desired from your fairy godmother.

He was disappointed. Nye looked at him blankly for a long moment. Perhaps he was deaf, thought Joe. Or tone deaf. Or maybe it was his own poor pronunciation.

'The *Llanffugiol* Choral Festival,' he said carefully, blowing out the double-L sound with a singer's breath.

'Never heard of it,' said the Welshman indifferently. 'Pass me that wrench, will you, boyo?'

Boyo, Joe had learned from Starbright, wasn't a racist put-down but a term of familiarity in Welsh-speak. He passed the wrench and would have liked to discover whether it was just the festival or Llanffugiol itself Nye hadn't heard of, which would be odd as Merv had assured them they were only half an hour's drive away. But Merv was lurking menacingly and an enquiry could have sounded like a vote of no confidence in his navigation, so Joe held his peace.

It took almost an hour for Nye to finish and another ten minutes to tot up his bill. Merv looked at it and indulged in an intake of breath so sharp that in another it would have merited and very severe whipping from Percy.

A full and frank discussion followed with Joe as arbiter. Finally forced to admit the justice of the claims, Merv produced his clincher.

'Don't carry that kind of cash,' he said, producing his wallet to demonstrate its leanness. 'Joe, we'll need a whip-round.'

Joe, imagining Aunt Mirabelle's reaction if he went to her with a collection plate, shook his head firmly.

'It's your coach, Merv,' he said.

'It's your choir,' retorted Merv.

For a moment, deadlock. Then Nye broke it by reaching forward to pluck a credit card from the open wallet.

'Plastic's fine,' he said.

On the passenger seat of his van was a credit-card machine and a camera. As Merv with ill grace signed the counterfoil, Nye snapped him, then again full face as he looked up, and finally he took a couple of the coach after cleaning the dust from the numberplate.

'Souvenirs,' he said. 'I like to remember my customers.'

'Hope that card's good, Merv,' said Joe, as they watched the van hiccup into the distance.

'Makes no matter,' said Merv evilly. ''Cos I'm going to run that squat little bastard off the road when I overtake him. Everyone aboard! Let's get this wagon train a'rolling.'

It was now early evening with the sun lipping the western hills and curls of mist patterning the surface of the stream.

'How far to go, Mr Golightly?' enquired Rev. Pot as he climbed aboard.

'Fifteen, twenty miles, maybe a little more,' said Merv vaguely.

The Reverend Percy Potemkin had not spent half a lifetime curing souls without developing a sharp ear for human vaguenesses. But he was not a man to rush to judgement. His gaze met Joe's and asked for confirmation that this lack of precision was merely a form of speech. Joe loyally gave an optimistic smile. But he knew that if his friend had a fault, it was his reluctance to admit the possibility of anything being wrong till the trout came belly up in the milk churn.

At least the engine had a sweeter sound now. Someone started a chorus of 'To Be a Pilgrim', but their hearts weren't in it and after a while most of the travellers settled down to inner contemplation or sleep.

Joe studied his information sheet. Llanffugiol, it told him, was a substantial village which in recent years had become the focal point of musical life in this area of rural Wales. This was its very first Choral Festival so there was no list of previous winners, but there was an impressive roll-call of top choirs which had been invited to take part. It was a bit less impressive if you studied the small print and worked out those which had actually accepted at the time the info sheet was sent out, but it still contained enough first-class opposition, like the German *Guttenberg Singverein,* to make this a tough competition. But Boyling Corner's triumph three years in a row at the Bed and Bucks Choriad had clearly given the chapel choir the beginnings of a national reputation which they were determined to live up to. As Rev. Pot said, 'We sing for the Lord not for glory, but if the Lord fancies a bit of glory thrown in, who are we to argue?'

Their accommodation was in the dormitories of Branddreth College, a boys' boarding school a couple of miles out of Llanffugiol. There was a sketch map showing the relation of the college to the village, but nothing to relate the area to the outside world. Written directions had been sent and these were now in Merv's possession, so all should have been straightforward, but Joe's heart misgave him when he recalled Merv's cavalier attitude to route-finding in his taxi. During daylight hours he used the sun, at night the stars, and when the weather was overcast, he fell back on instinct. 'Salmon and swallows do it every year,' he said. 'And if man's no better than fish or fowl, he's got no right to be organizing the World Cup.'

Well, it would be instinct tonight, thought Joe, glancing out of the window.

Darkness was falling fast, accelerated by the mist which had long since escaped from the river and was now printing its bloomy patterns on the outside of the glass.

Merv's threat to the wellbeing of Nye Garage had proved empty as, despite the apparent debility of his van, they hadn't overtaken it. Indeed, they hadn't seen anybody to overtake or be overtaken by for over an hour, which was just as well as the roads seemed to be getting narrower and narrower.

Suddenly the coach halted. In the headlights through the mist it was just possible to see a triple parting of the ways. There was a signpost, and Joe's heart, always a buoyant organ, rose sharply as he made out the letters *Llan.* Merv got out with his flashlight to take a closer look and Joe joined him. It was crash-dive time again. True, each of the three arms pointed to somewhere beginning with *Llan* but none of them was Llanffugiol.

'Merv, don't you think it's time to look at a map?'

'Been looking at a sodding map for the past half-hour,' said Merv, like an atheist admitting to prayer. 'Trouble is, none of the funny names on the sodding map match any of the funny names on these sodding signposts!'

'What you going to do then?'

'Take the middle one till we reach the place mentioned then consult the natives,' he said. Then, his irrepressible optimism returning, he added, 'Maybe there'll be a pub!'

He climbed back in the coach and called, 'Not long now, folks.'

'So he knows where we are?' said Beryl as Joe returned to his seat.

'Don't think so,' said Joe.

'Don't think so? Joe, isn't it time you got on that phone of yours and rang someone to ask for directions?'

'Yeah, maybe. Only you can't ask for directions less'n you know where you are. Soon as we reach this village we're heading for, I'll give it a go.'

But no village appeared. The coach was now full of anxious and mutinous muttering. Rev. Pot went up the aisle and started talking to Merv. Joe knew it was strictly none of his business, but an accusatory glance from Aunt Mirabelle sent him to join the debate, which was getting so heated that Merv brought the bus to a halt in order to bring both arms to the discussion.

'Well, whose fault is it, then?' Rev. Pot was demanding. 'You're the driver.'

'That's right, I'm the driver. I just follow directions. You know so much, why don't you tell me where to go, Reverend?'

'If I wasn't a man of the cloth, I might just do that, brother,' thundered Rev. Pot.

Out of the corner of his eye, Joe thought he glimpsed a light moving way to his left. He blinked. Yes, there it was. Looked like a single headlight. On a tractor maybe. Some farmer out working late. Maybe some crops were best gathered at night. Joe was a little vague on matters agricultural.

Joe turned to the disputants and said, 'Why don't we ask that guy?'

'What guy?'

'That guy...where's he gone?'

The light had vanished.

'You seeing things now, Joe?' said Merv sceptically.

'No, I'm not. I'll go talk to him.'

He grabbed the flashlight Merv carried under the dash and got out of the coach. It was so dark and alien out there, he felt like he'd just been beamed down from the *Enterprise.* Hastily he switched on his light. That was better. Still alien but not so dark. There was a gate into the field where he'd seen the light. He unlatched it and stepped into what felt like a bog. Did the Welsh grow rice? He shone the torch down and saw it was a pungent mixture of mud and cow dung.

'Oh shoot,' he said. But he wasn't going to retreat. He reasoned all the farmer had done was switch off his light and engine till the coach went on its way. Reason? Maybe he was shy.

He aimed the beam forward and squinted along it. Nothing but its light reflected from the drifting mist wraiths. Then his straining eyes glimpsed something more solid. A shape. A sort of vehicle shape. He'd been right.

He began to move forward. As he got nearer he saw that it wasn't a tractor after all, but one of those farm buggies with the big tyres. But before he could take in any detail, the headlight blossomed again, full in his face, dazzling.

'Hi there,' he called, shielding his eyes. 'Sorry to trouble you but we're a bit lost. Wondered if you could give us some directions.'

Silence. Then a muffled voice said, 'Where to?'

'Place called Llanffugiol,' said Joe. 'Where the Choir Festival is.'

More silence.

'Never heard of it,' said the voice.

The buggy's engine burst into life and it started moving forward. For a second, Joe thought it was going to go straight over him, then it swung away in a semicircle and bounced off into the mist.

He raised his flashlight and for a second caught the driver's back full in its beam. Long narrow body in a black fleecy jacket. Matching narrow head, bald or close-shaven, could have passed for that guy who played the King of Siam in the old musical. Maybe I should've tried singing 'Getting to Know You', thought Joe.

Then the mist closed behind him.

Joe returned to the coach. He tried to clean his shoes on the grass verge, but the smell of the countryside came in with him and he didn't have any good news to compensate.

Merv rolled his eyes heavenwards as if the farmer's response was Joe's fault, engaged gear noisily and set the coach rolling forward along the narrow road once more.

Even Rev. Pot seemed to have forgotten his duty of Christian charity.

'Now that's real helpful, Joe,' he said sarcastically. 'So what's your guess? I mean, just how many miles away do you think we are if folk round here haven't even heard of the place?'

'Half a mile's a long way in the country,' said Joe, his anti-rural prejudices now in full cry. 'These natives probably never been out of their own village.'

Rev. Pot gave him a glance which had he been in the exorcism business would have cast Joe back into the outer darkness, no problem.

Then Merv said, 'Hang about. Look, that has to be civilization.'

He was looking ahead. The mist was of the ground-clinging variety which occasionally permitted glimpses of treetops while their bases were hidden at ten paces. Joe saw what had caught Merv's eye. There was a distinct glow in the sky, the kind of light which could only come from a substantial settlement.

The road ahead rose steeply and as the coach laboured up it, the mist began to fall away behind and the glow increased. Then they reached the crest and saw its source was much closer than they'd imagined.

Far from being a substantial settlement, it was a solitary house. And the reason it was casting such light was it was on fire.

Merv ran the coach through an open gate and came to a halt some thirty yards from the building. Joe got out. Even from this distance he could feel the heat.

The others crowded round him.

It wasn't his charisma that attracted them, it was his phone.

'Better ring for help,' said Beryl.

He pulled out the mobile. Someone said, 'You see that?' and pointed.

On the side of a small outbuilding someone had sprayed the words, ENGLISH GO HOME!

'This the welcome they keep in the hillside?' said Merv.

Joe stabbed 999.

'Shoot,' he said. 'Not getting anything.'

'Wouldn't say that,' said Merv. 'Best service I've ever seen.'

A car had come up behind the bus at speed and a uniformed police sergeant got out and came running to join them. Had a look of that Welsh movie actor who kept on getting married to Liz Taylor, thought Joe. The voice too.

'What the hell's going on here?' he demanded.

Merv, never one to miss the chance of sending up a copper, said, 'Could be a millennium bonfire, got the dates wrong.'

The cop ignored him. His face expressed a strange mixture of anger and bafflement. Might look like Richard Burton but he was far from word perfect in his role, which was to take charge of the situation, thought Joe. He punched 999 once more.

Beryl said, 'Joe, have you forgotten to switch on again?'

Now the cop found his lines.

'Leave this to me,' he snapped. 'And move back, will you? Now!'

He ran back to his car, presumably to call up help.

Joe examined his phone. Beryl was right. Again. He smiled sheepishly at her. He didn't mind being wrong. You got used to it. And it was nice that now he could relax and enjoy the fire without feeling he had to do anything about it.

Then Beryl screamed, 'Joe, there's someone in there!'

And looking up along the line indicated by her pointing finger, Joe saw a black outline of a human figure against the dark-red glow in one of the upstairs windows.

TWO

IF BERYL HADN'T prefaced her cry with *Joe!* he might not have done it.

And if he'd taken thought, he certainly wouldn't have done it, not because thought would have brought self-interest into play and there was a presumably fully paid-up public servant in calling distance, but simply because for Joe problem-solving by the cerebral route usually involved a paper and pencil and two pints of Guinness.

But pausing only to thrust the phone into Beryl's hand, he'd set off running around the back of the house before he'd had time to work out by reason alone that just because the front of the house was an inferno didn't mean the back was burning fiercely too.

It wasn't. Not yet. At least not upstairs, though the flicker of the flames was clearly visible through the ground-floor windows. Meaning it was pointless going in at that level.

Against the rear wall stood a lean-to wash house with a sloping roof angling up to a first-floor window. There was a large aluminium water butt under the wash house downspout. With difficulty Joe clambered on it and used it as a step up on to the roof.

Here he paused. Through the chill night air he could feel draughts of heat drifting from the house. Must be hot as hell in there. He looked down into the water butt. From the black mirror of the water's surface, cold-eyed stars stared back at him.

Again, no thought. Just a deep breath, then he crouched down and slid off the roof.

Spring might be bursting out all over but winter was still lurking here. He shot out like a missile from a nuclear sub and found himself back on top of the lean-to with no recollection of how he'd got there.

Dripping water from every orifice, he knelt on the slates, looking up at the first-floor window. A taller man could easily have reached the sill by stretching out his arm, but Joe wasn't a taller man. In fact, he was a good inch shorter than Beryl Boddington, and when she wore her nurse's cap, he felt a good foot shorter. But uniforms generally had that effect on him.

He tried to scramble up the roof. It was like being a squirrel in a wheel. The slates started sliding under his knees so that he had to scramble even faster just to stay on the spot. Much more of this and he was going to be back in the water butt. He flung himself forward, caught at the lip of the sill with the tips of his fingers, and got just enough purchase to draw himself up.

The window was open, which was good. It was also very small, which was bad. For while no man by taking thought can add one cubit to his stature, any man by taking the Great British Breakfast and lunching regularly on cheeseburgers with double chips can add a couple to his girth.

There was a moment when he thought he was stuck and he tried to reconcile himself to the prospect of having his head toasted crisp while his legs kicked wildly in the chilly air. Far from composing himself, the notion made him struggle so violently, he erupted through the window like a cork from a bottle and found himself lying on a rug in a small but nicely furnished bedroom.

He felt beneath the rug. The floorboards felt warm but still well this side of combustion. The closed door was not so promising. It felt definitely hot to the touch and he'd seen enough disaster movies to know that opening it could be like throwing a canful of paraffin on to a bonfire.

But having got so far, he couldn't just retreat. Could he?

He looked up for inspiration.

And found himself looking at a small trap door in the ceiling.

Fortunately, like most old farmhouses this one had been built for sixteenth-century dwarves, and standing on a chest of drawers elevated him right to the low ceiling.

The trap was a tight fit. As he pushed up with all his strength, it occurred to him that if the flames had got into the attic via the front bedrooms, this too could produce the can of paraffin effect.

Then all at once it gave way and he was standing with his head in the roof space, and it wasn't being burnt off.

But there was smoke up here. It caught at his throat and made him cough in a manner which would have had Rev. Pot glaring. In the Rev.'s eyes, all ailments which affected the larynx were self-induced and totally undeserving of sympathy.

He ducked his head back into the bedroom, pulled off his sodden jacket and draped it over his head. Then he took a deep breath of air and dragged himself through the narrow gap into the attic.

It was unboarded so he had to lie flat across a couple of beams till his eyesight adjusted. Something scuttled over his outstretched arm. Mouse, or maybe a rat, getting the message there was trouble on the way and looking for an exit. He hoped it made it.

He rose to his feet and tore a couple of slates out of the roof. Air might feed fire but it also fed humans and anyway it was good to take a last look at the starry sky. He edited out *last,* took a deep breath and started moving forward.

Lack of height was now an advantage. If he'd been built like Arnie Schwarzenegger he'd have been bent double. On the other hand, he guessed the poor devil trapped in the fire would probably have preferred even a contorted Arnie.

Where he was moving to he didn't know. What he needed was

a plan. Break through the ceiling below him was an option. He considered it. Probably go up like a Roman Candle as the fire funnelled through the hole, and in any case it only made sense if he had some idea where the trapped man was situated.

Which, he realized, he might have.

There was a water tank up ahead. Not very big, looked like the header tank for a shower, and the water in it was bubbling like the shower was switched on. Meaning maybe the trapped man had sought refuge here from the flames.

He checked the fall of the pipes. Chances were they went straight down into the shower room. He touched the plasterboard around them. Still cool.

He raised his right foot and stamped. The plasterboard cracked. He stamped again, harder. His left foot slipped off the narrow beam, his whole body hit the floor and he went through the ceiling in an avalanche of dust and plaster. And water.

He landed soft and noisy. The softness was a human body. The noise was the human whose body it was, shrieking.

He'd have felt please with himself if there'd been time. It *was* a shower room and the trapped man *had* sought refuge here. Only it wasn't a man. It was a young woman. He knew that because she was naked.

She was in a bad way. She'd probably breathed in too much of the smoke which was gradually filling the cubicle for anything but incoherent shrieks to come out. Her arms were gashed like she'd pushed them through a windowpane, and her face and body were heat-blistered, but worst of all was her left leg which was both burnt and torn. Went through a burning floorboard, he guessed. If she'd headed for the back of the house she might have made it the way he'd come in. Instead she'd headed into the shower, *back* into the shower most likely, which would explain both why she had no clothes on and why she hadn't heard any noise as the fire took a hold below.

Shoot, here he was thinking like a detective when what he should be doing was thinking like big Arnie. The heat in here was growing by the second and it couldn't be long before the flames came licking through and all that the rapidly diminishing flow of water would do was let them boil before they burnt.

He said, 'We've got to get out. Can you move at all?'

Her eyes struggled to focus. They were grey and he could see that her face, even though blistered, was the face of a pretty girl, late teens maybe.

The eyes had got him now. They registered puzzlement for a moment. Couldn't blame her. Even if he had been Arnie, she'd still have wondered where the shoot he came from.

He said, 'I've come down from the attic. We've got to get back up there. Are you ready?'

Stupid question. Her gaze went up to the hole in the ceiling then back to his face. She nodded. He could see that even that movement caused pain. He knew there was worse to come and he guessed she knew it too.

He stood up and pulled her upright with him. She let out what was a shriek in any language but she wasn't a deadweight, not quite. She was giving what help she could. He looked up at the hole into the attic. Even with munchkin-level ceilings, this was going to be the impossible side of difficult. What he needed was a ladder. He looked down. Best he could find was a low plastic stool, presumably for Arnie-sized showerers to sit on so they didn't bang their heads. He propped the woman up against the wall, which was getting hotter by the second. Then he squatted down, positioned the stool, thrust his head between her legs from behind, took her weight on his shoulders and stood upright like a weight-lifter doing a lift-and-press.

He presumed she shrieked some more but he couldn't hear for the sound of the blood drumming in his ears, or maybe it was the fire raging beyond the wall.

'Try to pull yourself up,' he yelled.

He didn't know if she could hear or, if she could, whether she'd have the strength or the will to obey.

But she was brave, braver than he guessed he'd have been in like circumstances. And she had the resilience of youth. He felt her body move, and he stepped up on to the stool and grabbed her thighs in his hands and thrust upwards with all his might.

There was a moment when he thought she was stuck, and all his strength was gone, and there was nothing to do but subside into the cubicle and pray they suffocated before the flames got to them.

Then suddenly she was through, and the weight was off Joe's shoulders.

'Don't come off the beams!' he yelled, easing her legs through the hole.

Now it was his turn. He reached up, took a strong grip on the beams on either side of the hole, and hoisted himself through with the fluency of an Olympic gymnast on the parallel bars.

Gold medal? he thought. Piece of cake. All you need's a fire under your bum.

But there was no time for the National Anthem. With a series of cracks like an old sailing ship taking a broadside, the attic floor burst open at half a dozen points and tongues of flame came shooting through to lick greedily at the ancient beams.

Suddenly Joe was back in his childhood schoolroom. *If a nine-inch beam burns at one cubic inch every five seconds, how long will it be before the house collapses in on itself?* Answer: doesn't matter 'cos you'll have suffocated long before that.

OK, another problem. (Shoot! I must be dying. My life flashing before me, like they say in the books.) *If a middle-aged, out-of-condition, overweight PI picks up an eight-stone woman and tries to run along a narrow burning beam in dense smoke which reduces visibility to nil and breathing to less, how does someone explain to his pet cat, Whitey, why he never came home again?*

Answer: not applicable. Man would have to be mad to try it. Man would have to be very stupid indeed not to work out that one life was preferable to two deaths and abandon the woman to her fate.

Such was the verdict of rational thought. But Joe was a slow thinker and he'd been up and running before good old rational thought had even got out of its blocks. The woman was in his arms. He hit the slope of the roof at the point where he'd already removed the slates to make a breathing hole, erupted into the cold Welsh night like a comet, went straight over the edge, crash-landed on the lean-to roof, bounced twice, caught the edge of the water butt with his heels, twisted in the air to give the woman the soft landing, and found himself lying on the blessed ground, looking up at a sky so packed with stars, he felt he was trembling on the brink of eternity.

Earth beneath him, water pouring over him, fire behind him, and the bright clear air above. The four first things. It was right they should be the four last things also. He felt his whole being drawn up towards that starry infinity.

Then this peace was disturbed by the arrival of moving shapes and chattering voices, growing ever louder and calling his name, all trying to get him back to the world of here and now. But his wise old body knew that this world was full of pain and tribulation, so it gave commands.

Joe closed his eyes, and light and noise and thought and feeling all died together.

THREE

WHEN HE AWOKE he was still on his back and he still had a naked female body in his arms.

Only now it was Beryl Boddington's and it smelled of wild strawberries and honey and she was sighing with pleasure, like a cello accompanying a Brahms love song. And, amazingly, he could see this marvellous body, every bit of it, even as his other four senses took their perfect pleasure.

Even their minds seemed twined. He yearned towards her, eager for consummation, and in his head he heard her laugh as she pulled away a little.

'No need to rush, Joe, boy. Not here, this is for ever, this is the place where you can pick all the flowers along the way, and see them grow again even while you're drinking in their scent.'

This was beyond anything Rev. Pot had ever promised in his most optimistic sermons. If Joe had known heaven was going to be like this he'd have paid a lot more heed to Aunt Mirabelle and never turned over and gone back to sleep on a Sunday morning. Let word of this get around, and there'd be queues forming at first light outside chapels and churches and mosques and temples and tabernacles and synagogues...

He looked at Beryl's smiling loving face above his, felt her warm scented breath on his lips. He strained up to press his hungry mouth to hers, got so close that her beloved features blurred. He relaxed and blinked once, twice, and smiled as that lovely, loving, beloved visage slowly came back into focus, till once more he saw clearly those big brown eyes, so full of compassion and concern...

'Oh shoot!' said Joe. At least that's what he tried to say, only his throat was so rough it came out halfway between a cough and a groan.

'Joe, you're awake,' said Merv Golightly.

Joe blinked again, but it was no use. Merv remained. He let his gaze drift slowly round the room. There were half a dozen other beds in it, though no one in them moved. It was either a hospital ward or a mortuary.

He pushed himself up in the bed and groaned again as the movement set off a small symphony of aches and pains. When Merv tried to help him, he shook his head and pointed to a jug of water on the bedside locker. The big man poured him a glassful and he drank it greedily.

Then he tried his voice again and this time got a result, though it sounded like something coming out of an old-fashioned gramophone that needed winding up.

'Where am I?' he said,

'Some place called Caerlindys, think that's how you say it, but I couldn't swear. Joe, my friend, it's really great to have you back. But how come, all these years, and you never told me your big secret?'

'Eh?' croaked Joe.

'Last night, we'd just got you definitely down for dead and long gone, then you come bursting through the roof of that burning building and fly through the air with this rescued lady in your arms, and even twist round so it's you who hits hard and her who lands soft. Joe, your secret is out. Everyone knows now you're really Superman!'

'You're a real joker, Merv,' croaked Joe. 'No wonder folk throw themselves out of your taxi while it's still moving.'

Merv laughed loud enough to raise a couple of heads off pillows, which was a relief. Then he leaned close and murmured, 'Seriously, man, though I ain't putting this in writing, I'm truly proud to know you.'

Embarrassed, Joe downed another half-pint of water and asked, 'So where's the others? Where'd you all end up last night?'

Merv put his head on one side and gave a modest shrug.

'That burning house, just another half-mile on, and there it was.

Branddreth College, place where we're staying. Didn't I say I had the instinct?'

'And where's this place we're at now, Caerlindys, is it?'

'Sound like a native, Joe. Twenty miles going on seventy from the college, depending whether you know the lingo. Bad news is the town's not much bigger than the Hypermart back home, good news is the hospital's almost as big as the town.'

'You bring me here, Merv?'

'No. That cop, never caught his name, conjured up the whole circus, cop cars, ambulance and fire engine turned up. Too late to do any good, mind. House is ashes, which you'd have been too if you hadn't pulled your Y-fronts over your trousers and done the switch. You're a hero, Joe, but don't be surprised if the cops treat you like an idiot or a suspect. Guy in charge is a DI called Ursell, pronounced arsehole from the sound of him. I've met some miserable bastards but he beats them all. He's like Chivers without the charm.'

This was a poor recommendation, Sergeant Chivers of Luton CID being the founder member of the Sixsmith-sucks club.

'He around, is he?'

'Oh yes. Asking more questions than Ruby Wax and cheekier with it. He'll surely want to talk to you, Joe. Numero duo on his list after the woman, and she's not talking to anyone.'

'The woman? Oh shoot.' Joe was racked with guilt he hadn't thought about the woman till now. 'How's she doing, Merv? You're not saying she's out of it?'

'No, still with us, they say, but only just. She looked a real mess last night. Then so did you and look at you now! Hey, here's something to cheer you up.'

Joe looked towards the door and groaned, but only inwardly. Groaning outwardly at Aunt Mirabelle was never a good idea. In a hospital bed, it could have you on your belly receiving an enema. In her eyes, any treatment that didn't start with a good clear-out was doomed to failure.

Then his spirits lifted as he spotted Beryl close behind her, talking to a tiny nurse who looked about twelve, with an elfin face and the brightest red hair he'd ever seen, bursting out of the confines of her cap like tongues of fire. Not a comfortable image.

'You awake at last, Joseph?' said Mirabelle. ''Bout time. Doctor says there's not much wrong with you.'

'Now that's not exactly true,' said Beryl, breaking off her conversation.

Mirabelle gave her a reprimanding glare, then stooped to kiss Joe on the cheek, at the same time whispering in his ear, 'You did real well, Joseph. Your ma, God rest her soul, would have been real proud of you.'

'Thanks, Auntie,' said Joe, touched.

She straightened up and at her normal volume said, 'Why you speaking that funny way? You ain't gone and done something to that voice of yours, I hope. It's rough enough the way the Lord made it without you sticking in your sixpenn'th.'

Joe sighed. He had no desire to play the big hero, but he didn't really see why everyone should find it necessary to hide *his* light under *their* bushel. Surely modesty was his prerogative?

Rescue was close. Beryl gently moved Mirabelle aside and stood smiling down at him.

'Hi, Joe,' she said. 'Reckon you owe me an apology.'

'Huh?'

'There we are, middle of a conversation, suddenly you take off without a pardon-me-ma'am, next time I see you, you're flying out of a burning house with a naked woman in your arms. Hope you'd do the same for me if the occasion arose.'

The memory of his waking dream rose in Joe's mind and he felt himself blushing.

'You got a fever, Joe?' she said anxiously.

Then she stooped and kissed him full on the lips.

'No, that feels about normal,' she said.

'This a new NHS economy measure?' he croaked. 'All the nurses taking my temperature this way?'

'In your dreams,' she laughed. And Joe blushed again.

He took another drink of water. The red-headed nurse came forward and picked up the empty jug. She wore a name badge which told him he was being cared for by Nurse Tilly Butler, which was nice. Made it feel like a user-friendly hospital.

'Throat bad, is it?' she said sympathetically. 'Doctor will be along shortly, get you something to soothe it then.'

'Guinness?' said Joe hopefully.

She laughed and said to Beryl, 'You were right about him then. Back in a mo.'

'What you been saying?'

'Nothing that needs bother you. She's a nice kid.'

'I noticed. Shouldn't she be at school?'

'You think? Maybe she thinks you should be in the gerry ward.'

'Sorry,' said Joe, reproved. 'So how's it look to an expert, this place? They got chloroform yet?'

'There you go again, Joe,' sighed Beryl. 'You and that lady you saved hit real lucky. Nurse Butler was telling me, they closed a lot of small hospitals round the region and put all their resources into this one. State of the art is what you got here. Makes where I work look ancient.'

'Yeah, but they got you to keep them young,' croaked Joe gallantly.

It got him a smile. Then a voice said, 'Excuse me,' and Beryl was edged aside by a weary-looking young man in a white coat whose name badge said he was Dr Godsip, though from the way he glanced down at it from time to time, Joe got the impression he wouldn't have minded finding he was somebody else.

After a yawn which looked like it might be terminal, he started checking off Joe's ailments. Joe was reminded of a mechanic doing an MOT.

'Superficial burns to the face and hands; dislocated left shoulder, replaced; wrenched right knee; heavy bruising to the back and buttocks; various other minor strains, sprains, and contusions of the arms and legs; nothing life-threatening; I'd say you've been very lucky, Mr Sixsmith.'

It didn't feel that way. Like warning lights on a test circuit, each of the injuries flashed pain as the doctor listed them, and by the time he finished, Joe felt much worse than he had before.

'What about his lungs and throat, Doctor?' asked Mirabelle. 'He sounds real funny.'

'Yes, that was the most worrying thing. Often it's not fire that does the real damage, but smoke inhalation. But as far as we can see, he's been lucky there too. There'll be some discomfort if he breathes too deeply, and his oesophagus will feel like it's been pulled through with a pineapple for a while, but no lasting damage. Now, normally we'd keep him in for observation for another day or two, but if he's happy to discharge himself...'

Joe sat straight up, ignoring the pain.

'Hey, man,' he said. 'What is this? I know you folk get short of beds, but how many legs do I need amputated before you let me stay here?'

It was Beryl who answered.

'Don't be exciting yourself, Joe,' she said. 'Yes, they are short of beds, but no, they're not throwing you out. Only there's a nice little sickbay at Branddreth College, and with me being a nurse, the doc'll be happy to let me take care of your medication. Also there'll be a doctor in attendance at the festival who'll be able to check you out if necessary. We thought you might like it better to be close to the others rather than stuck here, miles away. But it's your say-so.'

Joe scowled thoughtfully, but inside he was chortling with delight. Cosy little sickbay with Beryl as his private nurse or stuck here among the living dead with hospital hours and hospital food...no contest!

'Where do I sign?' he wheezed.

Godsip, who was still young enough to feel guilty at giving a patient the bum's rush, wanted to put him in a wheelchair but Joe insisted on getting dressed and walking under his own steam.

He regretted it the moment he stood up but he wasn't going to back off now and by the time he'd got into his clothes, he'd adjusted to the discomfort, but tying his shoelaces made him wince.

'I'll get that,' said Merv, kneeling before him.

'Heard you English were into hero worship but didn't realize how far it went,' said a sardonic Welsh voice.

It came from a tall thin man with eyes screwed up as if against the sun and a weathered face who looked like Clint Eastwood at early Dirty Harry age. His suit looked about the same vintage too.

Brynner, Burton and Eastwood, all in the same neck of the woods. Maybe I've wandered into an old movie, thought Joe, and these burns and bruises are just make-up.

Merv stood up. He didn't tower over the newcomer but he had a couple of inches advantage which he used to good effect.

'Joe, this is DI Ursell I told you about, but I expect you'd have recognized him anyway.'

Ursell regarded Joe as though thinking about inviting him to make his day.

'Glad to meet you,' said Joe. 'How's the lady?'

'I'm a copper not a quack,' said Ursell. 'What bothers me isn't how she is but who she is. Thought you could help me there.'

'Sorry?' said Joe.

Ursell rolled his eyes and said very slowly, as to a backward foreigner, 'Did she say anything which might give us a clue who she is?'

'Not a thing,' said Joe. 'Didn't have time for introductions and she wasn't in a fit state anyway. But don't you folk keep records of who lives round here, council tax, electoral register, that sort of thing?'

It was a genuine question. Joe knew the Scots had a different legal system because it had come up in an episode of *Dr Finlay's Casebook*, so maybe the Welsh moved in their own mysterious way too.

Ursell, however, looked like he was taking it as a crack.

'Oh, yes, we keep very good records, as you may find, Mr Sixsmith. We like to know all about everyone who lives round here, or comes visiting for that matter. But nothing's known about this woman, nothing at all, which I find very puzzling. I suppose everyone on your coach is accounted for?'

He glared accusingly at Merv, but it was Mirabelle who leapt into the breach.

'What you saying? This poor lady jumped off our coach and ran into that burning house just so my nephew could risk his life saving her? And while we're disputing the matter, how come that other policeman who was there didn't do the saving? Ain't that what we pay our taxes for?'

Even without the backing of rational argument, Mirabelle was a fearsome disputant. With it, she towered like the sons of Anak, and Ursell became as a grasshopper in her sight.

'Sorry, no, you misunderstand me,' he said, trying without much success for a placating smile. 'Far as I understand it, Sergeant Prince was in his car, summoning help, and didn't know there was anyone in the house till a few minutes later when he rejoined you all. House should have been empty, see? So what we have here is a woman nobody knows, and she's in a bad way, and all of us are very keen to let her next of kin know what's happened, so as they can get here to give her support and comfort.'

He didn't sound very convincing but he suddenly sounded very Welsh, in the same way the Scots become very Scottish and the Irish very Irish at times they want to be defensively disarming. This was a phenomenon Joe's radical solicitor friend, Butcher, had pointed out in reference to himself. 'You saying I come over all Uncle Tommish?' he'd demanded indignantly. 'Worse than that,' she replied. 'You come over all poor-me-deprived-Luton-laddish.'

Mirabelle wasn't disarmed.

'If that wasn't her own house burning, why you not hassling the folk whose house it is?' she demanded.

'That's Mr and Mrs Haggard of Islington, London,' said Ursell. 'They're on their way but over the phone they've made it clear no one was staying in Copa Cottage with their permission.'

He made Islington, London, sound like Gomorrah, thought Joe. And also he got an impression that this Mr and Mrs Haggard were not people of good standing in Ursell's eyes. Of course it could be it was just this anti-Anglo-colonization thing he'd once read about in a magazine at the dentist's.

'Maybe they got children,' said Mirabelle. 'Young 'uns can be pretty free with what ain't their own.'

She shot Joe an unjustifiably significant glance.

'Thank you ma'am,' said Ursell, clearly tiring of being disarming. 'Now, if I could have a quick word with Mr Sixsmith alone...'

There was resistance, but the DI was good at crowd control and in less than a minute he had everyone else out into the corridor. He now looked at the other patients as if considering pushing them out too but decided against it.

Joe said, 'There was some writing on a wall, something about GO HOME ENGLISH. Maybe this wasn't an accident, is that what you're thinking?'

Ursell let out the long-suffering sigh of one who is fed up with being taught how to suck eggs.

'Someone mentioned you were some kind of investigator, Mr Sixsmith,' he said with a neutrality worse than sarcasm. Not that it mattered to Joe who'd been put down by men with research degrees in down-putting.

'Not trying to investigate anything,' he said. 'Specially not when you had one of your own men right on the spot. Prince, did someone say his name was? He the local bobby?'

Ursell took his time answering.

'Not really,' he said finally. 'Just happened to be in the area on another matter, it seems. And not one of my men. Uniformed, or perhaps you didn't notice?'

Joe, familiar with the often strained relationship between CID and the rest back in Luton, said provocatively, 'In, out, always a cop, isn't that what they say?'

Ursell said softly, 'We can certainly count ourselves lucky having two pairs of trained eyes at the scene of the crime.'

That unsarcastic sarcasm again.

'So it was definitely a crime?' said Joe.

Ursell hesitated then shrugged.

'It's no secret, not round here anyway. Yes, it was arson. Traces of an accelerant, probably petrol.'

'So maybe if this woman shouldn't have been in the house, these fire raisers thought the place was empty?' suggested Joe.

'Could be,' admitted Ursell. 'Why she didn't hear something and get out quick is the puzzle.'

'Oh, that's easy,' said Joe, very superior. 'She was naked when I found her. I reckon she was in the shower when it happened, probably didn't hear a thing. Came out, found the place full of smoke. Ran into the front bedroom which was when we spotted her. Saw there was no way out there. Headed back, ceiling beneath already on fire, and her foot went through the floorboards. After that, best she could manage was to drag herself back into the shower, turn the cold water full on, and lie there waiting for the end.'

The long speech brought on a fit of coughing which spared Ursell the angst of having to agree.

'You here to sing, you say? Interesting,' he observed when Joe regained control. 'Rest of the choir coughs in tune too, I daresay.'

'Come along and listen if you've a spare moment,' snapped Joe, irritated at the sneer against the choir. 'You might learn something.'

'Oh yes? About as much chance as I have of having a spare moment, with all this in my lap.'

Now Joe was thoroughly incensed, not a condition he was very familiar with.

'Listen, Inspector. I'm sorry you've been inconvenienced, but this fire, whoever's responsible, it's not me or my choir, and it's almost certainly not that poor woman who's got herself nearly burnt to death. Now, if you need to talk to me again, you'll find me at Branddreth College.'

He strode to the door. It was an effort not to show what an effort striding was, but he managed it.

With Merv's strength at one side, and Beryl's warmth at the other, he set off down a long corridor.

Ursell overtook them without a glance and turned down a side corridor. When they reached it, Joe looked along it and saw the inspector talking to a uniformed policeman who'd just risen from a chair outside a door.

'Hang on a sec,' said Joe.

He abandoned his supporters and walked down the side corridor. Ursell and the uniformed man watched his approach in silence. When he reached them, Joe peered in through the glass panel of the door. He'd anticipated what he would see there, but the sight of that deathly still figure lying on a bed, hooked up to a variety of drips and monitoring apparatus, still caught at his throat worse than the smoke from the fire.

'How's she doing?' he asked.

'No change,' said Ursell.

'I hope that...I hope...'

Joe broke off. What had this cop, who looked like he thought life was a form of irritable bowel syndrome, to do with his hopes?

He turned away, but he'd only gone a few paces when the inspector came alongside.

'Mr Sixsmith.'

'Yes?' said Joe, halting.

'I don't think I said, you did OK.'

Saying it seemed to hurt his throat as much as speaking hurt Joe's.

'Yeah,' said Joe. 'Maybe not OK enough, eh? You'll let me know if anything...'

'Rest assured,' said the inspector. 'I'll let you know.'

Maybe it was just the accent, but the words sounded very final.

FOUR

In *The Lost Traveller's Guide,* the famous travel book devoted to places unlikely to be visited on purpose, Branddreth Hall, the seat of Branddreth College, is described thus:

> *Here we have a building which achieves the remarkable feat of spanning six centuries, from medieval stronghold through Tudor hall, Georgian manor and Victorian mansion, to twentieth-century school, without once coming within welly-hurling distance of distinction. Succeeding generations have recorded their disappointment that, despite all attempts at contemporaneous improvement, the complete building sullenly insists on remaining less than the sum of its parts, and in this unrepentant ugliness, the Lady House, an Edwardian dower house built in what might best be called the Mock-Tudor Council Estate style, shows an almost touching family resemblance.*

Joe, whose architectural acme was the green and yellow marble clad ziggurat housing the new Malayan restaurant in Luton High, viewed the hall with no such critical eye. All he saw was the gift-wrapping round the cosy little sickbay where Beryl was going to act as his personal nurse.

On their way, they had passed the burnt-out shell of the farmhouse, or Copa Cottage as he now knew it was called. Only a jagged shell of outer wall remained standing and firemen were still picking their way through the ashes. A real inferno, thought Joe. And nearly my pyre.

A fire engine and two police cars were parked in front of the ruin with a plum-coloured Daimler standing a little to one side, like a duchess keeping her skirts out of the heavy tread of the hired help.

Next to it stood four people, watching the firemen at their work. Two of them, a man and a woman, thirtysomethings, smartly tweeded in the way posh townies dress for the country, he with his arm comfortingly round her shoulders, Joe guessed to be the Haggards from Islington. A little to one side, regarding them with grave concern, stood a tall distinguished man, with aquiline nose, silvering hair, and a walking stick.

And set back from this trio, regarding them all with unreadable blankness, was Detective Inspector Ursell.

Who'd had time to finish his business at the hospital, leave after them, and still get here before they did. Which meant that Merv could still be a long way from sussing out these winding country roads, a suspicion confirmed when Mirabelle hissed, 'What you doing bringing us past here?'

Thinks seeing the place again might do my head in, thought Joe, not altogether displeased at being regarded as such a sensitive plant. Then Beryl's arm went around him, and he realized his body was shivering. Maybe he was that sensitive plant after all!

The rest of the journey (less than a mile—Merv had got that right at least) passed in melancholy silence. But when they got out of the coach and heard the sound of singing voices drifting through the bright spring air, interrupted from time to time by Rev. Pot's cries of encouragement or abuse, Joe's heart bounded and he felt like he'd come home.

Even the discovery that the cosy little sickbay was more barrack room than BUPA didn't depress his spirits. Meekly he allowed Beryl to check him over for damage in transit then put him to bed, with Aunt Mirabelle playing gooseberry, more, he thought generously, out of concern for his condition than suspicion it wouldn't debar him from unclean thoughts.

He drank some thin soup and a cup of tea. A high liquid intake was prescribed till his throat eased. Hopefully he enquired about the availability of Guinness. Beryl pursed her lips (oh, how he longed to open that purse) but Mirabelle, God bless her, said, 'That black stout supposed to be good for nursing mothers, isn't it? Don't see how it can do you any harm. But sleep first.'

Upon which promise, and the imagined promise contained in the kiss which Beryl brushed across his mouth, Joe closed his eyes obediently and, to what would have been his surprise if he'd been awake to appreciate it, he fell asleep immediately.

He woke in semi-darkness and the knowledge that there was someone in the room.

Like most of Joe's instant certainties, evidence came a good way second. His occasional good friend, Superintendent Willie Woodbine of Luton CID, justified his plagiarism of Joe's occasional detective triumphs (the same occasions on which he became a good friend) by saying, 'God knows how you get there, Joe, but you've got to understand, the real work starts with me having to plot a logical path that won't get laughed out of court.'

While Joe didn't see how this entitled Willie to take ninety per cent of the credit, he did see that a lowly PI couldn't afford to turn down any offer of goodwill from the fuzz on no matter what extortionate terms.

Now he didn't waste time working out what combination of sound, smell and sixth or seventh sense was giving him this info, but focused on the two main issues: one, he wasn't alone; two, he didn't know who it was he wasn't alone with.

He kept his breathing natural. Not as easy as it sounded. It had taken the great American gumshoe, Endo Venera, whose book *Not So Private Eye* had become Joe's professional Bible, to point out that not many folk had the faintest idea what their natural breathing sounded like when asleep. 'Only way to check if you gurgle like a baby or grunt like a hog is to use your VAT,' said Venera.

It had taken Joe a very confused five minutes to work out that the American didn't mean value-added tax but voice-activated tape. Such hi-tech aids weren't in his armoury, but he managed to rig up a conventional recorder on a timer so that he got an hour's worth of the weird noises he made in bed. Even then he had to separate the basso continuo of his cat, Whitey, from his own surprisingly high-pitched plainsong. So now he was able to avoid the giveaway error of an imitation baritone snore as he lay there, and felt the intruder moving stealthily closer.

Very close now. His mental eye was seeing a mad Welsh nationalist with a can of petrol in one hand and a lighter in the other, bent on getting rid of this potential witness to last night's crime. It was hard, but he kept his nerve and waited. The intruder had come to a stop. So, Joe realized, had his own breathing. Dead giveaway! Showtime!

He shot upright, flung out his arms, grappled his assailant to his body in a weapon-neutralizing bearhug, rolled out of the bed and wrestled him to the floor.

Various parts of his body sent out signals. Conflicting signals. His injured shoulder, back and knee registered what-the-shoot-are-you-doing-dickhead? shafts of pain, while his face and chest acknowledged gratefully that what they were pressing down on was pleasantly soft and yielding.

Then his ears got in on the act, picking up a high-pitched shriek of shock and indignation which confirmed what his torso was telling him.

This *him* he'd got hold of was a her, and a well-built one at that.

Ignoring his pain, he rolled off, stood up, and pulled the curtains aside to let in a torrent of bright sunlight.

It fell on a young woman in her mid teens with long blonde hair and a surprised expression. She was wearing a red skirt and a white blouse, both of which had ridden up under the pressure of his attack. She had strong well-fleshed legs and a bosom to match.

'Hey, man,' he said. 'I mean, hey...I'm sorry.'

He bent over her and offered his hand to help her rise. It occurred to him too late that if her purpose *were* offensive, he was laying himself wide open to a kick in the crutch or a blade in the belly.

But all she did was take his hand and draw herself upright, saying, 'Bloody hell, boyo, they told me you were ill.'

Joe's aches, temporarily anaesthetized by his chivalric guilt, came flooding back, and he sat on the bed with a groan.

'Too late playing for sympathy now,' she said. 'Not when you've indecently assaulted me already.'

She had a voice like a Welsh stream, bubbling with gently mocking laughter.

Joe said, 'Really am sorry. Thought you were a burglar or something.'

'So it was just self-defence, not irresistible desire. There's disappointing. Is it your back is hurting, then?'

'Among other places,' admitted Joe.

'Let's take a look, shall we?'

She came round the bed and before he could protest she had pushed his pyjama jacket up round his neck and her fingers were pressing up and down his spine, lightly at first, then probing ever deeper. He opened his mouth to cry out in pain, then realized there wasn't any, or at least a lot less than there'd been a few seconds ago.

'Going, is it?' she asked. 'That's good. Let's hope it goes to somebody who deserves it. Not a real hero. First time I got my hands on a real hero.'

'You the district nurse or something?' enquired Joe.

This produced a cascade of laughter.

'No way! You try that wrestling trick on Gladys Two-bars and she'd snap you like a twig, hero or not.'

'Gladys...?'

'Two-bars. Gave her a lady's bike when she started, but twice out and the frame buckled under the weight of her, so they had to get her a man's, and even then she needed a double crossbar.'

Joe offered up a prayer of thanks he'd been spared that encounter and asked, 'So who are you, then?'

'Bron, that's Bronwen, Williams. My da's caretaker here at the college, and when your friends had to go off, they asked if we'd keep an eye on you. I would never have said yes if I'd known what sort of man you were going to turn out to be.'

Joe didn't enquire what sort of man that was, but asked instead, 'So where've they gone, my friends?'

'Down into Llanffugiol, silly. Festival proper starts tomorrow and they got to register, see what's what, more rules than a lawyers' union these choir contests, my da says.'

'Yes, but it's the singing that counts,' said Joe defensively.

'You think so? Easy to tell you're not from round here. Could sing like an angel and they'd disqualify you for not having wings if they felt like it. Here, lie down, will you, else I'll be doing my own back in.'

Obediently, Joe stretched prone on the bed and next thing the girl was straddling him, her bum warm against his buttocks as she leaned her fingers deep into his back.

'You trained for this?' he croaked.

'No. You complaining? Send you back to that fancy hospital if you like. But you won't find any of those puffed-up little nurses can give you this treatment. Nothing but a bunch of skivvies, that lot, just about fit for cleaning bedpans. Chuck you out before you can hardly walk, too. 'Spect they'll be chucking that woman out you rescued any time now.'

'Don't think so,' said Joe, wondering what experience of Caerlindys Hospital had given Bronwen such a jaundiced opinion of the place. 'She looks to be in a pretty bad way.'

'You talk to her then?'

'Not me. Police are trying but she's in no state.'

'Police are useless,' she said dismissively. She was, thought Joe, a very dismissive young woman. 'So they don't know who she is, then? What she was doing there?'

'Not yet. What's the word locally?'

'Sorry?'

'Back home, everyone would have a theory,' said Joe. 'Can't be much different here, I shouldn't have thought.'

'Mind our own business round here,' she said sharply. 'Got enough to do looking after ourselves without wasting time on strangers.'

In the circumstances, which were that her bare thighs were gripping the bare back of a complete stranger, this seemed a questionable disclaimer, thought Joe. But he wasn't about to raise the objection.

The massage, temporarily suspended, now resumed, with the girl sliding back and forth above him like a rower pulling on an oar, as she let her hands run in long slow strokes the whole length of his back from bum to shoulders.

'How's that feel?' she asked.

'Lot better,' said Joe, his voice now husky with more than just smoke damage.

'Turn over and I'll do your front then,' she said.

'No,' he said explosively. 'Front's fine, really.'

'You sure?' she said, her voice husky as his own. 'It's all down to tension, you know, get rid of the tension and you get rid of the pain...'

She's taking the mickey, thought Joe. She knows exactly what's going on and she's taking the mickey.

Before he could decide how to respond there was a sound like the polite cough well-brought-up folk use when less well-brought-up folk would shout, 'Oy!'

The girl dismounted like a pro jockey. Joe turned his head to see what had made the sound and rather to his surprise, because being right first time wasn't something he was used to, he saw what looked like the very model of a well-brought-up polite cougher in the doorway.

It was the silver-haired man with the eagle's beak he'd seen in the group by the ruined cottage.

'Mr Sixsmith, I presume,' he said, advancing. 'I'm glad to see Bronwen's looking after you. I'm Leon Lewis, High Master of Branddreth.'

He approached the bed with his hand outstretched. Joe, though already gratefully acknowledging the deflating effect of the interruption, was not yet in a position to do more than flap his hand out sideways.

'Please,' said the newcomer, brushing his fingers against Joe's. 'Don't disturb yourself. I just wanted to check that all was well, and of course congratulate you on what from all accounts must have been a spectacular act of courage, worthy, I would say, of one of our country's official awards for gallantry.'

His gaze moved from Joe to Bronwen.

What's he thinking? thought Joe. Medal or maiden?

He took the chance to pull the bedspread over his bottom half, roll over, and sit up.

Lewis was smiling benevolently at the girl, who was looking at the same time resentful and embarrassed.

Good, thought Joe. Bit of embarrassment won't harm you, my girl.

'Best be off now,' she said abruptly. 'They'll be wondering where I am.'

She left the room without a glance at Joe.

Story of my life, he thought. One minute they're sitting on top of you, next they won't give you the time of day.

'So, Mr Sixsmith, well done, and welcome to Wales in general and Llanffugiol in particular.'

Lewis had a fine voice, musical and rich-timbred. Headmaster needed a good voice, thought Joe, remembering his own at Luton Comp. who in full throat could drown a departing jumbo.

But this guy hadn't called himself a head.

'Thanks,' said Joe. 'Glad to be here. High Master same as headmaster, is it?'

He'd never discovered a better way of finding out things than asking, but Lewis viewed him narrowly for a second as though in search of satire.

Then he smiled and said, 'Indeed. Such a variation of title is not unknown even beyond the border, I believe. May I ask what the medical prognosis is, Mr Sixsmith?'

Sounded to Joe like something that doctors shoved into you.

He said, 'You mean, how'm I doing? Pretty well. In fact, very well.'

To demonstrate he slipped out of bed. The embarrassing effects of Bronwen's massage had vanished, but happily the therapeutic effects remained. Though not feeling completely back to normal, normality now felt like a gainable goal.

'Like you can hear, voice is no good, though,' he said. 'Won't be able to sing.'

'And does it hurt you to talk?'

'Not as much as it probably hurts you to listen,' said Joe.

'On the contrary, it's a very great pleasure,' said Lewis. 'In fact, I would be delighted to hear your own version of events. We've been given the official account of what happened, of course—the constabulary are very accommodating...'

'Mr Ursell, you mean?' said Joe, unable easily to fit the DI and *accommodating* into the same sentence.

'Ah. You've met the inspector, have you? An excellent officer at his level, I do not doubt, but one who tends to be rather officiously silent on what he regards as police business. Protecting his position, I suppose. Fortunately my good friend Deputy Chief Constable Penty-Hooser who is O/C Crime takes a rather more open view and has put me fully in the picture. The only thing better, of course, would be to get the full story from the horse's mouth, as 'twere, especially when, as I gather, the horse in question can lay claim to the professional expertise of a private investigator. To which end my wife and I hope you might feel able to join us at the Lady House for dinner tonight.'

'Tonight?' echoed Joe, thinking this was the first time he'd ever heard anyone say *as 'twere* and wondering how the High Master had caught on he was a PI. His mate the DCC most likely.

'I know it's short notice, especially in view of your ordeal. But there is another reason for pressing you. Fran and Franny Haggard, who own Copa Cottage, are staying with us and they would dearly like to meet you before they go back to London tomorrow. So if it were at all possible...'

'Don't know if I'm up to going out to some restaurant,' said Joe, foolishly avoiding the refusal direct.

'What? Ah, I see. No, the Lady House is in fact where I live. It's only a step from the college, but of course I would be more than happy to pick you up in my car...'

'Think I can manage a step,' said Joe sturdily, before he realized this was as good as an acceptance.

'Excellent. Shall we say seven for seven thirty? Informal, of course. Don't dream of dressing. Pleasure to meet you, Mr Sixsmith. Now I'll let you get back to your rest.'

He touched his silver-topped stick to his silver-topped head and left.

Don't dream of dressing? thought Joe, looking down at his red and yellow striped pyjamas. He knew things were different in Wales, but surely not that different!

It was the kind of jokey remark he'd have addressed to Whitey if Whitey had been present. Unfortunately, Rev. Pot had declared choir transport a petless zone ever since the great MI dogfight, in which two border terriers, a whippet and a labrador-cross had assaulted each other and anyone who came near, obliging the coach driver to veer off the road on to a police-only parking site which was already fully occupied by a police car.

Whitey had taken no part in the action, contenting himself with sitting on Joe's lap, sneering at the idiocies of canine behaviour and the inadequacies of human control. Nevertheless, he had been included in the general ban and was presently in police custody, meaning he was being looked after by Detective Constable Dylan Doberley.

Doberley, nicknamed Dildo by the wits of Luton CID, was a member of the choir. He had first come to Boyling Corner in lustful pursuit of a young mezzo and would have been indignantly ejected by Rev. Pot if he hadn't turned out to have a genuine basso profundo voice. 'Does not the Good Book teach us tolerance?' proclaimed the Rev. But it was a lesson he'd been hard put to remember when Doberley announced he couldn't make the Welsh trip.

He'd backed up his own anger with the wrath of God, but Doberley had been unmoved.

'Sorry to be letting down you and God both,' he'd said. 'But with Sergeant Chivers it's more, like, personal.'

Joe knew what he meant. Having Rev. Pot and God on your back would be burdensome, but couldn't come close to the personal pressure Chivers was capable of exerting. Joe knew all about this. The sergeant took his presence on the mean streets of Luton *masquerading* as a PI very personally.

It wasn't all bad news on the Doberley front, however. The DC was between accommodations, having left the police Section House because it inhibited his private life and having been let down about a bedsit he hoped to rent. So he'd jumped at the offer of a bed in Joe's flat in return for seeing to all the needs and comforts of Whitey.

This was an arrangement which caused Joe no little unease, mistrusting as he did both parties.

Better ring and check how things are working out, he thought.

Which should have been easy for a hi-tech tec with a mobile.

Except the last time he'd seen said mobile was when he'd shoved it into Beryl's hands prior to his 'heroics'.

Fortunately there wasn't far to look, as the sickbay's furnishings consisted of a metal locker. Its khaki colour suggested that it was army surplus and the young inmates of the sickbay had salved their convalescent boredom by scratching their names in the paint. An attempt had been made to blot them out but as the overpaint was a different shade, all it did was give the inscriptions a ghostly dimension, like they were trying to convey a message from the shadow world. The convention seemed to be that you scratched your name and the condition which had put you in here. Some were straightforward: *Billy Johnstone, broken leg. Eric Pollinger, flu.* Others oblique: *Michael K. Tully, faintings. Sam Annetwell, spots.* And some downright cryptic: *Henry Loomis, sights. Simon Sillcroft, sadness.* In fact, Simon Sillcroft and his sadness were regular attenders, his name appearing at least three times that Joe could see. Poor kid. He hoped he got over it. And Henry Loomis over his sights!

He thought of scratching his own name. *Joe Sixsmith, heroics.* Better not! Instead he opened the locker and found his spare clothing all neatly arranged on hangers and shelves. He was pleased but not surprised. The kindness of women still delighted him but had long since ceased to be unexpected. Beryl's hand, he guessed, only because if Mirabelle had got *her* hands on the mobile, she'd have chucked it in the nearest pond, not positioned it suggestively on a pile of Y-fronts.

Maybe he was reaching for *suggestively.* But a guy could hope.

He punched in his home number, got nothing, remembered to switch on, and heard it ring for nearly a minute before there was a response.

'Yeah?'

'That the user-friendly way they teach you to answer the phone down the nick?' said Joe.

'Wha'? Who's that?'

'It's me, Joe.'

'You sure? You sound like a frog with laryngitis.'

'Don't sound so hot yourself.'

'That's because you just dragged me out of my pit which I'd just fallen into.'

'Hey, you not fornicating in my bed, I hope, Dildo?'

'Chance would be a fine thing. Chivers got me on nights and I'm trying to catch up on sleep, which ain't easy what with the phone ringing and that crazy cat of yours always wanting something but not letting on what.'

'Yeah,' said Joe, recognizing the problem. 'But you're getting on OK?'

'Yeah, yeah. Eats everything I give it and anything else I don't actually lock up. And keeps funnier hours than me. Joe, I've gotta get some sleep, I'm on again tonight. Things OK with you in the Wild West?'

Joe considered the events of the past twenty-four hours and said, 'Fine.'

'Great. You do sound rough, though. Could have told you that Welsh beer would take the skin off your tonsils. Regards to all. Cheers.'

Joe switched off the phone. Should he have asked to talk to Whitey? he wondered. Probably not. Dildo would have thought he was insane, and the cat wouldn't have disagreed.

He turned his attention to the more immediate problem of whether his hopes for Beryl would be better furthered as a bed-ridden invalid or a plucky convalescent.

Being in bed already could be regarded as half the battle, except it left you vulnerable to the attentions of undesirable visitors from Auntie Mirabelle to Bronwen Williams.

Not that Bron was altogether undesirable, but he doubted if it would help his cause with Beryl to be caught straddled by a Celtic masseuse. There was *bedridden* and *bed-ridden.*

He smiled at his joke, and stored it up for later retrieval. It was OK if you were Oscar Wilde, shooting out off-the-cuff-one-liners, but less gifted mortals had to work at it.

So it was plucky convalescent. And in any case, if he was dining with the High Master tonight *as 'twere,* he'd better start getting his sea-legs as 'twere.

There was no lock on the door so he placed the wooden chair

against it. No point taking risks with Bronwen on the loose. Then he stripped off his pyjamas and stepped into the narrow open shower cubicle. The water came out more in a spout than a jet, but it was nice and hot and helped soothe his aches to a distant nag. He glanced through the steam at the round white plastic hospital clock on the wall opposite. High noon. He tried his Tex Ritter imitation which usually went down well on Karaoke Nite at his local, but after a couple of notes acknowledged that his current voice was fit only for Lee Marvin's 'Wand'rin' Star'. More suitable anyway. He might be footloose in the Wild West, but to the best of his knowledge there was no one out there looking to blow him away.

But maybe he'd better stick to whistling till he got his voice back.

You know how to whistle, Joe?

Now who had said that?

Stepping out of the shower he began to towel himself down carefully to avoid reactivating the sensitive areas. Then, dried off, he put on his clothes, combed his hair and went out to explore.

FIVE

OUTSIDE THE SICKBAY, Joe found himself in a stone flagged corridor which magnified the slap of his trainers and set up an echo so strong he looked back to see if he were being followed. He must have passed along it when he arrived, but the press of company and his own fragility meant he hadn't paid much attention. To one side a line of high narrow windows with pointed arches looked out on to a rolling, wooded landscape, but it wasn't the light they admitted that you noticed, rather the shadows they threw, creating the effect of a medieval cloister which Joe recollected from some old Robin Hood film on the telly. The only hint to the casual visitor that this was the twentieth century was the winking light of a security camera high on the walls at either end.

Maybe any kid spotted running instead of walking got shot with an arrow.

On the other side were classrooms. He pushed open a couple of doors and peered in. Rows of old-fashioned one-piece desks stood on carefully measured parade. The floorboards, though scrubbed clean, were old, uneven, and splintered, and the white-washed walls were devoid of ornament and peeling.

People paid for their kids to come here? thought Joe. They managed things better in Luton.

A flight of stairs almost tempted him upwards but he decided best to keep his feet planted firm on the ground till he sussed out the geography, which didn't promise to be easy. He turned a couple of corners and lost contact with the outside world for a while. Once more only the security cameras kept him reassured that he hadn't time-travelled. Finally a narrow door opened on to what looked like a scaled-down version of the kind of baronial hall he recalled from that same old TV movie, its walls decorated with ragged banners, battered shields, rusty weapons and mouldering animal heads, plus (presumably the modern equivalent) photographs of scenes from college life, most featuring the High Master in close proximity to visiting dignitaries. One showed a sunlit group of boys in running shorts, flanked by a blazered Lewis and a tall angular, strawberry-nosed man in top-brass police uniform, looking like he was suffering from prickly heat. The legend beneath confirmed what Joe guessed, that this was DCC Penty-Hooser, who had presented the prizes at the last sports day.

No point having important friends if you can't use them, thought Joe, heading across the hall to a huge oak door, solid enough to deter a peasants' revolt. But first impressions, especially Joe's, weren't always right. At the merest touch of his finger the door swung smoothly open and he stepped out into the light.

As even *The Lost Traveller's Guide* acknowledges, whatever the architectural shortcomings of Branddreth Hall, the guy who chose the site knew a thing or two.

Built on the other side of the ridge from the burnt-out cottage, it looked out westward across a tumble of wooded hills to a line of high mountains whose every detail was swept clear by the house-proud sun.

It was a great view. Even Joe, a devout bricks-and-mortar-man, was impressed.

Then a wisp of cloud floated across the sun, running its shadow towards him over the white fields like a wolf loping towards a lost traveller. Joe shivered and quickly turned his head to look at something closer.

It turned out to be Frank Sinatra's face, only a foot or so away.

Joe took a step backwards, thinking, is there some big Welsh lookalike convention going on? Or has Ol' Blue Eyes really made it back?

'Shoot,' he said, recovering. 'Where you drop from, friend?'

'You the one from the fire?' demanded the man, who was in his forties, wearing dungarees and the kind of look Sinatra might have worn if he'd flown in from the States to discover he'd been booked for Karaoke Nite at the Llanffugiol Working Men's Club.

Or maybe it was just he was clearly suffering from a bad cold.

'Suppose I am,' said Joe distrustfully.

The aggressive distrust vanished to be replaced by a broad smile showing the kind of teeth that probably got you jailed in Hollywood.

'Dai Williams,' said the man, wiping his running nose on the back of the hand he then thrust out to Joe. 'I'm the caretaker. Glad to meet you, Mr...?'

'Sixsmith,' said Joe, reluctantly touching the proffered hand.

'Sixsmith? That all?' said Williams.

'Joe to my friends.'

'And I hope I can be one of those, Joe. What you did last night was the act of a man I'd be proud to call my friend.'

'Thanks,' said Joe, embarrassed. 'The caretaker? Think I met your daughter.'

'Bron. Not been bothering you, has she?' said Williams, frowning.

Oh, yes, thought Joe. But not in a way I can tell a protective dad. Not that the caretaker looked too protective, but with dads you could never tell.

'No, no. Just dropped by to see I was OK. Mr Lewis came too.'

Just to underline, no hanky-panky.

'Did he? Well, it's his school, and welcome to it. Less I see the better. Had to come back early from Barmouth to see to your lot.'

This came over as an accusation.

'Sorry about that,' said Joe, who sometimes wondered how he

came to be apologizing so often for things which he didn't really feel responsible for.

'That's OK,' snuffled Williams magnanimously. 'Just as well you were coming, way things turned out. You hungry?'

Joe consulted his stomach and got a big yes vote. Nothing but that bowl of soup since Mirabelle's sandwiches yesterday. It was a wonder he could still stand upright!

He said, 'Think I could manage a bite.'

'Yes, her the nurse said you'd be hungry when you woke,' said Williams.

'Beryl, you mean?' said Joe, moved at her foresight.

'That's the one. Fine-looking girl, that,' said Williams, with an appreciative crinkling of his runny nose.

Joe regarded him sharply. Was this pint-sized Sinatra imitation the local Pal Joey? He wondered as he followed him down the long west facade of the building and round the corner into a courtyard formed by the two main wings. The caretaker led him through a doorway which was probably the tradesman's entrance in the old days. And probably the new days too, thought Joe, for didn't places like this exist to keep the old days fresh?

'Ella!' called Williams. 'You in there, girl? Got a hungry hero out here who needs feeding up.'

Joe's incipient jealousy quickly evaporated when he saw Mrs Williams. A broad-shouldered, strong-featured woman a good six inches taller than Dai, she didn't look the kind of wife a wise husband would mess with.

She told Dai sharply to take his germs elsewhere, then sat Joe at a well-scrubbed kitchen table and without prompting (or maybe Beryl had briefed her) she produced a mountain of scrambled eggs, mushrooms and tomatoes which filled Joe's stomach without offending his tender throat. This was followed by soft white bread, fresh butter and home-made marmalade washed down with strong tea. And she didn't trouble him with talk while he was eating.

A jewel among women, he told himself.

'That was the goods,' he told her fervently as he held out his cup for a refill.

The cup was a fine piece of Wedgwood china matching his plate, the best set, he guessed. A childhood spent observing Mirabelle in her natural habitat had taught him it wasn't what a visitor ate that signified status, it was what they ate it off. His hostess, he noticed, was drinking her tea from a plain white breakfast cup.

'More where that came from,' she offered.

Joe was tempted but shook his head.

'Better not,' he said. 'Mr Lewis has asked me to eat with them tonight and if his lady is as generous with the grub as you, I'd better leave a space.'

A knowing smile flickered across her lips but the only comment she offered on her employers' cuisine was, 'They'll be wanting you to sing for your supper, I expect.'

'Shan't be doing any of that for a while,' said Joe.

'Pity. That Beryl says you always hit the notes on the head. Here, I've just been baking some scones, they won't take up much space.'

Joe felt a warm glow at this reported praise. Many choristers do good service by being able to take a note when given it, but a choir needs at least one member of each section who can actually give the notes first time.

'But what I meant was, they'll be wanting you to tell them about the fire,' continued the woman as she put a plateful of scones and a potful of jam in front of Joe.

'Expect so,' said Joe. 'Good folk to work for, the Lewises, are they?'

She viewed him thoughtfully for a moment as if trying to assess his motive in asking the question. He gave her a wide-eyed smile of one who had no ulterior motive, which was easy because he hadn't.

'Williams seems settled,' she said finally.

'And you?' asked Joe, trying a scone. It was as delicious as it looked.

She smiled.

'My gran always said, complaining loses old friends and doesn't make new,' she replied.

'Name wasn't Mirabelle, was it?' said Joe. 'Sorry. My auntie. You may have noticed her?'

'Now you mention it, I think I did spot someone who reminded me of Gran.'

They laughed together and things got even easier between them. Joe took another scone, promising himself it would be the last, and said, 'Sorry we messed up your holiday, having to come back early for us.'

'Williams been moaning? He never got on with Gran. Pay him no heed. Couple of days less in a boarding house in Barmouth is no great loss, specially when it's run by my sister-in-law. Expects me to help in exchange for special rates, least that's what she calls them. If that's a holiday, give me home every time.'

'Yeah, I'm not great on holidays either,' said Joe. 'Lot of folk are, though. Buying up country cottages for a few weekends a year. Can get up local folks' noses, that, I've read.'

'That what they're saying about the fire up at Copa?' she asked, circumnavigating his subtlety as if it wasn't there. 'May be something in it. Beer talk for most, but there's always someone daft enough to take their little boys' games further. She going to be all right, this woman?'

'I hope so,' said Joe. 'She deserves to make it. She was very brave.'

'Thought that was your line.'

Joe thought of the injured woman's attempts to draw herself up into the attic, the pain she must have felt.

'No, she was the brave one. I just did it on the run. She had to make herself do what she did. And there's no way I could have got her out less'n she'd helped.'

Mrs Williams took a reflective sip of tea.

'You'd just have left her then?' she asked.

It occurred to Joe that if the injured woman hadn't been able to pull herself through the hole in the ceiling, the only way he could have got out was to pull her back down.

Would he have done that?

Could he have done that?

'Man don't know what he'll do till he finds out,' said Joe.

'Well, what you found out is what I call brave,' said the woman. 'Who is she anyway, this woman?'

'No one knows,' said Joe. 'The Haggards, who own the cottage, are here so maybe they can help. Specially if they've got kids, or close friends with kids. Word soon gets around; you ever in Wales, there's this cottage only gets used in a blue moon. Kids are like that. Empty place is an invite to squat.'

'You sound sort of expert,' she said.

'Watch a lot of TV,' said Joe, thinking, this is a sharp-eyed and -eared lady. Would probably find out he was a PI, no bother, but he wasn't going to advertise the fact. Like with a doctor, being off duty didn't stop people parading their symptoms.

'Anyway, I think you're wrong,' she said. 'Anyone getting into Copa would need a key. I heard Electricity Sample charged them Haggards a fortune for making the place secure.'

'Who?'

'Edwin Sample. Runs a security business in Caerlindys, but everyone remembers him when he had a little back-street shop repairing hoovers and kettles. Now he's up there hobnobbing with Mr Lewis and his other jee-um mates.'

'Jee-um?' said Joe. 'Sorry, don't know Welsh unless it's in a song.'

'No,' she said, laughing. 'Gee Em. General Motors. Little local joke. Someone in the States once said, what's good for General Motors is good for the country. Well, there's some round here look at things that way too, what's good for them is good for the rest of us. Don't know who started GM, but it stuck.'

'So who are they?' asked Joe.

'Councillors, Chamber of Commerce, Freemasons, top-cops, the usual. They look after themselves and we look after their tail-lights. But none of this is your concern, Mr Sixsmith. Day after tomorrow, you'll be back over the border, safe and sound. Will you have some more? If not, I'd better get on. Lots to do, what with your lot and the reception...'

'Reception? What's that?' asked Joe, noticing with surprise that the scone plate was empty. He was tempted to take up her offer of more, but virtuously decided against it.

'Tomorrow night, in the college assembly hall. Haven't you read your welcome pack? No, maybe you've been otherwise engaged. It's a get-together for everyone concerned in the Choir Festival. Better to have it after everyone's settled in and got the opening nerves out of the way, says Mr Lewis. Keep everyone interested and on their toes. Keeping me on my toes, that's for sure.'

'I bet. Sorry to have held you up. That was really great,' said Joe.

He stood up and headed for the door. Except there were three of them and he couldn't recall which he'd come in by. Not good for a trained PI. Well, self-trained.

He chose one confidently and opened it. He found he was looking into a small windowless room occupied by a chair and a bank of four TV monitors.

'Sorry,' he said. 'Enjoy television, do you?'

'What? Oh, them. It's the security,' she said scornfully. 'Waste of money, I think, but I wasn't asked, was I? Not my money, anyway.'

'Bet it was you had to do the clearing up after the workmen though,' said Joe. 'And keep them topped up with tea and stuff. Worth spinning a job out an extra week for them scones of yours.'

She smiled and said, 'You trying to get on the right side of me, Mr Sixsmith? Well, you're succeeding. But fair do's to Mr Lewis, he had Electricity Sample do the job while we were on holiday a few years back. That's right, Barmouth, where else? Everything done and tidied when we came back. At first I hated the idea of those cameras looking at me as I went round the school but I don't notice them now. Mr Lewis said it was a good selling point to parents, knowing their kids were being watched over all the time. Could be right. Not that Williams bothers checking the screens that much, and if he did see an intruder, he'd probably send me or Bron to check him out!'

Joe laughed and said, 'Bet you'd sort him out too. Thanks again.'

He reached for another door handle.

'Want to get back into the college, do you?' said Mrs Williams.

Joe had made another wrong choice. Faced with only one remaining door, he finally made it into the rear courtyard formed by the college's two main wings.

He spotted Dai Williams at the corner of the left wing, in what looked like lively debate with a youth of about eighteen or nineteen. They stopped talking as Joe approached, then the young man, who was slim to the point of emaciation and had a pale poet's face in a net of fine black hair, turned and moved away at a pace just short of running.

'Dai, your wife's a treasure,' said Joe. 'That boy looks like he could use some of her tender loving cooking.'

'Young Wain? Don't feed you up over at the Lady House, that's for sure.'

'He lives at the Lady House?' said Joe, concerned at the implications for his dinner.

'Well, he would, being their son. Got a damn sight better fed when he was with the other boys being looked after by my missus, I tell you.'

And now Joe recalled Mrs Williams's knowing smile when he'd refused her offer of seconds.

'So he went to the college, did he?'

'For a bit, till his ma sent him off to one of those posh English places where they train you up to rule the working classes. Lewis said it wouldn't look good running a school and not letting your own boy be educated there, but he didn't object, not when it was her money, not his, paying the bills.'

'Help them with their finances, do you?' enquired Joe.

Williams showed his home-grown teeth in a grin and said, 'Could say that. For certain I know how much it hurts Mr Lewis to part with money, believe me. Very close relationship we have. Feudal, I mean. Master and servant. Doesn't fancy any closer relationship between our families though.'

He cocked his head on one side as though inviting Joe to work this out.

Joe worked it out.

'His son and your girl, you mean?'

'Sharp,' said Williams approvingly. 'Yes, young Wain was sniffing around there a while back. Mrs Williams got upset, like she was leading him on. Took them both by surprise, I think, when I made it clear last thing I wanted was any child of mine getting mixed up with Wain. I sent the boy away with a flea in his ear and promised him a boot up the arse if he bothered Bron again. Don't think the High Master liked the way I talked, but seeing as we were in total agreement for once, he didn't complain.'

Joe, who wondered how much real understanding of his daughter the caretaker had, said, 'Ever think of moving on?'

'Why should I?' demanded Williams sharply.

'Well, all this hassle, you don't seem crazy about the Lewis family, and this is all right for an afternoon out'—he made a gesture which comprehended all the visible landscape in *this*—'but it's not what you'd call lively, is it?'

'My missus been saying something, has she?' said Williams. 'Or our Bron? Oh yes, they'd like the bright lights and the big shops, but me, I'm all for the quiet country life, see, so long as

I'm head of the family, this is where we stay. Anyway, what's it to you?'

'Nothing,' said Joe. 'Just chatting. None of my business. Sorry.'

'No, that's all right,' said the man magnanimously. 'I like a good natter. You ask all the questions you like, Joe.'

Remember, a Private Eye is also a Private Ear, said Endo Venera, Joe's American guru. *Never miss a chance to get people talking. You never know when it will come in useful.*

He said, 'So what's this Wain do now?'

'Bloody student, what else? Went off to America after he finished at school, working holiday they called it, more holiday than work if I know him, then back to some English university, Manchester, is it? Welsh university not good enough for him. He'll end up a bloody Englishman. Started already. Few months over there and he's back here telling us how to do things, just the way those bastards have always done. Useless load of wankers, the whole bleeding race of them. Best argument in favour of ethnic cleansing there's ever been.'

Joe was momentarily knocked back by what felt like a Pearl Harbor attack out of a clear blue sky. Then it dawned on him that Williams was speaking to him as one member of a disadvantaged ethnic group to another. He thought of pointing out that the only disadvantaged group he belonged to was Luton Town Supporters' Club, but decided against it. There were interesting tribal relationships here he'd like to find out about before he declared an interest.

'So how does Mr Lewis take all this? I mean, he's Welsh, isn't he?'

'Cardiff Welsh,' said Williams dismissively. 'Learnt the language from books and now you'd think he was descended from Cadwalader. Hates it when he hears Wain called Wain.'

Joe considered this for a moment but it was beyond him.

'Why? When it's his given name?' he asked.

Williams wiped his nose on the back of his hand and laughed snuffily.

'*Owain*'s his given name. Like in *Owain Glynn Dŵr,* see? But the boy started calling himself Wain soon as he got old enough to see what a prat his da was. Gets right up Lewis's nose, I tell you. Best not to take notice, I say, but he's not easy-going like me. You got kids, Joe?'

'Er, no.'

'Wise man. Meant to bring joy, they say, but look around you, what do you see with parents and kids? Lot more sadness than joy, I tell you. Oh, yes, sadness whichever way you look.'

He's going to start singing, *It's quarter to three and there's nobody in this bar but you and me, Joe,* any moment, thought Joe. He'd heard the Welsh were a melancholic race but this was getting real heavy for such a bright sunny day.

Time to lighten things up.

'Sadness, eh? Few nights in the sickbay with your wife would soon sort that out.'

It struck him as he spoke that there was some slight ambiguity here. He'd certainly caught Williams's attention.

'What's that?' he demanded.

'No, just meant that she acts as matron, doesn't she? And you talking of sadness made me think of something I just saw, some kid called Sillcroft, I think it was...'

Now all traces of melancholy had vanished from the caretaker's face to be replaced by cold menace.

'You some kind of reporter, Joe? You here sniffing around for a story?'

'No!' denied Joe indignantly. 'Just saw this kid's name scratched on the sickbay locker, and it said *sadness* alongside it, and I thought that with Mrs Williams taking care of him, and her cooking and all, that would soon cheer up most kids I know.'

Being transparently honest wasn't much help when you wanted to deceive but when you wanted to persuade someone you were telling the truth, it came in real handy.

Williams's face cleared.

'Sorry, Joe. It was just that...well, never mind. Nothing to bother yourself about. Tell you what, fancy a drink tonight? I know a lot of the boys down the Goat and Axle would like to make your acquaintance. If you feel up to it, that is.'

It would have been easy to plead weakness or a prior engagement, but when a man's trying to make amends, it's a pity to turn him down.

'Quick one early on, maybe. I need to be back...'

'To get yourself an early night. Point taken. Suits nicely. We keep country hours round here, early to bed, early to rise. I'll take you down about five thirty, then. Now I'd better get some work done. Never know who's watching, do you?'

He glanced sideways towards a distant copse of trees with a house behind them. The Lady House?

'Mr Lewis, you mean?'

'That's right, Joe. Don't want the High Master on my back, do I?'

The idea seemed to put him in a good humour and he went off chuckling.

Joe watched him go, then set out himself in the opposite direction to ponder these matters. But not for too long. He was temperamentally unsuited to pondering for more than a few minutes at a time. If a panful of puzzles didn't come to the boil quickly, best thing to do was stop watching it and leave it to get on under its own steam.

He turned his attention to more personal strategies. Now he'd accepted two invitations out, his picture of Beryl returning from the village to find him lying pale and interesting on his sickbed was fading fast. Even if he'd been the kind of lowlife who could play on a woman's tender feelings to get his wicked way, then glance at his watch and say, 'Oh, sorry, gotta run, they're expecting me down the boozer then I'm going on to dinner,' he doubted if he could have got away without a lot more fire damage.

This needed thinking about. Also he was beginning to feel quite knackered. As horizontal was his best thinking position as well as being therapeutically attractive, he returned to the sickbay and lay on his bed to think about it.

It was here that Beryl found him a few hours later, fast asleep, looking pale and interesting. She lay down beside him and woke him with a kiss.

'Oh, shoot,' said Joe when he realized what was happening.

'Shoot yourself,' said Beryl. 'Don't you know it's bad manners to sound disappointed when a girl kisses you? And what are you doing with your clothes on?'

'Soon get them off,' said Joe hopefully.

'No, thanks. You're well enough to put your clothes on, you're well enough to keep them on,' said Beryl rolling off the bed. 'So what have you been up to?'

He told her, giving a pretty full account, except it didn't seem worth mentioning Bron's massage.

'Don't know why I bother with you, Joe,' she said, shaking her head. 'You fool us all into thinking you're sick, then you pack your social calendar fuller than Fergie's.'

'It just sort of happened,' he said. 'Sorry.'

Beryl laughed a deep throaty laugh which ran over a man's libido like a hot tongue.

'Nothing to apologize to me for,' she said. 'I'm just glad you're feeling so much better. Not sure if Mirabelle will see it that way, though.'

'So how was your day?' asked Joe.

'Interesting. We were greeted by the head of the Festival Organizing Committee, the Reverend David Davies...' She smiled at something.

Joe said, 'What?'

Beryl said, 'They call him Dai Bard 'cos it seems he writes poetry and he won the crown at some eisteddfod. Only the young ones thought of him when that Bruce Willis film *Die Hard* came out way back and they started calling him Bruce the Juice 'cos he likes the old claret. They got a good sense of humour, this lot, if you listen closely.'

'I'd laugh only it hurts,' said Joe with uncharacteristic sourness which he immediately regretted. 'Sorry. Only there hasn't been a lot to laugh at since we crossed the border. So he's a bundle of fun, is he, this Dai Bard? Talks in limericks, maybe?'

'Well, no,' admitted Beryl. 'Certainly talks a lot, but doesn't look like he's having fun. In fact, he looks more like Hermann Goering having to tell Hitler the war's not going so well.'

Joe pondered this. Beryl could be pretty round-the-houses sometimes.

'Worried?' he concluded.

'You got it. He kept on being interrupted to go into a huddle with some other committee member. I got the feeling there's a lot of crisis management going on which they're not too keen to let anyone know about. Like the time they found the dead bat in the operating theatre.'

'Down Luton 'Firmary? I never heard about that.'

'There you go,' said Beryl. 'But the hospital management were lucky. They didn't have Mirabelle on their case.'

Joe knew what she meant. His aunt had antennae like antlers and a sunflower's objection to being kept in the dark.

'So what's the word?' he asked.

'Lot of snarl-ups. Mobile toilet people turned up with nothing but men's urinals. Herd of cows got into the main competition field so it was covered with cow pies. French choir thought the dates had changed and almost didn't make it. And the Germans arrived a day early and found there was nothing ready for them. Took the Dai Bard half a day to persuade them not to head for home.'

'Probably helped looking like Goering then,' said Joe. 'Well, let's hope they've got their bad luck out of their system.'

'Mirabelle doesn't believe in bad luck, she thinks God's trying to tell them something.'

'Like what?'

'Like they should stop worrying about these foreigners and concentrate on seeing a home-grown team wins.'

'Maybe someone is,' said Joe lightly. 'We probably count as foreigners ourselves, and I recall we had a hard time finding anyone who'd tell us how to get here. Even the signposts had been bust.'

'Joe, you're not getting a fit of the great detectives again, are you?' she said warningly.

'This Welsh air's turning you into a comedian,' he answered, grabbing her hand and pulling her towards him.

She wasn't putting up much resistance when the door opened and Bronwen looked in.

'Ooo, sorry,' she said, smiling broadly and running her delicate pink tongue round her vibrantly red lips. 'Thought I might finish that massage, Joe, but I see you're in good hands. Da says he'll pick you up round the back in twenty minutes. That be long enough for you?'

'Yes, thanks. I'll be there,' said Joe.

The girl mouthed, 'Bye', and withdrew.

So did Beryl.

'That, I assume, is the caretaker's *kid* you mentioned,' she said. 'And what was this *massage* you didn't mention?'

'Massage? Thought she said message,' said Joe unconvincingly.

'Don't think so, Joe,' said Beryl. 'And if you've only got twenty minutes, I think you should come with me to make your confession to Rev. Pot and Aunt Mirabelle. Though from the sound of it, twenty minutes ain't going to be half long enough.'

SIX

BERYL WAS RIGHT. Mirabelle in particular wanted to nail Joe to the floor till she'd finished quizzing him, and in the end he had to do a runner in mid-sentence, and even then he was late getting into the courtyard.

An old red pick-up was being revved impatiently on the cobbles, shedding a shower of rust with each vibration. Joe climbed into the passenger seat, apologizing profusely and trying to keep as much distance as he could between himself and the snuffling Williams.

Then he was hit by something soft on his left side, and Bronwen's voice said, 'Shove up, won't you?'

Rev. Pot could have made a sermon out of the competing claims of the yielding warmth of Bron's haunch on the one side and the hard angularity of the handbrake on the other, but both sensations were rapidly relegated to the realm of the inconsequential by the furiousness of Dai's driving. Alongside him, Jehu was a slouch.

The hedgerows were so overgrown that there scarcely seemed room for one vehicle, yet soon they were hitting fifty which felt like eighty in these narrow winding tunnels.

It took Joe three mouth-moistening attempts to say, 'Know I was late, but I ain't in this much of a hurry.'

'Hurry?' said Williams, surprised 'Who says we're hurrying?'

'Your speedo for one.'

The caretaker took one hand off the wheel and blew his nose into what looked like an oily rag.

'Round here you don't drive by the speedo, Joe,' he said. 'You drive by the clock. Two minutes later and I'd be driving round this bend at two miles an hour.'

They took it on two wheels, or so it seemed to Joe. To his right he caught a glimpse of an open gate and a stampede of full-uddered cows about to emerge.

'Ifor James's beasts,' said Williams. 'Brings them to the milking parlour same time, spot on, every evening. You can put your life on it.'

'Think we just did,' said Joe, thinking nostalgically of the quiet pleasure of doing the ton down the Luton bypass in Merv Golightly's taxi.

He contemplated drawing attention to a potentially fatal flaw in Dai's road-safety strategy, to wit, the intrusion of strangers, but a sign saying Llanffugiol flashed by and thinking they'd soon be stopping, he held his peace.

It wasn't a very big place but it seemed to have everything necessary to a not-very-big place, like a little shop, a little chapel, a little church, a little village hall, a little war memorial, and, the Lord be praised, a sizeable pub.

Only it was called the Grey Mare not the Goat and Axle. Also it was receding fast, as was a field full of marquees which must be the site of the festival.

'Not going to the village pub, then?' said Joe hopelessly.

'No. More at home in the Goat, you'll be, Joe,' said Williams. 'Your kind of people, see.'

The renewal of terror as they plunged back into a green tunnel prevented Joe from riddling this assertion. After what seemed an age, they drew up in front of a long single-storeyed building in leprous whitewash standing alone at a five-lane crossroads, and Joe climbed out with the unsteadiness of a round-the-world sailor finally hitting home.

'Don't know about you, boy, but I'm ready for a drink,' said Dai, heading for the open door beneath a weatherbeaten sign proclaiming this was the *Goat and Axle, prop. John Dawe Esquire.*

A chorus of greeting swelled at his entrance, cut off as by a conductor's baton when Joe followed.

'Boys, meet Joe Sixsmith,' said Williams. 'You'll have heard about the woman who got trapped in Copa Cottage last night. Well, Joe's the hero who pulled her out.'

'Bloody hot fire,' said someone. 'It's grilled the bugger black.'

No one was given the chance to laugh as the tall barrel-chested man behind the bar, presumably John Dawe Esquire, brought his hand down on the polished oak with a crack that set the ashtrays jumping and said in a basso profundo, 'Anyone thinks that's clever can find another pub to drink in. Mr Sixsmith, you're most welcome. Let me draw you a pint. And take heed, Danny Edwards, this is going on your slate.'

Edwards, Joe presumed, was the young man who'd made the crack.

He remained seated, looking resentful, and there were others who didn't move either, but sat there either indifferent or neutral. Some—two or maybe three, he only got a fleeting impression of retreating forms—felt the need to leave as he came in, their exit marked by a sudden gust of rock music as an inner door opened then closed behind them. Joe hoped their exit was coincidence rather than comment, but his unease was soon dissipated in the unmistakably genuine warmth of the half dozen or so who crowded round to shake his hand.

They were all men in the bar. Bronwen had vanished, presumably heading straight for the source of the music. Certainly there was little here to attract such a bright young denizen of the modern era. In fact, Joe doubted if this particular bar had changed much in the past hundred years. Its small windows created perpetual dusk, which was no great deprivation unless you wanted a good look at the uncarpeted floorboards, the low ceiling stained with enough nicotine to dye a thousand lungs, or the dusty photos of depressed-looking men in stiff collars which crowded the flaking walls. Was sadness endemic in these parts? Joe wondered. Like one of them cancer clusters some folk reckoned existed round nuclear power stations. Or maybe some apparition of something bad that had once happened appeared from time to time and sent you plunging into the depths. Sights and sadness. He recalled the two odd ailments scratched into the sickbay locker's paint. Perhaps there was a connection, cause and effect, the sights bringing on the sadness.

But the jollity of the chief welcomers quickly seemed to communicate itself to the others, and he began to feel that maybe there were worse places to be than sitting here among Dai Williams's cronies, modestly retailing details of the Copa Cottage rescue to a continuo of admiring applause.

Even Danny Edwards had come out of his sulk and was showing a lively interest. At one point he turned to a neighbour and said something in Welsh. Instantly the landlord, who was addressed familiarly as Long John, said, 'English, boyo. Show some manners. We don't have much to be grateful for, but at least the bas-

white supremacists who'd burnt down their own cottage for the insurance...

Shoot! Prejudice like this could get him done under the Race Relations Act. And rightly too. Also he knew he was just evading the issue.

Had he heard anything that he ought to pass on to Ursell?

Not really. OK, that was what he wanted to think, but what in fact had he heard? Bunch of barroom hotheads, shouting their mouths off, mainly in a language he didn't understand. So they were rude about the English. Should listen to the lads in the pub back home when England were getting beat on the telly. Now that really was abuse!

'Thinking 'bout what?' Bron persisted.

'Things,' he said vaguely.

'Ooh, my man of mystery. So where'm I taking you? Or is that a mystery too? Back to the college, is it?'

'Yeah. The Lady House. Mr Lewis asked me for dinner.'

He saw her look surprised, and went on, as if excusing himself, 'Wants me to meet the Haggards and tell them about last night.'

'Here the conquering hero comes,' she mocked. 'Not that you're not entitled, Joe, but you don't strike me as the ticker-tape welcome type.'

'No,' he said. 'Rather have an early night with a good book.'

'That what they call it in England?' she said pertly.

Joe wondered how real all this sexy been-there-done-that line was. Maybe there wasn't all that much else to do round here. Or maybe like a lot of kids she was just reaching forward into what she imagined the sophisticated grown-up world would be like.

He said, 'So what do you do for fun round here? Goat the hot nite-spot, is it?'

'You seen it,' she said gloomily. 'And I need a lift out there if Da won't lend me the pick-up. You're from Luton, is that right? What's it like there?'

'Like every night's mardis gras night,' said Joe, with slightly hyperbolical nostalgia. 'Lots going on, something to suit everyone, and you can be down in the Smoke in a jiff if that's your fancy.'

'Sounds great,' she said enviously.

'Well, maybe your father will move to town eventually. I didn't get the impression he was mad keen on his job here.'

'No, not him,' she said with force. 'Keeps on moaning, but if me and Mam mention moving, he changes his tune and says that at least we've got security here. Like in jail, you mean? I say. And he says that he doesn't know what I'm moaning about as I'll be up and away in a year or so. And then I see Mam looking at him funny as if she's thinking what it's going to be like just the two of them stuck out here.'

'So what do you do, Bronwen? Got a job?'

'No, I'm still at the comp. I help Mam out in the hols. Thought I might fancy being a physio, something like that, but I'm not sure.'

'Massaging people, you mean?'

'Right.' She grinned at him slyly. 'Hope I didn't get you in bother with your girl.'

'No way,' he lied. 'Hey, I thought you said it was dead round here. Looks lively enough to me.'

They had reached Llanffugiol, which was bustling with life.

'Isn't like this normally,' said Bron. 'Not seen so many people here since they stopped burning witches three or four years back. Festival's put it on the map for a couple of days, I suppose.'

'Just as well. Didn't seem to be on no map yesterday,' said Joe.

'Sorry?'

He explained their difficulty in getting directions and she laughed.

'You must have asked the wrong people, Joe.'

'So who are the right people?'

She hesitated. Wondering whether she should be washing dirty linen in public, Joe guessed. He made no further attempt to prompt her verbally. He'd learned that a man could make up a lot of deficiency in the incisive questioning department by being a very good listener, so he put on his good-listening face, like an affectionate dog hoping for a walk.

She said, 'The festival's caused a bit of bother locally. There's half a dozen villages round here, Llanffugiol and Llanffaith the biggest, and when the idea first came up about three years ago, it was going to be the whole area involved. Musical side of things was going to be looked after by this guy from Llanffaith, Glyn Matthias. He teaches music at the comp., used to do some here at the college.'

Another hesitation. Time for a prompt. Glyn...teacher at the comp....

'Was that him in the pub tonight. You were talking to him as you came out?'

It did the trick.

'Yeah. That's right. Wasn't full time at the college. Does a bit here and there, and private tuition. So he was in charge of that side of the festival, Mr Lewis and the Reverend Davies looking after organization.'

'That would be Dai Bard, Bruce and Juice,' said Joe, showing off.

It was almost counterproductive.

'Yeah,' she said frowning. 'You got big ears for a little fellow, Joe.'

'Less of the cheek. That the way they teach you to talk to people old enough to be your father?'

'No one's that old,' she said feelingly. 'Anyway, there was some bother at the college. There was this boy, he got taken away, and there was all kinds of stories, and the police came out to the college, but like most things round here, just when it looked like getting interesting, everything went quiet. People said Mr Lewis must have had a word with his chum Pantyhose and got things swept under the carpet.'

'His chum *who?*'

'Don't know everything then,' she observed slyly. 'Mr Penty-Hooser, the Deputy Chief Constable, always gets called Pantyhose, but I won't tell you the joke with you singing in a chapel choir. Him and Mr Lewis are friends from way back, went to the same fancy school together, they say, as well as being GM, of course.'

'General Motors,' said Joe, reclaiming some of the high ground. 'Look, what are we talking here? Some kind of abuse?'

'Depends who's talking,' said Bron. 'All I know is the Sillcroft boy got taken away, and there was talk, and one or two other boys got taken away, then Mr Matthias got his cards.'

Sillcroft. He was recalling her father's aggressive question when he'd mentioned the name in relation to the weird inscription in the sickbay: *You a reporter?*

'That be Simon Sillcroft?' he asked.

'You heard about him already, have you?' she said. 'Don't know why I'm bothering to tell you things when you know more about them than I do.'

It sounded more like time out to regroup than genuine pique.

Joe was glad of the time out too. *Simon Sillcroft, sadness.* It had bothered him a bit when he first spotted the words. Now they were bothering him a lot more.

They passed beneath the mouldering arch which marked the entrance to Branddreth Hall and almost immediately turned sharp left along a bumpy unmetalled track winding through a beech copse which led to the kind of house which would have looked great in an old Hammer movie. It had a timber frame filled with narrow bricks the colour of dried blood and it stood three storeys tall, the top one gabled. The narrow windows looked out blankly like dead eyes and to Joe's fairly expert engineer's gaze, the structure didn't look quite square-built, but gave an impression of sagging, like an old man, or lady, who's stood in the heat too long.

The track lassoed a circle of desiccated lawn, the hub of which was marked by a magnolia tree that looked like it was missing home. Bron brought the pick-up to a halt at the foot of a flight of incongruously grandiose granite steps which led to a flaking front door flanked by a pair of marble cupids, one headless.

'This Simon Sillcroft, you knew him?' he asked.

'A bit. Only 'cos he was a bit sickly and spent a lot of time in the sickbay, where you are, and sometimes I helped Mam in there. Otherwise Da kept me well away from the collegers. Can't imagine what he thought they were going to do.'

She spoke with a childish innocence which wouldn't have fooled a naive vicar. Joe guessed that it was a long time since Bron hadn't been fully aware what it was the young collegers were dreaming of whenever they caught a glimpse of her.

'And what did he say happened?'

'Don't know. Can't imagine him saying much at all, to be honest. I never got a word out of him, that's for sure. He was a bit weird.'

Girl of fourteen or fifteen exerting her charms on a young lad and getting no response *would* think he was a bit weird, thought Joe. Especially with charms like Bron's.

'So nothing happened in the end?' he said.

'Don't be silly,' she laughed. 'Nothing happened to bother folk in Luton maybe, but round here a lot happened and it's still happening. Don't you listen when someone talks to you, then? Everyone was up in arms one way or another when Mr Matthias got his cards. It was like pointing a finger at him, see? Mr Lewis had to do it to reassure the parents, some said, but that wasn't the point, said others. You don't point the finger at an innocent man just to stay in business. So who's innocent? the first lot asked. No smoke without fire, and it's Mr Matthias himself who lit the flames, not making any secret he's queer as a chocolate chafing-dish. That's in his favour, said the others. It's the secret ones you've got to watch out for, and in any case, what's supposed to have happened? It's all in the mind of that DI from Birmingham, only got transferred back here because his foster mam was sick in Caerlindys, and when she died they wouldn't have him back on his old patch, so he's always looking around for some big scandal to make his name...'

Joe cleared his throat noisily, partly because it needed clearing, partly because he felt that if he let Bron get fully into her stride, he was soon going to see the smoke from his burnt dinner rising from the kitchen chimney of the Lady House.

And partly too because he liked to keep things clear.

'This DI wouldn't be called Ursell, would he?' he croaked.

'That's him. You *do* know everything...hey, you're not from the papers or the telly, are you?'

The question came across very different from the way her father had put it, less snarling accusation and much more dewy eyed hope.

'Sorry,' said Joe. 'Just nosy. So Mr Matthias is gay and everyone knows about it? And him getting the sack meant that he wasn't involved with organizing the festival any more, but the others went ahead anyway, only now there was an opposition party.'

'That's right. Mainly it's those who live around Llanffaith who are anti and those round Llanffugiol who are for, and that's why it's just the Llanffugiol Festival now...'

'And why there's a lot of people altering signposts and giving misdirections,' concluded Joe. 'Bron, I gotta go. Thanks a lot for the lift. And for filling me in.'

'Didn't seem to me you needed much filling,' she said.

'Well, my stomach certainly does,' he said, laughing. 'Maybe we'll get the chance to talk some more later.'

'Sure,' she said.

He got out of the car, and groaned as his straightening body reminded him of the beating it had taken last night.

'You OK?' she said through the open window.

'Nothing that a good nosh won't cure.'

'Maybe you should have brought a doggie bag,' she said.

'Big helpings, you mean?' he said hopefully.

'No. I mean, maybe you should have brought a full doggie bag.'

She laughed at his expression, then said something in Welsh.

'Sorry?' he said, stooping to the window.

She said, nice and slow, *'Sugnwch fy nhethau, bachgen bach.'*

'Sorry,' he said again. 'You'll have to translate.'

'Oh, it's just something we say when we leave someone,' she said vaguely. 'Like, thanks for your company.'

'Thanks for yours too,' he said, touched.

She stretched up to him and brushed his cheek with her lips, then drove away.

He watched her go. Interesting girl, he thought. Sixteen going on thirty, depending how you caught her. And very attractive whatever age you caught her at. He knew he liked her, though he knew equally well he didn't understand her. As for fancying her, Joe was too much the realist ever to confuse fantasy and fact.

Don't box outside your weight, and what can't be puzzled can always be postponed, were the twin pillars of his social philosophy.

Now it was showtime. He turned to survey the forbidding facade of the Lady House. Not just the door could do with a lick of paint, the window frames too, plus the main timbers all had a wormeaten look, and a bit of pointing wouldn't come amiss either. He caught a movement behind one of the first-floor windows, then a brief glimpse of a pale face in a nest of black hair. As he looked, it vanished. Wain Lewis, most like, now off to warn his dad there was a dodgy character casing the joint.

Joe marched up the granite steps.

'Consider yourself cased,' he said to the complete cupid. And to the headless one he said, 'As for you, seems to me you need your head looked at, hanging around outside a joint like this.'

'Good evening, Mr Sixsmith. Welcome to the Lady House.'

Joe jumped so high that for a moment he was almost at eye level with Leon Lewis, who had quietly opened the front door and was standing on the threshold, smiling benevolently at him.

And probably, thought Joe, laughing like a drain inside.

EIGHT

THINGS DIDN'T GET better, not immediately anyway.

'Just admiring the statues,' said Joe lamely.

'So I noticed. There are many to admire around the grounds. Some Victorian squire was a collector. All copies, so far as I can ascertain, though I do not doubt he was occasionally conned into paying for an original, and of course they have suffered the depredations of many Welsh winters, plus latterly the slings and arrows of adolescent schoolboys. I do what I can by way of repair; indeed, it has become quite a hobby of mine and I think I can say with all modesty that when I'm finished with this young fellow, you will not be able to see the join.'

He caressed the disfigured cupid lovingly, then stood aside to usher Joe through the doorway.

'If you too are an enthusiast of the plastic arts, perhaps you might care to look at my little workshop later,' Lewis went on.

Joe, who during this long-winded welcome, had suddenly become very aware of the three pints of beer he'd consumed during his honeymoon period at the Goat, said, 'Thanks, but I wouldn't mind looking at a toilet first.'

With only the slightest crinkling of the silvery eyebrows, Lewis directed him upstairs.

By the time his aching limbs had borne his heavy bladder up the long staircase, he'd forgotten the directions. The first door he opened revealed a bedroom so chaotically untidy that at first he didn't notice Owain Lewis lying on the bed.

'Sorry,' said Joe. 'I'm here for dinner.'

It was, he realized, not a complete explanation, but in the circumstances it would have to do.

The next door revealed a bathroom in much the same state of chaos as the bedroom, but Joe was in no state to be choosy.

He couldn't recall having drunk quite as much as that, but some evidence there's no arguing with. Relieved, he pressed the flush handle and discovered it was one of those specially designed to embarrass strangers. After three clanking wheezes loud enough to alert everyone in the house to his dilemma, Joe removed the cistern lid and peered in.

He spotted the cause of the problem straight off. A plastic bag, rolled into a tight cylinder and secured by two elastic bands, had got wedged against the plunger.

Joe removed it and pressed the handle. Perfect. Now replace it and go eat your dinner. This was high-class advice even though he had no one but himself to give it to. It was his experience that things hidden in toilet cisterns were not good news. On a case, it might be different. This knack he had of making discoveries by accident, which had some long word to describe it, often came in useful and his lawyer friend Butcher claimed it was the nearest thing he had to a qualification. But off the job, it could sometimes be a pain.

Still, it was a gift of God and, as Mirabelle said, you should never kick a gift horse in the teeth.

He removed the elastic bands and opened the bag.

It contained another sealed bag. He opened this one too.

It contained several Cellophane bubble strips of small lozenge-shaped pale-blue tablets.

'Oh shoot,' said Joe, wishing he hadn't started this. But no point stopping now. From his wallet he took a piece of clear plastic the size of a credit card and held it an inch over the lozenges. This magnifying aid was one of his few PI devices. He'd got it out of a packet of breakfast cereal.

On one side of the lozenge he read DECORAX. And the bubble strip had the name *Charon* printed on it.

He made a note, then rewrapped the packet, put it back in the cistern, pressed the handle again for the benefit of Lewis who must be getting very impatient down below, washed his hands, and set off to be the perfect dinner guest.

He walked straight into Wain Lewis.

'That's my bathroom,' said the youth accusingly.

'Yeah? Ever thought of tidying it up?' retorted Joe. 'Or do you think your ma's got nothing better to do?'

This response, whose tartness covered up his sense of guilty unease, was a great tribute to the conditioning effect of growing up under Mirabelle's strict regime. It clearly took the young man by surprise.

He stepped back and said, 'None of...I don't...what's it to...' then broke off and went back into his bedroom, slamming the door behind him.

'Mr Sixsmith, there you are. Thought you'd got lost.'

It was Lewis senior, halfway up the stairs.

'Everything OK?' he went on. 'Good. Come down and meet the others.'

The others consisted of his wife, Morna; the Haggards, Fran and Franny; the Reverend David Davies, a.k.a. Dai Bard a.k.a. Bruce the Juice; and a man called Edwin Sample, presumably the 'Electricity' Sample Mrs Williams had mentioned, who had so little presence or conversation that after a while you forgot he was there, till suddenly you became aware of his bright sharp eyes fixed on the person talking like a thrush's on a wormcast.

Morna Lewis was also as self-effacing as her hostessly duties would allow her.

She was, Joe reckoned, the illest woman he'd ever seen moving under her own steam. No; correction. Whatever she was moving under it wasn't as warm as steam. She was like a figure drawn by frost on a sheet of glass, so thin and icy white, you felt a warm breath might melt her away. The family resemblance between herself and her son was strong. With the same black hair and thin pale features, she could have been his ghost. But when she smiled on being introduced to Joe, her face lit up like Audrey Hepburn's, and Joe felt truly welcome.

The Haggards made greater demands on his attention, not least because they were as alike in person as in name. In fact, remembering which name belonged to which looked like being a real problem till Joe fell back on the old mnemonic device of rhyme. Fran the Man.

They were both medium build, medium height, with elegantly coiffured light-brown hair, light-blue eyes, matching suntan, and sets of perfect teeth which looked like they could have come out of the same glass. Her creamy dress was slightly paler than his creamy suit, but both looked to Joe's inexpert eye like they'd been designed by the same expensive French hand. They were both media people. Fran the Man was a TV producer, and Joe was assured that there was no need to feel confused every time he looked at Franny as she was indeed Zelda Lavall, the actress.

Joe, who wasn't in the least confused as he'd never heard the name nor to his knowledge seen her act, said, 'Hey. Zelda Lavall. Wait till I tell them back home.'

He won a brilliant smile, which pleased him. It wasn't often his efforts at deception met with such success.

But not for long was Franny/Zelda allowed to hold his or anyone's attention. It soon became clear that in the Llanffugiol firmament, only one star was allowed to shine.

The Reverend David Davies, had he been a missionary, would have been a good argument for cannibalism. He was so well fleshed that, turned on a spit, he would have been self-basting. More to the point, a boiled head is a silent head. The trouble was that Lewis, though ready enough to act the High Master in relation to his wife and other guests, seemed in some slight awe of the man who was introduced not only as the festival's organizing genius but as the author of something called *The Third Door,* mention of which was evidently expected to provoke an admiring intake of breath from those present. Intakes of breath, however, were something which did not seem necessary to Dai Bard, who talked non-stop on any and every subject, no matter how peripheral to it his own experience seemed to be.

Mention of the events at Copa Cottage, far from putting Joe centre-stage, inspired the reverend tongue to a series of small but intense lectures on subjects as various as the historical antecedents of New Age travellers, the evidence for and biological explanations of spontaneous combustion, and the delicate balance between the greater heat-resistant properties of Negroid skin and the instinctual fear of fire inherent in most members of the more primitive races.

At this point, even Lewis felt his hostly duty required him to run a bit of interference, but it took the ringing of the telephone to bring the monologue to a complete halt.

'It's for you, David,' said Morna Lewis, who left the room to answer it. 'Some problem with the caterer.'

With a look of self-important exasperation on his face, the Bard went out.

'Come and sit here, Joe,' said Franny Haggard, patting the deeply indented sofa cushion next to her which Davies had just vacated. 'I'm dying to hear every last little detail of what went down last night.'

She meant it too, hanging on to his every word like the white chick who married the black guy in the opera, and urging him on with admiring questions whenever he flagged, plus generous refills of Lewis's sherry (which was dry enough to seal shaving cuts) whenever his voice got too croaky.

'And did the girl actually say anything to you?' asked Franny.

Joe saw her again, saw the mouth gape in agony, saw the eyes fixed on him, saw the naked will urging the naked, burnt, hurting limbs to move...

Oh yes, she'd said things to him, but nothing he could tell these people.

'No,' he said. 'Nothing.'

Franny was regarding him like she'd noticed his hesitation.

'What about in hospital?' she asked. 'You saw her there?'

'Just a glimpse. And she wasn't speaking then either, but the cops have got someone on hand so they can talk to her soon as she recovers.'

'Will she recover?' asked Morna Lewis, who'd been hanging on his words almost as intently as Franny Haggard.

'Hope so,' said Joe fervently. 'But like I say, you'd need to ask the hospital for an update. Or the cops.'

'The cops!' said Fran the Man with a dismissive sneer. 'Last to know anything in my experience.'

'They were pretty quick on the scene,' said Joe defensively, though why he should feel defensive on their behalf he didn't know. 'That guy, Prince, arrived almost as soon as we did.'

'Prince?' said Haggard looking towards Lewis.

'Sergeant Tom Prince,' said Lewis, smiling. 'Happened to be in the area. Nice chap. Very helpful.'

'Then it's a pity he's not in charge,' complained Haggard. 'Getting information out of that Ursell creature is like getting a decision out of the BBC. Seems to have a chip on his shoulder. Anything known, Leon?'

'Ursell? Well, he's from these parts, somewhere. Went off to England but got transferred back here a couple of years ago. Allegedly to look after some elderly relation, I believe, but of course it might simply have been that he couldn't cut the mustard out there in the mad urban world, and he's been taking it out on us poor rustics ever since. I recall when he was here before, on another matter, he was shall we say uncooperative. I had a word with John Penty-Hooser and that got things back on line.'

Pantyhose, thought Joe, registering that while Prince seemed to meet with GM approval, Ursell clearly didn't. Point in his favour, maybe?

'Perhaps your chum could have another word now,' said Haggard.

'Doesn't like to interfere too much with the chaps on the ground, but he'll keep me informed,' said Lewis confidently. 'At the moment, they're working on the theory that the woman was some itinerant who'd broken into Copa, and was the accidental victim of some mindless nationalist group who torched the place, thinking it was empty.'

'That what you think, Joe?' asked Franny.

'Well, that message sprayed on the outhouse makes it the best bet,' he said.

'But not the only bet?' persisted the woman.

All eyes were on Joe, and he didn't feel they were all friendly. He hated it when he was forced publicly to translate vague feelings into firm theories. Somehow they always came out like the ramblings of a dimwit trying to sound smart.

'Could be the woman started the fire herself by accident and the message on the wall was someone trying to cash in on it,' he offered.

'Someone who just happened to be passing with a spray-can,' murmured Lewis, his mockery all the more evident because his tone was perfectly polite.

'There was someone wandering around,' insisted Joe, forced against his will to defend what he had never really wanted to say.

He told them about the man on the farm buggy.

This seemed like news to Lewis. Maybe his line to pantyhose wasn't as open as he imagined, thought Joe. Or maybe Ursell wasn't telling his DCC everything. In which case, I may have just dropped the DI in it, Joe thought with sinking heart.

'Well, thank you for the benefit of your professional insights, Mr Sixsmith,' said Lewis with the decisiveness of a man who thinks it's time for a new subject. 'I'm sure we don't want to fatigue you with any further questioning.'

Any sense of insincerity in the High Master's words was removed by Franny Haggard, who squeezed his knee gently and murmured, 'I thank you too, Joe. And it's a real privilege to talk to someone who did what you did. If there's any decency left in the world, they'll give you a medal for it.'

Through the closed door, they'd been able to hear the distant rumble of the Bard's telephone conversation, or rather conversations, as the phone had been replaced at least once and another number dialled. Now the man's voice soared high, and though the words were still indistinguishable, Joe, who had some experience of passionate preaching, had no difficulty in recognizing a hellfire climax.

As if in acknowledgement that this might be their last chance for some time to exercise their tongues, everyone started talking to each other, except for Edwin Sample who remained silent and watchful, till Joe, who'd been brought up to feel it was rude to leave people out of a conversation said, 'You the one they call Electricity, Mr Sample?'

Such a look of alarm came over the man's face, Joe had to elaborate.

'Someone said it was you installed the security system. At the college.'

He'd been going to say *cottage,* but it occurred to him this might sound like a criticism. As it was, he'd managed to stop all the other conversations.

He soldiered on, 'Being in the surveillance business myself, sort of, I was interested...'

Sample didn't look like he was going to answer, but Lewis came smoothly in.

'You're quite right, Mr Sixsmith. It was Edwin's firm who did the work for me. These days when we read daily of intrusions into schools, hospitals and other semi-open institutions, we can't be too careful, can we?'

Joe nodded agreement, Sample sat back in his chair and started rubbing his hands together, Morna gave everyone her Hepburn smile.

Then Fran the Man broke this moment of concord by saying, 'And it was, of course, Mr Sample, who did the electrical and security work for me at Copa Cottage. State of the art, I think was the term used.'

There was, if not accusation, certainly complaint in his voice.

Lewis frowned at him warningly, as if to say that this was not the time or place to bring up such matters. But it was certainly a matter the police would bring up, thought Joe. And with the subject opened, he saw no need to be shy about pursuing it.

'So it wouldn't have been easy to break into Copa?' he said.

'Without a Sherman tank, impossible,' said Haggard.

It sounded like a quote.

'So who had keys?' asked Joe.

'Me, naturally,' said Fran the Man.

'And I also. Naturally,' said Lewis. 'In my capacity as local keyholder in case of any problem requiring instant attention. And, in answer to your next question, Mr Sixsmith, it is in a place of safety known only to me where it still remains. Naturally I have checked.'

'What about the police? Don't they have a key?' asked Joe.

'Of course not,' said Fran the Man. 'Why should they have?'

'Well, if there's a direct alarm line to the station...'

He saw from Haggard's face there wasn't. So much for state of the art.

There were other questions he'd have liked to ask if he'd been on the case, and maybe even though he wasn't. But at this moment the door burst open and Dai Bard re-entered on a wave of indignation.

'That was Mrs Pontin in charge of catering to say she's at Mr Jonas's slide show of his trip to the Holy Land—don't rush to see it; he spent most of his time in bed with his stomach and what he did take is mostly out of focus anyway—and she ran into Mrs Jones from Penfyn whose husband's firm got the sandwich contract, and she cut her dead, so naturally she asked why, and it all came out that someone had phoned her husband and cancelled the contract, saying that I'd given it instead to a cousin of mine in Wrexham!'

'Oh dear,' said Lewis. 'But you managed to sort it out, I do not doubt.'

'Yes, of course I did, though not without considerable difficulty,' said Davies, torn between being super-efficient and overworked. 'But I shall not rest till I discover the scoundrel who has dared to take my name in vain!'

Joe reckoned that what ought to be rattling the Bard's cage was the notion someone was trying to sabotage the festival rather than having his name taken in vain, which he seemed to recall was one of the Almighty's no-go areas.

t. Everyone waited expectantly. This time there was
and he reappeared after less than a minute.
almost happy.
e now,' he announced. 'I told Mrs Pontin to check
ering arrangements just in case. All cancelled. Except
cer. He's been told to deliver seven hundredweight of
three cauliflowers. Thought it was odd but put it down
oreigners coming. Mrs Pontin is hysterical. I have to
you, Mrs Lewis, for a delicious meal. No, don't get up.
self out.'
. Distantly they heard the front door open and close.
aid, 'Dai is at his best in a crisis which is perhaps why
mes gives the impression of wanting to cause one. Also
e poet. His bardic ode *The Third Door* will I think take
among the classics of our literature.'
t reproved for his uncharitable thoughts about the Rev-
e looked down at his plate and tried to feel ashamed. Mrs
perhaps misinterpreting his gaze, said in her quiet voice,
you finish off the casserole, Mr Sixsmith?'
nds! Not for everyone, he gauged from the low level of the
laybe this had been marked down for Davies and his early
ire had put it back on the market.
a shame to waste it,' said Joe fervently.
e tipped up the dish and filled her ladle with all that remained
n appeared to be another pair of the tiny lamb chops. Joe held
is plate. The ladle hovered over it.
hen the door opened and Wain Lewis entered and slipped into
eighth place at the table.
His mother froze.
Joe often needed an icepack and a pocket calculator to work out
complex situation, but this one he grasped instantly.
Morna Lewis had prepared precisely enough for eight and had
ecided that as her son hadn't appeared by the end of the main
ourse, he wasn't coming.
Joe wanted to withdraw his plate, but a drop of gravy was swell-
ing on the end of the ladle and if he moved, it would fall on to
the unblemished rosewood surface.
Lewis said, 'A little early for breakfast, aren't we, Owain?'
The gravy drop fell. Joe caught it, withdrew his plate, and said,

Still, it had nothing to do with him, and even Lewis, with whom it did, seemed to be taking it all very laid-back.

Dai Bard let his fierce gaze move slowly round the room, as if debating whether any here present might be in the conspiracy. Joe, who was perhaps the easiest man in the world to make feel guilty even when totally innocent, looked away. So did most of the others, except for Morna Lewis whose tragic grey eyes looked unblinkingly into the Bard's fiery orbs as she murmured those most welcome of words to a hungry PI, 'I think we can go in to dinner now.'

NINE

In the dining room an elegant rosewood table, agleam with the deep lustre of age and loving care, was set for eight. Joe had noticed that the furniture everywhere looked to be in a better state than the fabric and decor of the house. The once gilded ceiling cornices were now faded and flaking and the wooden wall panelling looked as if it was held together by a coat of varnish. This was definitely a Lady who'd seen better days.

The first course was a portion of smoked mackerel hardly large enough for a single bite, which was what the Reverend gave it, ramming it down his throat with a bread roll, like a musketeer loading his gun.

Joe took the chance offered by the temporary gagging to ask, 'Why's it called the Lady House?'

Dai Bard's eyes bulged as he tried to swallow quickly to answer but Lewis was there before him.

'It seems that before the first war, the Squire of Branddreth found the hall wasn't large enough to contain both his wife and his mother. He tried moving the latter into Copa Cottage but that proved far too small and inconvenient to match her sense of personal worth, so he had this place built for her, hence its name, the Lady House.'

'So Copa used to belong to the estate?' said Joe.

'That's right. We bought it off Leon a couple of years ago,' said Fran the Man.

'It was a real wreck,' said Franny. 'We put so much work into it to turn it into something really nice, and now this...'

'It's particularly galling as we made sure we got all the work done locally,' said her husband. 'Took twice as long and cost twice as much as getting outside contractors, but we wanted to make a statement. It wasn't as if we were depriving some local couple of a house either. I've talked to the youngster in the Grey Mare. What they want is a modern council house with all mod cons and good streetlighting between them and the local supermarket. Until I spent a fortune digging a well and installing a pump, the only water supply at Copa was what you could catch in a rain barrel.'

'I'm glad you hung on to the rain barrel,' said Joe, thinking maybe Haggard should have talked to the regulars at the Goat and Axle as well as those at the Grey Mare.

'So you can see why we find it so hard to believe anyone from round here would be involved in arson,' Fran the Man went on. 'Perhaps after all it will turn out to be an electrical fault.'

This seemed an undiplomatic thing to say with Electricity Sample, whose firm was presumably responsible for the electrics as well as the security, sitting at the table. Security too. The poor devil was vulnerable on all fronts. Haggard had the look of a man who wouldn't be backward about suing his best friend in a matter of substantial loss.

'Fire chief will be checking out how it started,' he said. 'Did they manage to save much?'

His memory of the ruined cottage as Merv drove him past it that morning didn't give much cause for hope.

'Much?' echoed Haggard. 'No, not much. In fact, so far as I can gather, absolutely nothing usable. To track down the culprit, I mean.'

It seemed a slightly odd way of putting it, nor did he utter the words with the tragic force of a man broken by total loss. Maybe like a lot of folk with holiday cottages, they'd just filled it with a lot of old junk. Except Franny Haggard didn't strike him as the old-junk type.

She seemed to confirm this by saying with some force, 'If it was deliberate, I hope whoever did it rots in hell.'

'The ways of God are mysterious and we must not rush to

judgement, for often out of a
through pain and peril we find

Dai Bard was back in busine
course offered little hope of ano
casserole dish two small lamb cho
on each plate, and to them were
spoonful of string beans.

There was wine too, two bottles
gave promise of being at least as nu
most of those present were likely
seemed to be generally accepted that
tween six of them while the other wa
Dai Bard, bringing to mind his other ni

Lewis must need this guy badly to invi
Joe. Even a dinner like this. Then he repr
unkind thought. Mrs Lewis, he guessed, w
what she could afford. Things going badly
Sillcroft thing, selling off assets like Copa
of spare cash, not enough spare, though, to se
Lady House—poor woman was probably hav
shoestring. Which was what these beans remin

But for all their tastelessness his hunger had b
allowed his drift of thought under the constant dr
monologue to so distract him that he'd forgotten
he'd finished his meal way ahead of the field.

Embarrassed, he raised an empty fork to his mo
it as if he were taking a mouthful of burger in L
Grill & Burn It. Once when a stranger expressed c
the meat's provenance at the height of the BSE sca
ataxic waitress, had replied, 'Relax, friend. When the
beast that provided this meat, they hadn't invented ma
ease.'

Lewis caught his eye as he chewed on air and smiled
appreciation of the charade. Mrs Lewis was looking des
into the casserole dish.

The phone rang once more.

Dai Bard pushed what little remained of his meal into his m
and said, 'It will be for me,' with the certainty of one who kn
the voice of God when he hears it.

'On second thoughts, better leave room for the pudding. That was real lovely, Mrs Lewis.'

This got him the Audrey Hepburn smile.

Wain said, 'It's all right, I'm not hungry.'

Joe, who didn't mind a sacrifice but hated an empty gesture, said, 'Hi. I'm Joe Sixsmith. And if you're not hungry, I've forgotten what it's like to be young.'

The youth gave Joe a glance which said this wouldn't surprise him in the least, but he accepted the plateful of casserole his mother offered him and began to pick at it with a fork as if determined to demonstrate his indifference to food.

'Long time no see, Owain,' said Fran the Man. 'The States last year, and now you're at university whenever we visit.'

Wain looked as if he could bear the separation.

'So how was America?' enquired Franny.

'American,' said the young man laconically. Joe noticed he was eating his food in the American manner, fork in right hand, and guessed this was done to disoblige his father.

'So what are you studying at college?' Franny went on.

'Sociology.'

'Heavy,' she said admiringly.

'Not really,' said Leon Lewis. 'Basic second-class postage will cover carriage of a sociology degree if you follow the conventional route of applying to a mail order firm. Owain, however, for reasons best known to himself, has opted to spend three years on it.'

His son, who did not acknowledge the sarcasm by so much as a glance, said to Joe, 'You the big hero, then?'

'Watch your manners, sir,' thundered Lewis. 'Mr Sixsmith is our honoured guest.'

'Gotta be a first for everything,' muttered Wain into his plate.

'It's OK,' said Joe. 'Not so big. Not so heroic either. Just plain stupid really.'

'Saving people's lives is stupid?'

'Didn't mean to say that,' said Joe. 'Just that I acted before my brain got engaged, know what I mean? Thinking about doing something and being scared, then doing it, that's brave.'

Franny's hand was squeezing his knee again, or maybe this time a few inches above his knee.

'Now that is one of the loveliest things I've ever heard,' she said. 'Darling, why can't you find me plays in which people say lovely things like that?'

Fran the Man seemed to consider an answer but contented himself with a helpless shrug. Mrs Lewis started clearing the plates away. Joe observed with some amusement that despite her son's claimed indifference, his was completely empty.

A bread pudding which wouldn't have made above two decent sandwiches was soon polished off. Then came coffee in an elegant silver jug, but Joe recognized the flavour as belonging to the supermarket instant he himself favoured. He piled in two sugars and an inch of cream and drank it quick. He was beginning to feel seriously knackered and the sooner this evening was done, the better.

He waited for his moment, then coughed, which was easy with his throat, and said, 'Time for me to be off. Still a bit achy from, you know, last night...'

Sounded like he was wanting to milk the applause, he thought.

'Of course, my dear chap. How inconsiderate of us to keep you so long,' said Lewis.

'No, that's OK. I mean, I've enjoyed it. Thanks for a lovely dinner, Mrs Lewis. And thanks everyone...'

For the second time that night he sought a good exit line. The quote from 'Men of Harlech' that had got him out of the Goat didn't quite fit here, but there was that other bit of Welsh Bronwen had used. *Thanks for your company,* she said it meant.

He conjured up the memory of her voice and said carefully, '*Sugnsch fy nhethau, bachgen bach.*'

He thought he'd got it just about perfect. Certainly everyone looked amazed.

Franny said, 'Joe, am I right, is that Welsh? My, my, you even speak the lingo. What a man of hidden talents you are.'

That hand on his leg again, this time unambiguously on the upper thigh. This rate of progress, it was definitely time to leave.

'So are we going to be let into the secret?' said Fran the Man. 'What does it mean?'

'Perhaps you should do the honours, Mr Sixsmith,' said Lewis.

Maybe his book-learned Welsh didn't run to everyday conversation, thought Joe.

'Don't really speak the language,' he said to Franny. 'Just a phrase I picked up earlier. It means, thanks for your company, something like that.'

'Well, I'm still very impressed,' said the woman. 'All the time I've been coming here and I've never picked up a word. Don't you think it's amazing, Leon?'

'Indeed I do,' said Lewis. 'Mr Sixsmith, I compliment you on the excellence of your ear.'

Wain stood up so abruptly he knocked his chair over.

'You're not going to tell him then?' he demanded. 'You're going to wait till he's gone, then have a quiet little chuckle at his expense?'

'Owain, that's enough,' thundered Lewis in a voice which probably had the sixth form trembling and the first form wetting themselves. But it had no effect on his son.

'You disgust me, you know that?' said the youth, suddenly sounding more mature than his father. 'Mr Sixsmith, someone's been playing a joke on you and my father obviously thinks it would be funny to let it happen again. But if you spend all your life with children, that's how you end up—childish—isn't it?'

'Sorry?' said Joe.

'What you said doesn't mean anything like thanks for your company,' said Wain. 'What it actually means is *Suck my tits, little man.*'

TEN

WHEN JOE WAS consternated, he stepped in consternation deeply, but he didn't track it next door. Though he left the Lady House apologizing, and being apologized to, within a very short time he had regained his normal equanimity and was able to laugh out loud at what had just transpired, causing some consternation in a swarm of gnats enjoying the balmy air.

It was an evening to make even a devout anti-pantheist sigh appreciatively at its beauty, with the sun perched on the horizon like the ball on West Germany's goal-line in the '66 World Cup, not certain whether it was all over or not. Across the azure sky a passing jet had left a twin vapour trail which the sunset rays had flushed a delicate pink. Not much given to poetry unless it had a good tune, Joe was inspired by weariness to think it looked like a cherry-blossom-strewn path to slumberland.

Pity Beryl wasn't around to try the image on. Nothing like a flight of flowery fancy for softening up the ladies. At least that was the gospel according to Big Merv Golightly, who claimed to have softened up more leathery hearts than a barrelful of dubbin.

So immersed was Joe in this dream of a softened-up Beryl drifting to sleep with him on a bed of cherry blossom, he didn't notice the figure lurking in the shrubbery till it was too late.

'Gotcha!' cried his ambusher, leaping out and wrapping his arms about Joe from behind and lifting him high in the air.

Lesson 16 in Mr Takeushi's martial arts class at the Luton Sports Centre had been all about dealing with the attacks from behind. Trouble was it assumed that your feet remained firm on the ground. Nor did it mention the fact that being lifted violently into the air could instantly undo the analgesic effect of Welsh bitter, dry sherry and red wine.

He screamed very loud. Perhaps Lesson 17, which he'd missed, went into the use of scream as defensive technique. Whatever, it certainly worked.

His attacker placed him gently on the ground, released him and began apologizing profusely.

'Joe, I'm sorry...I didn't think...you OK, man?'

'Merv! No, I'm not OK. If anything I feel worse than I did last night.'

'I'm real sorry...here, try a shot of this...it's Welsh whisky...'

'What you trying to do? Case you haven't crushed me to death, you want to finish me off with some moonshine brewed in the hills?'

'No, this stuff comes in a proper bottle, all legal,' said Merv. 'Here, try it.'

Joe took the bottle and drank cautiously, then with more abandon.

'You're right,' he admitted. 'Tastes like real Scotch.'

'Why shouldn't it? Just like Scotland, this place,' said Merv without noticeable enthusiasm. 'All hills and sheep crap and people speaking like they had their throats slit, which wouldn't surprise me.'

Joe felt a general sympathy with this analysis, but he never liked rushing to judgement without examining all available evidence.

'You ever been to Scotland?' he asked.

'Not conscious,' said Merv. 'You?'

'Went to Cumberland once.'

'Is that in Scotland?'

'Might as well be,' said Joe.

Having established his superiority of knowledge, he now showed his generosity of spirit by saying, 'Live and let live, Merv. There's good things everywhere if you look hard enough.'

'Yeah? Name one good thing about Wales.'

'Well, Paul Robeson was very fond of it,' said Joe.

Robeson was one of his all-time heroes. Merv knew he'd get nowhere arguing with Joe once he'd cited the great man on his side.

He said, 'OK, I'll keep on looking. What you been doing anyway? I went looking for you in that sickbay and got told you were out living it up. Thought you made a miraculous recovery or something, else I wouldn't have jumped you.'

'Miraculous don't come into it.'

He gave Merv a rundown of his evening.

The taxi driver was much amused at Joe's discomfiture over Bronwen's Welsh phrase.

'Next time she says *anything* to you in Welsh, you grab her tit, man. Tell her you took a rain check. She a good looker, you say?'

'Oh yes. But young. Younger than she looks, maybe, playing a kid's trick like that.'

'Don't sound like no trick to me, Joe,' said Merv. 'Didn't you say you spoke some Welsh just to wind up those guys in the pub? Maybe they wanted to find out how much you'd really understood of what they were saying and got the girl to check you out.'

Now Joe recollected waiting for Bron in the car park and seeing her in the doorway with Glyn Matthias speaking earnestly in her ear. Maybe something had been said they didn't like the idea of him understanding. Shoot! Did this mean he ought to speak to Ursell after all?

'Another thing,' said Merv. 'I've been down the Grey Mare in Llanffugiol. You know that wide boy who fixed my bus...'

Joe grinned his appreciation that Merv was using *wide boy* in every sense.

'Nye Garage, you mean?'

'Yeah. Him. Well, he got talking to me and he was asking a lot of questions about you. He wasn't at the Goat, was he?'

'Thought I saw his van in the car park,' admitted Joe. 'And there were a couple of guys left the bar pretty quick as I went in, one tall and thin, one short, could've been Nye. How come you two are so friendly anyway? Thought you were going to run him off the road next time you saw him?'

'Got told if I wanted a bet on the singing, there was this guy ran a book locally coming in later, and it turned out to be Nye.' His expression darkened, and he went on. 'Not going running to the Old Bill with any of this stuff, are you, Joe? I mean, it's all guessing, isn't it? Nothing firm to link Nye to those guys in the Goat, or any of them to anything dodgy either.'

'Why are you so worried? No, let me guess, you put a big bet on, and Nye Garage wouldn't be paying out if he was behind bars!'

'Not so big, just a pony. But I'm right, aren't I?'

'Yeah, you're right,' said Joe, glad of another reason for not talking to Ursell. 'Hope you win. Sorry I won't be singing, it's bad enough all this talking, but the others are in good voice and they'll do their best to see your money's safe.'

He regarded his friend fondly, touched that the big man who was a notoriously careful punter, should have put his money where the Boyling Corner mouths were. Then a certain evasiveness in Merv's return gaze sparked suspicion.

'It is the Corner you're backing, isn't it, Merv?' he asked.

The big man raised his arms defensively.

'There's this little Irish girl from Donegal. I heard her singing in the bar. Voice like an angel, Joe, and she says the rest of her lot are even better. I was chatting her up when Nye appeared and said he'd heard I was looking to place a bet. Well, what else could I do but ask the odds on Donegal? But she really does sing like an angel.'

'So you've bet against your friends for the sake of carnal pleasure,' said Joe primly. 'Rev. Pot is going to love that. I just hope she was worth it.'

'Didn't have no chance to find out,' said Merv gloomily. 'These two guys turned up, built like barrels of Guinness. One's her brother, other's her fiancé, didn't stay around long enough to work out which was which. That's why I'm back early.'

'Well, it may be early for you, Merv, but it's bedtime for me,' said Joe yawning. 'You see Mirabelle or the others, tell them I'm getting my head down and don't want no tucking up.'

'Not ever Beryl?' leered Merv.

'Five minutes past, maybe, but since this lunatic attacked me, all I want under me is my mattress.'

They parted company, Joe carrying on down the drive to the hall, Merv branching off to his coach. He insisted on sleeping in it, for security, he claimed, but Joe guessed it was partly so he could play his usual lullaby of heavy rock, and partly in case he struck lucky.

The sun had finally decided it was all over, though the pale sky was still not pimpled by stars. A few birds were twittering. Joe presumed they were saying good night.

'You too,' said Joe, then stopped dead in his tracks when what he'd taken for a piece of statuary came to life ahead of him.

It took him only a nervous second to recognize Fran the Man, so presumably he was safe from even a mock-attack.

'Saw you talking to your friend and I didn't want to interrupt,' said Haggard.

'Nice of you,' said Joe. 'I'm just on my way to bed. It's been a hard day's night.'

'I'll walk you to the college,' said Haggard, falling into step beside him. 'Let me come straight to the point. I've a proposition for you. It's about the cottage. I had a lot of valuable stuff in there, equipment, papers that are going to cost me time and money to get replaced, even a fair amount of the folding stuff put aside for a rainy day.'

He paused as if totting up mentally the extent of his loss.

Joe said, 'And you kept all this valuable stuff in an old cottage out in the sticks?'

'I know. Sounds stupid, doesn't it? But it's a lot safer than our London flat, I tell you. So many break-ins round us, I think the agent must be issuing keys. Anyway, I thought I'd got maximum security after Sample's firm finished the job. But that's another story. And of course I've got insurance. Trouble is, there's the usual exclusion clause about acts of civil disobedience and terrorist activity. If it turns out this was definitely down to some bunch of nationalist nutters, my company won't pay a penny. The police are being almost obstructively cagey. They refer me to the fire chief and he refers me back to the police. It wouldn't surprise me if the local rep of my insurance company isn't in cahoots with both. Or am I being paranoid?'

Joe recalled Ella Williams's remarks about GM and said, 'Probably. But it don't mean you're wrong.'

'That's how I see it. What I don't want is this thing being wrapped up nice and tidy just to save the paperwork. I'd like to be sure someone was working hard at finding out exactly who this woman was, how she got in, what contribution if any she made to starting the fire. OK, I may be wrong about the police and they'll do the job. But I'd feel a lot happier if I had someone on my payroll looking out for my interests.'

'Me?' said Joe. 'You mean me?'

'Why so surprised? You're a PI, aren't you? And you've got an inside track on this woman. No one's going to be surprised if you show an interest. OK, I know you'll only be here for a couple of days, but they're the significant days, with the iron still hot, if you'll pardon the expression. So what do you say?'

Joe opened his mouth to list all his objections.

Instead, weariness plus a bit of exasperation that this guy wasn't showing the least concern for the wellbeing of the burnt woman, only for his own financial health, made him say, 'I charge one fifty a day plus expenses.'

'Fine. Two days' advance be OK plus a ton on account of expenses?'

A wallet appeared bulging like a sumo's bum.

Should've asked for two hundred, thought Joe as he took the crisp new notes.

'Here's my card. We're heading back to town tomorrow. Ring me at my office number, not home, OK? This is something I'd prefer not to bother my wife with. She's upset enough about the fire as it is.'

Why shouldn't she be when it nearly killed someone? thought Joe. They had reached the college door. Haggard said good night and set off back up the drive. Joe pushed open the well-oiled door and stepped inside.

It was very dark. The residual light didn't penetrate in here. He tried without success to find a light switch. Probably used rush-lights or something. He conjured up a picture of his earlier passage through the hall and set off across its centre with his hands out-stretched before him. With luck he should hit the opposite wall somewhere close to the doorway he'd come through that morning.

He was more than lucky, he was dead on target. He opened the door and went through. A long gloomy corridor stretched ahead. He couldn't find a light switch but who needs light in a straight corridor?

Me, he answered himself after a little while. It seemed to go on for ever. Then he saw a faint rectangle ahead, traced in light. When he reached it he saw a notice stuck to it which he could just make out. PRIVATE. NO ADMITTANCE TO COLLEGIANS.

Oh, shoot, thought Joe. This must be the door into the Williamses' kitchen he'd opened that morning. He could hear voices behind it. Nothing to do but knock and admit to Ella Williams that he was lost again. Then one of the voices was upraised and he could make out words.

'Whatever that stuff is, I want it out of there.'

It was Mrs Williams.

'Don't get your knickers in a twist, Mam. I'll get rid of it tomorrow. I'm just looking after it for him.'

'That all you're doing for him? I thought I heard voices from your room last night...'

'The radio, Mam, like I told you.'

'It better had have been. If your father thought you'd started that up again...'

'What would he do? Take to drink or something? Anyway, I'm not sure he'd know what it was all about, it's so long since I heard any noises from your room—'

There was the sound of a slap. A cry of pain. And anger. Then a door opening and slamming.

Joe turned around. Not a good time to be asking directions, he thought.

He made his way back along the corridor and opened the door into the pitch darkness of the hall. There had to be a light switch here somewhere. He reached out and groped against the wall.

His hand touched something, but it didn't feel like a switch. Fabric. Maybe one of those tatty banners hanging around. He pressed harder. Soft and yielding. Also warm.

Light came on in his mind at exactly the same moment it came on in the hall, and he found himself facing Franny Haggard with his hand resting on her breast, and hers on a light switch by the door he should have taken.

He whipped his hand back like he'd touched a snake.

She smiled and said, 'Joe, I'm so glad it's you.'

Take that any way you like, thought Joe.

He said, 'Sorry. Didn't realize you were in here.'

'I wanted a word, so I came looking for you. Hope you don't mind.'

'Good-looking film star comes looking for me, what's to mind?' asked Joe.

'You say the sweetest things,' she said coyly, then, very businesslike, 'Joe, it's about that girl you pulled out of the cottage—'

He interrupted, thinking that he was too tired to cover the same ground twice.

'If it's about the insurance—' he began.

'Insurance? Hell, no,' she interrupted back. 'Listen, Joe, I'll lay it on the line. I think there's a good chance Fran knows who this woman really is. I've suspected for some time that he's got something going, without being able to point my finger at a prime suspect. It seems to me altogether possible this woman had a date to meet Fran in the cottage. How else could she have got inside, unless he'd given her a key? He's always having to take off on unexpected urgent business meetings, and I bet he'd have been called away today, then high-tailed it up here for a bit of humpty on my waterbed, the bastard!'

Waterbed, thought Joe.

He said, 'Look, Mrs Haggard...'

'Franny,' she said.

'Look, if this woman's a friend of your husband's, surely he'd be all broken up by what's happened? I mean, really broken up.'

'Fran can be a cold son of a bitch,' she said, without any heat herself, as though this wasn't a condition which seriously offended her. 'Prides himself on rolling with the punches, know what I mean? When push comes to shove, it's everyone else out of the balloon without a parachute, no regrets, so long as Fran gets a soft landing. It's just the way he is. Any tears he's got for this tottie he'll save till he feels he's got himself in the clear.'

'Yes, but...'

...but if the burnt woman was Fran the Man's bit on the side, why had he hired Luton's top tec to (a) find out who she was and (b) if possible prove she started the fire?

'But what?' said Franny.

Maybe she had seen him talking to her husband and was simply trying to provoke him into telling her what had passed between them?

Joe shook his head to clear it. Trying to follow the convolutions of other people's thought processes always gave him the grey crinklies.

'But why are you telling me this?' he asked.

'Because I want you to find out all you can about her for me, Joe,' she said. 'Fran can play real rough and I need to keep ahead of the game. So anything you can find out, I'd be really grateful. I mean really.'

Her tongue ran round her magenta lips and her hand went into her blouse. For a second Joe thought she was going to offer to pay him in kind; before he could work out a way to get free of this with his dignity and virtue intact, the hand emerged clutching a thin cylinder of paper.

'I've written a cheque to cover two days' retainer,' she said.

'But you don't know what I charge,' said Joe weakly.

'I've used London rates,' she said. 'If it's not enough, add it on to your expenses bill.'

She took his right hand and pressed the cheque into his palm. It felt warm.

'The number on the back's my mobile,' she said. 'Let me hear from you, Joe.'

'Yes, but...' said Joe again.

He was pretty sure he was going to come clean about his deal with Fran the Man, but into the gap between *pretty* and *sure* fell a noise like a stifled sneeze.

The woman's hand shot out and the room was once more plunged into darkness.

After a moment Joe hissed, 'You there?'

No reply.

He commenced a careful groping for the switch, ready to jump back a mile if his fingers encountered anything soft and yielding.

They did. But even as he jumped, he registered that though

definitely flesh, what he had just touched was a lot harder and rougher than any part of Franny ought to be.

Then the light came back on and he found himself looking into Ol' Blue Eyes' ol' red eyes.

Behind Dai Williams the door Joe had come through that morning was open. Of Franny Haggard there was no sign except for a faint wisp of expensive perfume which was presumably beyond the scope of the caretaker's blocked-up nose.

'Cat's eyes you must have,' said Williams, 'to be wandering around in the dark.'

'Couldn't find the light switch,' said Joe.

'Enjoy your fancy dinner, did you?'

'Very nice. You enjoy your night out with the boyos?'

'Yeah. Joe, I'm sorry how it ended. Reason I stayed on and let Bron drive you back was there were a couple of things I needed to say while the iron was hot, so to speak. Real ashamed they are, one or two of them, for getting so excited. It's in the blood, see, doesn't mean anything, and they send their apologies, hope you'll come back for another drink if you have the time.'

He's spoken to Bron, found out just how little Welsh I really know, thought Joe.

But he doesn't know I've worked that one out.

He smiled and said, 'No problem, Dai. They seemed a nice bunch of guys. Give them my best.'

'Will do,' said Williams. 'Now I'd better do my rounds.'

'And I'd better get to bed,' yawned Joe. 'Good night.'

He went through the doorway. In the light from the hall he saw a switch on the flaking brown wall. He clicked it on and closed the door behind him.

There was a faint damp patch on it, about four and a half feet up, just where a man standing in the dark with his head pressed close against the woodwork, listening, might have sneezed.

It felt like it might be a significant deduction. But all it meant to Joe at this moment was that he must remember to have a good antiseptic gargle before he climbed back into the bed he was wishing he'd never left.

One last task, though.

He picked up his mobile and dialled.

'Luton Police. Can I help?'

'Speak to DC Doberley, please.'

ne, Dai,' called Joe, and realized he was in duet with
vho'd come out of the kitchen door and was shouting,
Da!'
in no mood to make it a trio. Without a glance in their
he accelerated away at a rate which had Joe wincing
nbered terror.
e remembers what time of day it is,' he said to the girl,
ne running forward to join him.
wearing an old woolen dressing gown. She may have
hing on under it, but Joe didn't think so. He looked her
the eyes to make sure he didn't find out.
d, 'Where's he gone? He promised me the pick-up this

know. Maybe he'll be back in a moment.'
e the English will give us back Cheshire,' she snarled,
way and striding back to the house.
good time to enquire about breakfast, thought Joe, sadly.
atched the girl go. A casual observer might have thought
s something prurient about his gaze, but it was the yawn-
ties in his stomach not in his sex life that his mind was
g. So rapt was he that when a hand touched his shoulder
oice said, 'Mr Sixsmith,' in his ear, his feet leapt six inches
ground and his heart even higher.
ot!' he exclaimed when he'd returned to earth and identified
urce of the shock. 'You on commission from a cardiac
'
rry,' said Owain Lewis. 'Didn't think.'
way he looked, thinking probably hurt his head, thought
le recalled the tablets he'd found in the Lady House loo, but
y looked more just knackered than spaced out.
u all right?' he asked.
ah, fine. Can I have a word?'
n't normally talk to anyone till I've had breakfast, but that
eem likely round here,' said Joe.
didn't mean it as a plea. Not much point in trying for an
o the Lady House, not on last night's evidence.
God hears even the unspoken prayers of the pure in heart.
e'll be a good refreshment tent down at the festival,' said
could give you a lift.'

'Who's calling?'

'Never mind that. He knows me.'

He hoped his huskiness made him sound like a snout.

A long pause, then Dildo's voice said, 'Doberley.'

'Dildo, it's me. Joe.'

'Joe Sixsmith? You still sound like shit. What's up, ringing me here?'

'Nothing's up. Just something I'd like you to check. Just listen if you can't talk.'

'It's OK, I got the place to myself. But it don't make no difference, Joe. I've told you before. I can't be acting as your in-house gofer. Chivers would have my guts!'

'Don't want you to gofer nothing. Just have a look in one of them big books you got, tell you everything about everything, and see if there's anything there about some pills, colour blue, diamond-shaped, got the name Decorax on them, made by some outfit called Charon. Got that? I'll be in touch. Love to Whitey. Cheers.'

He rang off before Dildo could tell him to get knotted. He knew the young cop well enough to put money on some small accident having occurred during his occupation of Joe's apartment—broken crockery, overflowing bath, exploding oven. With luck and on reflection, it might strike his wheeling-dealing mind that putting Joe a favour in debit would be no bad thing.

And if he didn't bother, so what? Probably best if he didn't. Generally speaking, it was Joe's experience that the more you knew, the bigger the trouble you got into.

And all he wanted to get into now was his bed.

ELEVEN

JOE WOKE UP next morning full of high moral resolve that the right thing to do was give up both the Haggards' commissions.

He climbed gingerly out of bed and was delighted to find that far from setting him back, last night's activity seemed to have reduced his aches and pains to a distant nag, no worse than a moderate hangover.

There was a note on the mirror above the hand basin.

Hi, Dozy. Us workers are off to the village to get down to work. 'Sets' today. Hope you'll be fit enough to come and applaud. Love B xxx

'Shoot,' said Joe, annoyed he'd slept through Beryl's visit to his bedside.

'Sets' were set pieces designed to test the various strengths of a choir. Formats at festivals varied. Here at Llanffugiol, there were two sets marked by a judging panel of three, whose marks made up fifty per cent of the total. The other fifty per cent came from the two freely chosen pieces to be sung tomorrow, whose only limitation was of length (twenty-minute maximum) and which would be judged by another panel with no knowledge of the 'sets' marks.

Ever since the great Dyfed scandal of two years ago when accusations of fix were hurled around like custard pies in a silent movie, festival organizers had been at pains to demonstrate impartiality.

Brushing his teeth, Joe returned to the moral problem of the retainers.

Upright things looked a little different. OK, so he couldn't keep them both, but he was a pro, this was his living, and he'd be mad to turn down a job which ran parallel to his own inclination. He wanted to find out all he could about the burnt woman. What was it the Chinese said? Save a life and it's yours for life? Or was that one of the medics in *ER?*

Choice of which client was easy. First come, first served. Also Fran the Man had paid in hard cash. Much easier to return a cheque than part with hard cash.

He looked through his pockets to make sure he'd still got it. There it was, still in the tight little cylinder which Franny had rolled to store in her cleavage.

The thought made him languid and he quickly unrolled the cheque to suppress unclean thoughts.

Then he saw the figures she had written and discovered as many before him that money can be more potent than sex.

'Shoot!' he said.

What was it she'd said? *London r*
been using in London but the guy su
Suddenly it seemed silly to be stick
he could be getting so much more f
wife.
But the man had been first. And he
Franny to check out something which
husband wouldn't have hired him in the
Unless, of course, what Fran the Man
was reassurance the cops were nowhere n
between him and the burnt lady...
Far-fetched, maybe, but he'd come acr
fetched a lot further.
Anyway, politicians and lawyers made a
ing able to believe two or three different th
so why shouldn't a PI?
He looked in the mirror to comb his thinn
there was no silver-tongued spin doctor or sha
round brown face that had always failed A
detector test during childhood.
Best he could do was postpone a decision
anything, he turned up.
Anyway, there was a more important matter
ductive powers, which was, where did a man g
here?
His instincts and his nose took him to a room l
where tables, benches and a serving hatch to a large k
him hope. But though his nose caught traces of the G
Breakfast, that was all he could find.
His best bet, he decided, was Ella Williams, but
to do anything as blatant as knock on her door ar
She'd been good to him yesterday and he hat
looked like taking generosity of spirit for grante
He made his way outside and as he turned i
yard he thought he might have struck lucky.
there, standing by his pick-up, talking into a
didn't look happy and as Joe approached, wo
for bringing the conversation round to hungry
wives, he said something short and savage in
the pick-up and started the engine.

'Excuse
Bronwen,
'Hang on,
Dai was
directions
with reme
'Hope
who'd co
She w
had som
straight
She s
morning
'Don'
'May
turning
Not
He
there
ing ca
explor
and a
off th
'Sh
the s
clinic
'S
Th
Joe.
the b
'Yo
'Ye
'Do
don't
He
invite
But
'The
Wain.

It was such an obvious solution that even with Joe's record, he didn't know how he'd missed it.

'Man, I'm so hungry I could run down there, but a lift would be great,' he said.

He slightly revised his estimate a few moments later when he found himself looking at what seemed a very fast, very low, bright-red Mazda MX-5.

As he squeezed into the passenger seat with some difficulty, a voice called the boy's name. Bronwen came running after them full pelt, her speed sufficient to pull the old dressing gown open and confirm Joe's earlier conjecture.

Embarrassed, he found something intensely interesting in the car's dashboard to occupy his attention.

Neither the girl nor the youth seemed to share his embarrassment.

'Wain, not going anywhere near Caerlindys this morning, are you?' said Bron.

'Don't know,' said the young man ungraciously. 'Why?'

'I need a lift. My stupid dad promised me the pick-up but he's taken off in it and God knows when he'll be back and I've got a hair appointment...'

'Real emergency, then,' said Wain. 'Listen, I'm not sure what I'm doing...'

'Yeah, it is a real emergency, boyo, like yours the other night. And another thing, my ma says she doesn't think my room's cut out to be a chemist's storehouse...'

'OK, OK,' said Wain, with an anxious glance at Joe. 'I'll take you. About an hour?'

'That'll be lovely. Thanks.'

She was gracious in triumph and gave him a kiss which Joe heard rather than saw. Then she turned and moved away and Joe was able to look up again.

'Nice girl,' he said, as Wain slid in beside him.

The youth gave him a sharp look.

'Yeah? You fancy her?'

This was not the way a mere lad should talk to his elders.

'No. Heard you did, though,' retorted Joe.

'Don't be fooled by all that flesh, she's just a kid,' said Wain negligently. 'Chucked herself my way a while back, but I had to chuck her back. You going to fasten your seat belt?'

An implied threat? wondered Joe nervously as he complied. It seemed a good idea to be on the best possible terms with his driver.

'Nice wheels,' he said.

'Eighteenth birthday,' said Wain.

'Your parents?' said Joe.

'Mum.'

That figured. Joe couldn't imagine Leon Lewis dipping into his pocket for this kind of toy.

'She well-heeled then?' he asked, thinking of last night's frugal repast.

None of his business really, but the engine had started with a threatening roar and nervousness made him rude.

'She inherited some money and stuff from her family and managed to keep my father's hands off it.'

But not yours, thought Joe as the car began to move. Nothing too much for her beloved son, but she saw no reason to supplement her housekeeping allowance from her personal funds.

'The furniture's hers then?' he said, recalling the contrast between the fabric of the Lady House and its contents.

'Right.'

They reached about twenty m.p.h. and to Joe's amazement and relief, showed every sign of sticking there.

'Is it right you're a detective?' said Wain.

'It's right,' said Joe.

'Not police, though?'

'Definitely not police.'

Silence. Time to enjoy the countryside moving slowly past. By now Joe had worked out that the boy wanted to ask something and this was the reason they were crawling along.

But even crawling didn't give them for ever to cover the shortish distance to the village, and if they went any slower they'd stop.

He thought of the food awaiting him and said, 'Wain, you got something you want to ask me?'

'Could I hire you? Are you that kind of detective?' said the boy at a rush.

'And here's me thinking Wales was a high unemployment area,' said Joe.

'Sorry?'

'Nothing,' said Joe, who knew his jokes rarely survived explanation, which in this case he couldn't give anyway. 'Hire me to do what?'

'Find out about the fire in the cottage. Copa Cottage. Where the girl got burnt,' said Wain.

'Oh, *that* cottage,' said Joe. 'Police are trying to do that, Wain. And they come better equipped than me.'

'Police!' He spat the word out like a worm in an apple.

Was this the conventional reaction of a student who hid funny pills in the lavvy or something more personal?

'I'd have thought with the DCC being a close family friend...' he probed.

'Oh yes, my father's so close to old Pantyhose, they could crack each other's lice,' snapped Wain.

Definitely personal. Could it be his motive was similar to Franny Haggard's and he suspected his father of putting his fancy woman into the cottage? OK, it was right on his doorstep, but arrogant bastards often reckoned they were clever enough to ignore obvious risks.

'Don't like the police much, then?' he asked.

'What's to like?'

'They come in all shapes and sizes. I take them as I find them. Like DI Ursell. Seems to be a conscientious kind of cop.'

'And that makes him man's best friend, does it?'

Oh dear. Try again, Joe.

'What about Sergeant Prince? You know him?'

'No. Heard of him, though. Sounds like a fully paid up member of GM. Look, you want this job or not?'

'Depends. Why are you so keen to find out what happened, Wain?' he asked.

Suddenly the boy was sensitive.

'What's that got to do with anything? Are you always so nosy when someone offers you work?'

'Being nosy is usually what they're paying me for,' said Joe mildly. 'Talking of which, how you going to pay? I don't take no student vouchers.'

This was mere prevarication, in the hope of finding out more about the boy's motives before turning him down. It had the effect of causing Wain to bang his foot down hard on the accelerator, flinging Joe back into his seat. After their sedate progress along the narrow road, they now passed down the village street at fifty and rising, and turned into the festival field with no sign of slowing till Wain stood on the brake and brought them to a grass-burning halt a couple of yards in front a large marquee marked *Refreshments.*

'Not that hungry,' gasped Joe.

Wain was paying no attention. Out of his back pocket, he pulled a roll of notes.

'You want cash, cash it is. What do you want as a retainer? Fifty, a hundred? Let's make it a hundred. Takes more, there'll be more, don't worry.'

He pushed the notes into Joe's hand.

At the same time a figure appeared at the driver's side of the car and Joe instinctively, though not without some painful contortion, thrust the money into his back pocket.

'Owain, long time no see. How are things with you?'

It was Glyn Matthias, his tone friendly without being effusive, a faint smile on his lips. Elegantly dressed in pale-blue slacks and a lemon shirt, his slim figure and pale face looked positively robust against Wain Lewis's anorexic pallor.

'Fine, I'm fine. Mr Sixsmith, we'll talk later, OK?'

The engine revved. It sounded like a firm promise that sometime in the next couple of seconds, the Mazda was out of here, and Joe shot out of his seat like he'd hit an ejector button.

'What it is to be young, eh?' said Matthias, watching the car vanish from the field at the same speed it had entered it.

'Good way of staying young, driving like that,' said Joe.

He looked around. The festival fields were a fine sight, tents gleaming white in the morning sun, flags and pennants of all kinds and nationalities fluttering in the gentlest of breezes, and already lots of cars in the car park and plenty of punters wandering round in that semi-deshabille with which the Brits signal their distrust of even the brightest weather.

A signpost in Welsh, English, French and German pointed the way to the competition field. That was for later. Just now, with the good smell of bacon drifting from the refreshment tent, Joe needed no signpost.

'Excuse me,' he said. 'Missed my breakfast.'

'Mind if I join you?' said Matthias.

Joe shrugged. He bore no grudge, or very little, against this guy for putting Bron up to the trick which had made him look so stupid at the Lady House dinner, and he thought that folk who objected to gays for the sake of it were as daft as women who objected to men for the sake of it. But child molestation was something else, and till he got the true ins-and-outs of the Sillcroft story, he was withholding judgement on Matthias.

At least the guy knew when to hold his peace. He sat opposite Joe, nursing a mug of coffee and saying nothing till Joe had made huge inroads into a plate crammed with a very satisfying Welsh variant of the Great British Breakfast.

The Welsh bit he cautiously left till the end.

'Not going to eat your lava bread?' asked Matthias.

'Depends what it is.'

'Only what it says, more or less.'

'That right? I don't speak Welsh. As you know.'

Matthias frowned as if puzzled how Joe should have worked this out, then said, 'It's not Welsh, actually. English. Laver's seaweed. It's boiled, rolled in oatmeal and fried. Hence laver or lava bread. Try it.'

Joe tried it. It was OK.

His plate empty, he gave the Welshman his full attention and said, 'OK, so what do you want, Mr Matthias? Not going to offer me a job, are you?'

'No. I just wanted to apologize if anything in the Goat last night gave you offence. We are an emotional people, and sometimes misunderstood because of it.'

'You an official spokesman or something?' said Joe.

'That makes us sound like a corporate body,' said Matthias with a smile.

'When really you're just a bunch of regular guys who get together for a drink?' said Joe. 'Well, not speaking the language, I can't say anything different, can I?'

'I suppose not. I'm looking forward to hearing your choir sing. I've heard very good reports of them.'

Change of subject, thought Joe. But from what?

'Yeah, well, lots of good choirs here,' he said. 'The Guttenbergers, the French. And singing in Wales is a bit like playing Man United at Old Trafford. But I didn't think you'd be taking an interest.'

This was hardly diplomatic, but Joe liked things out on the table. To his credit, Matthias didn't play dumb.

'Because of my uneasy relationship with Branddreth, you mean? What have you heard, I wonder? Of course, it depends who you heard it from, and even then I doubt if anyone will have said anything direct enough to be slanderous, though I'd be interested to hear if they had.'

He spoke lightly, but Joe detected a strong current of feeling beneath his words.

'No, nothing slanderous, or even close. In fact they thought you had a raw deal.'

'*They,* in that case, being the lovely Bronwen rather than anyone you met at the Lady House,' said Matthias. 'But you were clearly not convinced.'

'Don't know enough about it,' said Joe. 'All I know is where there's kids concerned, adult feelings don't rate.'

He spoke with some vigour.

Matthias nodded and said, 'You're right, of course. But, forgive me, you sound almost as if you had a personal concern here, rather than just stating a general principle.'

'Not really. Except, something I saw in the sickbay. The kids who were in there scratched their names on a locker, plus what they were in there for, flu and sprains and stuff. Only this kid Simon Sillcroft all the fuss was about, I saw his name, three times. And after it he'd scratched *sadness.* Yes, I felt that personal when I saw it, and when I heard what had happened, I felt it even more personal.'

He'd got the man's full attention and every trace of that faint private smile which had hovered round his lips up till now had vanished.

'Sadness,' he echoed. 'Oh, the poor little devil. Sadness all the way for him.'

'You knew him well, did you?' challenged Joe.

'I knew him. He had a good treble, not strong but very pure. And he played the violin well. He didn't have music paid for in his fees—it's an extra at Branddreth—but I fitted him into lessons when I could.'

'Mr Lewis didn't object?'

'Oh, no. Said he was pleased I had a special interest in the boy, they were all a little worried about him, he was so quiet and unforthcoming, almost repressed.' The smile flickered. '*Special in-*

terest. That phrase came back to haunt me. Funny how different it sounds when there's unspoken accusations hovering in the air.'

'So what happened?' asked Joe.

'The boy's state of mind got worse. He really seemed to have retreated right into himself. I was only at the school a couple of times a week, but I noticed, and I said something. That came out as more evidence of my *special interest,* I believe.'

'What about his parents, weren't they told?' asked Joe.

'Eventually, though, to be fair, it was difficult,' said Matthias. 'The mother is dead, the father's an engineer working mainly in Argentina, the boy spent the holidays in the care of an aunt in Bexhill, on the south coast, who wasn't herself in the best of health. Eventually a doctor was sent on behalf of the family to examine Simon. That's when things were said, accusations hinted...'

'We're talking abuse?' said Joe.

'Yes, we are. But whether the boy was depressed because of abuse, or whether the idea of abuse came up because of things the boy's depressed state of mind made him say, I'm not expert enough to say and unlike some people I'll wait till I have firm evidence before I start making accusations...'

He was speaking with great force till, suddenly becoming aware of it, he visibly reined himself in and went on in his earlier laid-back mode, 'Well, it makes no difference now, does it? In a better place, isn't that what they say, the professional comforters, the ones who are born knowing everything?'

Seemed an odd thing for a comforter to have said, Bexhill a better place than Branddreth Hall, but Joe wasn't going to argue with it, though he was a Brighton man himself. He examined Matthias closely, which was easy as the man seemed to have fallen into a fit of melancholy introspection. If his concern for young Sillcroft's wellbeing was an act, it was a good one. But Joe knew that in this field the craft of deception—perhaps because in many cases it was grounded in self-deception—had been refined to high art.

'Was there an enquiry?' he asked.

'What? Oh yes,' said Matthias, returning with a visible effort to the here and now. 'Our wonderful police went through the motions...'

'Why do you say that? Didn't get the impression someone like DI Ursell was a motions man,' said Joe.

'Ursell? Yes, I recollect he was involved at an early stage. His attitude to people like myself seemed just as prejudiced and illiberal as most of his colleagues and he vanished from the scene fairly quickly, meaning, I presumed, he didn't think the enquiry was worth his attention. Social services showed their face, but it was all very low key, very GM, if you know what I mean?'

He looked at Joe to see if he needed explanation, saw he didn't, and went on, 'It ended with the boy being withdrawn, on medical grounds, and with me being sent down the road at about the same time, because there wasn't the demand for a specialist music teacher any more. I had no formal contract so no formal ground for complaint. Nothing was ever said openly to link my departure and young Simon's, but there was no one round here who didn't make the connection, and I'm sure that whenever parents got a whiff of what had happened and rang up to make enquiries, they were assured that there was nothing to worry about as the only possible source of the problem, if there were a problem, had been rooted out.'

He sat back and examined Joe. For approval? Why should he be bothered?

Joe said, 'You seem to be OK.'

This surprised the Welshman.

'Why shouldn't I be?'

'Something like this...back home it would be bad enough...the rumours, I mean...I'd have thought round here...'

'That me being gay and living here in wild Wales, I run the risk of getting tarred and feathered every Sabbath night? Not so, Mr Sixsmith. Narrow-minded many of my compatriots may be, but having a narrow mind doesn't stop you having a broad heart, and they judge by what they feel not by what they're told, not even when it's the police and so-called leaders of our community doing the telling.'

'Yeah, well, I heard you had a job at the comp., and I thought, yeah, well, that's good, that shows something...'

There he went again, starting down a thought road without looking to where it led.

'You thought that maybe I was allowed to retain it out of sympathy? Or perhaps to make a point in the local battle against the

High Master?' Matthias shook his head sadly. 'Oh, Mr Sixsmith, what kind of people has your prejudiced English press led you to believe inhabit this beautiful land of ours? The kind who out of pity or politics would put their own children at risk?'

'Sorry,' said Joe, who was beginning to feel that if he'd got himself insured against being abashed, he'd be a rich man. 'Didn't really think that. Didn't really think at all.'

'No. Any more than my friends at the Goat and Axle thought last night when they made those assumptions about you. Which, like I said, is one reason I have for approaching you now, to apologize on their behalf. Sorry.'

'That's OK,' said Joe, glad to be back on firm ground. 'Look, they'll be starting the "sets" soon, I don't want to miss my lot. Or the others for that matter. I'm looking forward to hearing if this Welsh singing's all it's cracked up to be.'

'Don't think you'll be disappointed, though it may not show in the "sets",' said Matthias. 'It's the feeling rather than the technicalities where we shine, Mr Sixsmith. And certain kinds of feeling too.'

'Nationalistic, you mean?' said Joe challengingly.

'Oh yes. That. But I was thinking of things more properly Celtic, more to do with loss than triumph. That word Simon Sillcroft wrote, poor boy. *Sadness.* As a people we know a deal about sadness in all its many and sometimes horrifying forms. All kinds of ways to deal with such knowledge. Drink your way out of it, if that's your fancy. Try to spend your way out of it, if you have the money. Politicize your way out of it, maybe, if you have the vote. We realized a long time ago there's no real way out of it, so we sing it. I don't mean sing our way out of it, more sing our way into it so we can make something different of it. Singing the sadness, that's what most of our music is about.'

'Singing the sadness,' echoed Joe. 'I like that.'

'Not mine,' smiled Matthias. 'It's the title of one of the poems the Reverend Davies won his bardic crown for.'

'Thought it was called *The Third Door,*' said Joe.

'How clever of you to know that. But of course you'd have met him at dinner last night.'

And how clever of *you* to know *that,* thought Joe.

'Yeah, we met.'

'And you thought he was a bit of a blow bag? Well, so he is. But he's a poet too, and a very good one.'

So this at least was one thing that Matthias and the High Master had in common. Joe, who'd never been in company before where being a poet excited anything but demands for a good mucky limerick, was curious to know why the Welsh placed so high a value on the talent.

'So what's this poem about, then?' he asked.

'I suppose it's about us, the Welsh, our origins, our soul,' said Matthias seriously.

That was one thing Joe had noticed about the Welsh which he liked. They could talk about themselves seriously without embarrassment, whereas back home in Luton, this seemed impossible without frequent apology or self-putting-down joke.

Matthias continued, 'The whole sequence was called *The Third Door* in reference to a story in *The Mabinogion,* that's a collection of our folk tales. I won't bore you with details, but seven heroes bearing the head of King Bran to London spend eighty years in an enchanted hall at Gwales in Pembrokeshire where they experience unalloyed happiness with no memory whatsoever of all the sorrows they have seen and suffered. There are three doors in the hall, one of which they are forbidden to open. Of course, one of them finally opens it and the moment he does so, every pain and distress they have ever suffered, all the loved ones they have lost, all the sadness which is at the heart of life in the real world, comes rushing back into their souls and minds, and they have to continue the quest. Sorry. I'm letting myself get carried away.'

'No problem, man,' said Joe, genuinely interested. 'I loved stories like that when I was a kid. Still do. And this *Singing the Sadness* was part of this long poem about the third door. Nice title.'

'Indeed. Sounds even better in the original. Pity you don't speak any Welsh, Mr Sixsmith. A man who speaks from his heart like you needs a truly poetic language to speak in.'

'Man like me is more interested in putting things right than making them sound pretty,' said Joe, with a force that surprised himself.

'Well, you did insist last night you were English,' said Matthias, rising. 'But don't mistake me. Singing the sadness doesn't make us feel the pain any the less. Keeps it in our hearts, see, so that when the time comes for retribution, that comes out fiery hot too. We'll talk again, I'm sure.'

He offered his hand.

Joe took it. No logic, but it didn't feel like he was shaking the hand of a child molester.

TWELVE

OUTSIDE THE refreshment tent, the sun still shone as bright and the air was still as balmy, but Joe felt like there was some kind of web over the sun, casting a shadow across his mind.

Why the shoot had he got mixed up with any of this? It was all down to Merv. If the big man had had a decent bus or even a decent map, they'd have got to their destination a lot earlier and instead of going around feeling low with his vocal cords filed rough by smoke, he'd have been looking forward to singing his first notes in the competition.

And the woman in Copa Cottage would be a pile of ashes.

'So you managed to get here. Good of you to make the effort.'

It was Beryl's voice. He turned to see her standing behind him, the look on her face matching the mild sarcasm of her tone. But her expression softened before the unrestrained warmth of Joe's welcoming smile.

'Beryl, great to see you. How're you doing?'

'I'm OK. How're you feeling?'

'All the better for seeing you,' he said. 'Seems ages. I got a lot to tell you.'

'Yeah, thought you might have. Saw you going through the village last evening, being driven by your personal masseuse.'

'She was taking me to dinner at the Lewises, I told you about that.'

'I know. Lives next to the school. You taking the short cut, were you?'

No mistaking. She was pissed off about something. But she'd come to his room that morning, left a note on the mirror.

'We'd been out to this pub for a drink. Not us, I don't mean. Me and her father. He wanted me to meet some people.'

'One of the family, feet under the table already, Joe. You're a fast worker.'

'I wish. No, sorry, I don't mean I wish...what I meant was, she's a kid. Dropped me at the Lady House, ain't seen her since.'

Not strictly true. A picture of Bron with the old dressing gown flapping loose around her shapely body flashed across his mind and he blinked hard, as if the image might somehow show through his eyes.

'No. You wearing that shirt last night?'

Joe looked down at his black short-sleeved polo. He'd chosen the colour because it was supposed to be slimming. After the full Welsh breakfast, there were definite signs of strain around the belly.

'No. Fresh on this morning,' he said.

'Which means these are fresh on this morning too, unless the great detective's got some other explanation.'

She reached over his shoulder and plucked three or four long strands of hair from his back.

So this is what had caused the big freeze as she came up behind him.

He said, 'Hey, look, I got a lift here, no, not with Bron, with Wain Lewis, the High Master's kid. Must've picked them up from the seat of his car.'

Into which he'd been crushed so tight, it was a wonder he didn't have the maker's name stamped on his back.

She was still regarding him doubtfully so he offered what felt like a clincher.

'Anyway, they ain't Bron's. She's blonde, these are bright ginger.'

'Oh yes? Maybe this is the colour she was before she got at the bleach.'

'Oh no. She's...'

He was going to say genuine blonde, only for once his mind jumped ahead to the next hurdle, which was explaining how he knew.

Time to fall off and hope that Beryl's vocational instinct would take over.

He put his hand to his back and winced.

It worked, if not quite the way he'd intended.

Beryl laughed out loud and said, 'Joe, you're the easiest man to wind up, and the worst actor I ever met.'

'Mean you're not really jealous?'

'Do I look green-eyed?' she said, bringing her big brown eyes close to his.

He felt a small pang of disappointment that he hadn't caused her to feel jealous, but it was quickly swallowed by the big wave of pleasure at being back in her good books and at such close quarters too.

'No. Just great, like always.'

She stepped back from him and said, 'You can get that look off your face, though. These are decent God-loving people and they won't take kindly to public displays of unbridled passion.'

'OK, bridle's back on, but I can't promise to keep it there. What time do you reckon you'll be finished here?'

'Well, we're on second for the first "set", but then they reverse the order for the second, so I can't see us being done till three at the earliest.'

'Meet you in the refreshment tent at half past,' he said. 'Maybe we can take that walk we talked about.'

'Maybe,' she said. 'But you're staying to listen to us, aren't you?'

'Couldn't keep me away,' he assured her. 'You see a good-looking black guy being thrown out for applauding too loud, that'll be me.'

She gave him a quick kiss then headed away towards the choir marshalling area.

He watched her go then turned away and ran straight into Big Merv.

'Been watching you,' grinned the driver. 'You'd better be careful. Back in Luton, you can't go to jail for what you're thinking, but out here it may be different.'

'Ha ha.'

'Another thing. Ain't never seen you look so attractive from behind before. Should take more care, Joe, going around tempting folk.'

Was he going to go on about hairs on his shirt too? wondered Joe. But the big man reached round to his rear pocket and brought his hand back into sight clutching a bunch of banknotes Wain Lewis had given him.

'Oh, shoot. Forgot about those. Got to give them back,' said Joe.

'Give them back? What's that mean? You so rich you're giving refunds?'

'No, it's complicated.'

'I'm good at complicated,' said Merv. 'Also, as your partner, sort of, I got a right to know what you're into that involves giving money back.'

Joe regarded him doubtfully. The sort of partners they were had no sort of legal basis. It was like the sort of friends they were, outspokenly critical and unspokenly loyal. Merv felt Joe was an innocent abroad in the murky world of investigation, and Joe knew that letting Merv in on a case was like getting into his cab—unless you were very strong-willed or threatened him with a gun, you took his route with scant regard for speed limits or traffic restrictions.

So back home, Joe treated Merv's claims to a business relationship with great caution. Here in the wilds, however, it felt good to have a friend.

He told Merv about his unexpected queue of clients.

'Jeez!' said the driver with admiration. 'That's like me taking three passengers to the airport in the same run and charging them all full whack. Where's your problem?'

'Called professional ethics,' said Joe solemnly. 'Can't see no way of doing a proper job for one of them, let alone all three.'

'Since when did you do no-result no-fee jobs, Joe? You say they all paid?'

'Yeah. Cash from two, cheque from the lady.'

'Then the only problem you got is getting the cheque cleared before she changes her mind. Hop in the bus and I'll run you somewhere they got a bank.'

'Thanks, Merv. You're right about one thing. I could do with some wheels, but I'm not sure that battleship of yours is the best thing for cruising these so-called roads.'

Which was both true and a polite way of saying he didn't care to be at the mercy of either Merv's driving or the unreliability of his coach.

Plus the main reason he wanted transport wasn't to get to a

bank but to do enough poking around to justify hanging on to at least one of his advances. Merv's coach was about as anonymous as a chariot of fire in a WI car park.

'You could be right,' said Merv. 'But no sweat. Cometh the hour, cometh the man. Hi there, Nye, my man, you so sure of losing, you've come to pay my winnings in advance?'

The greeting was aimed at Nye Garage who was getting out of his air-polluting van a few yards away.

He looked blankly at Merv, then nodded slowly and said, 'A joke, is it? I like a laugh.'

Merv winked at Joe and said, 'You remember Nye who came galloping to our aid day before yesterday.'

'Sure,' said Joe. 'Nice to meet you again, Nye.'

The Welshman said, 'And you. Heard what happened. You OK now?'

'Yes, fine.'

'Good. I'm pleased.'

It wasn't much but it came across more sincere than a much more fulsome congratulation.

Merv, very sensitive to atmosphere in a bargaining situation, said, 'Yes, and Joe's being very brave about it, but as he can't sing on account of he now sounds even more like a dying frog, he'd like to see a bit more of your lovely countryside. Walking's a bit hard, with his injuries and all, so he needs some wheels and it strikes me a man in your line of business might know where he could borrow a car.'

'Hire,' said Joe firmly. He had more scruples than Merv about turning the compassion screw. Also it would be a legitimate expense for one of his clients.

'Easy sorted,' said Nye.

He got back into the van, a process rather like sliding a substantial piece into a three-dimensional puzzle, and pressed buttons on his car phone. Merv gave Joe a wink and a thumbs-up. Joe, embarrassed, looked the other way.

'All fixed,' said Nye after a brief conversation in Welsh. 'My boy will bring it over.'

'Great. Settle up then, right?'

Nye nodded.

'See the goods first, then pay, always the best policy. Looks like they're getting the show on the road. Only half an hour late. Not bad.'

Joe followed his gaze. The festival site consisted of several fields, with car-parking nearest the road, then the commercial tents, next the administration tents, and finally, furthest from the road and its threat of noise, the competition area proper. This was a rising meadow at the foot of a small hill. At its lower end under a high canvas awning, a platform had been raised about five feet off the ground on a framework of scaffolding, which was concealed at the front by a row of large earthenware tubs crammed with spring shrubs and flowers. Behind, a backcloth was provided by a small copse of new-budding trees. In the bright morning sunlight, it was, thought Joe, as pretty as a picture. What it would be like if it rained didn't bear thinking of.

In front of the stage were two rows of moderately comfortable looking chairs. Judges and VIPs, Joe guessed. Behind them, banked up by the rise of the hill, were a couple of dozen rows of backless wooden benches for the mob, with quite a lot of the mob already in position.

As Joe and his two companions moved forward, a procession of men and women with the selfconsciously important look of those trying to look unselfconscious about their importance were ushered into the front rows of chairs by the Reverend David Davies. The noble grey head of Leon Lewis was not among them. Maybe he had better things to do. But there were some familiar faces, if not among the VIPs, certainly on the benches. Danny Edwards he spotted, and one or two more he was sure he'd seen in the Goat last night. He felt quite touched. They really loved their music, these Welsh. Even though these men were almost certainly allied with Glyn Matthias in the anti-festival faction, and some of them were probably actively involved in the niggling sabotage attempts which had taken place, this didn't prevent them from coming along like Matthias himself to hear the singing.

'Not going to sit down?' Joe said to Nye Garage, who'd come to a halt at the entrance to the competition field.

'No. Need to keep an eye for my boy with your wheels,' explained the man. 'Can hear just as well here, if they're any good.'

'Oh, these are good, believe me,' said Merv.

The first choir was mounting the platform. From the green feather they all wore at their breasts or in their buttonholes, Joe guessed this was the Donegal contingent, a judgement confirmed when Merv led the applause and pressed forward to get a better view.

They quickly got under way. The first set piece was arranged to put each section of a choir on show in turn. The sopranos had a lovely tone. Joe tried to guess which one it was that had taken Merv's fancy. One slim fresh-faced girl with an explosion of bright red hair came closest to the big man's description, but when it came to objects of desire, Merv was a notoriously unreliable witness. But she was certainly very pretty. Good job Beryl wasn't close to catch a hint of his admiration, Joe thought, else she might have started having serious suspicions about the origins of those ginger hairs on his shirt!

The baritones were OK, but the tenors had problems. One guy with John McCormack pretensions towing along the rest. He glanced at Nye and caught the hint of a smile. Knows that Merv's money's safe in his pocket, thought Joe.

The Irish finished. The applause was polite rather than overwhelming from the majority of the audience, but one pair of hands kept it going a good ten seconds after everyone else had stopped.

It was, of course, Merv, who'd either forgotten the brother and the fiancé, or was trying to applaud up his investment.

Nye, who'd turned his attention backwards to the car park, said, 'Your transport's here.'

'Give me a minute,' said Joe, his eyes fixed forward. 'This is my lot.'

The Boyling Corner Chapel Choir were approaching the stage. They looked a little nervous, thought Joe. They'd sung before bigger audiences, but out of doors in a strange country was always going to be a test.

He could see Mirabelle giving last-minute instructions. Word was that way back Rev. Pot had once tried to shut her up, but had rapidly realized that the old lady's voice had become such a part of the pre-match build-up, the others lost their rhythm without it.

Now they were off. He saw Beryl's face, a mask of concentration as she watched the Rev.'s waving baton. His heart stirred but he wasn't absolutely sure what the stirring signified. She was great, yeah, no problem with that. And he really enjoyed being with her. And as for desire, or lust, or whatever you liked to call it, oh yes, he felt the stirrings even now, just looking and thinking.

But that other thing, *love*, with all it implied of long-term relationships and marriage or at least cohabitation (though whether Mirabelle would let him get away with that, he wasn't sure!), all that stuff was dangerous emotional territory where he was reluctant to let his thoughts stray too wide.

He made himself concentrate on the singing and felt guilty when he detected a lack of weight among the men in the lower registers. Not just vanity either. Biggest miss was Dildo Doberley, their star bass, whom he needed to check with about the pills in the Lady House loo.

But he really did think his own voice would have made a significant difference. Maybe.

Even without it, though, they got a good hand from this knowledgeable audience.

He joined in enthusiastically and was pleased to see that both Merv and Nye kept it going as long as he did.

'Right, let's take a look-see at this vehicle then,' he said.

They turned away and started moving back towards the car park.

Merv's hand suddenly gripped his elbow.

'Jesus Christ,' he said in a low voice. 'It's a ghost.'

Joe didn't reply. His heart had leapt into his mouth when he spotted it. A Morris Oxford, 1960 vintage, black paint possibly original, bodywork in fair nick. Someone had taken care of this baby.

It was to the untutored eye the twin of the car which had been Joe's pride and joy till it had plunged into the pit beneath a broken cattle grid and been bombarded with falling masonry. Repair was proving problematical, involving as it did trawling the junkyards of England for authentic parts. Meanwhile, Joe was stuck with a loan car, the infamous Magic Mini whose swinging sixties psychedelic paintwork made tailing a suspect even more difficult than Joe usually found it.

And now, here it was, like at the end of one of those old plays, finding someone you thought was dead wasn't.

Nye Garage, long inured to satire and gobsmackery when customers realized the antiquity of his proposed hire car, was momentarily flummoxed when Joe ran his hand over the bonnet like a collector of porcelain assessing the glaze on a vase.

But he quickly recovered.

'Real craftsmanship there, isn't it?' he said. 'Don't make them like this any more.'

'That's because they couldn't sell them if they did,' said Merv, who'd learned out of friendship to be kind to Joe about his old wreck but saw no need to extend the courtesy to a Welshman.

'See under the bonnet?' said Joe.

Nye raised it with the flourish of a man who had nothing to hide. Which indeed he didn't. Or not a lot, thought Joe, his expert eye checking the engine. And with what he could salvage from his own wrecked car...

'There's lovely, isn't it?' said Nye complacently.

'Depends what you're asking,' said Joe, a savage ankle tap from Merv reminding him of the first law of negotiation, don't look keen.

'Well now,' said Nye thoughtfully. 'Tenner a day to a hero, how's that sound?'

'Sounds very fair. Very, very fair. What do you think, Merv?'

Merv, who had a very reliable eye indeed when it wasn't fixed on an object of carnal desire, was thinking about sprats and mackerel.

Smart little sod's worked out that once Joe gets in the driving seat, they'll be into sales talk tomorrow, and then we'll see how very fair his prices are!

But he knew how much the old Morris meant to Joe.

'Yeah, sounds fair.'

Joe reached into his pocket and produced a roll of notes which he recollected were Wain's only after he'd peeled off a twenty and handed it to Nye.

'Lovely,' said Nye. 'Stirling, give him the keys.'

Only now did Joe pay any attention to the driver who proved to be an exact copy of Nye, reduced by a third. Hard to gauge his age, but probably thirteen or fourteen. Maybe the law was different in Wales. Most other things seemed to be.

He slipped into the driving seat. Felt good. He started exploring the controls while Merv wandered round the vehicle, idly kicking the tyres like he hoped he might put his foot through one of them. A man walking by paused and addressed Nye.

'Come on, boyo,' he said. 'Germans next.'

Joe stuck his head out of the car window and said, 'That the Guttenbergers you mean?'

The man, who was tall and thin and wearing a striped rugby shirt and a baseball cap, looked down at him. Joe had small charismatic conceit and rarely anticipated being made welcome as flowers that bloom in the spring on first encounter, but he felt the guy could have made a little more effort to conceal his unenthusiasm.

'Only one set of Krauts here that I know of,' he said brusquely, and turned and hurried away.

In retreat, he scratched at Joe's memory. One of the guys exiting from the bar at the Goat as he entered last night...?

'Wasn't he in the pub last night?' he said to Nye.

'Was he?' said Nye innocently. 'Don't recall.'

'You were there then,' said Joe. 'Thought I saw your van. And I'm sure I saw you and your friend heading out the back door as I came in the front.'

It wasn't a guess, he realized as he said it. He really was sure.

'Oh yes?' said Nye. 'Now why should we want to do that?'

It didn't sound altogether a rhetorical question. More like Nye Garage really wanted to know if he had an answer. Which he didn't. Not yet.

'Don't know,' said Joe. 'But if I think of something, I'll get in touch.'

'I'd appreciate it,' said the Welshman. 'I'm off now. Don't want to miss the Germans. Enjoy the car, Joe.'

He hurried away towards the competition field.

Joe got out of the car, torn between his desire to hear the Guttenbergers and his eagerness to put the Morris through her paces.

Merv viewed him fondly and said, 'Joe, do me a favour. You start thinking about buying this heap, let me be your negotiator, else Nye No-neck is going to take you to the cleaners.'

'This ain't no heap,' said Joe indignantly. Then, recognizing his friend's real concern, he added, 'And I can do my own haggling, but if you want to stand behind me looking mean and moody, I'd appreciate it.'

He strolled slowly round the car, feeling already the pride of ownership. He stopped to peer beneath the chassis. Bit of work needed, but he wasn't at all unhappy with what he saw. It would be good to say goodbye to the Magic Mini and once more drive the mean streets of Luton in the discreet style proper to his calling.

A distant outbreak of applause broke through his reverie. The German choir must be taking the stage.

Merv said, 'So are we going on a test run?'

'I'll just hear this lot first,' said Joe. 'Coming?'

Merv, who, good-looking colleens apart, had no real interest in choral performance, yawned and said, 'You're a real glutton, Joe. OK, one more won't hurt.'

They set off back towards the competition field. As they approached, the first notes of the singing came to them, borne on the clear air. Sounded very classy, thought Joe. Very classy indeed. Maybe we'll get them on feeling. Welsh were big on feeling. Singing the sadness, like that guy Matthias had said.

Then suddenly the notes changed and didn't sound so classy any more.

Merv, whose great height gave him a view of the stage, said, 'Thought this was all about warbling, Joe. Didn't know they allowed dancing as well.'

'What're you talking about?' demanded Joe.

Then he pushed through the people standing by the field entrance and saw for himself.

For a moment he thought Merv was right and the Guttenbergers were swaying from side to side like Deep South gospel singers.

Then he realized it wasn't the singers who were swaying but the stage. And the noise they were making was no longer just musical discord but an outcry of alarm and fright.

The scaffolding frame must have come loose. This shifting weight of the choristers as they reacted to its movement was making things worse. A couple of them jumped off the front, crashing into the flower urns and scattering earth and pot shards and torn blossoms over the VIPs.

Now the scaffolding collapsed completely and a universal shriek arose, from singers and spectators alike. Several of the former grabbed at the canvas awning for support. Their weight tore it loose. Down it billowed to cover the ruined stage and the figures still on it like a great shroud, stifling their cries. There was, it seemed to Joe, a split second of utter stillness and silence, but it may have been just in his imagination. Then spectators surged forward and began to drag the canvas away.

Joe and Merv joined them. It was a natural instinct. But not for everyone.

Nye Garage was standing there like a sea rock, letting the tide of people wash around him. And moving away from him against the tide was the man in the rugger shirt and baseball cap.

Nye looked back and his gaze met Joe's. Then Joe turned his head to watch the long man go by. As he retreated he removed his baseball cap and scratched his head. He was completely bald. And seeing that Yul Brynner silhouette in retreat threw a switch in Joe's memory.

Here was the source of that half-recognition, and the explanation of the man's lack of enthusiasm when they met face to face just now. It wasn't just the possible glimpse at the Goat that was confirmed either, though he felt sure he'd been there too.

He turned to meet Nye's gaze again and share his recognition with him.

Impossible maybe to stand up in court and swear to it, but Joe would have put cash money on Nye's friend being the unhelpful fellow he'd seen driving the farm buggy over the hill from Copa Cottage on the night of their arrival.

THIRTEEN

GOOD NEWS was no one was seriously hurt. Enough strains, sprains, cuts and bruises to pack the St John Ambulance tent, but no breakages.

Bad news was the Guttenbergers were seriously disgruntled. Even while the rescue operation was still under way, their executive organizer, whose title in German almost outstretched Llanfairpwllgwyngyllgogerychwyrndrobwllllantysilliogogogoch, was telling an untypically subdued Dai Bard that this was the worst-organized festival since time began, that the Guttenbergers had withdrawn as from now, that they would be expecting substantial immediate compensation without prejudice to any further claims that might be made via the European Court, and that they would be using their not inconsiderable influence to ensure that the first Llanffugiol Festival was also the last.

His English was excellent, his voice was loud, and pressmen up to fifty yards away were able to take notes without difficulty.

As the confusion subsided, Joe spotted Beryl talking to a St John Ambulance man who looked ancient enough to have bandaged Owain Glyn Dŵr.

He guessed she was offering help, but not very successfully, it seemed.

'Thank you, my lovely,' the old man was saying, 'but I think we can manage without any outside help. Amateurs can cause more harm than do good, if you'll forgive my frankness. Besides, it's not half as bad as it might have been. Strong people these Germans. Like my da used to say in the war, need to shoot the buggers twice to make sure they're dead.'

Beryl said sternly, 'It's not just injuries, they'll all need treating for shock.'

'Shock, is it?' said the old man sceptically. 'Oh yes. Lots of that around these days. Time was when all shock meant was England had scored a try. Don't you be worrying your pretty head, dearie, just concentrate on your singing. Daresay this won't hurt your chances at all, will it? It's an ill wind, as my old da used to say when Cliff Morgan missed touch.'

He patted her arm and wandered away leaving Beryl looking furious.

Joe said, 'Who the shoot's Cliff Morgan?'

'Don't know and don't want to know if he's anything to do with that stupid git and his old da,' she exclaimed.

'You mad 'cos he talked about your pretty head?' said Joe. 'Well, he's right.'

'Don't go gallant on me, Joe. No, it was that crack about not hurting our chances. As if anyone would do something like this to hurt another outfit!'

'Some people round here take things pretty serious,' said Joe. 'And he's right, isn't he? I mean about our chances if the Guttenbergers pull out.'

She looked at him disbelievingly.

'Joe, you'd better give up on the heroics, it's affecting the way your head works.'

She strode away, magnificent in retreat.

Order was being re-established. Dai Bard was talking earnestly into the ear of the German organizer as he made a tour of his injured troops. Joe got the impression it was more like oil being poured on leaping flames than troubled waters.

Leon Lewis had put in an appearance at some point and was concentrating his attention on the VIPs. He looked as ever totally unflustered by what had happened.

The crowd around the collapsed stage had thinned, though several onlookers remained to savour the heady brew of near disaster, murmuring that it could have been much worse in that tone which has almost as much of regret in it as relief.

What struck Joe as he joined them was the relative neatness with which the framework had folded. He walked slowly round it, stooping occasionally to touch the nuts and bolts which had failed to hold it together.

'Now that'll be handy when we're dusting for prints,' said a voice.

He looked up to find Dirty Harry in the person of DI Ursell looming over him.

'Why'd you want to do that, Inspector?' he asked.

'You a racing man, Mr Sixsmith? If so, you'll know that when an odds-on favourite trips over the first hurdle, everyone starts shouting fix.'

'This isn't a horse race,' he said mildly.

'No. Tell that to your friend running the book. Interesting to see his odds on the Germans,' said Ursell.

Interesting also to see that somehow the man had observed his encounter with Nye Garage. And perhaps most interesting of all to observe that, though still far from conciliatory, the man's manner had modified a lot from the life-in-general-and-amateur-tecs-in-particular-make-me-sick impression he gave at the hospital.

The change was underlined by his next remark.

'So how are you feeling, Mr Sixsmith? Looking a lot better than when I saw you yesterday.'

'Feeling a lot better,' said Joe. 'Nice hospital, but can't say I was sorry to be out of it.'

'I know how you feel,' said Ursell with some passion. 'I hate that bloody place. Just the smell of it makes me want to puke. Try to hide it, but I daresay it shows.'

This was close to an apology, thought Joe.

'Just a touch,' he agreed. 'You got here quick. Better service than we get back home.'

'You say so? Though you got pretty good service yourself, Mr Sixsmith.'

That sounded significant, but Ursell didn't give him time to think about it, going on, 'In fact, I was here already.'

'For the singing?'

'No, I'm a Tom Jones man myself. Duty, Mr Sixsmith. Little case of arson, or have you forgotten?'

'Not likely to forget,' said Joe. 'How is she?'

'The same. Critical but stable is how they put it.'

'I hope she makes it. Any word on who she is, how she got there?'

It struck him that if Ursell said yes and gave him chapter and verse, this could be the three easiest investigative fees he'd ever earned.

'Not a thing. You got any new ideas, Mr Sixsmith?'

Joe checked for hidden sarcasm, found none, and said cautiously, 'You'll have covered all the obvious things.'

'Like?'

'Like checking out the folk with access to Copa.'

'The Haggards, you mean? Oh yes, I've been looking very closely at the Haggards. Maybe too close for comfort.'

This again sounded significant. And again Joe had no idea what it signified.

He said, 'Mr Lewis has a key too, I gather.'

'Mr Lewis?' The policeman turned so that he was looking at Lewis, who was ushering the VIPs towards one of the admin. tents, doubtless to be treated for shock with injections of champagne. Morna Lewis was with them. Her gaze turned towards the wrecked stage and met Joe's, but her pale face gave no sign of recognition.

'Need to be careful there, Mr Sixsmith, saying anything that sounds like casting aspersions on Mr Lewis,' continued Ursell. 'Big man round here, highly regarded, friends in high places, same lodge as Mr Penty-Hooser, our DCC, God bless him. Need to be a very brave investigator who started poking round the High Master, I tell you. Need a very good excuse indeed before someone in my line with a career to think of could take a step in that direction. You look like a man who might have found a good excuse or two in his time, Mr Sixsmith. I daresay you've left quite a trail of cut corners behind you.'

There was definitely something going on here, but Joe was a blind horse when it came to subtle nods and winks.

He said, 'I'm only here for the singing, Inspector. You want the best brambles, you ask a local rabbit, that's what my auntie always says.'

'That could be the picturesque old lady? Wise woman. Gather you had the chance to sample some of the brambles for yourself last night, Mr Sixsmith. Little bird told me you had a drink down the Goat before going off to dinner at the Lady House. You're a popular man.'

Little bird? Great clacking beak! thought Joe, wondering whose.

He was getting a vague sense of the direction he was being nudged in. Not that he altogether trusted his vague sense, which in the past had led him further astray than a Tilbury tart. Nudge would have to come to push then shove before he let himself be moved.

'People have been very kind,' he said. 'And it's been nice to meet some of the locals, see some of the sights.'

'And there are some fine sights to see,' said Ursell. 'The hall's very historical, of course. And the Lady House is worth a close look too, I would say. Built by local craftsmen. I would guess there's many a little gem of design and ornament lying around in there, true diamonds, indeed, if only you know where to look. And can be sure they're where you expected to find them.'

This was a nudge-nudge know-what-I-mean like a wedding speech joke, thought Joe. And he didn't like the direction it was pushing him in one little bit. That stuff about diamonds and knowing where to look, what could it mean other than that Ursell knew about those tablets in the cistern?

He dismissed the thought as rapidly as it came.

How could he know? No, it had to be something else. Mustn't let himself be double-talked into unnecessary trouble.

He said, 'Sounds like treasure trove. Get a reward for that, do you?'

'Adding to the sum of human knowledge is its own reward,' said Ursell reprovingly. 'But such unselfish acts often do have a spin-off on the personal plane, Mr Sixsmith. Like ensuring the continued welfare of an old friend, for instance. Ah, here come the ice-cream boys. I'd better make sure they don't drive over too many clues. You'll be wanting to go for a drive in that new car of yours, I daresay. Good time, this is. Won't be much to get in your way with everyone here. As a bit of a collector myself I'd be interested to take a look at anything you come across. Not all of it, you understand. Just enough to give me or anyone else interested a *taste* of what we might expect to find. I hope we get the chance for a real heart-to-heart later, Mr Sixsmith.'

Hope sounded like it meant something a bit more definite in Wales than it did in Luton, thought Joe as he watched the DI go to meet the two police cars which were nosing their way towards the competition field, lights flashing, sirens wailing.

The inside of Joe's head felt like it was in much the same state. He was beginning to feel that maybe he'd been right after all, and it wasn't a good feeling. All that stuff about *taste,* it had to be the tablets in the cistern Ursell was talking about. And for whatever reason, he'd like to use them as an excuse to get into the Lady House with a search warrant. So why didn't he do what Sergeant Chivers would have done in like circumstances, i.e. put Joe up against a cell wall and invite him to make a statement which could then be used to persuade a justice to issue a warrant?

It was all headachingly complex so Joe did what he usually did with things that were too hard and tucked it into the back of his mind to let it soften up in its own time.

Next question. What was all that stuff about the welfare of a friend? Which of his friends was likely to have put his welfare at risk from the police?

Like an answer from above, Merv's voice spoke in his ear.

'You and old Arsehole looked very cosy,' he said. 'Gotta watch that, Joe. Man gets known by the company he keeps.'

'So why do I hang out with you?' said Joe.

'Ooh, aren't we sharp?'

'Sharp enough to know that stage didn't collapse by accident,' said Joe. 'It had been fixed.'

'You reckon? How?'

'Looked to me like most of the nuts were loosened so's all that was holding it together were a couple at the back with their bolts well greased. Quick twist of the spanner from someone lurking in them trees would leave it ready to start swaying soon as anyone started moving around up there.'

Merv had too much respect for Joe's mechanical expertise to

argue with his conclusions. He said, 'That what you were telling the cop?'

'No, he's worked it out for himself, I think. Merv, apart from your illegal bet with Nye, you got anything going with any of the locals? Them funny cigarettes, anything like that?'

'No way. Not when I'm driving a bus for Rev. Pot.' He laughed out loud. 'No pot for Rev. Pot. Not bad, eh?'

'Ha ha. So you've not been up to anything?'

'What is this, Joe? That Arsehole been saying something? Maybe I'd better have a polite word with him.'

'No, no, he hasn't said anything,' said Joe, who'd mopped up the blood too often after Merv's polite words. 'Wonder what's happening now?'

Again his question was answered by words from on high. This time it was the speaker system which told them in English, Welsh and French, but not German, that proceedings had been temporarily interrupted because of a minor accident in which no one had been seriously hurt and it was hoped to resume the competition within the hour.

'Show goes on,' said Merv. 'What are you going to do, Joe?'

'Thought I might take the Morris for a trial run,' said Joe.

'Oh yeah? Expect you'd like me along to give you a push?'

Joe hesitated. If he was right, DI Ursell had been nudging him to return to the Lady House, check whether the Decorax tablets were still in the cistern, remove a couple and bring them out with him. He still couldn't see any good reason why he should go along with this. Maybe the DI's threat was just the kind of bluff cops everywhere liked to throw around to get their own way. But if he did do it, then someone to act as lookout would be very useful. On the other hand, if the cop did have something on Merv, he was the last guy he ought to take along.

He was saved from decision by the passage of a group of pretty young women wearing the Irish green feather, one of whom smiled Merv's way in a manner which could only be called inviting. They vanished into the refreshment tent.

'Suddenly I feel very thirsty,' said Merv. 'Joe, you keep driving downhill, you won't need a push. And you've always got your mobile if you need to call up help. See you!'

One thing about Merv, he made no secret of his priorities, thought Joe. Then reproached himself, knowing that if he ever really needed the big man, he'd drop everything including his trousers and come running.

He went to the car park and climbed into the Morris. It had got a bit warm standing in the sun so he opened all the doors to get a bit of ventilation. Merv's mention of his mobile reminded him he hadn't checked the battery status for a while. He drew it out of his trouser pocket with some difficulty, and switched it on. Still OK. Might as well check for messages, he thought. Not that he ever had any messages. He dialled the code, and to his pleasurable surprise, the breathless female voice of the operator said, 'You have five messages.'

But his pleasure at suddenly being so important was shortlived.

'Joe, where the hell are you? What's the use of having that sodding thing if you're never going to answer it? Listen, soon as you get this message, if you ever do, you ring me. This is urgent, life and death. I do not joke. I'm at the flat. Ring me!'

While he was still paralysed by shock and speculation, the next message began. It was Dildo Doberley again. And the remaining three. Each more hysterically urgent than the one before.

It had to be Whitey, thought Joe as his trembling fingers punched his Luton number. An accident. From the sound of Dildo's voice, a bad accident. Oh, God, don't let him be dead. Please God. Was it OK to pray for an animal? Would Rev. Pot and Mirabelle approve? To hell with them both! Any god that wasn't in the market for prayers about Whitey wasn't a god that he wanted anything to do with!

'Hello?'

'Dildo, it's Joe...'

'Where the hell have you been? I've been trying to get you for hours.'

'Yeah, I know. Listen, what's happened? Is it Whitey? He's not dead, is he? Please don't tell me he's dead.'

'What the hell are you talking about? Your precious mog's in pissing good health, which is more than you can say for me. God, how did I ever let myself get mixed up with a trouble-stirrer like you? Rev. Pot is right. You touch pitch, you'll get yourself defiled, he said...'

'Hold on!' commanded Joe. 'You weren't ringing me about Whitey?'

'Of course I wasn't. I'm ringing about those sodding pills you asked me about, that's what I'm ringing about.'

'Thank you, God,' said Joe joyfully. 'Thanks a lot.'

'What are you thanking God for, Sixsmith?' yelled Dildo. 'I'm in trouble, and that means you're in trouble too, you'd better believe me.'

Joe believed him. The cloud which had lifted from him cleared his vision in all directions and all at once he saw what should have been obvious when he was talking to Ursell. The only possible source of the DI's info about Joe's discovery of the tablets had to be the only other person Joe had mentioned them to. Dildo.

He said, 'What's happened?'

'Like an idiot, and because I was bored out of my skull sitting around the station knowing everyone else was out on an op., I thought I'd just run that stuff you asked me about through the computer. Normally this is just routine. Accessing a drug-details file for info, no one pays any heed. But soon as I entered Decorax, I saw this could be trouble. It was flagged...'

'Sorry, what's that mean?'

'Means that it's part of an ongoing investigation and any queries about it would be registered, that's what it means.'

'Dildo, I'm sorry. But can't you just say you'd heard someone mention the drug and were checking it out of curiosity...'

'Now what a clever idea that is! I can see why you're so highly thought of in the detection business,' said Doberley. 'Only I don't have that option, do I? Oh no. Let me tell you what happened. First off, the drug. Decorax, the file told me, is manufactured by the Charon Corporation in Detroit and it's just been licensed for use in the States. Far as I can make out it helps cut down inflammation, whatever that means, but there's been a bit of concern over there about misuse, 'cos one of the side effects can be euphoria, you know, a high, and the kids are always on the lookout for some new quick fix. It's been licensed on a trial basis over here for the past six months at various hospitals, and round New Year a whole bunch of these pills went walkabout at this hospital in Wales...'

'What's it called?' asked Joe with sinking heart.

'Something unpronounceable. Hang on. Caerlindys General. That mean something to you, Joe?'

'No. How should it?' lied Joe, crossing his fingers.

'I don't know, but you're in Wales, aren't you? And that's where this sodding DI was ringing from just before I came off shift this morning. Wanted to know what my interest was in Decorax. I flannelled, of course. I said I was just bringing myself up to speed on what was going off, that sort of thing. But he wouldn't let it alone. And pretty soon I got the feeling it wasn't just Decorax that had caught his interest, it was someone in Luton being interested in Decorax. He started coming on really heavy, asked who my guv'nor was, did he know what his subordinates were up to? Then out of the blue, he said. "You don't have a snout called Sixsmith, do you?"'

'Oh shoot,' said Joe. It was all clear now. Ursell, made aware that someone in Luton was interested in Decorax, and provoked to suspicion by Doberley's unconvincing evasions, had flown a kite. Which Dildo, he guessed, had grabbed at with both hands.

'So what did you say, Dildo?' he asked.

'Well, it was obvious he knew about you, wasn't it? So I said, yeah, that's right. Joe Sixsmith. Licensed PI. Not really a snout, but he likes to keep us sweet by feeding us a bit of intelligence from time to time, and yes, it was him brought Decorax to my attention.'

'Oh great,' said Joe. 'Thanks a bunch, Dildo.'

'Now don't come over all injured party with me, Joe,' yelled the young constable. 'It's my career that's on the line here. Your mate Chivers isn't going to believe any of this snout crap, is he? And if ever he gets to hear I've been using the computer to dig up information for you, my balls are really on the block. This could finish me in CID.'

'I'm sorry,' said Joe sincerely. Then, picking up on the significant word in Doberley's complaint, 'You said *if.* How did Ursell leave it?'

'Ursell? I never mentioned his name. How do you know that, Joe?'

My big mouth, thought Joe.

'Lucky guess,' he said. 'Just tell me how he left it.'

'He told me to keep my mouth shut, not to say a thing to anyone. I said I'd be silent as the grave, he could rely on that, but what if my snout—that's you—rang? And he laughed and said, "Oh you can tell him everything. In fact, it's probably a good

idea if you give him a ring yourself and make sure he knows."
And then he rang off. Joe, what are you into down there?'

'Dildo, you don't want to know,' said Joe. 'Listen, I've got to go. Something that needs doing. But don't worry. I'm sorry I got you into this, but the good news is, I think I can keep you out of it from now on in. You shouldn't be hearing from DI Ursell again.'

'You sure?' said Doberley doubtfully.

'Pretty sure. And Dildo, thanks.'

'For what?'

'For being a friend. Love to Whitey. Cheers.'

He rang off.

So now he knew it all. If he didn't play along with Ursell, Dildo was going to be dropped right in it. The welfare of an old friend. Sharp man, Ursell. Hadn't taken him long to work out which buttons made Joe Sixsmith jump.

He closed the car doors and turned the key in the ignition.

FOURTEEN

THE MORRIS WAS A JOY to drive. Whatever else Nye Garage got up to, he knew how to keep an engine sweet.

Joe was not an acquisitive man. If his flat was on fire, he'd rush in, grab Whitey, then probably get himself burned to death standing around working out what else he wanted to save. But he knew he had to have this motor.

With the insurance money from his wrecked machine, plus what he could earn from his current clients...

Earn! That was the key word. What the shoot was he doing to earn a fee from even one of them? Maybe if he returned to Ursell like a good dog bearing a gift in his mouth, the DI might toss him some scraps of information about the Copa Cottage investigation which he could feed to the Haggards...

And Wain? No, he didn't feel he could hang on to Wain's money. Whatever its source.

He turned through the college gates and kept turning up the

track that led to the Lady House. He parked right at the foot of the steps leading up to the front door. Get caught burgling with your car parked where a genuine visitor would park it and you might talk yourself out of trouble. Hide your car in the shrubbery and you had more explaining to do than a bishop in a bordello.

He got out, slammed the door loudly (oh, that satisfying clunk!) and went up the pretentious portico steps. Of course, there shouldn't be anyone here to hear the clunk. Leon and Morna Lewis were at the festival and Wain had had his arm twisted to take Bronwen to her hair appointment in Caerlindys. Ursell was right. This ought to be the perfect window of opportunity for a nervous burglar to climb through. No one home.

All the same, belts and braces, he reached up to the bell pull above the headless cupid.

But he didn't pull it. Instead he stood with his arm raised like another piece of statuary and stared at the flaking door.

It was slightly ajar.

Windows of opportunity were one thing. Doors of opportunity were another pail of prawns.

Finally he rang the bell. If there were someone inside with a right to be there, fine. If on the other hand the Mad Axeman of Llanffugiol was lurking in the lobby, this gave him fair warning to exit out the back.

Not that there were any signs of forced entry. Which was reassuring. Nor were there any signs of response to the bell, which wasn't.

Time for the shout.

He pushed the door wide open and shouted.

'Hi! Anyone home?'

Anyone clearly wasn't.

The bell again and the shout again, just for the record.

What record was that? he asked himself as he stepped inside. He didn't think anyone able to support his account was going to make a reliable witness.

Despite the pleasant sunshine, the house felt really cold. It had felt chilly enough last night when presumably some heed had been paid to the comfort of the guests, but this struck real deep.

What was it Mirabelle used to say when he came downstairs complaining of feeling frightened in his bedroom?

'You just curl up tight and warm under your blankets, Joseph.

Long as you're tight and warm under your blankets, them ha'nts can't touch you. They like it cold, them ha'nts, can't abide the heat. Always tell a house where the ha'nts hang out. Like winter in summer.'

That was how it felt now. Winter in summer.

Still, on the whole a ha'nt was preferable to a mad axeman.

His instinct was to head straight upstairs, check out the lavatory cistern, then get out of here. But that would be a bad move if there really was anyone hanging around down here, legitimate or not. So he forced himself to go through the ground floor, checking each room in turn.

Nothing. Nobody. It didn't just feel empty, it felt like a house no one had inhabited for a long time, with a faint odour of old decaying woodwork tainting the chilly air. He moved fast, resisting all temptation to poke around in drawers, despite Endo Venera's recommendation that it was a snoop's bounden duty never to pass on a chance to snoop.

The kitchen which he'd grown up to regard as the warm heart of a house, was little improvement. He couldn't imagine that many people sat round this cheap Formica-topped table comfortably gossiping over a pot of tea with the kettle singing merrily on top of the ancient stove. Indeed, as the stove used cylinder gas and there were a couple of spare cylinders lying alongside, it felt unsafe as well as uncomfortable.

There were three doors here. The one he'd come through; one which led to the outside, locked, barred and bolted; and one more, standing slightly ajar.

He approached it stealthily and peered through. He didn't much care for what he saw. Steps leading down into the darkness of a cellar.

A cellar, he quickly decided, was not a place a man of nervous disposition wanted to be. Ground floor, he could run out of the door. First floor, he could jump out of a window. But in a cellar...

He closed the door firmly. There was a lock with a key in it and a solid-looking bolt. He turned the key and slid the bolt home.

Now he felt able though still not keen to go upstairs.

He didn't know if he was relieved or not when he explored the lavatory cistern and found it empty. He saw Ursell's sceptical face when he came back empty-handed. Maybe he ought to take something to prove he'd been here, but what? A bar of soap? A toothbrush? What would they prove? It would have to be something a lot more personal, something that would prove he'd definitely been inside the house...

Are you crazy? he heard the distant voice of common sense (which in Luton he called Whitey) demand. You want to present a cop with evidence you've done a burglary?

It was bad enough Ursell having him by the short and curlies over Dildo without giving the guy the wherewithal to bang him up if he felt like it.

Best thing to do was rely on his honest face. If the DI didn't believe him, tough.

But it seemed a good move to give him the fullest report possible, to which end Joe set out in search of other cisterns to check.

There were two more lavatories upstairs. Seemed a bit excessive, specially in view of the minimalist diet the Lewises seemed to exist on. Neither of them contained anything more suspicious than a leaky ballcock.

His search for them took him into the bedrooms. Wain's he'd seen briefly already, and a second look confirmed the impression of confusion just this side of squalor. Probably his mam snuck in when he was away at college and cleaned up anything likely to actually decay. By contrast, what looked like the master bedroom was like a barrack room before an inspection. And a glance in the wardrobe revealed that it was indeed the master bedroom. Men's clothes only. In fact, it was a master floor, as he couldn't find any sign of female residence. Then he opened a door which revealed a further flight of stairs, narrower than those from the main hallway. Probably they'd led up to the servants' quarters in the good ol' days. Where else should he expect to find that pale self-effacing woman?

He began to climb, then stopped. Was that a noise he'd heard or just something his nervous stomach had sent echoing up to his nervous ears? It certainly came from below, not above. Carefully he retraced his steps and peered over the landing balustrade.

Nothing to see, or to hear. And out of the landing window no other vehicle stood in front of the house but the dear old Morris, calling to him like a chapel bell to an old-time villain in search of sanctuary.

Finish the job, he told himself sternly, and turned back to the stairs.

He quickly established that this was indeed where the lady of the house slept. He felt a pang of indignation on her behalf, though, to be fair, she did have two smallish rooms to herself, one for sleeping in, the other a dressing room. Plus a fairly Spartan bathroom with another pill-free cistern.

Poking into a woman's rooms made him feel much uneasier than the men's so he got out of there quick. It took him a few more minutes to establish that the other rooms up there were empty except for dust and the odd tea-chest. There was a trap in one of them obviously leading to the attic but even if he'd had a ladder, he didn't fancy going up there. Leave that to them as had a warrant.

A noise again. This time not so frightening, as it was outside and, to his mechanically fine-tuned ear, identifiable. Sounded like a 250cc bike engine. Important thing was, it was receding. He peered though the small cobwebby window and saw nothing but cobwebs. A small spider ran down a silken ladder and began to dress the corpse of a large fly. It felt like time to go.

He headed downstairs, light-hearted (and footed) with relief that he was going to get out of here unscathed and leaving no trace of his passage.

Except, he recalled in the entrance hall, the cellar door. Would someone recall they'd left it open and wonder how it came to be locked? Probably not. But, as Endo Venera said, there's guys breaking big rocks 'cos they couldn't be bothered looking after small details.

He went into the kitchen.

And stopped dead.

The bolt he'd slid home was now slid back and the door was once more ajar.

Someone had been in here while he was gumshoe-ing around upstairs and gone down into the cellar.

Question was, were they still down there?

Instinct said, run!

But man did not live by instinct alone otherwise he wouldn't have got the vote.

No, sometimes a choice had to be made based on the greatest good of the greatest number. The greatest number in this case was one, himself. And his greatest good was knowing what the shoot was going on here.

At least, he thought that that was his greatest good, but he was open to argument.

None came. He went to the door and pulled it full open. It moved easily on well-oiled hinges. If there was someone down there, he didn't want to surprise them so he made a lot of noise with his feet and coughed loudly, not difficult considering the still rough state of his throat.

Then he advanced to the head of the stairs.

If there was someone down there, they were in the dark. It was like looking down the devil's throat. He needed a torch, or a box of matches.

Or you could try that light switch on the wall, said an exasperated inner voice.

He tried the light switch on the wall. And felt like the Almighty on Day One.

This was very different from what he'd feared. No dusty low-watt bulb this, swinging on a frayed flex to illuminate a skeleton in a rocking chair, but a day-bright striplight, illuminating fresh white walls, a quarry-tiled floor, and a plastered ceiling high enough for even a tall man to walk beneath without stooping.

It wasn't a huge cellar; in fact, it was rather smaller than Joe expected. But its space was remarkably uncluttered. Same tidy mind at work here as was evidenced in the master bedroom, Joe guessed.

At one end there was a workbench with a vice and a tool rack on the wall behind it, while the wall at the other end was totally occupied by a wine rack.

There was nowhere Joe could see that a man could hide, so he went down the steps.

On the workbench he found a few shards of what looked like marble and he recalled Lewis saying that he made a hobby out of repairing antiques. Man of many talents. Also a man with a taste for better wine than his wife provided food to wash down with.

Not that Joe knew a lot about wine, but this stuff just had that look about it. Older the dearer was the rule, he recalled. He took hold of the neck of a bottle and pulled it out to check the date. At least he tried. It seemed firmly wedged. He gave it a good tug.

And the whole rack came moving towards him.

For a horrified moment, he thought he'd pulled the whole caboodle over and any second now he was going to be ankle deep in broken glass and pricey plonk.

Then he realized with mingled relief and puzzlement that rather than falling towards him, the rack had swung outwards, like a door. He pulled on the bottle neck again and the movement resumed. Stooping down, he saw that the whole frame rested on scarcely visible rubber castors which ran silently, leaving no trace on the quarry tiles. One more pull and there was enough space for him to see what lay behind.

He'd been right to feel the cellar was smaller than it ought to be. Behind the rack was another small room containing a tall metal locker and a padded office chair in front of a triple bank of television screens.

He stepped inside and sat down.

There was a control panel. He studied it for a moment then pressed a switch. The circuits of the human mind might be a constant puzzle to him, but Wilco Engineering had got a fingerhold on the electronics age before it lost its grip and tumbled into the abyss of lost dreams.

Green lights appeared. There were several numbered switches. He clicked One. A screen came to life and he smiled with satisfaction as he recognized the entrance hall to Branddreth College. This was, as he'd guessed, another terminal for the college CCTV security system. Lewis was not a man to put all his trust in the likes of Dai Williams.

He flicked idly around. Empty rooms. Almost as dull as daytime network telly. And then a figure appeared in one of the shots. It was Ella Williams walking along a corridor, with what looked like a pair of pristine white sheets folded over her arm. Heading where? To the sickbay, he guessed. Who else could merit having their sheets changed for such a short stay? Nice lady, he thought appreciatively. That Dai didn't know how lucky he was.

He flicked another switch and by the lucky chance which compensated for so many of his other deficiencies he saw he'd actually got himself a view of the sickbay. He realized to his shame that he hadn't even bothered to leave the bed looking tidy. At least he couldn't see any dirty underclothes lying around.

Then shame faded as something else caught his eye. The door was open and behind it he could see something...the edge of something...it moved...oh Lord, there was someone there...someone lurking with Ella Williams getting ever closer.

He opened his mouth to yell, closed it as he realized the futility of the sound, and watched in horror as the woman stepped inside.

The ambusher was out in a flash. He had a weapon in his hands...some sort of club...but he didn't need it, not yet, as he threw his arms around the woman from behind and grappled her to the bed.

Joe pushed himself up out of the chair. He had to get from the Lady House to the college. How long would it take? Three, four, five minutes...? At least! Quick enough to save her from the worst...maybe...maybe not...

For the worst seemed closer than he would have expected. The woman was on her back on the bed, her attacker was pulling her clothes off her, she was arching her back to resist him.

Or was it to help him...?

For now he was pushing himself away from her to enable him to pull off his own clothes. And she was reaching up to help him. Dear heaven, it was incredible how quickly two fully clothed human beings could render themselves completely naked if the incentive was right!

And now he identified two things. One was the 'attacker'. Long John Dawe, the jovial landlord of the Goat and Axle. No wonder he was so jovial!

The other was the club-like 'weapon' he'd been wielding which now lay disregarded on the pillow.

It was a bottle of champagne.

What, he wondered, were they celebrating?

And what could champagne add to what they were presently doing to celebrate it?

Everyday country folk they might be, but there was clearly little the sophisticates of downtown Luton could teach them about the fine art of making love.

Shoot, Sixsmith, you are starting to enjoy this! thought Joe with a sudden inrush of shame. Or was it envy?

Whatever, time to switch off in every sense.

He pressed the off switch to blank out the disturbing image. Not just the sex that disturbed him though...something else...but it was the tangle of limbs whose imprint he wanted to smudge from his mind. He sent his gaze wandering round the room in search of something to replace it.

Nothing much else to look at. Except the metal storage cabinet.

This was top gear, bolted firmly to the wall. Unremovable without a lot of noise and effort and impregnable without a lot more expertise or explosive than your average break-in artist had.

Except that it was unlocked.

What was it that Lewis wanted such an expensive item of equipment for? And having acquired it, why didn't he keep it locked?

Probably because it was empty, he answered himself.

He opened the door.

And wished he hadn't.

Looking up at him was the head of a young boy, blue eyes wide open, red lips pursed in what looked like a smile but had to be the rictus of death.

He might have shrieked out loud, but his throat had tightened as he took a staggering step backwards.

Only to find his progress impeded by something hard and metallic thrusting into the back of his head with a force that brought tears to his eyes.

He managed to twist round and saw mistily that it was the business end of an up-and-over shotgun.

Presumably there was someone at the other end, but he couldn't make out that far.

Now the barrels were under his chin, pushing upwards. In fact, they were probably the only thing holding him up.

And all he could think of as he teetered on the edge of eternity was that at last he was going to find the answer to the Great Philosophical Question which Endo Venera poses in the final reflective chapter of his book—

Did a stiff here the bang of the gun that killed him?

FIFTEEN

JOE SAT IN THE deepest armchair in the Lady House lounge, staring fixedly at the shotgun even though it was now leaning up against the wall, and drank great gobfuls of whisky.

No rubbing whisky this, unimportant guests for the use of, but the real Macallan, old enough to be someone's father.

Leon Lewis was too well brought up to say it, but Joe guessed this was the first time he'd realized that black men too can go pale with terror.

As well as the whisky, this revelation had brought another plus, Joe's terror for some reason inclining Lewis to believe his pleas of innocence. Why this should be Joe couldn't understand. Some of the most nervous characters he'd ever met were crooks. Dangerous crooks too, their jangling nerves urging them to get their retaliation in first. But he wasn't complaining, not with the High Master listening sympathetically to how he'd called round to have a chat with Owain, found the front door open, got worried when no one answered his call, entered to look around in case anyone was in trouble, found the cellar door open (a slight upping of the eyebrows at this), descended, found the wine rack pulled back and the cabinet open (another eyebrow quiver) '...and I'd just been frightened half out of my wits by seeing that chopped-off head when you scared me out of the other half with that scattergun.'

Lewis murmured, 'Sorry,' and looked down at the head which was resting in his lap.

It was made out of marble and had been removed not from a child but the cherub at the front door, though Lewis had had to bring it up from the cellar to convince him.

'So what's it doing in that cabinet?' demanded Joe, remembered shock making him aggressive.

Lewis smiled placatingly.

'My hobby, Mr Sixsmith, is restoring antiques. Didn't I mention it last night? You probably noticed my workbench in the cellar.'

Sounded reasonable, thought Joe.

'Why's it coloured?' he asked, looking with curiosity at the head whose blue eyes and bright red lips still made him feel queasy.

'Ancient Greek statuary usually was coloured. Of course, by the time it reaches us, after centuries of exposure to the air, or sometimes even to sea water, the original pigment has long vanished. But we do have written descriptions which suggest that the colouring erred as you might expect on the side of Mediterranean primary exuberance rather than Nordic pastel restraint. The past may be another country, but true antiquarianism stamps its own passport. Re-creation has always been the better part of recreation, as 'twere.'

He'd lost Joe some way before the *as 'twere,* but he didn't mind. Try as he might, he found it hard to lie, and even harder to lie well. Endo Venera had no good advice here. He seemed to assume that anyone getting into the PI business would have a natural talent to deceive. Joe found it easier to practise evasion than deceit. But he recognized deceptiveness in others and he was getting a feeling that Lewis had been as taken aback to find the cupid's head as himself.

More hard stuff to set aside for softening. Main thing was the High Master seemed inclined to believe his story. But there were still questions that needed answering, especially if, as seemed highly likely, DI Ursell was going to be asking them.

'So nothing was stolen then?' he said.

Lewis fixed him with a gaze which if not inscrutable certainly gave Joe some difficulty in scruting.

'Not so far as I can see,' he said. 'What makes you think something might have been?'

'Well, just the doors being open and everything,' said Joe lamely.

'Making you think, *burglar.* I can see why a man in your line of business might make such an assumption, but as my own error indicates, it is not one to rush into rashly. No, if it were the front door alone, I would have no problem in seeing an explanation. Morna is a trusting soul, still inhabiting that mainly mythical bygone era when no one needed to lock their doors and a naked virgin with a bag of gold could walk the length of Offa's Dyke untroubled by anything worse than blisters and a chest cold. As for Owain, not even the best education money can buy has been able to persuade him that doors do not close automatically behind him. But the cellar door, and the wine rack...unless I myself am in the early stages of Alzheimer's, I see no immediate explanation. How about you, Mr Sixsmith?'

'Eh?' said Joe, feeling the hot breath of accusation.

'You are a detective after all. Much of your working life must be spent in propounding hypotheses.'

'Yeah, well, I'm mainly out and about,' said Joe.

'Of course. *Cogito ergo sum, sed laboro ergo vivo,* eh?'

'Sorry, like you saw last night, I don't speak Welsh.'

This gave Lewis the pleasure of a superior smile. Joe didn't mind. He'd long since given up trying to close the gap between clever devils and himself, but he'd found that letting them think it was even wider than it was often worked to his advantage. He'd sung too many requiems and the like not to recognize Latin when he heard it, and he could even have tried at a translation. *I think therefore I am, but I work therefore I live.*

'So you saw nothing suspicious in or around the house? Nobody lurking in the shrubbery? No car parked off the drive?'

Joe thought about the intruder in the school but decided that was too complicated to raise just now. He saw that Lewis had clocked the hesitation and tried to look like a trained PI running a sequence of events through the VTR of his mind.

'Sorry. It all looked normal. Probably like you say. Mrs Lewis forgot. Hey, what gives at the festival, you back so early? I thought things were going to be back on course pretty soon?'

Subtle change of subject.

'They would have been,' said Lewis, 'but that chap Ursell seems unhappy to accept it was probably just an accident caused by those cowboy scaffolders. Strange fellow that. Came here from the Midlands a couple of years back and has never seemed fully to adapt to our comparatively crime-free atmosphere. Rather look under a rock than sit on it, if you know what I mean. What do you make of him, as a fellow professional?'

'Hardy know him really,' said Joe.

'Oh? I thought I saw you deep in conversation with him after the accident.'

'Just passing the time of day,' said Joe. 'I asked him about the woman in Copa.'

'Ah yes. And how's she doing?'

'No change. They seem hopeful, though.'

'As are we all. Something special you wanted to talk to Owain about, was there?'

It took Joe a second to recall his excuse for being in the Lady House.

He thought he caught a glimpse of that superior caught-you-out expression on Lewis's face and decided he'd been on the back foot long enough.

'Can't tell you that,' he said. 'Client confidentiality.'

'Client?' Lewis pursed his lips in a silent whistle. 'Do you mean you are a client of Owain's? Hardly. So I presume that someone else has hired you and you believe my son can help you with your enquiries, whatever they may be. Am I right?'

'Sorry. Not at liberty,' said Joe, wishing he had stayed on the back foot.

'Don't worry. I quite understand about professional ethics. Such thorny problems constantly strew the path of us professional men, eh?'

Some boring fart in Luton Reference Library had once tried to explain postmodern irony to Joe, but he'd nodded off before he could get to grips with it. Good old-fashioned sarcasm he could smell a mile off, though.

'Yeah, man, must have been like that for you with Glyn Matthias,' he said. He regretted it instantly. Man playing dumb should never let himself be provoked into being a smartass.

He saw Lewis's gaze flicker momentarily to the shotgun as though he too were having regrets.

'Fascinating,' he said. 'Barely two days here and already you are in professional employment and the local gossips have taken you into their confidence. Either you are a prince in your profession or, as I have often suspected, rural Wales's reputation for being a close and secretive society is merely an invention of the kind of literary exile who writes plays for Radio 4.'

'Just I met this guy at the Goat and Axle,' Joe heard himself explaining while that inner voice which at home ventriloquized Whitey was saying, 'Hold your peace, dickhead.'

'Good Lord,' said Lewis, mock-amazement sitting not very comfortably on something else that might have been genuine shock. 'Depths within depths. In a trice you have gone where few strangers penetrate and whence fewer return, the inner sanctum of disinformation and disaffection. Naturally I cannot discuss with you the details of Mr Matthias's professional relationship with Branddreth, except to say how sorry I was to lose the services of such a distinguished musician. However, my overriding concern as High Master must always be for the welfare of my pupils.'

'I can see that,' said Joe, thinking that as he'd come this far, he might as well push a bit further. 'Should have thought, you being so friendly with Mr Penty-Hooser, you could see anyone threatening your pupils got put away like he deserves. Always supposing you had the evidence, that is.'

'I see. That's the way the Goat and Axle spin doctors are presenting things, is it? Yes, I'm happy to claim John Penty-Hooser as an old and close friend, but you should understand this, Mr Sixsmith—any influence I might have with the authorities was used to dissuade them from bringing charges against Matthias. Once he was removed from the orbit of Branddreth, I could not find any satisfaction at the prospect of seeing a man of his talents publicly disgraced and possibly jailed for what is simply a genetic weakness.'

He finished with the modest self-deprecating gesture of a man who expects, though he doesn't desire, applause.

Joe said, 'But the guy's still teaching at the comp., right?'

'Oh, the public sector,' said Lewis dismissively. 'Try giving *them* advice. Even in our rural fastness, the liberal trendies have long since penetrated there. Wasted breath, Mr Sixsmith. Wasted breath. Which like your time I must not waste any more of. Let me apologize again for so distressing you. It may be some small retrospective consolation to know the shotgun was not loaded.'

'Now that's a real comfort,' said Joe.

He didn't mean it.

Partly because it made no difference to a man who'd been scared just this side of fouling his pants to hear there'd been no real danger after all.

But mainly because when Lewis had gone back down to the cellar to collect the head, Joe had checked the gun.

It was loaded all right, both barrels.

Suddenly, as he drove away from the Lady House, it felt very good to be alive.

SIXTEEN

JOE'S EUPHORIA only lasted as far as up the hill to Copa Cottage.

He'd instinctively turned away from Llanffugiol. Ursell was

probably still there and he didn't have any answers yet for the DI.

There was no sign of anyone around the burnt-out shell, so he pulled in and got out of the car. Despite the warm sun, he shivered as he walked around the ruin. If the coach hadn't broken down...if Big Merv hadn't got lost...if...

There were a thousand *ifs,* each of them ending with the mystery woman and an even more mysterious pile of ashes. And there seemed almost as many unanswered questions, most of which looked like they'd have to wait on her recovering consciousness...if she ever did.

He pushed that last unthinkable *if* to the back of his mind and examined some of the questions.

What the shoot was DI Ursell playing at? Were the Goat and Axle boys into burning English-owned cottages to make a political point? Or were they simply so anti-Lewis because of this festival thing that they'd burn down Copa just to disoblige him anyway? And all these people eager to hire him to find out about the woman, what did they really want to know about her? And where did poor student Wain Lewis get all that folding money he'd handed over as deposit?

Joe pulled out the boy's money and looked at it as if in hope of an answer. The notes were all well used. He checked to see if they were numbered in order, like they'd come from a bank, and wasn't surprised to find they weren't. As he started to push them back into his pocket, one fell loose, and a light breeze gusted up to carry it away from him over the burnt-out cottage, fading away to drop it right in the middle of the ashes.

'Shoot,' said Joe.

For some reason he felt reluctant to tread over the ashes, but it was crazy to leave a fiver lying out there, especially when he had every intention of returning the money to the boy soon as he saw him. In any case, what was bugging him? It wasn't as if anyone had actually died here. Nothing in these ashes that had once been living.

Delicately, in order to cause as little disturbance as possible, he moved towards the note.

As he stooped to pick it up, he saw a faint shape outlined in the ash beneath. He used the banknote to brush the grey deposit away. Something metallic. Gingerly he picked it up and shook it clean. A bracelet. Or what had once been a bracelet, with a small chain, its links now fused by the fire's searing heat, and a buckled lozenge of metal which might have once had something etched into it but which was now utterly illegible. He was going to throw it down when suddenly he realized he knew what it was, or might have been. He'd seen a barmaid at his Luton local wearing something like this. When he'd made a comment, she'd explained it was an allergy-alert bracelet, so that if she was ever in an accident and unable to speak, the medics would know that penicillin did nasty things to her. 'Makes me all swell up,' she confided to Joe, who'd looked at her well-developed figure and agreed that this would be gilding the lily.

Chances of it belonging to the burnt woman were slight, and chances of it being any help to the cops were slighter still. But Joe had come to understand he was as likely to stumble on significant things by accident as he was to work them out by intellect. He pocketed it with the banknote and made his way back to the Morris and considered his next move.

He felt curiously out of sorts with himself, restless, rather depressed. Back home he rarely felt like this, or at least not for long. Maybe that was because back home there was always something to be getting on with, even if it was only strolling down to the pub for a pint. Man who felt at a loose end in Luton was probably at a loose end in life. But here in the sticks there was nothing to be at but loose ends. Pointless going for a stroll even, 'less you had a girl and a blanket. Nothing to look at but trees and sheep. Joe could tell a sheep from a tree but further distinction seemed neither profitable nor pleasurable. Paul Robeson must have visited a different part of the Principality, he told himself, feeling a sharp pang of longing for the sound of traffic, the drift of a crowded pavement, the sweet smell of fat and vinegar from a passing chippie; buildings, machines, humanity.

Nearest he'd get to that round here was Caerlindys. Excuse for going there? To check up on the woman in the hospital. Also to give thanks for the care he'd received during his short stay.

In fact, not excuses, but good reasons.

Cheered, he got into the Morris which cheered him some more. This was one area in which the country had it over the city. Not much fun edging your way through Luton's notorious one-way maze in the rush hour.

Taking his bearings vaguely from the sun, he kept going till he hit a road wide enough to have a white line painted on it and main enough to have a real signpost instead of a bit of wood nailed to a tree.

According to this, Caerlindys was only ten miles away. He made it nearer fifteen on the clock, but maybe a Welsh mile was different. Or maybe he'd better get the clock checked.

He'd not paid much attention to the place last time he was here, but now he saw it was a country town small enough for him to take in at a glance as he motored down the slope of the valley in which it was set. He didn't complain. After twenty-four hours around Llanffugiol, it looked like a metropolis.

He drove right into the middle till the street spread itself out into a sort of square and parked in a line of classy-looking cars along the kerb. Then he got out and looked around, just for the pleasure of seeing traffic and people and shops.

'Can't leave your car there,' said a voice in his ear.

He looked round to see he was being addressed by a traffic warden. This was feeling more like being at home every minute, he thought. Luton's traffic wardens were known as the wolf pack from their ability to sniff out an illegally parked vehicle while the engine was still hot.

This one was a woman, square enough to be Nye Garage's sister, with eyes like hammer drills.

Joe smiled at her sweetly.

'Sorry,' he said. 'Didn't realize this was no parking.'

He glanced with only mild irony at the other cars, but the warden took it as an aggressive argument.

'Well, you know now, don't you, sir,' she said, pronouncing *sir* with a sibilance which made it sound like a term of abuse.

'Hello there, Rita. Having trouble?' said a male voice.

'Not yet,' said the woman.

Joe glanced round to see a uniformed sergeant approaching. Now he felt really at home. Then his gaze took in the face as well as the uniform.

Recognition was mutual. Richard Burton.

'Sergeant Prince, isn't it?' he said.

He got an impression of debate and decision, almost simultaneous, then the man's face split in a smile and he said, 'It's Mr

Sixsmith, isn't it? How are you, sir? I never had a chance to shake you by the hand.'

Which he now proceeded to do with such vigour that passers-by paused, probably in the hope of witnessing a novel form of pre-arrest restraint. But once the cop made clear what he was doing and why, smiles became universal and a small queue formed to follow his example.

Joe was touched but more than a little embarrassed. Being a hero was nice, but like birthdays, once a year was enough, and yesterday had overdosed him.

Prince seemed to sense this and intervened, putting his arm round Joe's shoulders protectively and saying, 'That'll do now, wear him out, you will, and him not long out of his sickbed. You just taking the chance to have a look round our little town, Mr Sixsmith?'

'Looking to find the hospital, actually,' said Joe, as the little crowd moved away.

'For treatment, is it?' asked the sergeant solicitously.

'Oh no. I'm fine, well, I'm OK. But thought I'd like to find out how the young woman is, the one from the cottage.'

'Oh. I see. Very commendable, if I may say so. Tell you what, I've got to go up there to check her out myself. Why don't we walk together? It's just a step and it'll save you getting mobbed by your fans, eh?'

This seemed a long shot to Joe, but he knew better than to turn down an offer of help from the police.

He said, 'What about the car? Shouldn't I move it?'

'Don't be daft. Right as rain there, it is, long as you like. I'll leave a little note just in case Rita here goes off duty and one of her chums wanders along.'

Rita didn't look happy but she watched in silence as the sergeant scribbled something on a yellow sticky notepad, tore off the sheet, then studied the window carefully in search of the best place to stick it. It was at this point that Joe noticed the tax disc was three years out of date.

'There,' said the cop, placing the yellow square precisely over the disc. 'That'll keep everybody happy.'

'Thanks, Sarge,' said Joe. 'You've got the right name.'

'Wish you'd tell my missus that,' laughed the sergeant.

As they moved away, Joe nodded towards the other cars.

'Don't see many more notes to teacher,' he commented.

'What? Ah, I'm with you. No need. Councillors' cars, see? By their numbers shall ye know them. Should be six six six in most cases.'

'Here is mystery,' said Joe, whose upbringing under Mirabelle's tutelage had left him no slouch at a biblical quotation. 'Don't look much like council offices to me.'

He glanced up at the long grey building before which the cars were parked. A sign over its imposing entrance read THE OLD DRAGON above a depiction of the fiery beast in bright red, with beneath it in smaller letters *Philip Feathers Prop and Licensee.*

'That's the thing, see, council chambers are closed for refurbishment so they're holding their meetings here pro tem, only there's no official parking here, public highway, isn't it? But we can't have our democratic representatives dissipating their energies having to walk maybe a hundred yards or more, can we? So Mr Feathers, who's on the council's police committee, asked our brass if they could help out, all unofficial like, of course, couldn't be official now, could it? That would be undemocratic, and they're all good democrats round here. That's the way we do things here in Wales, Mr Sixsmith.'

He spoke with an amused irony which implied he didn't see any harm in this.

Joe said, 'Not just Wales. We got councillors like that back home.'

In fact, generally speaking, Joe found the Luton politicos he knew personally were a nice enough bunch, always willing to give him the time of day and listen to his gripes and suggestions. He wasn't so naive not to recognize that most of them reckoned he had some kind of constituency it was worth their while to cultivate, but he reckoned he was well able to sort out the true tossers from the amiable flannellers. But playing the yeah-I've-been-there-too card with Prince seemed a good move. When you get a cop on your side, keep him there even if it takes verbal superglue.

'Bet you have. Same the whole world over. Doubt if you've got anyone like Rita Meter back there, though. Lucky I came along. I think she was about to put a wheel clamp on you.'

'Oh, our cars get clamped regular back home,' said Joe.

'No, I meant on you personally,' laughed Prince. 'Home's Luton, that right, Joe? OK to call you Joe? I'm Tom, by the way.'

Knows I'm from Luton. Knows I'm called Joe. Well, why not, probably in the local paper anyway, so everyone knows.

'Yeah, Luton,' he said. 'You know it, Tom?'

'Been there,' he said. 'Once.'

'Spent most of your career round here then?'

Joe was just making conversation but this got him a quick appraising glance before the man answered. 'No. Been here and there. Only been in these parts a few months.'

'Yeah? How do you like it?'

'Seems fine so far,' said Prince. 'Mind you, I'm still working out the lie of the land. Do as you're told, make no waves, not till you know who you'll be sinking, that's the way I was brought up. So when I'm told to keep parking spaces free for the council, that's what I do.'

'Seems a wise move to me,' said Joe. 'No point getting the wrong side of GM till you got to, is there?'

Prince didn't pause in his stride but Joe felt him go still.

'GM?' he said. 'Now what would that mean?'

'Just something I heard, way the locals talk about the boys with clout round here; maybe I picked it up wrong,' back-pedalled Joe.

'Maybe you did, Joe. So how are you finding things out at Branddreth College? Making you comfortable, are they?'

'It's fine,' said Joe.

'See anything of the fellow who runs it, Lewis, is that his name?'

Why would you be unsure? wondered Joe. In his experience, when cops started asking casual questions, they were pumping you. Easiest way to deal with that was hide nothing you weren't desperate to hide, then you couldn't be tripped up.

'Had dinner with him last night,' he said. 'Haggards, people who own Copa Cottage, were there too. Wanted to talk to me about what happened.'

'They did? Now why would they want to do that?'

'Well, it is...was theirs,' said Joe. 'Naturally they're interested in finding out how it came to get burnt down with an uninvited guest on the premises.'

'Definitely uninvited, they say?'

'Yeah,' said Joe. 'Why do you need to ask me, Tom? Thought it would only be civilians the DI didn't talk to.'

'The DI?'

'Ursell. He's in charge of the case, or didn't you know that?'

'Yes, I knew that. You've met him?'

'Of course I have. Twice. At the hospital, then at the festival this morning.'

'So he talks to you. Thought you said he wouldn't talk to civilians?'

Joe was getting a bit irritated. If the guy wanted to ask him questions why couldn't he come straight out? It was tiring for a guy who'd been through what Joe had been through having to perform this verbal square dance.

'Maybe he doesn't think I'm just a civilian,' he said.

'Not a civilian? Well, I suppose you're a witness too.'

It came out light, like he was some old lady who'd seen a car not stop at the crossing.

'Yeah, and also I'm a licensed PI who's worked the streets,' Joe said, coming as close to blowing his own trumpet as he was ever likely to.

'You're a *what?*' Prince was taken aback.

'A private investigator,' said Joe, pleased with the effect.

'Is that right? Said in the paper you were a lathe operator, made redundant through no fault of your own and keen to get back into work.'

Mirabelle! Joe had no difficulty identifying who'd done the talking to the local journalist.

He said, 'Well, don't like to shout it around.'

'When you're working, you mean?'

'When I'm not working, I mean. Like being a doctor on holiday. Everyone gets to know, they start telling you their symptoms.'

'And when old Perry Ursell got to know, did he start telling you his symptoms?' mocked Prince.

Perry. Short for what? wondered Joe. And the mental diversion was enough to give his tongue room to go wandering off the straight and narrow.

'In a manner of speaking. Leastways, he took it serious enough to...'

He tailed off into silence. Maybe it wasn't all that wise a move to advertise that he'd been blackmailed into feloniously entering the house of a distinguished member of the local community, especially to a sergeant who didn't seem to find anything too demeaning in keeping illicit parking spaces available for councillors enjoying a freebie.

'To do what, Joe?' said Prince, with that softness which in a spring breeze often presages a gale.

'Just asked me to help out a bit, you know, keep my eyes open,' Joe waffled. 'Not that I'm likely to see anything that helps, but maybe the DI, *Perry,* thinks people might be a bit more relaxed round me than him. I mean, he doesn't seem all that hot on public relations. Mr Haggard seems to think his best bet of finding out what's really happening is through Lewis having a quiet word with his mate, Pantyhose, sorry, Mr Penty-Hooser...'

This could be a good time to faint, he thought. And a good place too.

Their steady progress through the streets of Caerlindys had brought them to the hospital where Prince's presence had got them through the reception area with no more than a friendly wave at the man behind the desk. They were heading down a long corridor which on his previous visit, when he'd insisted on walking out under his own steam, had seemed to go on forever. It didn't feel quite as long today, but long enough. They were about halfway down it when a figure appeared at the far end, halted abruptly, did a smart about-turn, and vanished round the corner.

'Hello, hello,' said Prince. 'You know that lad, Joe?'

'What lad?' said Joe, peering round myopically.

'That one who's just disappeared. Five-nine, long black hair, slight build, blue jeans, red rugger shirt. One of us he didn't fancy meeting. Probably me. Often happens. It's the uniform.'

He sounded fairly complacent.

And he was probably right, thought Joe.

For he couldn't think of any good reason why the sight of his own unthreatening face should have set Owain Lewis running.

Nor could he think of any good reason why he didn't identify the boy to Prince.

'Your eyes always been bad, Joe?' enquired the sergeant.

'What? Nothing wrong with my eyes...except for long sight...bit of weakness there.'

It was a lame recovery. He was easier to trip than a man with a wooden leg.

He tried for diversion and asked, 'Any line yet on who she is, Tom, the lady in the cottage?'

'Not a thing, far as I know,' said the sergeant. 'Looks like either she'll have to tell us herself if she recovers, or we'll be matching dental records against reported missings and that can take forever. Ours is an easy society to drop out of, Joe, without anyone paying much heed. You're the only one who's been around her while she was still conscious. You sure she said nothing that could help?'

'Sure,' said Joe. 'Hey, I did find this though. I was up at the cottage earlier—what's left of it—and this was lying in the ashes. Think it might be one of them allergy warnings.'

He produced the buckled bracelet.

Prince took it and glanced at it without much interest.

'Can't see this helping much,' he said dismissively. 'Nothing to say who it belonged to anyway.'

But Joe noticed that he wrapped it in a handkerchief and deposited it carefully in his tunic pocket. And at least it had diverted him from the topic of Joe's failing eyesight.

They reached the unit where the burnt woman lay. He recognized the nurse there as the one who'd been tending him when he woke up. Nurse Butler, the red-headed girl who didn't look old enough to be out of school.

She smiled in pleasure at seeing him and said, 'Hello, Mr Sixsmith. How are you feeling?'

'Fine, thanks,' said Joe.

'You two know each other?' said Prince.

'Why not? No law against a girl having friends, even in Caerlindys, is there, Sergeant?' she said, with a toss of her head and a saucy smile which bumped her into late teens/early twenties.

'See what little respect the young round here have for authority, Joe,' said Prince. 'Butler, is it? Meaning you're probably Tilly Butler, the minister's daughter from the Primitive Chapel, right?'

'What if I am?'

'Nothing if you are, plenty if you're not,' said Prince enigmatically. 'So, Tilly, how's the patient?'

The nurse became serious.

'No change. Holding her own. Mr Winstanley, the consultant, should be along shortly, though. Best speak to him.'

'I will,' said Prince. 'Shouldn't there be a round blob of indolence masquerading as a policeman sitting in that chair outside the door?'

'Ollie, you mean?'

'Constable Purslaw, yes.'

'Oh, I told him he might as well go and get himself a sandwich while I was around,' said the girl. 'Better than having him sitting there staring at me like he got his eyes from radiography.'

'How long's he been gone?' asked Prince.

'Not long. You just missed him.'

'So he'd have been around if anyone had come visiting our lady in the past five minutes?'

'Visiting?' said the nurse as if she didn't recognize the word. Even Joe spotted her uneasiness, and Prince was suddenly like a cat who's heard a rustle in the grass.

'That's right. Visiting. What visitors do. I'm thinking of a young man in a red shirt, slight build, black hair. You see anyone like that, Tilly?'

Her expression said yes for her. Poor girl, thought Joe. Probably imagines she was covering up for the absent Ollie.

She said, 'Oh yes, there was someone. I saw him peering through the glass and I said, "Can I help you?" and he said, "How's she doing?" and I said, "Who's asking?" and he said, "Nobody really. Just curious." And I thought he must be a journalist or something so I said we couldn't give out information and anyway there was nothing to give out. I was going to mention it to Ollie when he got back.'

Her flow of words had become increasingly defensive in the face of the sergeant's darkening brow and the years her pertness had put on were wiped away till once more she looked about thirteen.

'Don't worry,' said Prince. 'I'll mention it for you. We'd have had him, Joe, if that Purslaw didn't think more of his belly than his job!'

In the interests of everyone concerned it seemed to Joe this might be a good time to come clean and give up Wain Lewis. But before he could speak there was a fanfare of trumpets and a celestial choir burst into the Hallelujah Chorus as Mr Winstanley and his train burst into the room. The music, of course, was in Joe's mind, an alcoholic fantasy he and Beryl had composed one night after she'd suffered a particularly virulent bout of consultantivitis during her shift a Luton Infirmary. 'He comes into the ward, it's like a Nuremberg Rally,' she'd declared, which had set them seeking the best musical accompaniment for the occasion.

In fact, Winstanley, a man of Joe's size whose prominent front teeth looked like they'd been designed for a much larger face, arrived accompanied by no more than five acolytes, among whom Joe recognized the still weary figure of Dr Godsip.

The procession was led by a large ward sister who looked as if she'd done her training on the set of a *Carry On* movie. She scowled at Prince, glowered threateningly at the red-headed nurse, hissed something like *Bovril* at Joe, then presented the patient's chart to Winstanley like Cupid offering Venus a mirror in one of those big paintings Joe had seen in some country house the choir had once sung in.

The consultant looked at the chart, looked at the patient, looked at the bits and pieces of equipment she was hooked up to, and let out a long whistling sigh through his teeth. It was not the sort of sound Joe ever hoped to hear a doctor treating *him* make. It had too much of keep-your-fingers-crossed-but-don't-hold-your-breath about it.

Prince took it as his cue and interposed his body between the consultant and the sister who looked ready to jump on his back but instead turned her irritation on young Tilly.

Godsip came up to Joe, yawned and said, 'How're you doing, Mr Sixsmith? Good to see you out and about.'

'Few aches and pains,' said Joe. 'Voice still a bit rough, like you can hear.'

'Yes, no singing for a while, eh? Here for a check-up, is it? Didn't see your name on my list, but I'm sure I can fit you in...'

'No, thanks,' said Joe. 'I'm here with Sergeant Prince. We came to see the lady from the cottage. She going to be OK?'

'It'll be a long haul, but she's holding her own. I'm glad the sergeant's here. I've got a lab report that might interest him.'

The ward sister had decided she needed a bit more *Lebensraum* to blitz poor Tilly and was urging her out into the corridor. As she pushed past Joe, she hissed, 'Bovril!' at him again.

'Why's she keep saying Bovril to me?' asked Joe, bemused.

Godsip grinned.

'Not Bovril. *Overall.* She thinks you're an improperly dressed porter. Sorry. She's new. Thinks she's going to sweep us cleaner. Oh damn.'

A pager was beeping in his pocket. He checked it and switched it off.

'Gotta go. Look, give this to the sergeant when he's done, will you? And don't forget to see your GP when you get home. Bye now.'

He put a folded sheet of paper into Joe's hand and left. Prince was still deep in conversation with Winstanley. Not a man who relaxed his grip till he got what he wanted, the sergeant. And Joe guessed he didn't much mind whether he charmed the birds out of the trees or blew them out with a scattergun.

He unfolded the sheet of paper and glanced down at it.

It was all a bit technical but not so much he couldn't make out there'd been traces of alcohol in the woman's bloodstream, though well below non-driving level.

Some other stuff that was gobbledygook.

Then something leapt from the page and hit him in the eye.

Traces found of some stuff as long and unpronounceable as a Welsh place name followed by a handwritten note in brackets.

(Could be Decorax?)

Oh Wain, Wain, thought Joe. You and me gotta have a heart-to-heart talk real soon.

SEVENTEEN

JOE DID NOT SPEND a lot of time bemoaning the fact that God, who could easily have created him six foot six, rippling with muscles and coruscating with charisma, had opted instead for five foot five, a sagging waist, and social invisibility except maybe in a convention of white supremacists. What did gripe him a bit was there was no consistency. Man who could spend twenty minutes trying to catch the waiter's eye in a half-empty restaurant ought to be able to slip out of a crowded hospital ward without attracting attention, but the long eye of the law was not to be denied.

'Joe, where are you rushing off to?' said Prince, taking his elbow as he stepped into the corridor.

'Not rushing anywhere,' said Joe, which was true. More sidling. 'Just thought there were too many people in there, all standing over that poor woman, talking about her. Just because she ain't speaking don't mean she's not listening.'

'You're right, Joe. Wouldn't be so bad if all them white coats meant they could tell me any more than young Tilly, but they can't. Saw you were talking to Doc Godsip. Gave you a clean bill, I hope?'

These Welsh cops must have wing mirrors, thought Joe. He'd been thinking about 'forgetting' about the lab report which Godsip had asked him to pass on, but now it didn't seem such a good idea.

He said, 'Yeah. Asked me to give you this too.'

He handed over the sheet.

Prince glanced at it. Joe waited for his face to register the Decorax but there was nothing. Maybe it wasn't a case he was involved in. Or maybe he didn't just look like Richard Burton but could act like him too.

'So what are you up to now?' enquired Prince genially.

'Head back to the festival, see how we're doing,' said Joe.

'Lunchtime now, Joe,' said Prince. 'Stick with me, I'll show you where to get the best mutton pie in the Principality.'

The grip on his elbow felt more like arrest than invitation. Then a uniformed figure appeared at the far end of the corridor and stopped like it had hit a glass door at the sight of Prince.

'Constable Purslaw, I've been looking forward to a word with you,' said Prince, with the sort of anticipatory purr Whitey gave whenever Joe opened the fridge.

The elbow lock relaxed.

Joe said, 'Thanks all the same, but I gotta watch what I eat. Diet. Catch you later, maybe.'

He did a smart about-turn, shouldered his way between Nurse Butler and the *Carry On* Sister, who was still giving her a bad time, and headed down the corridor.

Getting out of the hospital this way involved passing through the Maternity Ward, which was very busy. What else was there to do out in the sticks, thought Joe with the false superiority of one who'd have swapped a lot of dull nights watching the telly for a couple of hours doing what else. He tried to look like an anxious father and must have got it half right as he finally made it to the outside world without being challenged.

He retraced his steps to the square to shift the Morris. If Prince was really keen to keep him close, this was the first place he'd look once he'd finished demolishing the unfortunate Purslaw. Every parking space was now occupied, with a second row of cars parallel to the first. Through the windows of the Old Dragon came the sound of merry voices and clinking glasses. Presumably the council meeting was now well under way.

Rita Meter was still on duty. She greeted him with what passed for a smile which Joe returned, thinking it was an attempt at reconciliation till he looked beyond it and saw the real cause.

A sparkling new Jaguar was parked alongside the Morris, firmly blocking him in.

'Excuse me,' said Joe to Rita. 'Any chance of me getting out?'

'Not till the meeting's over,' she said. 'Stuck here till then, you are.'

She clearly found much consolation in this.

'But this guy's double-parked,' protested Joe, pointing at the Jaguar.

'Doesn't matter. They all come out the same time, see, that's why we keep these places clear for councillors.'

'To save the public from inconvenience, you mean? Hey, that's real thoughtful of these guys, no wonder they got elected.'

She regarded him suspiciously as she digested his words and, because he'd found that giving petty bureaucrats unnecessary hassle rarely got you more than the merest flash of satisfaction, he went on hastily, 'So I'll come back later then. Couldn't tell me if there's a hairdresser's close by, could you?'

'Get a trim, is it?' she said, regarding Joe's close-cropped skull with interest. 'More like a polish you need, I'd say. Bill Barber's the man for you. Used to work at the prison before they started all this telly in their rooms and weekly perms stuff. Now the way you go is—'

'No,' interrupted Joe, though he would like to have found out if Barber was a real name or a work description, like Nye Garage. 'What I want is a ladies' hairdresser.'

She took a hasty step back. If she'd been wearing long skirts, she'd have whipped them away.

'A ladies' hairdresser?' she echoed.

'Not for me,' Joe reassured her. 'I'm meeting a friend. Forgot the name of the salon. Is there more than one?'

'Only two that matter. This friend, she'll be your age, will she?'

'Younger,' said Joe. 'A lot younger.'

She gave him a you-dirty-old-sod look, then said, 'Snips, it will be then. Other side of the square, first left down Tenter Street.'

Joe said thanks and moved off. Chances of Bronwen still being at the hairdresser's weren't high, and even if she was, chances of her having made an arrangement to meet Wain later probably weren't all that good either, but he still felt quite proud of himself for having thought of it. This was the way Endo Venera's mind worked, making connections, always looking for an angle. Maybe he was growing into the job.

It got better. As he spotted the sign saying Snips, the salon door opened and Bronwen came out, looking very attractive in a plastic Hollywood kind of way. She spotted him immediately. Not surprising. The streets of Caerlindys weren't exactly crowded with short, black, balding PIs.

'Joe,' she said. 'What are you doing here?'

'Looking for you,' he said.

She didn't seem surprised, more shamefacedly guilty.

'Joe, I'm really sorry. I didn't mean it like that, you know, to make a fool of you. It was just my da said it was worth a tenner to find out just how much Welsh you really spoke. I never thought you would say what I said in company.'

Joe worked it out almost instantaneously.

'Wain told you what happened, did he?'

'Yes, when he gave me a lift here, we got to talking about you...'

'Yeah? How come?'

She put her hand on his arm, fluttered her (new?) eyelashes, and said huskily, 'Well, you're the most interesting thing to happen round here for a long time, Joe.'

Must show a lot of old movies on Welsh telly, thought Joe. Maybe that explained all the lookalikes, strong impressions made during pregnancy.

'More interesting than burning down houses with people in them?' he said.

He wished he hadn't as the pouting lips started to tremble and he saw tears moisten her eyes.

'That was really terrible,' she said. 'I didn't mean...I was just joking...I hope with all my heart she'll be all right.'

'I've just been up to the hospital,' said Joe. 'No change, but she's still hanging in. Thought I saw Wain up there. Did he say anything about going to see how the woman was doing?'

'No, he did not,' she said with indignant anger. 'And if he had, I wouldn't have believed him!'

Joe tried to look as if this made some sense to him.

'Say anything about giving you a lift back later?' he asked.

'Said he wasn't sure what he was doing, the lying sod. Men, you can't trust them. Like my rotten da, said I could have the pick-up, and then he just buggered off, never a word to anyone. My ma's right, you got to get your retaliation in first, else they're all over you.'

Ella Williams on last sighting had certainly been trying to get her retaliation in first, thought Joe, but it hadn't stopped the man in question from being all over her.

Then he felt ashamed of himself for thinking so frivolously about something which could have a devastating effect on this girl. Mature for her years she might appear, but we're all kids when it comes to crises between our parents.

He said, 'So you're not meeting him?'

'Said I'd be in the Dragon lounge lunchtime if he was still around.'

'And how would you get home if he wasn't?' Joe asked.

'Council meeting on, isn't there? No shortage of good-hearted gents willing to give a girl a lift 'long as she votes the right way. And now there's you as well, Joe. You must be getting back somehow and you wouldn't see me stranded, would you?'

She tucked her arm through his and leaned up close against his side, urging them back across the square towards the hotel. The traffic warden was still on guard there and Joe was glad her duties didn't extend to monitoring moral as well as traffic violations, else he'd have had tickets stuck all over him.

The lounge of the Dragon was empty, though the proceedings of the council meeting which a stranger might have mistaken for the noise of a lively office party were clearly audible through the wall behind the bar.

'Sounds like they're enjoying themselves,' said Joe. 'Maybe we should join them.'

'In your dreams,' said Bronwen. 'That's a private room with a buffet bar and Big Eddie, the disco bouncer, on the door.'

She didn't sound critical.

'Doesn't bother you then?' said Joe.

'What?'

'Elected officers enjoying themselves on public money.'

She giggled as if he'd made a joke, or at least said something silly.

'Need their perks, don't they? Else why would they do it?'

'Do what?'

'The job. Mending roads, collecting rubbish, taking old folk on trips, building schools, all that stuff.'

'Lot of bin men and navvies in there, is there?' asked Joe.

'Don't be silly. They're the ones who see it gets done, and you can't expect people to do that for nothing, can you? Not telling me you're all Holy Joes back in England, are you, Joe?'

Joe considered. Plenty of noses in the public trough back home, he couldn't deny it. But on the whole it was done with discretion, they covered their tracks, and when they went over the top, they got done for it. Though, to be fair, there was that place in Yorkshire a year back where the troughing had been going on pretty blatantly for a decade or more before someone blew the whistle. It must be geography, he decided. The North as he understood it was very like Wales. Great wodges of emptiness filled with sheep and trees, and so near the edge of things that when a comet passed close, bits fell off into space.

He said, 'None of my business. And how does a Holy Joe get a drink round here?'

This made her laugh, a pleasant bubbly contralto accompanied by the treble of the bell on the bar which she shook vigorously.

After a moment, a door opened behind the bar to admit an increase of the party sound effects, a glimpse of the civic fathers of Caerlindys at their deliberations, and a harassed-looking barman.

'Hello, Bron,' he said. 'Not been ringing long, have you? There's enough noise in there to wake my Auntie Mag and she's stone deaf.'

'Not long,' said Bronwen. 'This is my friend Joe. Joe, meet Shorty, my favourite barman. Joe? You taking a nap?'

'Sorry,' said Joe, staring at the door which had closed behind the barman. 'Hi, Shorty. Good to meet you. Pint of Guinness and whatever Bron drinks.'

'Don't really want a pint of crème de menthe, do you?'

'If she can drink it, I'll buy it,' said Joe gallantly.

Shorty pulled the drinks. He wasn't all that short, in fact he was a good three inches taller than Joe.

'Anyone been asking for me?' asked Bronwen.

'No,' said the barman. 'But then we don't stock you, do we?'

Joe laughed as he paid. It was a good rule of life to appreciate a barman's jokes.

There was an upsurge of noise from next door and Shorty said, 'Better get back in there before they start on Any Other Business.'

He went back through the door, and its brief opening and shutting confirmed what Joe thought he'd spotted before.

The tall angular figure with the heavy whisky tumbler in his hand was in civvies rather than the uniform he'd been wearing in the college sports day photo. But unless there was a specially rich crop of strawberry noses in Caerlindys, Deputy Chief Constable Penty-Hooser was present at this private council meeting, in deep confabulation with Electricity Sample.

'Penny for them, Joe,' said Bronwen.

'What? Oh yes. Just wondering how come Shorty when he's not so short?'

'Not his size, silly,' she said. 'No, what's short is the pint in your glass and the change in your pocket.'

Joe started to check and she added, 'Not now, not when there's just the two of us, and you're with me anyway. But Saturday nights when there's a rush on, I reckon he makes a hundred in short change and another in short measure.'

Again that easy acceptance. Again Joe made the comparison with back home in Luton. Barmen looked for the perks there too, but anyone so blatant he was named for it would soon be even shorter by dint of being driven into the ground.

He said, 'Why's his boss not do something about it?'

'Mr Feathers? None of his business, is it? I mean, it's not like someone's dipping his hand in the till. Try that and Mr Feathers would soon chop it off at the wrist.'

'So what if someone complains?'

'Big Eddie sorts out troublemakers and you get banned.'

'So go somewhere else.'

'Nowhere else to go, is there? Need a licence from the council to hold discos.'

These are murky waters you're swimming in, Joe, he thought.

He longed to be strolling along Luton High on his way for a drink with Whitey on his shoulder, the traffic purring by, the spring sun bouncing off the green marble of the KL restaurant, the Clint Eastwood inflatable over Dirty Harry's bobbing in the breeze, the jets high overhead unwinding their long, long trails to far-away places across the sky.

'You OK, Joe? You've gone funny on me again,' said Bron.

'Just thinking. You and Wain, him and you were making out, right?'

The directness of the question surprised him as much as it surprised her. Must've been thinking about home that did it, and realizing that tomorrow was his last day here and he was still a million miles from finding anything out, or even understanding what in fact there was to find out.

So no more Mr Polite Guy, he told himself ferociously. Straight to the point, don't make no matter how people take it, the lies they tell are just as revealing as the truth they don't to a good PI, according to Endo Venera.

Bronwen said, 'Joe, you're not going to turn out to be one of these old guys who like to talk dirty, are you?'

He said, 'I don't think a pair of nice kids loving each other is dirty, do you?'

She shook her head fiercely, then said, 'Not the way some people see it round here, though.'

'So what happened?'

She looked at him over her glass of crème de menthe (straight out of the movies again) and said, 'So why do you want to know?'

'Don't know,' said Joe honestly. 'Just I'm working on something and the more I know about what's going on round here, the better.'

It didn't sound all that persuasive, but she nodded and said in a rush, 'We've known each other since we were kids. Couple of years ago I, you know, filled out and he started acting different and I was curious, so after that we did it a lot, it was like we felt this was just the start of us being together for ever.'

'But it wasn't.'

'No,' she said. 'We got caught. There was a row. I wasn't sixteen, see? And she said Wain could go to jail, it was the law.'

'She? Your mother caught you?'

'Not mine. Wain's. She said she wouldn't tell his father, or mine, but we had to stop, at least till we were old enough to make our minds up.'

'And this persuaded you?' said Joe dubiously. His own observation of teenage behaviour was that the only pressures they took notice of came from brute force and blatant bribery, and not always then.

'Well, I was scared, and so was Wain. She may not look it, but Mrs Lewis can be pretty scary when she wants.'

Joe tried to imagine this without much success, but then he wasn't a teenager caught with his pants down.

'How old are you now, Bron?' he asked.

'Seventeen.'

'Old enough to make your mind up?'

'Legally, maybe,' she said, managing a smile. 'I turned sixteen a couple of weeks after Mrs Lewis caught us, but Wain had finished his A levels then and he got sent straight off to America, so I didn't see him for over a year, and when he came back he went off to university almost straightaway. It wasn't really till the Christmas hols that we had the chance to talk.'

'So you talked,' Joe prompted.

'Yes, and we did the other, if that's what you're interested in,' she said coldly.

'But you didn't stay together, I mean, not as an item?' said Joe. 'Was that because Mrs Lewis still didn't approve?'

'Oh no. Not scared of her any more,' said Bron dismissively. 'It was because I didn't approve, see?'

'Sorry? Thought you said...'

'I said we slept together, no commitment, just for the fun of it, OK? But there are rules. Rule One is, you go to a party with a boy, you don't expect to find him halfway through the evening with his arm up someone else's skirt. Different in America and at university, maybe, but round here, that's the rule. He said it meant nothing, and *she* always looks like butter wouldn't melt, but I told him where to get off. So if anyone tells you he gave me the push, you can tell them you know different, can't you?'

She spoke with the vehemence of remembered hurt.

Joe said gently, 'Anyone can see he'd have been mad to do that, girl. But this morning I got an impression you were back together, sort of...'

She took a long pull at her drink then said in a rush, 'That's what I thought...he came to see me the night before last and it was just like it was before...better...and I thought...but then he's gone all funny on me...and now you tell me he's been up at the hospital...don't know why I'm telling you this.'

The world, or at least South Bedfordshire, was full of people who weren't sure why they'd told Joe Sixsmith all this. Joe didn't know either, but he wasn't complaining. All he wished was that God would have fitted him with a decoder up to the same standard as his receiver.

'Not working out then?' he said.

'I don't know. Why should I know anything? Like everyone keeps telling me, I'm just a kid.'

Many a true word spoken in anger, thought Joe.

He said, 'Shouldn't let it worry you. Nice, bright, beautiful kid like you, I bet there's lads standing in line to get their names in your appointments book.'

'You in the line, Joe?' she said, smiling at him.

'Couldn't stand the competition,' he replied. 'Much going off in the way of drugs round here?'

This was meant to be casually slipped in on the back of this wave of intimacy. Instead it acted like a breakwater.

'Who you been talking to, then?' she demanded, anger back tinged with deep suspicion.

'No one,' he said. 'Just a sort of professional interest.'

'Oh yes? Fancy keeping in with the pigs, is that it? Well, you'd better not expect favours back, believe me. Pigs round here eat their young.'

'Hey, I'm not trying to get no favours from the cops,' protested Joe. 'Just making conversation. But maybe you shouldn't lump them all together anyway. There're still some good cops around, even here!'

'You reckon? Name three.'

'Well, DI Ursell. And Sergeant Prince...'

The only other he knew by name was Pantyhose and he didn't think he was going to impress by putting his name on the list, but it didn't matter as Bron laughed as if he'd already gone one cop too far.

'Tom Prince? That the best you can manage, Joe?'

'Why? What's wrong with Prince?'

'Oh, nothing proved or he wouldn't still have his stripes. But you don't get moved from being a detective in Cardiff to being in uniform here without there's something going on. Know what I mean, hand in the till, everyone knows but he left no prints.'

'Who told you this, Bron?' asked Joe.

'Oh someone, I don't know. Everyone gossips round here, forget what time you're meeting your mate, just ask the first person you see in the street and they'll be able to tell you. I've seen him myself in here having his drink in the snug with Phil Feathers half an hour after proper closing time except to residents. So don't tell me to put my trust in the police.'

Joe said, 'I'm sorry. Listen, you're reading me wrong. All I want...'

...is to find out how close Wain is linked to the stolen Decorax and whether there's a direct link between the Decorax he'd found in the Lady House cistern and the traces they'd found in the burnt woman's system. That was all he wanted, but it wasn't easy to explain.

But as so often, inarticulate confusion worked better for him than eloquent explanation.

Bronwen suddenly smiled at him and shook her head in mock exasperation, as if he were the troubled teenager and she the mature man.

'Joe, you're a nice man, kind of man who'd take a girl home and not expect favours along the way, and that's pretty rare in these parts. And you've only been here no time at all but you've managed to do a good thing, which is more than most of them who rate important round here will manage in a lifetime. And that's got them taking notice of you which is not always a good thing, believe me. So why not rest quiet and go home safe and sound soon as the festival's over? But first of all, why not take me home and maybe we'll find a little favour for you along the way even if you don't expect it?'

Now Joe saw strong what he hadn't been able to see before, the resemblance between Bron and her mother.

He grinned and said, 'Love to. Only there's a problem.'

He explained about the Morris being blocked.

She said, 'Big silver Jag, is it? Fluffy skeleton in the window?'

'That's right.'

'Andy Quilter. See his name everywhere. His firm does most of the big building contracts round here.'

'Including the new council offices?' Joe guessed.

'Of course.' She looked at him as if he'd said something naive, which he supposed he had.

'So will he move it if I ask him nicely?'

'Not if you ask him nicely, no way,' said Bron. 'You got your mobile with you, Joe?'

He produced it, she took it from him and went through the door marked Ladies.

A few minutes passed, then the phone behind the bar began to ring and after a while Shorty emerged to answer it.

The conversation was in Welsh but the consternation on the barman's face needed no interpreter.

He banged the phone down and went back into the meeting room. Bronwen came out of the toilet and slipped the phone back to Joe. The door behind the bar burst open and a fat man, his face flushed with drink and anger, emerged, followed by Shorty who was gabbling, 'Only a scratch, Mr Quilter, that's what she said, nothing that a bit of polish and a smidgen of filler wouldn't hide...'

They passed through the bar without a glance at Joe and Bron. The girl finished her drink.

'Time to go home, Joe,' she said.

Outside they found Shorty and Quilter examining the Jag like a pair of customs officials.

'You sure she said it was mine?' said Quilter.

'No, well, it was the way she described it...she did sound pretty old and very distressed and you know how women are about makes of car...so no harm done after all, Mr Quilter, all's well that ends well.'

The builder nodded, relief at the lack of damage momentarily dominating irritation at being dragged from his enjoyment.

Bron nudged Joe and he stepped forward to the Morris.

'Excuse me, sir,' he said politely to Quilter. 'I seem to be blocked in. Couldn't move this lovely machine of yours, could you?'

The builder glowered at Joe and did not look at all inclined to concede. Then Bronwen stepped forward and caressed the Jaguar mascot on the bonnet sensuously with the palm of her left hand.

'Oh, it's lovely, isn't it? I'd love a ride in one of these. Maybe some day when you're not too busy, Mr Quilter...'

The builder looked at her assessingly. Bron's performance was way over the top, judged Joe. Man would need to be a real idiot not to see he was being sent up.

'I'm not too busy right now as it happens, young lady,' said Quilter with a leer, producing his keys and clicking the door locks open.

'What a pity, my mam's expecting me home half an hour ago, but we'll call that a date, shall we, Mr Quilter? Now, Joe, you drive fast as you can or I'll be in real trouble.'

Quilter got into his car and moved it away with as much grace as he could muster. What else could a real idiot do? Joe asked himself as he waved an acknowledgement.

He drove the Morris out of the square, then glanced at Bron who sank back in her seat and screamed with the uninhibited laughter of a child and Joe, who had never travelled very far from the child in himself, had no problem joining in.

EIGHTEEN

BACK IN LLANFFUGIOL, Joe found that normal service had been resumed. The stage had been reassembled, the shattered flower urns replaced, and once more the sound of sweet voices in unison enhanced the balmy air.

He'd offered to drop the girl off at the college but she had said she'd prefer to go to the village. She turned to him with a smile and said, 'Thanks a lot, Joe bach.'

'My pleasure.'

She began to open the passenger door, then turned back.

'Nearly forgot. Promised you a favour in return, didn't I?'

Leaning over the gear lever, she took him in her arms and kissed him hard, with lots of tongue. It was like having a hot goldfish in his mouth. Finally it withdrew, only to resume its assault on his left ear as she whispered something in Welsh.

'Do I want to know what it means this time?' he gasped.

She released him, got out of the car, then stooped back down to look into his eyes.

'Means you'd better think of something fast to tell your girlfriend,' she said. 'Ta-ta, Joe.'

She walked away, rear penduluming provocatively.

'That girl needs to be careful else she'll slip a disc by the time she's twenty,' said a familiar voice. 'So what she been massaging today, Joe? Apart from your vocal cords.'

Joe turned and found himself looking up at Beryl.

'Shoot!' he exclaimed. 'You shouldn't come sneaking up on a guy like that.'

'Not me who's the sneak round here. Thought you'd come to listen to the singing, then I find you've gone sneaking off to do heaven knows what.'

Joe was good at listening to the voices of those he loved. He could tell Aunt Mirabelle's state of mind from a couple of syllables heard distantly. Not that this was hard, seeing that, far as he was concerned, she didn't have much more than three states of mind—suspicious, exasperated, and despairing. With Beryl, when she was accusing him of playing around, he could usually identify a kind of affectionate mockery. It wasn't there now. Maybe he ought to feel flattered. All he felt was indignant.

He got out of the car and said, 'Now hold right there. I'm old enough to be that girl's...'

'Know what you're old enough to be, Joe. Pity you're not old enough to have more sense. Must be the primitive company you keep.'

Last time Beryl had had a go at him about Bron, she'd had her tongue in her cheek, but now there was a look in her eyes which told him this was no wind-up. The crack about primitive company had to refer to Merv.

He could see what had happened. Beryl must've asked Merv where he was and got the jokey explanation that he said he'd got a date with a lovely lady, meaning the car. Only Beryl didn't altogether approve of Merv on account of he made taxi-driver jokes like, *You know why they call them the fair sex? 'Cos if you want the sex, you gotta pay the fare!* And Merv, recognizing the disapproval, reacted by really playing up the bold bad ladykiller who didn't like the way his old hunting mate Joe Sixsmith was being hijacked off the pleasant primrose path on to the straight and narrow. So he'd probably made a big production of Joe's alleged date, which normally Beryl would pay no mind to, not till she caught him snogging Bron in the car park.

Working it out and explaining it to Beryl were different things. He opted for a change of subject.

He said, 'You ain't said nothing about the car, don't tell me you've not noticed? Was just trying it out...'

'I noticed. Often wondered why you were so stuck on them old juggernauts. Now I know. They got room for a double bed.'

It was too good a line not to exit on. She turned and strode away, her back view as expressive as Bron's. Normally she could do a pretty good pendulum thing herself, but today it would have needed a seismograph to detect a tremor.

There is a time for everything under the sun, says the Good Book, and there would be time for a repair job, but it wasn't now.

'Mr Sixsmith, good afternoon.'

Another female voice behind him. Like being stalked by Apaches. He turned, and adjusted the example. By spirits.

'Hello, Mrs Lewis,' he said.

Morna Lewis had looked like she might fade away in the confines of her own house by night. Outside under the spotlight of the sun, she had such a slight presence that Joe was glad to see she still threw a shadow.

But when he said, 'Wanted to tell you thanks for having me last night. Real nice dinner,' her face lit up with the Audrey Hepburn smile which gave the sun as good as it got.

'You were very welcome,' she said. 'That was Bronwen just now, wasn't it?'

So she'd been standing there invisible, watching the whole little drama. He didn't mind. Way he read this lady, she wasn't one to be entertained by other folks' troubles.

'Yeah. Gave her a lift from town.'

'Caerlindys?' she said, like there might be some other town in this wilderness. 'You didn't go to the hospital, did you? I was wondering how that poor woman was.'

'Did, as a matter of fact. Not much change but they're hopeful.'

Her tiny face puckered with concern.

'It's a terrible thing, fire,' she said softly.

She looked like she might cry.

Joe said, 'Hey, it's OK, Mrs Lewis. She'll probably make it. It's in the Lord's hands.'

This was one of Mirabelle's comfortable sayings, and it was her conviction that Joe put into it.

Mrs Lewis looked at him closely.

'Are you religious, Mr Sixsmith?' she asked. 'You don't mind me asking? I know yours is a chapel choir, but there is a saying in choral circles round here, it's not the vice that keeps you out, it's the voice that gets you in. I'm sorry. That was very impertinent of me. I did not mean to suggest...'

'It's OK, Mrs Lewis,' said Joe. 'No need to apologize. Much the same back home.'

He was thinking of Dildo Doberley whose fine bass obliterated many other disqualifications to membership of Boyling Corner Choir. Thought of Dildo brought the problem of the Decorax into his mind and his need to get hold of Wain Lewis. Maybe his mother could help. But first there was her question.

'No, I'd not say I'm all that religious, not in an on-my-knees praying and hallelujahing kind of way. In fact, my Auntie Mirabelle—she's here with the choir—would say I ain't religious at all. But I believe there's something out there bigger than us and sometimes when it's in the right frame of mind it can put the pieces together in a way nothing we understand allows for.'

He came to a halt, not wanting to get too heavy, certainly not wanting to get into personal stuff, like his feeling that sometimes his PI work couldn't work without this *something out there* gave everything a good shake up and showed him how the bits and pieces he scraped together could shape into some kind of picture. Once when he'd said something of this to Butcher who ran the Bullpat Square Law Centre back in Luton, she'd said with mock-awe, 'You mean you're really working for God? How's He pay?' She'd then started to suggest that maybe Joe was selling himself short, and the human mind was a very complex thing, even in lathe operators, and maybe the faculty, dear Brutus, lay not in his stars but in himself, at which point Joe had asked was that the Brutus who played for Brazil and Butcher had lit another of her smoke-screen cheroots and told him to sod off, she had work to do without expectation of a helping hand from the Almighty.

'Yes,' said Mrs Lewis, who'd been listening to him with a concentration which he'd have found troubling if he'd been trying to sell her insurance. 'I think I see what you mean. God is His own interpreter and He will make it plain. Thank you, Mr Sixsmith, that's a comfort.'

Gratitude really was troubling. Joe, who'd caught the reference here without difficulty as he'd sung the hymn plenty of times, guessed that the lady was thinking about her own lot, stuck out here in the sticks with an oddball like Lewis. Or maybe she was the oddball. Depended how you looked at it. Joe had seen too many ill-matched couples to dish out blame over-quickly, but on the whole he'd guess that in Mrs Lewis he was looking at one of the fearful saints the hymn went on about.

One thing he was sure of. Wain was the apple of her eye so he'd better box clever in enquiring after him. No point in giving her cause for concern. DI Ursell would do that soon enough once he got on the case.

He said, 'I'm glad they got things sorted so quick after the trouble this morning.'

'Trouble?'

'Yeah. You know. The stage. Mr Lewis must've been worried.'

'Oh yes. That.'

She didn't sound like she shared her husband's concerns.

'Yeah, well, it's nice to see everything's back on course. You going to listen to the singing?'

She shook her head impatiently, then, as if feeling this needed explanation, she said, 'I fear I'm not very musical, Mr Sixsmith.'

This was an opening.

Joe said, 'What about Wain? Who does he take after?'

'In this regard, me, I think.'

'So he won't spend much time at the festival then?'

'Not because of the music perhaps, but it is a happening, and there aren't many of those round here, not such as might interest young people anyway. Yes, I see his car parked over there, so he must be around somewhere.'

Joe followed her gaze along the row of cars in which he was parked and spotted the red Mazda MX-5. Morna Lewis moved towards the car and stood peering into it with a frowning intensity, as if trying to conjure up her son in the driving seat. Joe joined her.

'Nice wheels,' he said. 'Lucky boy. His age, I was saving for a bike. What did you say he was studying at college?'

'Sociology, to start with. I think he wants to go on to do child psychology.'

'Sounds heavy,' said Joe. 'Must be a bright kid.'

He meant it. People clever enough to learn that kind of stuff he genuinely admired, though rarely to the point of envy. You played the cards the dealer gave you, and as the game was more like poker than bridge, the way you played was as important as the hand you were dealt. But the way to a mother's heart is through her kid's praise and his remark got him the sunburst smile.

Then the face clouded over and he turned to see Glyn Matthias coming towards them. He recalled Lewis's dismissive reaction to the man's name at the Lady House that morning and wondered how Morna Lewis would respond.

He stopped in front of them and said, 'Good day, Mrs Lewis,' in his gentle, musical voice.

'Good day, Mr Matthias,' said the woman evenly.

'And good day once more to you, Mr Sixsmith.'

This got a reaction.

She looked from Joe to the music teacher with interest and said, 'You know each other?'

'We...ran into each other last evening,' said Matthias. 'I wonder, might we have a quick word?'

The words were addressed to Joe but the man was looking with earnest appeal at the High Master's wife. She responded with an unfocused gaze which seemed to go right through him to the furthermost horizon.

'Excuse me,' she said, after a pause which had gone on too long. 'I really must join my husband. There are arrangements to discuss. For this evening. There is a reception, you know. In the college hall. For the choirs and special guests.'

This was addressed to Joe.

He said, 'I'm looking forward to it.'

Matthias said, 'So am I.'

This got him a fully focused gaze.

'You?'

'Oh yes, I'm the voice coach for the Caerlindys Cantors, didn't you know?'

Clearly she didn't. And her husband? Probably. Joe didn't doubt that GM had its moles everywhere.

'It will be very nice to see you, Mr Matthias,' said Morna Lewis, recovered from her momentary lapse of surprise. 'You too, Mr Sixsmith. Good day now.'

She walked away. The two men watched her go.

'Nice lady,' said Joe.

'Yes. But poor judgement.'

Joe considered this. Sounded like an invitation to gossip.

'The High Master, you mean? Seems to me more likely you'd reckon him for the poor judgement.'

It was Matthias's turn for consideration.

'Because he gave me my cards? Well, as I indicated to you earlier, the High Master may have his reasons that reason wots not of. How about Mrs Lewis, I wonder. You and she seemed in deep debate just now.'

'We weren't talking about you,' said Joe firmly. 'I can't imagine her bad-mouthing you, though. And even if she had, I'd not have paid it no mind. Man's business is his own business, is what we say back home in the big city.'

He'd never actually heard anyone say anything remotely like that, but it seemed worth establishing his sophisticated urban credentials before he got down to the subtle cross-questioning.

'Should I be impressed?' mused Matthias. 'Or grateful even that such a metropolitan luminary as yourself, Mr Sixsmith, is willing to give me the benefit of the doubt?'

'Sorry. I just thought...' stammered Joe, then gave up because experience had taught him that saying aloud what he'd just thought was rarely the way to improve a bad situation. 'You just going to stand there, making me feel bad, you should know I've been made to feel bad by experts. So if you've got something sensible you want to say, best speak up, 'cos I'm going deaf with thirst.'

Matthias smiled and said, 'Now there's a sentiment worth putting in Welsh and declaiming at an eisteddfod. Joe—all right to call you Joe?—let me buy you a drink.'

'Best offer I've had all day,' said Joe.

'Including having your throat plumbed by the beautiful Bron?'

Had anyone missed that? Probably be on the local TV news!

'That wasn't an offer,' said Joe. 'That was repaying a favour.'

'Ooh, was it now?' said Matthias, suddenly very camp. 'Remind me to get in your debt, Joe.'

Then he laughed at the alarm on Joe's face and said, 'But we don't count drinks as favours in Wales, Joe. So let's see if these thirsty singers have left anything in the barrel, shall we?'

He turned towards the refreshment tent. Joe didn't follow immediately but stood looking down into the passenger seat of the sports car. He took a comb out of his pocket and slowly ran it over the back rest. Matthias had paused and was looking back curiously.

'Something the matter, Mr Sixsmith?' he enquired. 'You don't look too happy.'

'Just a bit of that sadness we were talking about before, Mr Matthias,' said Joe. 'And with my voice in the state it is, I'm not sure that singing it's going to do any good.'

NINETEEN

THE SMELL IN THE refreshment tent reminded Joe he hadn't accepted Sergeant Prince's kind invitation to sample the best mutton pie in the Principality and at the bar he added a bacon sandwich to the drinks order.

'I'll pay for it myself,' he offered.

'In case food turns out to be a favour?' murmured Matthias. 'Only joking. Make that two, will you?'

The Welshman led the way to a table by the entrance. Most people preferred to sit at the outside tables in the sun on a day like this, and Joe would have too, but he said nothing, guessing the reason was the greater privacy the uncrowded interior gave them.

The bacon was as good as Joe had remembered from breakfast and, also as at breakfast, Matthias had the good manners to let him savour his butty in silence. This had another advantage. Joe had the kind of mind which often works best when left to its own devices and eating good grub usually put it into suspend mode. As he'd once explained to Butcher, it wasn't that he couldn't eat and think at the same time, but he couldn't see why a man would want to. So the unproductive speculation filling his mind as to what Matthias wanted from him, by being switched off had worked its way to a conclusion by the time normal service was resumed.

He's got something to tell me, but only if I want to know it.

Or rather, he emended, if he thinks I need to know it.

Better try a subtle bluff.

'So are you going to tell me or not?'

'Tell you what?' said Matthias, looking puzzled.

Joe glanced around the beer tent in search of an answer. In another man this might have been evidence of complete bafflement. But Joe's experience had taught him that if God chose to make something plain, He wasn't choosy as to place and circumstance.

And found he was staring the answer in the face. Or rather in the back.

A man hoping not to be identified might imagine that to sit facing the blank canvas wall with his back to the body of the tent was pretty foolproof. But not when it was his bald head seen from behind that triggered the alarm bells.

'About him,' said Joe pointing. 'About what he was doing driving round on one of them buggy contraptions up the hill the night that Copa Cottage got torched.'

Matthias tried to look blank then gave it up and smiled, saying, 'Nye Garage was right about you, Mr Sixsmith.'

Then he called, 'Harry, care to join us?'

The Yul Brynner lookalike rose and came over to the table. He didn't seem any more enthusiastic at the sight of Joe than he had when faced with him that morning.

'I think you two have met,' said Matthias.

'Several times,' said Joe. 'But we ain't been introduced. Joe Sixsmith.'

'Harry Herbert.'

The tall man's right arm twitched as if it had thoughts of reaching out in a handshake. Joe made no responding move. This guy was closely linked with the Goat and Axle mob who'd made such nationalistic anti-Anglo noises. And Joe had seen him within a quarter-mile of Copa Cottage the night it burnt. If it turned out he had any responsibility for that woman lying still as a corpse in Caerlindys Hospital, Joe didn't want to recall he'd shaken his hand.

'Sit down, won't you, Harry boy?' said Matthias.

Herbert obeyed, never taking his eyes off Joe.

'Now, Mr Sixsmith, let's put our cards on the table, shall we?' said Matthias. 'First thing to establish is what you've told the good Inspector Ursell about Harry here.'

Joe considered boxing clever and pretending all kinds of things. But then he'd have to remember what he was pretending, and why he was pretending it. Truth was usually the best option, until it wasn't an option at all.

He said, 'Told him I spoke to a guy on a buggy the night we got lost on the way here.'

'With description, no doubt.'

Joe shrugged.

'Told him you guys all look and sound the same to me.'

That got a smile from Matthias, not from Herbert.

'This, I presume, was at your first interview with the inspector and apropos your first encounter with Harry. But you met him again earlier today.'

'Yes.'

'And, if Nye Garage's judgement is correct, recognized him.'

'Yes. Eventually.'

'And soon after that encounter you were observed in long and earnest confabulation with Mr Ursell. What if anything did you tell him about Harry on that occasion?'

This, thought Joe, might be a good time to start lying if he'd been chained to the wall in a nationalist dungeon instead of sitting here in this airy beer tent with people all around and a pleasant mix of birdsong, sunshine and choral harmonies drifting through the open flap.

'Nothing,' said Joe.

'Really? Why not?'

'Didn't arise,' said Joe. 'We were talking about other things.'

Matthias nodded and said, 'There, you see, Harry. Told you there was no need to book plastic surgery and head for the hills. If Ursell had been on to you, he'd have had you in leg irons hours ago.'

Herbert didn't look convinced, but Joe wasn't much worried about his state of mind. He was working out the implications of what Matthias was saying and feeling indignant.

'Now hang about,' he said. 'I should have told the inspector I thought I recognized Mr Herbert but, like I said, other things got in the way. Nothing to stop me now though, and soon as I see him, that's the first thing I'll be telling him.'

He emptied his glass and set it down with an emphatic bang.

'Same again, is it?' asked Matthias.

'I'm not sure,' said Joe. 'I'm choosy about the company I drink in.'

He stared challengingly at Matthias, who didn't blink.

'Fair enough. But I'd put you down as the kind of man who'd want to be sure what kind of company that was before making such an important decision. Joe, I'm here to give you both an offer and an explanation.'

'I'm listening,' said Joe, thinking the more they talked, the more he'd learn. And the mention of an offer intrigued him. Assuming it wasn't an offer in the Mafia sense of one he couldn't afford to refuse, it had to be some kind of bribe. This was an area he'd had little experience in and it would be interesting to see how much they thought he was worth.

Or maybe not.

'I gather you are interested, both professionally and personally, in finding out how and why Copa Cottage came to be burning that night,' said Matthias. 'What I'd like to do is persuade you first of all that neither Harry here nor any of the gents you met at the Goat and Axle had anything to do with it. And then, in return for your assurance that you will neither identify Harry to Inspector Ursell nor implicate either of us as the source of anything I might tell you here, to offer you some information which might assist your own investigations.'

They couldn't half rabbit on, these people, thought Joe.

'I'm still listening,' he said.

'That is all I ask for. Let me start by admitting what your own powers of observation plus Dai Williams's mistaken assessment of your likely political position probably made you suspect, that several of the regulars at the Goat are indeed activists in the nationalist cause, though on the whole more active with the tongue than with the terrorism. But the conspiracy in which those present the other night are primarily engaged at the present time has a closer target than the English occupation of our country. It is the Llanffugiol Festival.'

Herbert looked around fearfully as if expecting the SAS to come crashing in, and hissed something in Welsh. Joe guessed it was a protest at the music teacher's frank avowal of criminality in a public place to a man who was unlikely to have much sympathy for a purely local feud.

Matthias sighed long-sufferingly and said, 'Harry is concerned you may be wearing a wire.'

'Couldn't get one my size,' said Joe. 'So let's get this straight. It's been your lot trying to mess things up? Like cancelling the caterers? And fixing the stage? After what you said this morning, I wondered.'

'I thought you might,' said Matthias. 'Harry and some friends had been down here at the festival field the night you saw him. The stage had been erected that day, but as the festival proper was not due to get under way for another twenty-four hours, there was minimal security that night. It was decided to take the chance offered of preparing the stage for its collapse by lubricating and loosening all but a couple of key joints so that when the moment came, it would require only a couple of quick twists of the spanner to destabilize the erection.'

'Destabilize?' said Joe. 'It folded like a deck chair. You could've killed someone.'

'It was rather more dramatic than we intended,' admitted Matthias. 'But in the event no one was seriously hurt, thank heaven. Your own friends were never at risk, of course. We targeted the German choir because they are the festival's real draw, begging your pardon. And also we knew they would make the biggest fuss. One thing all inhabitants of these islands have in common is a fairly laid-back attitude to minor disasters, and major too. On the continent they take themselves and their dignity rather more seriously.'

He paused again and looked enquiringly at Joe, as if asking, what do you think of it so far? A group of youngsters came in, a couple went up to the bar to order while the others stood in the doorway immediately behind Joe, debating whether they should sit inside or out. The outsiders won and they pushed a couple of tables together right up against the canvas next to Matthias's table, but they were making far too much noise to be an eavesdropping threat.

Joe said, 'You want I should cheer 'cos you're telling me you're trying to wreck the festival I came all the way from Luton to sing in?'

'No. But I'd like to think you believe me when I say we had nothing to do with the event which has prevented you from adding your doubtless mellifluous voice to the performance of your fellow choristers. I heard them earlier, by the way. Most impressive. I got the sense that your choirmaster really makes you search for the true feeling beneath the music and the words too.'

This could just have been flannel but it came over so sincere that Joe felt a glow of pleasure at hearing Boyling Corner praised and said, 'Thanks. Rev. Pot's been telling us, no use going to Wales unless we can sing from the heart.'

'Singing the sadness, eh? He sounds like my sort of man,' said Matthias.

'Don't think so,' said Joe anxiously. 'He can be a bit old-fashioned.'

'I was speaking musically,' grinned Matthias.

'Are you two going to rabbit on about the sodding singing all day or what?' demanded Herbert surlily.

'Sorry, Harry. Mr Sixsmith, I take it I have carried you with me so far. I realize that by confessing Harry here and the rest of us guilty of a different crime, albeit a lesser one, from that which you suspected us of, I have not necessarily removed from you the natural good citizen's impulse to help the police in their enquiries. So now we come to the offer. If Harry can tell you something which might further your personal enquiries, would you be willing not to identify him to Inspector Ursell?'

Joe considered. The kids at the table outside had finished their drinks and were moving on. He felt a sudden and surprising envy of them. To be young and careless, wandering around in the sunlight with your mates, nothing more on your mind than whether the bird of your choice fancied you as much as you fancied her... 'Stead of which he was sitting here debating whether to do a deal with a bunch of saboteurs. Not that it was such a big deal. All it came down to was, he didn't finger Herbert as the guy acting suspicious the night of the fire and in return he got...what?

He said, 'Depends what it is he tells me. Could be worth dick.'

It was Matthias's turn to consider.

'OK,' he said, ignoring a protesting growl from Herbert. 'Go ahead, Harry.'

Reluctantly, the tall man said, 'I was heading for home after'—he glared at Matthias as though still objecting to the transparency of his account of the sabotage, then, clearly feeling the damage was done, went on—'after we fixed the stage. I had the tools and the lubricant on the buggy, see, so I had to go roundabout over the fields so as not to be clocked by some nosy copper. Only two places where I needed to cross a road, and blow me if I didn't run into some bugger both times. Sod's law, they call it. Second time was your coach. Don't know how the hell you recognized me when you only saw me for a few seconds with the headlight in your eyes.'

He glowered at Joe as if suspecting him of some chicanery. Joe, looking suitably modest, prompted, 'And the first time?' guessing this was the crux of the offered deal.

'First time was just below Copa Cottage. I'd just got the gate on to the road opened when I heard a car coming up the hill. I switched off the lights and ducked down. Needn't have bothered. Was going too fast to pay any heed to me. Went on by, then suddenly its lights went off too, just before it reached the turn to Copa.'

There was a dramatic pause which Joe spoilt by inserting the question, 'Did anyone get out?'

'I was coming to that,' said Herbert disgruntledly. 'I heard the door open and shut, gently like, and then the boot. I counted to twenty, then I started up the buggy and got out of there fast.'

'So you weren't around when the fire started?'

'No way! Wouldn't have done much good if I had been.'

'Saving a woman's life not much good?' said Joe incredulously.

'Didn't know there was a woman's life to save, did I?' snarled Herbert. 'No. All I'd have thought if I'd seen the fire start is, expensive little holiday home owned by a pair of poxy Anglos, burning's the best thing for it.'

'Thank you, Harry,' said Matthias smoothly, possibly feeling he might be losing his audience. 'Mr Sixsmith?'

'Well, it's something,' said Joe grudgingly. 'But not a lot.'

'I wasn't asking you if we had a deal,' said Matthias. 'I was merely inviting further questions.'

Joe was momentarily baffled. Then it came to him. They were all prima donnas, these Welsh. They didn't tell a story to convey information in the most direct way possible, they turned it into a performance with the listener as straight man.

Which meant you kept the best for last.

He said, 'Didn't happen to recognize this car, did you?'

'Oh yes.'

'And the driver too?'

'Yes, indeed.'

This was worse than getting Whitey to take a tablet.

He said, 'So could you manage to tell me about them? Please.'

'Don't need to tell you, do I? Not when you can see for yourself.'

Herbert pointed dramatically.

'There they are,' he said. 'That's the car I saw. That poxy little red sporty job.'

Joe turned his head. But he knew already what he was going to be looking at.

Wain Lewis's MX-5.

Something else he saw too. He'd thought all the youngsters had left the table immediately outside, but there was a figure still sitting there, very close. No, not sitting now. Jumping up and moving swiftly away.

'And that's the bugger who was driving it,' exclaimed Herbert. 'Hell! Do you think he heard us?'

Joe, on his feet now and watching Wain Lewis vaulting into his MX-5, didn't have any doubt.

'Wain, stop!' he shouted, stepping out of the tent and waving.

He saw at once he didn't have a monopoly. From different angles, at least three others were converging on the Mazda—Ursell, and Leon Lewis, and Bronwen.

Not that it mattered. Wain wasn't in the mood for company. The engine roared into life, the boy glanced round once, his pale poet's face like a death mask. Then he was gone, doing fifty and rising as he exited from the parking field.

TWENTY

HAVING FAILED WITH Wain Lewis, it seemed to Joe that the three pursuers looked around for someone to blame and with one accord settled for him.

He'd had the same kind of experience before. One occasion in particular was printed on his memory. He'd been King Mechior in the school Nativity Play and during their one and only public performance the girl playing Mary had broken wind loudly, and everyone had turned to look at him. Including Mary. He still saw her round Luton. She'd married a salesman who fathered five kids on her then done a bunk, and she looked ten years older than she was, and she was always real grateful if he gave her a lift, and sometimes they'd chat about the old days when they were kids, but he'd never been able to bring up the Nativity Play fart. It would have seemed like taking advantage.

She came into his mind now as the trio joined him outside the refreshment tent. It would have been easy to cause a bit of consternation all round by declaring that he had reason to think that Wain was mixed up with the theft of the Decorax from Caerlindys Hospital, and that he was connected with the mystery woman in the cottage, and that he probably had something to do with the fire that had put her in Intensive Care. But it would have had nothing to do with the pursuit of truth or whatever it was he imagined he was doing, just a bit of self-indulgence at their expense, so when DI Ursell snarled at him, 'Recognize him this time, do you, Mr Sixsmith? So now your eyesight's miraculously improved, maybe you can tell me where he might be heading?' he looked blank and said, 'Sorry. Can't help.'

'Then maybe you can tell me why you were so keen to attract his attention. Or were you waving your arms to ward off the mosquitoes?'

That sounded like a pretty good excuse to Joe, but it had clearly been pre-empted, so he said, 'Just wanted to have a look at his wheels, is all. Interest of mine, motors.'

'And that was why you came to the Lady House this morning, to discuss automobiles with my son?' said Leon Lewis. 'A purpose which your strong sense of professional responsibility prevented you from sharing with me?'

Joe, after a bit of effort, recalled the line he'd shot the High Master in return for the High Master not shooting him.

'Oh yeah,' he said. 'No, not just that. But I got the other thing sorted without needing to talk to Wain. Sorry. *Owain.*'

'Seen him in the last half-hour, have you then?' said Bronwen. ''Cos you were dead keen to get hold of him in Caerlindys and you hadn't managed it when I said cheerio to you thirty minutes ago.'

It's a conspiracy, thought Joe. Maybe I should just come clean with everything, let them sort it out among themselves.

He glanced back into the tent as if in search of inspiration. The table he'd been sitting at was empty. Not a sign of Herbert and Matthias. How come everyone else could vanish so easily while he couldn't even sneak away from Sergeant Prince without a helping hand from fate? Thought of Prince brought him full circle to Ursell's opening remark. Prince must have been talking to the DI on the phone, and once Ursell had got a description of the burnt woman's mystery visitor, he'd have had little problem recognizing young Lewis, and even less working out that Joe must have recognized him too.

This, plus the fact that the DI was probably still hoping he was going to pull a handful of Decorax out of his pocket, made him a good man not to be left alone with.

Joe felt nauseous. For a second he put it down to the bacon sarnie, then he identified the feeling as simple homesickness. Life had never been complicated as this back in dear ol' Luton.

He said, 'Why's everyone so keen all of a sudden to get hold of Wain?'

'Owain,' said Lewis. 'His name is Owain.'

He turned away and headed back towards the competition field.

Bron said accusingly to Joe, 'You seen my da?'

'No. He not turned up yet?'

'I wouldn't be asking if he had, would I?' she snarled and moved off with the measured pace of a hunting tigress.

'Bron, hold on,' called Joe.

With an apologetic smile to Ursell, he set out after the girl.

'What?' she demanded as he caught up with her.

'Just wondered why you were so keen to get hold of Wain. You didn't seem much bothered about seeing him when I drove you back from town. In fact, you seemed like you'd made up your mind there was nothing there for you any more.'

She hesitated before answering, then Joe's open honest gaze did the trick.

'Might as well tell you as I've told you everything else. It was weird. I ran into his ma. We've always been dead formal since that time she broke us up. But today she was dead nice to me. Talked to me like I was somebody, not just a kid. She said she was sorry about what had happened way back then but now I was older, I'd understand she'd just been protecting both of us, and she hoped Wain and me could still be good friends.'

'She didn't know that you'd got back together during the Christmas hols?'

'Don't think so, but you can never tell with mothers, can you? She said she didn't think he was very happy just now and he could probably do with a real friend to cheer him up, and I said he'd given me a lift to town this morning but he didn't seem all that friendly, and she said that young men are never very good at expressing their feelings, and he was around the festival somewhere, she'd seen his car, and anything I could do to cheer him up...well, it sounded to me like she was saying it was open season on Wain as far as I was concerned, so when I saw him sitting on his lonesome outside the refreshment tent, I thought I might as well ask him straight out where we stood, only before I could get near him, he took off...'

'Bron, I don't think it was you he was taking off from,' said Joe gently. 'And his mother's right. I think Wain's got a lot of things on his mind just now and could do with a friend. One thing I gotta ask, I'm sorry but I need to know, this girl you found him with his hand up her skirt, was she a red-headed nurse from the hospital?'

Her expression gave him the answer without her words.

'That's right. Tilly Butler. Little cow. Looks so innocent but you know what they say about nurses. Seen it all and still can't get enough of it.'

'That what they say? I'll have to tell my friend Beryl.'

'Oh hell,' she said, crestfallen. 'Forgot she's a nurse. I'm sorry, I didn't mean...'

'I know you didn't,' said Joe, smiling. 'You take good care of yourself, Bron. Me, I think Wain lost himself a bargain.'

He meant it. She was a nice kid. But he didn't think there was much joy in prospect for anyone with an emotional interest in Owain Lewis.

The girl went on her way.

Joe glanced back to see if he'd shaken off DI Ursell and found himself looking into the man's face.

'Alone at last, Mr Sixsmith,' he said. 'Tom Prince tells me you've been telling him how closely you and me are working together. He got the impression we are real mates, no secrets from each other. I was pleased to hear it. Always nice to know who your friends really are, isn't it, Joe? All right if I call you Joe?'

Joe thought, if Prince is GM, what's he doing cosying up to Ursell who clearly isn't? And did it really matter? Policemen and their relationships wasn't any problem of his. Also he was suddenly fed up with tiptoeing round them like they were little tin gods. All right, back home it came with the job, but there was no need to make a habit of it. Another day and he'd be out of here.

'Fine,' he said. 'And I'll call you Perry, shall I?'

Ursell took it in his stride.

'Be my guest,' he said. 'Which you may yet be if you hold out on me, Joe. Let's take a little walk, shall we?'

He put his arm round Joe's shoulders in a manner which might have looked avuncular but felt like the preliminary to the best of three falls, and urged him away from the tents and the parked cars and activity in general.

'Hey, I don't want to miss my choir,' said Joe, glancing anxiously towards the show field.

'Got some money on it, have you? Wise man. Word is that everyone's been very impressed and the odds are shortening fast, especially since the favourites took their tumble this morning. So anyone who backed your lot first thing may have done themselves a bit of good.'

'Shouldn't think Nye will like that,' said Joe, not seeing any point in pretending he didn't know about Nye's book with Ursell making no secret of his knowledge.

'Oh, he'll survive. All that money he took on the Guttenbergers, he's got a nice cushion.'

'But won't those bets be void, money returned?'

'Not according to Nye. They'd sung, see, like coming under starter's orders. So the bets stand. Lucky for Nye they did withdraw, though. Very generous odds you could get right up till the stage collapsed, so that's where the smart money was pouring in. Suggest anything to you as an investigator, does it, Joe?'

It suggested a lot, but not anything he was going to share with the police about a man he hoped to talk into selling him the car of his dreams shortly.

He said, 'So what's the verdict on the stage? Accident?'

The fingers dug into his shoulder.

'Thought we were friends, Joe? You want to play charades, wait till Christmas. I saw you checking out those joints on the scaffolding and I'm sure a man with your engineering background spotted straightaway what even an ignoramus like me could see in a few minutes. It was a fix. And the way you've been getting around in the short time you've been with us, I don't doubt you could point your finger straight as mine at the people responsible. But pointing and proving are different things. And so is proving and wanting to prove, eh, Joe?'

Joe's natural reaction was to play naive because that came easiest, so playing smart required a bit of effort. Might as well double-check Matthias's version of events, he thought.

'So it don't look like the lot trying to sabotage the festival have got anything to do with setting fire to the cottage?' he said.

'I'd agree,' said Ursell. 'Different things entirely. Might be able to help us, though, if by chance they were creeping around the undergrowth doing their guerilla act that particular night.'

He was sharp, thought Joe. Or maybe he'd just noticed him buddying up with Herbert and Matthias in the refreshment tent.

'Could be to their advantage too,' Ursell added, watching Joe closely.

'You mean like a deal?'

'This isn't America, Joe,' said the DI reprovingly. 'Nor even Luton. Don't make deals in Wales. But we do make decisions about resources. See, I've got this situation at the moment with Mr Penty-Hooser really keen for me to concentrate everything on finding out who's trying to undermine the festival, but what I say is, no one got hurt when the stage collapsed so it's not like arson with a woman critical in hospital, *that* should be my priority.'

'No competition,' agreed Joe.

'Only it's bringing me a lot of flak. Easy thing would be to throw everything at the saboteurs, get that out of the way. Unless they were being real helpful in the more serious case.'

'Thought you didn't do deals,' said Joe.

'Not with criminals in custody. What I'm talking here is free citizens freely offering their help, anonymously through a third party if preferred.'

The crunch. He wants to use me as the unofficial amateur middleman again, thought Joe. Someone he can deny all knowledge of if I get caught burgling someone's house or doing deals with criminals, with the additional advantage I'm not going to be around long enough to cause any future embarrassment by shooting my mouth off.

But the thought had no rancour in it. For the first time he felt as smart as Ursell was pretending to believe he was. He was way ahead of the game. The guy was asking him to act as intermediary in a done deal!

He said, 'It's everyone's duty to help the police any way they can, Perry.'

'Knew you'd see it like that, Joe. But information's like fish, the fresher the better.'

'I'll get right on to it,' said Joe.

He knew he should be telling the cop now that Wain had been seen driving up to Copa the night of the fire, but he also knew he wanted to talk to the boy himself first, though he wasn't certain why. OK, he had Wain's money in his wallet, but he also had the Haggards', so claiming professional duty to a client was, if not double-talk, at least one-point-five-talk. But his gut told him loud and clear to speak with Wain before feeding him to the cops, and a man whose thoughts came through like Radio One on a rundown transistor in an electric storm needed a good strong signal to respond to.

He still felt guilty, but Ursell seemed content to leave things there and move on to the main item in his agenda.

'So, Joe, what have you been up to since we talked about your old friend in Luton this morning? Anything interesting?'

'You could say that,' Joe replied.

He gave an account of his adventures in the Lady House, omitting only his small-screen viewing of Long John Dawe and Ella Williams at their exercise in the sickbay.

Ursell made a good listener. Rapt almost, not speaking till Joe came to a finish.

'So, nothing in any of the cisterns, you say?'

'Not a thing.'

'You checked them all.'

'All I could find.'

Ursell seemed only mildly disappointed. If Prince had passed on the info about the Decorax in the girl's system, he probably felt that Joe's evidence gave him enough to go after Wain without needing to show his hand by applying for a search warrant.

'So, these TV screens. Hidden behind the wine rack, you say.'

'They're behind the wine rack and hidden by it,' said Joe firmly. He wasn't sure yet of Ursell's motives in wanting to get Leon Lewis in his sights, but he didn't see it as any of his business to feed what might be just another private feud.

'What's the difference?'

'Difference is if a guy wanted a set of security screens in his cellar, he'd have lost storage space for his vino if he'd put them in front of the rack instead of behind it.'

'Maybe. And you say they're linked to the college security system. How do you know that?'

'Switched on and had a look,' said Joe.

'Oh. You didn't mention that before.'

He was sharp, this guy.

'Didn't I? Sorry. Yeah, well, they're just a duplicate of the set Dai Williams has got in his flat. You must have noticed the cameras when you were looking over the college this morning. I suppose Mr Lewis wanted some cover for when Williams wasn't around.'

Ursell didn't look happy.

He said, 'And this head in the cabinet, marble, you say?'

'That's right. He said it came off that cupid he's got at the front door.'

'But it gave you a fright?'

'You ain't joking,' said Joe fervently. 'Well, I was a bit wound up, wandering around someone else's house without permission. Plus the colouring made it look, well, not real, but realler, if you know what I mean. But the real shock was having that shotgun pushed against my neck.'

'I can see how that would be an unpleasant experience,' said

Ursell, suddenly full of sympathy. 'Wouldn't care to make out a complaint against Lewis for threatening behaviour, would you? Serious offence, waving a loaded weapon at people.'

Joe shook his head.

'No,' he said firmly. 'No complaint.'

'OK,' said the DI, not sounding surprised. 'Hard to make it stick anyway in the circs, you wandering around his place uninvited. He'd probably bring a counter-charge against you. Then you'd really find out who your friends were.'

The threat again. Joe was almost glad to hear it. With his tendency to look for the best in people, it was always helpful if from time to time they themselves prompted him to remember the worst.

He said boldly, 'Look, man, I think I know who my friends are already. What I don't know is what it is you're after. You're twisting my arm to help. Ever stop to think a man with his arm twisted is only half as much use as a man with both arms free? At the least, if you tell me where you're looking to go, then I won't get in the way by accident.'

It was, he felt, a reasonable appeal, and for a moment it looked like DI Ursell was giving it reasonable consideration.

But he was saved the bother of making up his mind by the arrival on the scene of a panting and flustered uniformed constable with the probable causes of his fluster hot on his heels. These were Bronwen Williams and a wiry-framed man in dungarees and gumboots who looked even more out of breath than the copper.

'Sir,' gasped the constable. 'Sorry to trouble you, sir, but there's a report we've just had a car gone over the edge of Stanigord Quarry. Ifor James here it was who farms round there, and he saw the fence was broken and he looked down and could see something under the water and when he took a closer look it was a pick-up truck and he thinks it might be Dai Williams's...'

'And you told *her?*' exclaimed Ursell, glaring towards the distraught girl.

'Me it was who told her,' said the farmer. 'First person I saw when I got here and I couldn't not speak, could I?'

Ursell looked ready to give him an argument but postponed the moment.

'Right,' he said. 'Let's go take a look. Joe, you take care of Miss Williams, will you?'

He strode away with the constable close behind. Joe turned to

Bron but she was also on the move. He went after her and caught up with her by the side of the Morris.

'Come on,' she said, pulling at the door handle as if she intended to open it before it was unlocked.

'Bron, I don't think...'

'Come on!'

And Joe, who knew from long experience that there was no gainsaying a hellbent woman, came on.

TWENTY-ONE

IT TOOK ONLY A few minutes to reach the quarry, though without Bron to guide him, it might have taken Joe half a day.

They set out on the narrow road which led to the Goat and Axle, turned off this on to a lane which made a narrow road seem like a motorway, and then off the lane on to a track which Joe wouldn't have passed fit for ox-carts. But he didn't even wince as the Morris sank into ruts deep enough to lay a gas main or bounced over rocks high enough to make headstones. Bron's fear filled the car like nerve gas, paralysing all concerns save that of getting to the scene.

The scene of what? he asked himself. Accident? Suicide? Murder? Policemen waited till they got all the facts before they made a judgement, but PIs could let their speculations spiral free. He was recalling Dai's expression as he talked on his mobile that morning, the urgency with which he'd driven off, and the fact that he hadn't been seen since.

Ahead he saw Ursell's car parked on a piece of relatively level ground. He pulled up alongside. Bron was out of the passenger door before he'd stopped and running forward to where the DI stood with a constable and Ifor James, by a broken fence, looking down.

Joe joined them, looked down too, and immediately stepped back. He didn't suffer from vertigo, or anything like that, but this was a hole you could have dropped Luton town hall into and still had room for the car park. How could people live in places that had potholes like this littering the landscape? Thing was, of course, there was just so much landscape. He looked around. In a town you always had things up close. Here, your eyes were always at a strain to reach some distant horizon. At least it got things in a better proportion. Gingerly he moved forward again. Maybe the hole wasn't so big after all, but it was big enough. Been here a long time too. The sides which fell in three distinct overhangs, presumably marking where whatever had been taken out of them had been taken out of them, were covered with several decades' worth of thick vegetation. Joe shuddered at the sight of it. Didn't mind a nice neat garden, but stuff growing *sideways* into the air, that was jungle!

And through the jungle directly below his feet a track had been scored. The pick-up hadn't gone flying through the air like they did in the movies. Would have needed to be travelling at sixty plus to manage that. No, it had gone through the fence and bounced down the side of the quarry to end up where he could see it far below, nose down beneath the surprisingly clear waters.

'How do you know it's Da's truck?' demanded Bronwen.

'Can read the number, see,' said Ifor.

Joe screwed up his eyes and got the plate but couldn't make out any letters or figures. He looked at the farmer doubtfully. Man had to be rising seventy. Jones stared back indifferently through faded blue eyes. Ursell went to the car and came back with a pair of binoculars.

Slowly he read out a number and Bron's face confirmed the worst.

'Aren't you going to do something?' she screamed. 'He could be down there trapped.'

'It's in hand,' said Ursell. 'I got on the radio as we drove here. Listen, girl, don't be rushing to meet things. Nothing to say your father was still in the truck when it went over the edge, is there? Could have left it here and the brake slipped and it just rolled over.'

Joe studied the ground. There was a slight incline towards the edge of the quarry, true. And the fence was more warning than barrier. But was the DI wise to try and build up hope? Why the shoot would Dai have left his pick-up here and gone off someplace else? In fact, why would he have come here in the first place?

He looked more carefully at the area where the cars were parked. Surprisingly, that's what it looked like, a parking area. Lots of evidence, like tyre ruts and oil stains, that Dai's pick-up hadn't been the first vehicle here.

He said unthinkingly, 'Why do people come here anyway?'

Ursell gave him a sharp glance, but the old farmer said, 'Courting couples, it is, mainly. Come here to get up to their tricks, then throw their rubbish out of the window for me to clear up in case any of my sheep get their teeth into them.'

'You saying my da had a fancy woman, Ifor James?' demanded Bron angrily. 'You'd better be careful of that tongue of yours, get you into real trouble one of these days, you stupid old goat!'

The farmer turned his gaze upon her as if debating how to deal with this impertinent child, then decided that if there was ever a time to make allowances, this was it.

'Sorry I am,' he said. 'Didn't mean to say anything like that, I'm sure. Don't usually get up to their tricks in the mornings, anyway.'

This seemed a half-cocked sort of apology to Joe, but maybe it wasn't a bad thing that the old boy was providing a safety valve for the girl's pent-up emotions.

She strode away from them now right to the very edge of the quarry and Joe started after her, fearful that she was going to try to climb down to the water's edge. In fact, it looked as if some bold souls, or perhaps very hungry sheep, had picked a way down the quarry face at various places, but Joe wouldn't have fancied it. He took her arm but she pulled free angrily.

'It's not right what he says,' she insisted. 'He got up to a lot of things, I know that, but he wouldn't do that to Ma. He wouldn't. He really loves her. I've heard him say he doesn't know what he'd do without her. He'd never do anything to risk losing her, that's for sure.'

She glowered at Joe as if challenging him to deny her. He nodded and said, 'I'm sure you're right, Bron.'

But in his mind's eye he was seeing her mother rolling around the little sickbay bed with Long John. And he saw something else as well. The bottle of bubbly that he'd mistaken for a weapon. Why had Long John brought that with him? Natural gift from a publican? Or was it because they had something to celebrate?

Sometimes he thought the worst thing about being a PI was the nasty way it made you think about people.

No, he amended. Worst thing was having to share these thoughts with someone else. Like the police. Which he'd have to do if they found Dai in the truck below. He was still trying to think *if,* but he knew he really believed *when.*

Yet why should he be so sure? OK, Dai had certainly come here with the pick-up. And even if it had gone over the edge by accident without him in it, he wouldn't just have walked away and abandoned it, would he?

He looked down again, following the vehicle's progress marked in the jungle growing out of the rock face. A series of bounces intermixed with a series of slithers, depending on the varying steepness of the drop. That rust bucket of a machine would probably have started bursting apart at the first hard contact...doors flying open if not flying off...

He said, 'Bron...'

The girl seemed to have sunk into a semi-trance, her eyes fixed on the water far below.

'Bron,' he said more insistently.

'What?'

'You know your dad's mobile number?'

'What?'

'His mobile phone. You know the number?'

'What are you talking about, you black monkey? Think you can ring him under the water and see if he answers, is it?'

Joe was better at making allowances than Social Security. He made them now and said, 'Just the number, please, Bron if you can remember it.'

His mild manner and gentle voice did the trick. She closed her eyes and stumbling a little recited a number. Joe took out his mobile and keyed it in. Her eyes were open again and regarding him uncertainly. Doesn't know whether to apologize or call me worse, thought Joe. Why the shoot do I get myself into these situations?

He pressed the transmit button.

A pause. He waited for the voice telling him the number he'd rung wasn't obtainable.

Instead, miraculously, in his ear he heard the ringing tone.

There was no reply. He didn't expect it. But when he lowered the phone and strained his ear against the gentle warm breeze, there amidst the rural cacophony of cracklings and rustlings and baa-ing and birdsong he caught the tiny, comfortingly urban chirruping of a telephone.

'What's going on?' demanded Ursell, coming towards them.

'Listen. Can't you hear it?'

'What? Yes, I can... God, you mean... Keep it ringing, keep it ringing! And get a hold of my legs!'

He lay down at the edge of the quarry with his binoculars to his eyes and pushed himself so far out that Joe actually sat on his legs, fearful he was going to slide over.

'It's down there to the left...I think I can see something...right, pull me back, boyo, before I join him!'

Together Joe and Bronwen hauled the DI back to safety.

'What's happening, what's happening?' demanded the girl.

'I think your dad got thrown out of the truck,' said Joe. 'He must be caught up in them bushes down there...listen, he could still be...injured.'

He couldn't bring himself to say *dead,* not with the new hope dawning in her eyes.

'We've got to get down there,' she cried.

Once more Joe seized her arm as she made for the edge. This time she didn't shove him away.

'It's OK,' he said. 'The emergency folk will be here soon and they'll have all the right gear.'

He looked for confirmation to Ursell, who nodded.

'That's right,' he said. 'They know it's a quarry job. But I'll get on the radio to tell them the situation's altered.'

He looked as if he was going to say something more to Joe then changed his mind and headed for his car.

It took another fifteen minutes for the emergency services to start appearing but when they did they came mob-handed. A paramedic was lowered down the face of the quarry. He went out of sight beneath the first overhang, then they heard his voice.

'He's here!'

Bronwen gripped Joe's arm so tight he felt his fingers grow numb.

Then came the second shout.

'He's breathing!'

And this time she flung her arms round his neck and hugged

him so hard that his sight swam and there was a loud churring, beating noise in his ears.

It wasn't till she let him go that he realized it was a helicopter.

Ursell said to Bron, 'They're going to airlift your father straight to the hospital. You get in the ambulance now and you'll be there not long after him.'

'What about my ma? Someone should tell her.'

'Taken care of. She'll be on her way quick as you. I'll be along myself soon. Go now.'

With a last hug for Joe, Bronwen ran to the ambulance.

'Poor kid,' said Ursell. 'Hope it turns out all right.'

'What's the verdict?' asked Joe, who'd seen Ursell in close confabulation with the paramedic team.

'He's unconscious. Head injuries. Some broken bones but nothing spinal, they don't think. It's the head that bothers them. Can't say anything really till he comes round. If he comes round. Seems to be your specialty, Joe, putting people into hospital who can't talk. Great strain on my resources, it is, having men sitting around there all day twiddling their thumbs.'

He smiled to show he was joking. At least that's what Joe hoped his smile meant.

'So what do you think happened here?' he asked.

'Was going to ask you the same, Joe. Any ideas?'

Joe took a deep breath.

'Some,' he said gloomily.

He told the DI what he'd seen on the security screen in the Lady House.

'Didn't mention any of this when we were talking before, Joe,' observed Ursell.

'Didn't seem relevant then.'

'That's for me to say,' replied Ursell without heat. 'So your theory is, John Dawe lured Dai up here with a phone call, knocked him out, then pushed the pick-up over the edge.'

'Don't have no theory,' said Joe. 'Just telling you what I saw.'

'Just the facts, man, is that it?'

'Yeah,' said Joe. 'Just the facts. Which is all I want from you in return.'

Ursell said, 'Take a tip from me, Joe. You seem like a decent sort of man. Life can be a very pleasant thing for a decent sort of man if only he makes sure he doesn't get himself mixed up with facts.'

'Reckon I'm all mixed up already,' said Joe.

Ursell regarded him steadily then said rather sadly, 'Yes, I reckon you are too. All right. No time now, but if I see you tonight, maybe then I'll tell you a few facts, but nothing for your comfort, boy. And don't think I've forgotten you should have some facts for me in return. Fair exchange, OK?'

'OK,' said Joe without enthusiasm.

It might be a fair exchange, but it didn't sound like it was going to be a pleasant one.

He looked up as the helicopter which had been winching the unconscious figure of Dai Williams aboard banked away into the clear blue sky.

'Hope he makes it,' said Joe.

'Makes it, misses it, life goes on,' said Ursell heading for his car. 'See you, Joe.'

Sometimes Luton seemed a million miles away.

TWENTY-TWO

LIFE GOES ON.

Which means we all march to our own tune, thought Joe.

It was only professional idiots like him who got themselves in situations where different tunes were playing like a radio someone's twiddling the band selector on.

He drove slowly back from the quarry. He had no stomach to return to the festival so he went straight through the village and on to Branddreth Hall where he sat outside in the sun, till the bus brought the choir from the festival field.

He was half expecting to be a centre of attention and questioning when they got back and didn't know whether to be pleased or disappointed to find he wasn't. All the choristers wanted to talk about was the festival—the departure of the Guttenbergers, their own performance so far, where they felt they stood in relation to the other choirs. Dai Williams's 'accident' meant nothing to them except the minor inconvenience that his wife wasn't around to supply tea and biscuits when they got back to the college. But with Mirabelle, that high priestess of the life-goes-on school of philosophy, ready, willing and able to step into the breach and the kitchen, this wasn't really inconvenient at all.

What tune Ella Williams would be moving to Joe didn't know. Tragic march, celebration waltz? Maybe an uneasy mixture as she feared what Dai might remember if and when he woke up. Could she really be mixed up in a murder attempt? His judgement said no, but what did he really have to go on except the excellence of her cooking?

Leon Lewis, arriving shortly after the choir, did seek him out, however, full of the proper concern of a properly concerned employer, enquiring anxiously after his caretaker's wellbeing, and then taking off to the hospital to see for himself. And Morna Lewis took everyone by surprise, or at least Joe, by coming over from the Lady House to take over Ella's job of superintending the reception caterers. It wasn't so much that she came that surprised him, but the quiet efficiency she displayed, making him adjust his mental picture of her as put-upon wife, indulgent mother, and overstretched hostess.

He took the chance of asking her if she'd seen anything more of Wain. She said, no, not since the afternoon at the festival field.

Then she looked at him with a sharpness which meant another minor image adjustment and said, 'You seem very keen to catch up with my son, Mr Sixsmith. Any particular reason?'

Joe reached for some evasive formula, thought, *I'll be on my way home this time tomorrow so why am I lying?* and said, 'Got some money I want to return to him. He seemed to think I could help him find out about the woman in the cottage who got burnt, but I don't think I can, so he's due a refund.'

As he watched for Morna Lewis's reaction to the words, he found himself distracted by his own. If Wain had really set fire to Copa knowing it contained a woman to whom he'd supplied drugs, then wasn't it a bit late to be paying someone to find out about her?

She said, 'But surely that's a job for the police. Why on earth should Owain get involved?'

'You know kids,' said Joe, 'Ideals, all that stuff.'

'Yes, that must be it,' she said, giving him the smile full beam, like he'd said something significant instead of just bromide. Not that he didn't believe in kids having ideals, only it was hard to see how even a doting mum could imagine it applied in this case. Maybe if he could remember his own mum doing any doting, he'd have understood better.

She went back to her supervising work and Joe left the assembly hall. He was wandering around in the hope of bumping into Beryl alone. He'd glimpsed her, but only in company which she didn't seem keen to let herself be winkled out of. Could she really be jealous of Bronwen? He knew the idea shouldn't make him feel pleased, but he couldn't deny it did. Anyway, when she got the full picture, she'd understand. He felt the time had come to share everything he was into with someone, and telling Beryl would kill two priests with one confession. Or something.

But all the choristers seemed suddenly to have vanished off the face of the earth and the only Lutonite he could find was Merv.

'Hi,' he said. 'Where's everyone?'

'Getting their heads down so they can shine tonight, I expect,' said the big man. 'Which you oughta think of trying yourself, boy. You look real rough.'

It wasn't till his friend said it that Joe realized how much he felt it.

'Yea. Maybe you're right,' he said.

They strolled along together.

'So how've you been earning all that money you got?' asked Merv. 'Or have you given it back like you said?'

'No chance,' said Joe. 'Young Wain's harder to get hold of than a cup final ticket and the Haggards are back in the Smoke.'

'No, they're not,' said Merv. 'Turned up this afternoon. Leastways I think it must be them. Guy in a linen suit, arm and a leg cost an arm and a leg. Woman much the same, twenty-five going on fifty. I saw them getting out of this big Jag and going up to Lewis. Didn't look like Stanley finding Livingstone either. I was close enough to earwig. He said, *This better be good, Leon. We were almost at Oxford.* And Lewis said, *Your choice. Of course if you prefer that I make all the decisions.* Then they clocked me and moved away. Mean anything to you?'

It meant, thought Joe, that Lewis must've got Haggard on his car phone and suggested he turn round and come back. Why? Or, just as significant, when? He worked out the distances roughly. Could have been just after Lewis had caught him in the Lady House cellar. Or could have been an hour earlier, an hour later. No point guessing without he knew when the Haggards had left, plus the state of the roads.

'Hello, Joe. Anyone at home?' said Merv.

'Sorry. I was thinking.'

He started to tell Merv everything that had happened. Merv wasn't Beryl, but he brought his own brand of direct-action thought to most situations. True, you didn't always want to take too much notice, not unless you hankered after hard beds and striped sunlight. But sometimes he got to the meat of things while smarter asses were still grazing round the meadow.

Apart from a request for sharper graphics in regard to the activities of Long John and Ella Williams, he listened in silence. Then when Joe had finished, he said almost enviously, 'Joe, for a homely slippers-and-pipe sort of guy, you surely do see life.'

'You know I don't smoke,' protested Joe.

'When would you find the time?'

'So. What do you think?'

'I think you should keep your head down, and head off home soon as the festival's over without talking to anyone, especially anyone whose money you got, and leave no forwarding address,' said Merv. 'Nothing but trouble in all this for you. Trouble with the cops and trouble with God knows who else, and maybe you don't want to find out. Two folk in hospital already, Joe. You had a shotgun in your face. This is the Wild West out here, boy, and I don't think they take kindly to greenhorns riding in to clean up the town.'

'Not what I'm aiming to do,' denied Joe. 'But Ursell's not a man to run out on.'

'Because he can drop Doberley in it? Hey, Dildo's a cop, it's not like dropping a real human being. Anyway, this guy Ursell's playing his own private game from the sound of it. Doesn't trust this Pantyhose guy, right? And sounds like he can't be sure whose sty this other pig, Prince, is rooting in either. So if he starts making a fuss about Dildo, all kind of questions could get asked before he's ready to answer them. No, I think you can walk away from this clear and free and with a bit of profit for your troubles.'

It was, he had to admit, sound advice, and he had a feeling that for once Beryl's reaction would not have been so very different from Merv's. But neither of them had lifted that trapped woman in their arms, and pushed her through the hole in the shower ceiling, and seen those poor burnt limbs struggle to find strength to drag her poor burnt body into the attic of the flaming cottage. That had been the human spirit, the life force, call it whatever you like, at work. Man who walked away from that was walking away from himself. At the least he had to know who she was.

'Thanks, Merv,' he said. 'Think I'll take your advice.'

'And head on out? Now, you mean?'

'No. I mean take your advice and crash out. You're right. I feel really rough.'

It was as if the admission gave authority for all the overtaxed systems of his overtaxed body to turn off. By the time he got to his room he felt far worse than he had since waking up in hospital and he barely had strength to strip off his clothes and collapse on to his bed and into instant sleep.

Dreams came like a trailer for the latest blockbuster thriller, full of flames and gunshots and cars crashing over cliffs and sweating naked bodies writhing now in agony, now in ecstasy. These must have been the closing frames, for he awoke, bathed in sweat and sexually excited. Beneath him, a tangle of bedclothes showed how much he must have thrashed around in his sleep. But surprisingly it seemed to have done him good, for when he moved he felt little pain, as if the exercise and self-generated heat had eased the aches from his limbs.

All I need now is a good woman to complete the cure, he told himself. Or a bad one, even. He recalled Ella Lewis and Long John on this very bed and groaned with desire.

On this very bed...

'Oh shoot!' exclaimed Joe, sitting bolt upright and dragging a sheet over his bottom half.

If anyone was checking out the security screens, they'd have had a lovely view of all he'd got to offer for the past couple of hours or more.

Hugely embarrassed, he slid off the bed with the sheet wrapped around him, trying not to glance apologetically at the security camera. He scuttled into the bathroom and stood under an icy-cold shower till he had dampened his desire, then switched it over to hot to cleanse the remaining perspiration off him. Then, with a large towel modestly draped around his body, he went back into the bedroom.

Now he felt able to glance up at the camera.

Except there wasn't one.

Now he knew what had been bothering him when he'd found himself watching the loving couple on his bed, only he'd failed to work it out under the greater bother of being an accidental voyeur. He examined all the walls carefully, then conjured up in his mind's eye the picture he'd seen on the TV screen. From that angle, the camera had to be...*there.*

He was looking at the wall clock. A plain not very attractive electric clock in a white plastic case such as you might find in any school or office or hospital.

There was one in the bathroom too.

Quickly he got dressed and went out into the corridor.

His memory was right. There was a security camera here. He walked around and located other cameras where you'd expect to find them, covering corridors and outside doors. And he looked for and found more of the electric clocks too. In the dormitories. In the gym. In the changing rooms. In the showers. In the toilets.

Finally, whatever the risk of being observed, he had to know. He went back to the sickbay, pulled the bed to the wall beneath the clock, stood on it and, with the pocket screwdriver he always carried, unscrewed the case.

It took a single glance to show him he was right.

'Oh, Mr Lewis, you are a piece of work,' he said.

'Mr Sixsmith? Joe? What on earth are you doing?'

He nearly fell off the chair in shock.

Looking round he saw Ella Williams in the doorway. She looked pale and drawn.

Quickly, he replaced the plastic cover and stepped down.

'Sorry,' he said. 'Seemed to be losing, thought I'd put it right. What are you doing here, anyway? How's Dai? Is he going to be all right?'

'Yes, they think so,' she said. 'He's not in any danger, they say. He opened his eyes for a minute and recognized me and spoke to me, but then he went again. They say that's the best thing now, it's more like proper sleep, see, now that he's been properly conscious. But they'll need to keep him in, naturally, till they can give him a real check-over, so as Mr Lewis was coming back, it seemed a good chance for me to pick up some of Dai's things he'll need, and Bron's still there with him, of course, so there'll be a familiar face if he wakes again. She told me it was you who found him and I just wanted to come along and say thank you...'

Her words were coming in a torrent and her filling eyes showed tears were not far behind. She might not be about to collapse from grief, but she was clearly in some degree of shock and it didn't seem at this moment to matter much what it derived from. Joe put his arms around her and said, 'It's OK, it'll all be OK.'

Over her shoulder he saw Beryl Boddington appear in the doorway, shoot up her eyebrows, then step back out.

Now the tears came, but the words didn't stop.

'Why's it do this to us, life? Why's it always the same? Just when you think you've got it worked out, there it goes again, everything upside down, all your plans turned against you. You know what he said, Joe? He said, *You and me have got it made, girl. Bad times all behind us, no stopping us now.* It was like he knew...'

'Knew what?' said Joe.

Sometimes there were questions you had to ask even though you didn't really want an answer. Which was just as well, as he didn't get one.

The sobs died away and she drew back from his embrace.

'I'm sorry,' she said, drying her eyes. 'Not like me, this. You're a very kind man, Joe Sixsmith. I thank you.'

They stood there awkwardly. Joe tried to think of something to say. Something comforting and uplifting, maybe a bit philosophical, like a line from an old movie. But the best he could manage was, 'How long these clocks been up?'

'Sorry?' she said, amazed.

Her expression convinced him that she certainly had no idea of their double function. In fact, now he thought of it, there'd been a lot more TV screens in the Lady House cellar than in Dai's cubbyhole.

'Just thought, if they've started losing, they might still be under guarantee,' he said. He thought it was pretty good extempore, and at least her amazement faded to mere bewilderment.

'I don't recall...no, wait. Same time as the security cameras, yes, that's it, we came back from holiday summer before last—that's right, Dai's sister's at Barmouth—and it was all done. Mr

Lewis said he'd arranged it then to save us the inconvenience, not that I'd have let Electricity Sample inconvenience me. We laughed, Dai and me, when we saw all the clocks. Way back when Electricity just had the shop, before he became a big businessman, they always used to say, you go in there to buy a fuse, lucky if you don't come out with enough lights for the municipal Christmas tree in Caerlindys. As for guarantees, oh yes, Electricity gives them like a politician gives promises. But that's for Mr Lewis to sort out. I've got more to worry about than clocks. Thanks again, Joe.'

'Hey, nothing. Regards to Dai.'

She smiled wanly at him and went out of the room, turning left down the corridor. A moment later Joe followed her out. Just to the right of the door he found Beryl leaning up against the wall.

'Oh, Joe, Joe,' she said, shaking her head sadly.

'Yeah, yeah. How come every time some female lays a hand on me, I find you somewhere close, clocking the situation?'

'Clocking? Now that's a good word, Joe, coming from someone so interested in clocks. Or is that just the latest line in chat-up among the smart set?'

'Listen, there was no chatting-up going on there. All I was doing...'

'I know, Joe. Sorry, I didn't mean anything. You were doing a good job. She's right. You're a kind man, Joe Sixsmith.'

She smiled at him fondly. Which was nice.

He said, 'OK, just so's you know that was all that was going on.'

'Oh yes. With the mother. But the daughter that I saw sticking her tongue down your throat, was that just you being kind again? Like you had a premonition something was going to happen to her dad and were getting your comfort in before the event.'

'You so funny, you must have been taking lessons from Merv,' said Joe.

This was an underhand blow. Beryl found Merv's humour sad, sexist, and generally distasteful.

But she didn't react to the smear. Instead she said, 'So are you going to tell me what's really going on, Joe?'

'Might do. But only if you promise not to give me the usual.'

'Oh, and what might that be?'

'That I'm getting out of my depth and shouldn't get mixed up with things that don't concern me and maybe Mirabelle's right after all and I ought to start looking for a proper job.'

'I said that?'

'Only nine or ten times.'

'OK, I promise.'

So Joe told her everything.

She listened without interruption till he finished. Then she said quietly, 'You telling me this place is wired so that the kids are on camera in the showers and the lavs and the dorms and everywhere? For whose benefit? I can't believe that woman knew.'

'No, I reckon the terminal in Williams's flat is only wired up to the cameras you can see. The Lady House set-up is much bigger. I noticed it without really noticing it.'

'So it's down to the creep, Lewis,' said Beryl angrily. 'This is really sick. Joe, you've got to tell that inspector fellow. This is beyond anything you can do to fix. This is police business. You've got to pass it on straightaway. Nothing some DIY PI can do about this without getting right out of his depth!'

'Hey,' he protested. 'You promised you wouldn't say things like that.'

'Yeah, well, after I saw that chit tonguing you, I promised myself there was no way I was ever going to let those old chapped lips of yours come anywhere near mine again. You want I should keep all my promises?'

She was regarding him with a fondness which set Joe's hopes rising.

'No way,' he said, reaching for her.

'Hey, the camera.'

Joe dragged the bed to the wall, pulled a sheet off it, jumped up on the bed-end and draped the sheet over the clock.

'Let it roll,' said Joe Sixsmith.

TWENTY-THREE

ENDO VENERA, Joe's American guru, had pretty firm views about cooperating with the police.

'Dealing with the cops is like buying real estate in Florida. Makes no matter what kind of good deal you think you got, you've been screwed. Never tell a cop anything without the alternative is he hits you in the nuts with a length of hose, and maybe not even then. A PI is only as good as what he knows. You don't share information with a cop, you give it away.'

Well, even gurus got it wrong sometimes. He had a lot of stuff loading him down which he was going to be only too glad to unload on Ursell. And despite all their talk of a fair exchange, he was beginning to wonder if he really wanted anything back. A vague appreciation of what this was all about was beginning to form in his mind. How it all fitted together was a million miles from clear, but like the guy in the old school poem who gets the notion that a fearful fiend is coming up fast behind on a lonesome road, he had no desire to look again and see things plain.

Trouble was, he still had a professional involvement. Well, he could get out of that by returning the retainers. Anyway, professionally speaking he was out of his depth. Way things were going he was finding more loose ends than a trainee surgeon. Let Ursell have the messy job of tying them up all to himself. As for his still strong desire to know what there was to know about the burnt lady, he could read all about that eventually in the newspapers.

His resolve to step away from the case, plus his pulsating memory of the brief but explosive interlude he'd enjoyed with Beryl, sent him down to the assembly hall for the reception with a light step.

Soon as he saw Ursell, he was resolved to tell him everything he knew or suspected from A to Z, or more probably in the DI's view, from A to C. And it seemed like God was approving his resolution to clear the decks when the first people he saw as he entered the crowded room were the Haggards, who descended on him with mile-wide smiles, like he was a returned prodigal.

'Joe,' exclaimed Fran the Man. 'How are you? You look well, doesn't he look well, my dear?'

Franny agreed that Joe looked good enough to eat, running her tongue along her teeth like a pianist playing an arpeggio.

'So, have you made any progress on that little enquiry I commissioned you to do?' asked Fran.

'Yeah, well...' Joe recalling Haggard's insistence on confidentiality glanced towards his wife.

The man laughed, put his arm around her waist and squeezed.

'It's all right, speak freely. No secrets between man and wife.'

Joe avoided catching the woman's eye and said, 'No, I'm sorry, nothing more than the police have been able to find out. Probably less. They don't tell you everything. Listen, I'm glad you're here, I can give you your advance back...'

'Joe, I wouldn't dream of it. I've no doubt you've been most energetic in your enquiries. Not your fault if nothing has come of them, don't you agree, my dear?'

'Surely do. But we're letting this darling man stand here without a drink, and him with that poor sore throat. Could you whistle up one of those Nice Young Things, sweetie?'

'My pleasure.'

Drinks were being carried around on silver trays by a selection of teenage girls in Welsh costume who presumably were the Nice Young Things. Fran the Man reached out for one, missed, and went in enthusiastic pursuit.

'Mrs Haggard,' began Joe.

'Franny. It's OK. I know what you're going to say. No result for me either. But it doesn't matter. Soon as Fran told me he'd hired you too, I knew I was chasing wild geese up the wrong tree. Jeez, what an idiot you must think me.'

'No, 'course I don't...I mean, not because I think...look, I've got your cheque right here...'

'You keep it, Joe. That's yours.'

'But I haven't earned it. I haven't begun to earn it.'

'Joe, just dealing with someone so honest is worth twice the price,' she laughed. 'Don't say a word about this to Fran, then you've earned it, believe me. Now where's that drink?'

Fran reappeared, steering before him what had to be an NYT. She was certainly young, and nice enough to look resentful of the directional pats to her buttocks. She bore a tray carrying a choice of wine or orange juice. Joe took the orange. He was still trying to work out what was going on here.

'Didn't expect to see you here,' he said to Haggard. 'Thought you were going back to London.'

'Change of heart,' said Fran the Man. 'It's so lovely up here just now that we thought, let's turn this thing round, just because the circumstances are unpleasant doesn't mean we have to mope. So we decided to hang around a bit longer, take the air, drink in the scenery.'

Franny came in sharp, 'We mustn't hog Joe, I'm sure he wants to be among his friends, talking music.'

She don't know I know he's lying, thought Joe, but she's bright enough to see no point to it less you really have to.

He said, 'Catch you later then.'

Across the room he'd caught sight of a group consisting of Lewis, Penty-Hooser and Electricity Sample, deep in conversation. And there, approaching them from the side, was the man he really wanted to see, DI Ursell.

Joe set off on an interception course but the best he could manage was a dead heat.

'Inspector,' he said. 'Can I have a quick word?'

'Later,' said Ursell dismissively, his gaze fixed on the Deputy Chief Constable. 'Sir, can we talk?'

'Gentlemen, gentlemen,' said Lewis, smiling broadly. 'I really must insist, both as host and High Master, that no one talks shop tonight. Unless of course it's musical shop. Though I'm a fine one to talk, having been beating Edwin's ear for the past ten minutes with a little technical problem we're having. Could interest you two, your line of country, so to speak.'

He paused. Wants us to ask, thought Joe. Not my game, let Ursell call the shots.

The DI said, 'And what might that be, sir?'

'Oh, it's nothing earth-shattering, just a bit of bother we're having with the CCTB security system that Edwin's firm installed for us a little while ago.'

'I always said the clocks might be a problem,' said Sample. It was the longest sentence Joe had heard him say and it came out like a line learned by the kind of amateur actor who gets to play the second footman in the chapel drama group.

Suddenly Joe was on full alert.

'Clocks? This to do with the millennium bug?' said Ursell.

'Oh no. These are real clocks, Inspector,' said Lewis. 'You see, I felt that cameras in full view were fine for open-access areas like corridors and this room we're in...'

He gestured towards a camera winking red high in a corner before going on.

'...where the very sight of them is, in fact, a deterrent, and very reassuring to our parents, but in some areas they seemed inappropriate, dormitories, showers, that kind of place. Yet these too needed to be accessible for checking, perhaps even more than the other areas. So I looked for some form of camera less intrusive than these blinking monsters. And Edwin suggested a system concealed in clocks.'

Oh, you tricky teacher, thought Joe.

'I told you, all that steam, maintenance could be a problem, though,' said Sample in his high-pitched monotone. 'Can't say I didn't, can you?'

This, though evidently extempore, was no more convincing to Joe's ears.

'Very true, Edwin. Still, there is the little matter of guarantee, five years I believe it was? But I am doing what I have forbidden these gentlemen to do, and dragging mundane matters into what should be a uniquely artistic occasion. I apologize.'

Joe regarded him with something like admiration. For once he didn't need hours of deep thought and an icepack to work out what was happening. Lewis must have spotted him on one of his screens checking out the clocks and decided that, when concealment's impossible, best move is to get your revelation in first.

Ursell said, 'Very interesting,' in that way which means, *very boring*, 'but I'm afraid I too am going to have to talk shop. Mr Penty-Hooser, sir, I thought you'd want to know that we've identified the woman in the cottage.'

If this was meant to produce a shock/horror reaction in anyone, it failed miserably.

'Have you indeed?' said Penty-Hooser, with the weary politeness of a man who's enjoying a good night out and doesn't relish the intrusion of work. 'Well, that's good.'

The silence that followed stretched long enough to be noticeable. Ursell showed no sign of being about to break it. He's leaving it to Pantyhose to say whether he should speak here or somewhere more private, thought Joe.

He looked at Lewis, whose face wore an expression of polite curiosity perfectly fitted to the situation.

Sample said, 'Get myself another drink, shall I?' and moved away with the look of a man glad to be elsewhere.

Lewis said, 'If you two are going to talk police business, we'd better make ourselves scarce. Joe, I don't believe you've met our judges yet. I know they're dying to meet our festival hero, though I fear they are musically too incorruptible to let your absence affect their judgement of the Boyling Corner Choir's performance.'

He put his arm through Joe's and drew him away towards the dais at the head of the hall by which stood a group of people whom Joe recognized as the occupants of the front row in the competition field. Joe was introduced and received politely enough, but he didn't get the impression that he'd made their night. Over their shoulders, or rather, as they were generally somewhat taller than him, under their armpits, he saw the two policemen in close conversation. He surprised himself by feeling really resentful, like he had some earned right to be the first to know who the burnt woman was. He could see that whatever Ursell was telling Pantyhose wasn't to his comfort. Whatever he's hearing is changing the way he sees things, thought Joe. He's either going to have to face up to something or cut and run.

How he could be so sure of this, he didn't know and didn't try to know. Happiness lay in being grateful for what you'd got and not being resentful over what you hadn't got. And not wasting time trying to analyse either.

Pantyhose had made up his mind. He was speaking authoritatively to Ursell. The perfect picture of a man taking control. But Joe knew better.

He's running, he thought. Or maybe *swimming* was closer. The ship was scraping along the reef and suddenly elsewhere seemed a safer place to be.

The DCC had turned and was heading for the exit, like a man with important business in the next county. Electricity Sample got in his way. There was a brief interchange, then Pantyhose resumed his progress with Sample in his wake. Lewis had noticed all this too and didn't like it, though the easy flow of his conversation continued unchecked. Ursell watched Pantyhose and Electricity out of the room, then turned towards the dais and began to approach. His was a much more leisurely progress. If people spoke to him in passing, he paused, smiled and replied.

This is for the High Master's sake, thought Joe. He knows Lewis knows he's on his way, so he's spinning it out, making him suffer. But how? And why?

At last he was there, standing deferentially just outside the group. This time it was Lewis he was forcing to make the move. Patience. Joe was beginning to appreciate this quality in the inspector. He was still far from clear what made Ursell tick, but he recognized something very single-minded in the man. Like that guy in the white hat in *Butch Cassidy and the Sundance Kid,* he wasn't a guy you wanted chasing after you.

Finally Lewis broke off and turned to him.

'Ah, Inspector. Duty done? Then let me get you a drink.'

'Very kind of you, sir. Just an orange juice. Duty may be over, but driving isn't. Setting a good example is half the battle, in policing as in education, wouldn't you agree, sir?'

'No argument there,' said Lewis, raising a finger to one of the NYTs and taking a glass of orange from her tray. 'I don't see your boss any more. I hope he's not setting a bad example by leaving early.'

He stressed the word boss almost imperceptibly.

Ursell said, 'Mr Penty-Hooser presents his compliments and says that he's sorry to have to steal away, but duty calls.'

'And duty as we all know is the stern daughter of the voice of God,' said Lewis. 'So, tell me, Inspector, are we all to be let into the secret of the unfortunate woman's name, or is there some embargo upon it till her family have been informed?'

'In a way, sir. There is some difficulty in tracing her family.'

'Why's that? Can't she give you names and addresses?'

'Oh no, sir. Still not in a position to give us anything, the poor creature. In fact, it's only thanks to the sharp eyes of Mr Sixsmith here that we've got a line on her at all.'

He nodded appreciatively at Joe who was momentarily bewildered.

'I don't recall...hey, you don't mean that bracelet thing?'

'Exactly so,' said Ursell.

'And what bracelet thing is that?' enquired Lewis, who didn't look like he was ready to give Joe a good-citizen award.

'This thing I found up at Copa this morning. Don't know what made me pick it up,' said Joe. 'But it was all scorched and buckled. How'd you get anything useful off that?'

'We live in a hi-tech world,' said Ursell. 'At our police lab we have technology to read serial numbers that have been ground off engine blocks to a depth of several millimetres. This was fairly easy meat to them. You were right, Mr Sixsmith. This was an accident bracelet to alert anyone giving medical treatment that the wearer was allergic to certain antibiotics. Happily its absence was not important medically here, as these particular drugs were not among those used upon her at Caerlindys Hospital. But our technical boys were able to make out the personal reference code plus the telephone number of the organization doctors were asked to ring to get full details of the patient's allergy. After that, it was easy.'

'So it looks like once again you are the person we should all feel grateful to, Mr Sixsmith,' said Lewis. 'Clearly the gods were smiling the day we decided to invite the Boyling Corner Choir to our festival.'

He didn't sound like he shared this divine good humour.

'Well, Inspector,' he went on. 'May we now hear this poor woman's name, so that we have something positive to call her in our prayers?'

'Of course, though presumably the Almighty already knows her name,' said Ursell, his gaze fixed on Lewis like a darts player's on the treble twenty. 'And I think you may recognize it too.'

He paused dramatically. They were all actors at heart, Joe told himself again. But while dramatic pauses are OK in drama, in real life they're like safe braking distances in motorway traffic—there's usually some plonker who will slide himself into it.

'Time for my little outline of tomorrow's procedures, I think, High Master.'

It was the Reverend David Davies, looking very important.

'Yes, of course. Excuse me, Inspector. Back in a tick.'

Ursell glanced at Joe and gave him what felt like an inclusive smile, as if to say, *Don't worry. We'll have him back in a while.*

Lewis mounted what was during term the staff dais at one end of the hall and tapped on a live microphone till he reduced the guests to relative silence. He didn't look worried and he certainly didn't sound it.

'Honoured judges, distinguished guests, ladies, gentlemen, songsters out on a spree, though none of you doomed, I feel certain, from here to eternity, you are most welcome. I would like to thank you all for the fortitude and good humour with which you have faced all the vicissitudes of the day, and to assure you that with God's help and a fair wind, which is to say no wind at all, we hope that our final day tomorrow will pass with no interruption at all, save that of applause for songs well sung. And to bring you fully abreast with the order of events tomorrow, let me now hand you over to one who needs no introduction, our much loved pastor, our much honoured poet, and our superbly efficient festival organizer, David Davies.'

There was the kind of pattery applause people make with drinks in their hands and Lewis stepped down and rejoined Joe and Ursell.

'Now, where were we? Oh yes. The mystery woman's identity. Do spell it out, I beg you, Inspector.'

And Ursell took his revenge for the spoilt dramatic pause by now taking him quite literally.

'Ess eye ell ell sea are oh eff tee,' he said. 'Which spells Sillcroft.'

Again the dramatic pause, this time uninterrupted.

'Her name is Angela Maria Sillcroft.'

TWENTY-FOUR

TRUTH IS A WELL-STACKED blonde in a Turkish bath, says Endo Venera in one of his more poetic passages. For a second you see everything clearly, then the steam swirls round those gorgeous curves, and all you can do is take a bearing and plunge right on in.

Only he didn't go on to say that sometimes you may find you're grappling with a monster.

Angela Maria Sillcroft.

Who had to be related to that other Sillcroft.

Simon Sillcroft, sadness.

The boy at the centre of the hushed-up scandal which had cost Matthias his job.

The Reverend David Davies, Dai Bard, was getting into his stride on the dais. Joe wasn't listening. He was too busy trying to get a clear line of sight before the steam curtain fell.

The burnt woman—Angela, though somehow knowing her

name didn't make thinking about her easier—Angela's presence in Llanffugiol must have something to do with what had happened to her brother. Investigation? Revenge? Blackmail even? If it was Lewis who put her in the cottage, that made sense... But then there was the sighting of Wain's car, and the traces of Decorax in her system... So Wain must have a connection... But the fire, could Wain really have set the fire? Why? To protect his father? Didn't seem likely, considering their attitude to each other. Blood thicker than water though. Maybe by protecting his father, he thought he was protecting his mother?

And there was something else. Either Leon Lewis had all the acting ability Electricity Sample lacked plus a whole lot more, or the burnt woman's identity came as a complete surprise to him.

Maybe more than surprise, though. Maybe shock, rapidly disguised as the natural surprise of recognizing the name.

One advantage of Dai Bard's electrically magnified voice was that it provided plenty of noise cover for any number of private conversations.

'Sillcroft?' said Lewis. 'We had a boy here of that name, a rather troubled, indeed disturbed child. You may recall the business, Inspector? A coincidence, perhaps. But again, perhaps not. Perhaps that was what brought her to Branddreth. Though if that were the case, and to save you the embarrassment of asking, she never made her presence known to me, Inspector.'

'Thank you for that courtesy, sir,' said Ursell, who to Joe's eyes didn't look as if he'd be embarrassed by having to ask the Pope to blow into a Breathalyzer.

'Have her family been informed?' asked Lewis. 'If I recall right, there was only the father, whose job kept him more or less permanently occupied out in the wilds of Patagonia. Oil exploration, I think. Young Simon was looked after during the vacations by an aunt in Bexhill.'

'That's right, sir. The daughter, Angela, went to boarding school too, few years older than her brother, finished last year. Nineteen, she is. Took a year off before university to look after her aunt who's not been in good health. And her brother too.'

'So what on earth was she doing up here?' demanded Lewis.

'Entitled to go where she likes, isn't she, sir?' said Ursell.

'Yes, of course. All I meant was, with the responsibility of looking after her family...'

'Ah yes, sir. Pastoral responsibility sort of thing. Very much your line. Well, the thing is, the aunt went into a retirement home in the New Year. The accident knocked her back, see. Well, it would, thing like that. Plus the damage to the house...'

Lewis was looking as puzzled as Joe felt.

'What accident? What damage?' the High Master asked with some irritation.

'Sorry, sir. Just like me, getting things in a tangle, all about-face, like,' said the precise Ursell unconvincingly. 'No reason you should know about the accident, pastoral responsibility being finished, and all.'

'I wish you'd make yourself clear, Inspector,' said Lewis icily.

Ursell lowered his voice to the level and timbre favoured by the doorstep bearers of bad news. Only this time it wasn't an act.

'It was the boy, something happened, Bexhill police aren't quite sure what. But there was a fire started in his room. Lot of damage. And he died, poor kid. Quite ironic, really, seeing how his sister's ended up.'

The news hit Joe hard, like it concerned a member of his own family. Which, given the way he felt about the burnt woman—sorry, Angela Maria—it did, sort of.

Simon Sillcroft, sadness. What had been a schoolboy scratching was now an epitaph.

Who is it calls the shots up there in that heaven Rev. Pot and Mirabelle so firmly believe in? wondered Joe bitterly.

But there was another question of more immediate, less metaphysical import knocking at his mind's door.

How had Glyn Matthias known about the boy's death?

That he had known, Joe was now sure. There was no other explanation for those comments this morning which Joe had found vaguely puzzling but which were now quite clear...*sadness all the way for him...a better place...*

Not Bexhill after all.

Something else to pass on to Ursell.

Dai Bard was still droning on—no, not droning, that was quite the wrong word for the oceanic undulations of words which were surging over them like a spring tide—mainly in English but with a fair flotsam and jetsam of Welsh.

Lewis was shaking his head, as at the manifest unjustness of life.

'I didn't know, I didn't know. The poor, poor child. And now his sister. Terrible, terrible.'

Joe was convinced by the ignorance. The man hadn't known about the boy's death. But he wasn't at all convinced by the regret, perfectly pitched though it was. Simon Sillcroft dead, Angela Sillcroft like to die—these could just be loose ends tied up in the High Master's eyes.

But that was mere speculation and none of his business anyway. Now that he knew the one thing he'd set himself to find out, the girl's identity, all he had to do was spill his guts to Ursell, then relax and enjoy the rest of the festival.

But Ursell was not yet available. He was regarding Lewis with a curious mixture of polite attentiveness, repressed dislike, and underlying bafflement.

Joe recognized the condition because he'd seen it before. On Sergeant Chivers's face when he felt he was close to fingering Joe's collar but knew in his heart that it was still just out of reach of his grasping fingers.

The greater part of Dai Bard's audience were now showing something like the same symptoms, this time due to the fact that the flood of words now consisted entirely of Welsh. Very rhythmic Welsh, Joe registered. He guessed that the Reverend poet was taking the chance to give a captive audience a taste of his bardic poetry.

Suddenly Ursell made up his mind, or perhaps it was simply a turning away from temptation.

'Thank you very much for your time, Mr Lewis,' he said formally. 'We may need to talk again later.'

'It will be my pleasure, Inspector,' said Lewis.

There was nothing triumphant in his tone but he might as well have been standing on an Olympic podium.

Ursell moved away so abruptly, Joe was left standing.

'Now this is fine, fine,' said Lewis, focusing his attention on Dai Bard's incantation. 'A pity you do not have the Welsh, Mr Sixsmith. This is quite splendid stuff.'

He sounded so sincere that Joe bit back the sarcasm rising to his lips and set out after the inspector.

He caught up with him at the door, talking earnestly to Richard Burton, which was to say, Sergeant Tom Prince in civvies.

Their conversation ceased, and Prince didn't look all that happy as Joe joined them.

''Evening, Tom,' he said placatingly.

'Sergeant Prince to you, Sixsmith,' said the policeman, glowering. 'I don't stay on first names with people who muck me about, people I can't trust.'

No prizes for guessing what he was referring to.

'You're narked with me 'cos I didn't identify Wain Lewis, right? I'm sorry. Just didn't seem important at the time. And it made no matter anyway, did it?'

'When I spoke with the DI and showed him that hospital lab report, it made a lot of matter. You'd seen it first, Sixsmith. Maybe it wasn't important for you to say straight off that the lad in the corridor looked like young Lewis. But the second you made that drug connection between him and the woman in Copa, it was your bounden duty to tell me. In fact, it was a criminal omission not to.'

'So arrest me,' said Joe, who wasn't in the mood to be intimidated.

'I might just do that.'

'And I might just shout out to everyone here that you weren't transferred out of Cardiff CID 'cos you had your hand in the till, no, that was just the cover story so's Perry could get you up here to give him some back-up at ground level.'

Now where did that come from? Shoot, who cared? Again that moment of complete clarity.

He saw Prince glance at Ursell with something between accusation and threat in his eyes. No time to work that out. When you're on a roll, roll.

'One thing you both might as well get straight about me, just 'cos I'm a PI don't mean I'm in the market to be threatened with the law for not cooperating with you one minute then blacked into breaking the law for you the next. No need for either, anyway. All I'm interested in is the truth. Anything I find out about drugs or dirty movies or *anything* that hurts innocent people, I'll tell you open and free, maybe not straight off, but I'll tell you, OK?'

It was, he felt, not without embarrassment, the pretty moving statement of a pretty honest man.

But the reaction, or rather reactions, took him by surprise.

Prince was frowning in a mixture of puzzlement and suspicion. And Ursell was looking completely blank except for his eyes...there was something in his eyes...

Prince said, in a soft and friendly voice, 'Don't quite follow you, Joe. What's all this about me being transferred from Cardiff and you being blacked into breaking the law to help us? All right for these plain-clothes types but you need to spell things out for us uniformed plods.'

For a second, Joe thought he'd got it wrong and that Prince really was the GM loyalist he'd appeared to be. But that didn't make sense, else Ursell would have said something by now, instead of standing there, looking at him...pleadingly? Yes, no doubt about the expression in those narrow Clint Eastwood eyes. He was being asked for help.

Then he got it. Didn't matter that it was way-out. Man brought up in a religious household got used to believing three or four way-out things before breakfast every day. Tom Prince might be a uniformed three-striper and Perry Ursell might be a plain-clothes DI, but in this relationship it was the sergeant who called the shots. And Ursell had been pursuing some private agenda when he twisted Joe's arm to poke around the Lady House, and he'd prefer it if Prince didn't know.

So what do I owe Ursell? thought Joe.

Here was a perfect chance to get his own back. Except of course there was still Dildo's future to consider.

And except too (this *except* took him a little by surprise) he had this feeling that if he had to trust either of these guys with his immortal soul, there'd be no competition.

He said, 'Hey, man, the thing about your transfer was just a guess 'cos clearly you're on the side of the angels, right? As for me breaking the law, that was just about you covering up my out-of-date tax disc so as I'd cooperate, leastways, that's how it looked to me.'

Prince looked at him doubtfully.

Ursell yawned as if it was all very boring.

A NYT came up to them and smiled longingly at Prince.

'Sergeant Prince, is it? You're wanted on the phone.'

Not just on the phone, thought Joe, envious of that smile. Must help looking like the young Richard Burton.

'Better show me where it is then, girl,' said Prince jovially. 'Catch you later, Joe.'

'Not if I see you coming, you won't,' said Joe softly to his retreating back.

Ursell said, 'Thanks, Joe.'

Joe liked that. No pretending nothing had happened here.

But he still wanted to know what had happened.

He said, 'Time for a word?'

'You've earned it. But outside, eh? In here a man could go deaf of peotry.'

On the podium, Dai Bard had ended his Welsh declamation, but raised his hand to stay the relieved applause.

'For those of you who do not have the Welsh, I have essayed an English translation of a few stanzas,' he said, beaming like one who expects congratulation for his condescension.

Then he coughed and began:

Three birds there are of Rhiannon
Whose songs were heard of old.
One sang the glory of the sun
In notes of molten gold;

'Is he really a great poet?' asked Joe.

The second traced across the night
A mighty starry rune
And sang in notes of dark and bright
The magic of the moon.

'Welsh he may be; English, you tell me,' said Ursell.

But pain of death and pain of birth
Are music to the third.
She sings the sadness of the earth.
Her song can still be heard.

'But he certainly got that right,' concluded the policeman. 'Come on, Joe. We may not have long.'

And Joe, following the DI out of the hall, asked himself, long for what?

TWENTY-FIVE

OUTSIDE THEY MOVED a little way from the building then came to a halt. It was still light but fading fast. Somewhere a bird was singing, one of Dai Bard's birds of Rhiannon maybe. It certainly sounded like it had stuff to get off its chest before darkness fell. And Ursell too, Joe guessed. But he was finding it harder to get started than the bird.

'This to do with you being brought up in a kids' home?' he prompted.

'Real smartass PI, aren't you, Joe,' said the DI without heat. 'But you're right, that's what it's to do with.'

He seemed to make up his mind and took a deep breath.

'OK, here goes. I was born round here, Joe, and brought up in a Home. Funny. Home to most people brings a nostalgic tear to the eye. Not to me. Home is the original four-letter word. Anyway, I won't bore you with details, but I was taken into care when I was four. *Care!* There's another double-edged word. Can mean being looked after or being worn down. I got both, but a lot more of the latter. By the time I got to twelve, I was care-worn, I tell you, boy. Close to being care-worn away. Then I had one bit of luck. I got fostered to a woman in Caerlindys. Madge Cullingham. Temporary, it was, between Homes. But something in me saw the depths of the pit I was sliding into. I was well down already, but not so far I couldn't still tell the difference between up and down. And I knew this might be my last chance to cling on and climb out. So I clung. By God, it can't have been a pretty sight, an awkward, uncouth, loutish lad inspired by nothing but selfish self-interest, but Madge saw through to the desperation, and she hung on to me, and when it got near the time for me to go back, she asked if I'd like to stay. I said, How long? A week? A month? She said, Forever.'

He paused, contemplating, Joe guessed, the single most important moment in his life, with gratitude that it had happened, and sick horror at how things might have been if it hadn't.

He said, 'My ma died when I was real young. My pa couldn't take care of me, so my Aunt Mirabelle brought me up. Was a time though when I didn't know what was going to happen to me. Only a day, probably, but I've never forgot that feeling. Then Mirabelle took over.'

When a guy offered you stuff like this, you gave him what you had to give in return.

'She seems a good lady,' said Ursell. 'But you didn't come damaged goods, did you, Joe? I mean, not seriously damaged.'

'We talking abuse, no, I didn't,' said Joe. 'That what we're talking?'

The DI nodded, as if saying yes was beyond him.

'Lot of it came out about the Home I'd been in a few years later,' he said. 'I said nothing. There were plenty of old boys talking without me, and I knew the pain it would bring Madge. Me too. That was a door I'd shut behind me, or so I thought. Only you never really get it shut, no matter how hard you lean on it.'

'Right,' said Joe. 'Right.'

'OK, onward and upward,' said Ursell, shaking off his introspection with a visible effort. 'Thanks to Madge, I grew up normal as I could, went to school, passed some exams, and decided for reasons I've never understood to become a cop. I joined the local force, but when the time came for me to start moving forward, CID, promotion exams, that kind of thing, I decided I didn't want to stay round here to develop my career.'

He paused again and Joe said, 'Not much going on? Too quiet for an ambitious lad?'

'Something of that. But something else too. It was all a bit too—how shall I put it?—too *structured.* Not what you had in yourself, but how your face fitted, who you drank with...'

'What lodge you belonged to?' suggested Joe.

'Bit of that too. Well, it happens, not just in the police either. But I'd had enough of people hanging close together, whatever their reasons. This wasn't the kind of pond I wanted to swim in, so with Madge's blessing I headed out to the open sea.'

Deep down they're all bards, thought Joe.

'And I did well enough,' he continued. 'Came back for visits as often as I could. Never thought I'd come back to work. Then Madge took ill. Cancer. The medics couldn't say how long, but not long. Could be over a year, could be six months. I got myself transferred back here. Told them if I didn't get a transfer I'd resign and move back anyway. Madge kept going for twenty-one months. I like to think me being here got her that extra time. Not that the last three months when she was in the hospital was extra time I'd wish on my worst enemy. Know why she went into hospital, Joe?'

'Because she was too ill to stay at home?' offered Joe.

Ursell shook his head.

'Because she could see what it was doing to me and she got frightened I'd do something to help her out of her pain. Not frightened for her sake, you understand. Think she'd have liked that. But frightened for what it would do to me, to my career, if I got mixed up in a mercy killing. That's the kind of woman she was.'

'And would you have?' Joe had to ask.

'I think so,' said Ursell softly. 'I think so.'

'But after it was all over, you stayed on,' said Joe. 'Didn't head back to the big time. Why was that? Pond life changed?'

'Oh yes. The waters had become a lot murkier,' said Ursell grimly. 'Before, it had just been a bit of back-scratching, looking after your mates, that sort of thing.'

'GM,' said Joe.

'That's right. GM. Keeping the wheels oiled. I didn't really pay much attention till after Madge died, but then I began to sit up and take notice. And it felt like there was something else, something different, here now. But it was the business with the boy, Simon Sillcroft, that really focused my mind. Landed on my desk like a sort of initiation test, I think. Tuck this away quietly and we'll go on from there. Nothing said directly, of course, but it was never presented as a case to investigate, much more as a conclusion to reach. Disturbed and sickly child, unstable background, in need of special care, no one at fault.'

'What about Glyn Matthias? Didn't you investigate him?'

'Nothing to investigate. No accusations were ever made. Not overtly. Just quietly removed without any fuss which said it all for some people. Like telling the world we, that is school and police authorities, had our suspicions and even though there was nothing that could be done in law, we made damn sure the chief suspect was put out of harm's way.'

'Poor sod,' said Joe.

'Maybe,' said Ursell indifferently. 'Don't have much sympathy for people of his persuasion. OK, I know that's not the correct attitude these days, but it's the way I feel. A boy gets savaged by Rottweilers, he's never going to be crazy about dogs, is he?'

Works both ways, thought Joe, recalling Matthias's instinctive distrust of the police.

He said, 'You still got him in the frame then?'

'No,' said Ursell, frowning. 'I spoke to him. Wanted to think the worst but didn't come away feeling there was anything there. And he's got a lot of friends who stuck by him despite the GM rumour machine, people who wouldn't know political correctness if you gave it tight trousers and called it Tom Jones. But when I let it be known I didn't think Matthias was in the frame but I still had a frame, I found myself being eased off the case. I failed the test, see, and Mr Penty-Hooser found other things for me to do. And remember, there really was no evidence that was going to stand up in court.'

'But you still suspected Simon Sillcroft had been abused?'

Ursell said quietly, 'I didn't suspect, I knew. Remember that door I told you about, the one I've been leaning against all these years? Soon as I saw the boy, it flew wide open. Oh, in many ways, most ways, we were completely different. I was wild and rebellious and always in trouble, which was what made me vulnerable, while young Simon was an odd and sickly child which was what put him in harm's way, I suspect. But sadness calls to sadness, Joe. And there was something deeply sad at that boy's heart which I recognized because I've lived with it most of my life too...'

'Sadness,' said Joe. 'You're right, Perry. He knew all about sadness.'

He told Ursell about the inscription scratched on the sickbay locker. And at last he took the chance to tell him too about spotting the cameras in the clocks.

'So that's what Lewis and Electricity were on about,' exclaimed Ursell. 'They spotted you spotting the hidden cameras and got their explanation in before it was asked for.'

'So what is going on?' asked Joe, hoping that narrative was over and they could get down to some facts.

'It all fits the investigation. Boys in showers and bathrooms and changing rooms and toilets, God help us. Boys doing the things that boys herded together like this tend to get up to. Get them on video, put them on the Internet, oh, there's a big market for this kind of stuff.'

'But it's not abuse, is it?' said Joe. 'I mean, it stinks, but in law it's a long way short of actually touching and doing that sort of stuff, isn't it?'

'Watching's not a substitute, Joe. It's a stimulant,' said Ursell grimly. 'As for the really bad stuff, never doubt it happened. Lewis would generally speaking be very careful not to foul his own nest. But just think of the temptation. All these boys, all those images. So when one came along who was separable from the others, and didn't communicate much with them, and wasn't being visited by doting parents all the while, and was known to be a strange, repressed and depressed child, the chance must have seemed too good to pass up on.'

Joe had known this was where they were heading, but hearing the policeman say it brought it out of his mind and into his heart.

'The bastard,' he said passionately. 'Oh, the foul bastard. What's he doing still walking around free? What's he doing still walking at all? I'd like to break his legs myself.'

He meant it. It took a lot to bring his peaceable, tolerant make-up within hailing distance of violence, but this revelation took him there in a single stride.

'Evidence, Joe, evidence. What the kid said was too vague and got marked down as the ramblings of a disturbed child. Could be he said something to his sister and that's what brought her along here to find out for herself. She talks to Lewis, he sweet-talks her back, she's not sure whether there was anything going on or not, he offers her a bed in the cottage—he had a key, remember—and then he torches it. How's that sound?'

It didn't sound very good, thought Joe. And he guessed that, much as Ursell would like it to be true, it didn't sound all that good to him either, else he'd not have been trying it out on a passing PI.

'He looked genuinely surprised to me when you told him the girl's name,' said Joe. 'Also when you told him Simon was dead. Pleased, maybe. But certainly surprised. And as for killing Angela by setting fire to the cottage, seems a bit hit and miss for the High Master.'

The High Master's son was a different kettle of fish. It felt like a good time to pass on his info about Wain's visit that night.

But before he could, Ursell said, 'Maybe there was another reason he wanted to torch Copa Cottage. Simplest way of disposing of evidence, a good fire. If it's a really good fire.'

'Evidence...? Oh shoot. The Haggards. They in on this too?'

'We believe so.'

'We?'

Ursell took his arm and turned him so that their faces were close.

'Joe, don't know what it is about you, but I've already told you ten times more than I intended. It must be your honest face, which I personally will rearrange if ever you open your mouth about any of it without my say-so.'

'Hey, no need to get heavy,' said Joe, genuinely taken aback that suddenly they were back in hard-nosed-cop land.

'Heavy?' Ursell stepped back a pace. 'Sorry if I sound over the top, Joe, but you'd better believe me, this is light as a butterfly's kiss compared with the steroids-for-breakfast boys down in the Smoke.'

Joe took this in, digested it, then said, 'This is something to do with you jumping when Prince cracks the whip, right?'

'You're not just an honest face, are you?' said Ursell. 'Joe, you kept quiet about our little arrangement back there without knowing what was going on, for which I'm grateful. Now I'm telling you what's going on for your own good, OK?'

'OK,' said Joe, who thought that *little arrangement* was a pretty vague way of describing Ursell's arm-twisting threats but didn't feel that now was the time to be picking nits. 'So tell me.'

'Well, after I got sidelined from the Sillcroft case, I felt pretty pissed off and I was getting the feeling that there were people upstairs in my own force I couldn't altogether trust...'

'Like Pantyhose,' said Joe.

'He's one of them. Not because they are necessarily mixed up in Lewis's little games, but because they think looking after each other's backs is the best way of making sure their bread's buttered on the right side.'

'That from one of Dai Bard's poems?' wondered Joe.

'Watch it! No feeling for language, you English. Anyway, I talked to friends in my old force, people I could trust. They put out feelers. And a few months later, I'm being invited to an informal meeting with some people in the National Police Squad. Not because they liked the cut of my jib but because they wanted to be sure I wasn't going to step on their toes in an ongoing investigation into a national paedophile ring. It was the Haggards' connection with Llanffugiol that rang their alarm bells. The High Master wasn't in their frame at all. And just how the Haggards were involved they weren't sure. Porno movies, yes. That's where the woman made her name. Could have got an Oscar for Best Supporting Actress from what I've seen. But the paedophile thing, the connection wasn't too clear. And Haggard's home and business premises were clean...'

'They were searched, you mean? So he knew he was in your sights?'

'Not exactly. Pointless going in and giving the game away unless you're sure you're going to find something. So a sort of unofficial preliminary survey was done...'

'Like you got me to do on the Lady House?' said Joe indignantly. 'You pick up bad habits easily.'

'Sorry. But ends and means...all right, no need to look all self-righteous. I know that bad things can happen when cops start thinking like that. But sometimes there's such bad things happening already, Joe, you've got to do anything you can to put them right.'

'So you were planning a—what did you call it?—a preliminary survey on Copa?' said Joe. 'Who were you going to get to do your dirty work this time?'

'No one. Electricity Sample had really made that place secure. So we were going to use the alarm system to get us in, see? Or rather, get Tom Prince in. You were almost right about him, by the way, except he's National Squad and it was them who arranged for him to be transferred here under a cloud, not me. I don't have that kind of clout. His job was to get himself trusted by the GM element in the area, see what he could turn up.'

'And keep an eye on you,' suggested Joe.

'Oh yes. That too,' said Ursell. 'So you saved my skin by playing dumb back there, Joe, but you possibly saved your own too, which is why I'm telling you all this so's you can keep on saving it.'

'You're talking like they got hitmen!' said Joe incredulously.

'In a way. They might not hit your life but they could certainly hit your living. Joe, I've come so far, I might as well spell it out. These NPS people have got a different agenda from me, a bigger picture is how they'd put it. The Haggards are more important to them than the High Master. He's peripheral. Films of boys crapping or playing with each other in the showers is children's TV to the kind of thing they're really after. They'll be all too willing to cut a deal with Lewis to get a lead in towards the centre, and with the Haggards too, if it comes to that. This is big business they're investigating, this is international corporation stuff. That's the way they see things. Well, good for them, say I. Me, what I saw was poor Simon Sillcroft who's now dead. And what I see is Mr bloody Lewis high-mastering it on my patch. And he's the one I'm going to have, no matter what!'

Joe for once had got here already. He was Ursell's unofficial weapon and his accidental encounter with Tom Prince had caused the DI problems, compounded by his outburst accusing the sergeant of being a plant. So Ursell had opted to bind him in with frankness. Perhaps more frankness than he intended. He came across as a guy much in need of someone to talk to.

And like Detective Superintendent Willie Woodbine of Luton CID, he'd grasped that Joe was a guy who sometimes reached places official investigators couldn't dream of.

'So what do you think was in the cottage?' he asked.

'The place was full of computer equipment. We know that from the wreckage. And Haggard admits it freely. It was what may have been in the computers that we'd like to lay our hands on. I think it might have been a control centre for the Haggards' and Lewis's kiddy porn ring. And God knows what else. Only if there was anything incriminating there, it very handily went up in flames.'

It still didn't sound right to Joe. But at least the fact that the Haggards were in the frame to some extent explained their behaviour. Fran the Man, knowing that Lewis had a key to the cottage, hadn't been totally convinced after talking to his partner that the other didn't know more about both the woman and the fire than he was saying. As for Franny, her reason for wanting to find out about the burnt girl rang genuine. But all their mutual distrust had evaporated under the more potent threat of police investigation, which Lewis must have passed on to them by car phone as they drove back to London. Joe could imagine what he had said. Something along the lines of: *The cops are doing some serious sniffing around, someone's been poking around my hidden TV room, I don't know exactly what's going off but I'm getting bad feelings and I'm going to need all my energies to cover myself, so if you want to cover your arses, you'd better get yourselves back here tooty sweety.*

Only, of course, the High Master would have wrapped it up a little more elegant with the odd *as 'twere* tossed in.

'So Joe, I've kept my side of the bargain. What have you got for me?'

Ursell spoke lightly enough, but Joe caught the urgency in his voice. Way things stood at the moment, he hadn't been able to lay a finger on Lewis. Fate seemed bent on tantalizingly pulling away the evidence from under the DI's nose just as he got within sniffing distance. He must feel perilously close to ending up with egg on his face, his only achievement of note being the damage he'd done to the National Squad's broader investigation. And if that happened, Deputy Chief Constable Penty-Hooser might find himself with some unexpected allies when it came to putting the snuffer on the DI's career.

So any straw was graspable, even when it consisted of a redundant lathe operator from Luton.

Joe looked up at the sky for inspiration. The bird had stopped singing. It was twilight with a couple of stars just beginning to laser their way through the deepening blue.

His brain too felt a twinkle coming through.

He said, 'You talk to Long John yet?'

'Dawe from the Goat? Yes, Joe, he admits to rogering Mrs Williams, claims it's true love and he wants to marry her. But after divorce, not death, and he's got an alibi for the bit of the morning when you weren't watching him on the job. But it was all a waste of time anyway. When Williams came round, all he said was it was an accident, brake slipped while he was sitting up by the quarry, so no crime.'

'Talk to Dai again,' said Joe. 'Tell him you're about to pick the High Master up for kiddy porn. Tell him you know about the hidden cameras.'

Ursell considered.

'You think he's in on it?' he said doubtfully.

'No, but I think he probably spotted the cameras. He's the caretaker, isn't he? And when he worked out what was happening, he had a quiet word. I bet Lewis has been paying him off for the past year or more. So another loose end to be sorted out when Lewis felt the heat on.'

'But why didn't he say anything?'

'Because with attempted murder to add to his blackmail threat, he must have thought he could really put up the payments.'

'Joe,' said Ursell softly. 'You may just be a genius. What else?'

'Wain Lewis was seen driving up to Copa Cottage the night of the fire. And those pills I spotted in his lavatory cistern and they found traces of in Angela, they were stolen from the hospital, right? Well, Wain's got something going with a nurse called Tilly Butler. Red-haired girl, father's the minister at the Primitive Chapel.'

Ursell shook his head in incredulous awe.

'Be not forgetful to entertain strangers,' he said. 'For thereby some have entertained angels unawares. What more, Joe? Is there more?'

There may have been, Joe wasn't sure. But of time there was certainly no more.

Tom Prince came hurrying out of the college building.

'Perry,' he said. 'I've just been on the blower to the hospital. Angela Sillcroft's awake and talking.'

'What? Great. Joe, why don't you come too...'

'I don't think so,' said Prince coldly. 'Heroes and civilians have got their place, and it's not where we're going.'

In that moment Joe appreciated the seriousness of Ursell's warning. Prince was not a man to mess with. Ursell looked like he might be ready to try it but Joe felt the DI already had enough on his plate.

'I got other things to do,' he said to Ursell, 'Catch you later.'

'Surely,' said the DI as Prince practically manhandled him towards their car.

Joe watched their lights fade down the drive. As they passed out of sight, another single headlight came in view, moving fast.

His ears told him what it was before his eyes could make it out clearly.

A 250cc bike. The same engine he'd heard receding that morning as he tiptoed tremulously around the Lady House.

He didn't have time to work out the implications of that before it came to a gravel-spraying halt alongside him. Its rider raised the visor of his crash helmet to reveal the anxious face of Glyn Matthias.

'Mr Sixsmith,' he said. 'I need help. Wain Lewis is back at the Lady House. I think he's planning to burn the place down.'

TWENTY-SIX

IT SEEMED TO JOE that since arriving in Wales he'd spent more time than a sensitive man ought to hurtling through the countryside at breakneck speeds.

This time, though the distance was short, the terror was even more intense as he covered it perched on the pillion of a motorbike whose rider's head seemed permanently twisted round so that he could gasp out details of his story to his passenger.

Joe concentrated hard on Matthias's words. The alternative was imagining how it was going to feel if they didn't come out of one of their speedway skids and fetched up against the solid trunk of some rough-barked tree that had been standing there for a hundred years and wasn't about to give way now.

By the time they came to a halt alongside the Lady House steps, Joe had got a broad outline of the picture.

Some time after fleeing from the festival ground, Wain Lewis had turned up at the Goat and Axle. He had got down to some serious drinking, and after a while Long John Dawe had refused to serve him without he handed over his car keys. A little while later one of the other drinkers had spotted a police car pulling up in front of the pub. Wain, clearly thinking they were after him, had headed out of the door leading to the back of the pub where his Mazda was parked. Of course, he couldn't start it. The cops had wanted to question Long John about his possible involvement in the possible attack on Dai Williams. Satisfied with his alibi, they had left, and Dawe, full of concern for Ella Williams, had headed off for Caerlindys to try to see her at the hospital.

This was as far as Matthias had got by the time they arrived at the Lady House.

Silence and darkness reigned. The only sign of anything amiss was the Mazda, which had been abandoned across the centre circle of lawn after administering a *coup de grâce* to the ailing magnolia.

'Thought you said he didn't have the keys,' said Joe, as they banged at the flaking front door.

'He didn't. I went looking for him and found him sitting in the car. He wasn't unconscious but looked all played out. I thought it was just the booze but I wondered later if he'd been taking something. I told him the cops had gone and a couple of us got him back inside. We made him some coffee and he sat quietly in the corner, so quietly that after a while we forgot he was there.'

'He certainly knows how to be quiet,' agreed Joe. ''Cos if he's still in here, he's not making any noise.'

He crouched down with his ear to the letterbox.

'He's in there,' insisted Matthias. 'After Long John left, we just helped ourselves to what we wanted and put the money in the till. Then suddenly someone noticed Wain behind the bar. I said, "You want some more coffee?" but he just vaulted over the bar and shot off out of the back door. And then someone said, "He's got his car keys!" and we went after him. How he got here without crashing I don't know. Don't know how I managed it either, and I was a long way behind. I found the car like you see it and I could hear stuff being smashed up inside the house and Wain screaming, "Where are you? Where are you? Do you know what you've done?" I tried shouting to him but it was no use and I couldn't get in. Then I smelt it...'

Joe, who was now down on his knees with the letterbox pushed open, could smell it too. Petrol. He shuddered at the thought of what a spark could do. Thank God the bell worked off an old-fashioned pull system.

'I thought I'd better get help quick,' concluded Matthias. 'I'm glad I saw you.'

'You are? Why?' asked Joe, puzzled that he should be anyone's first choice in an emergency.

'If I'd had to go into the reception, Mr Lewis would have come rushing up here and as the boy's obviously blaming his father for something, God knows what he'd do if he actually saw him,' said Matthias. 'Maybe you can talk him out before he does any damage. You seem to get on well with youngsters.'

'You reckon?' said Joe. 'Well, I'm flattered. But this stuff can just go up by accident while I'm talking. We'd better rustle up some professional help.'

He reached into his pocket for his mobile. But when he switched it on, nothing happened. He checked his battery status and saw that sod's law had finally taken it over.

'Oh shoot,' he said. 'I'm flat.'

He could hear Mirabelle saying with some satisfaction, 'You buy your shoes from the devil, you end up with a hole in your sole.'

Or soul. Same thing.

'What do we do now?' said Matthias, regarding Joe with the expectation of a young subaltern awaiting orders from a battle-scarred veteran.

'You get back to the hall, ring for help. Fire brigade, police, ambulance, best take no chances.'

'Right,' said Matthias, heading down the steps to his bike.

Sod's law was working here too. It wouldn't start.

At least, though phones were way beyond his competence, this was something Joe could deal with.

He ran down the steps and began checking out the ignition. It had sounded to be misfiring a bit to his finely tuned ear.

As he worked something occurred to him.

'Mr Matthias, how come you knew Simon Sillcroft was dead?'

Matthias looked surprised. But he obviously felt his was not to reason why.

'His sister told me. I wrote to his aunt after he left saying he was very talented musically and ought to keep it up. I thought it might help having someone being positive about him instead of all the poor-mixed-up-kid stuff she must be getting. It was Angela who wrote back some time later. She said I was the only person her brother talked about with any fondness.'

'You ever meet her?'

'No. Spoke to her on the phone. She rang me to say he was dead.'

'Ask you a lot of questions about the Lewises?'

'Yes, she did. Why are you so interested?'

'No reason,' said Joe, pressing the starter. The engine burst into life. 'Go, go.'

He watched the bike out of sight then turned back to the house. Twilight was deepening rapidly to darkness and the unlit building no longer just looked ugly, it looked sinister. Maybe it was empty, he thought. Maybe when Wain realized his father wasn't there, he'd set out on foot for the hall taking the direct route through the trees, and they'd missed him. In which case he'd be there about the same time Matthias got back, and it would be someone else's problem.

That would be nice. Except that the dark house didn't feel empty.

He had to get in or get Wain out. How could he tempt him? Or at least get his attention?

Easy.

He went to the red Mazda, reached inside, and leaned on the horn.

It had a rather distinctive note, G in the bass clef, he thought.

Something on the passenger seat caught his eye. A long ribbon of cellophane.

He stopped pressing the horn and picked it up.

'Oh shoot,' he said.

It was a bubble strip of Decorax tablets, except all the tablets had been pressed out.

Now he pressed repeatedly on the horn, sending an urgent challenge which bounced back mockingly from the brick facade of the still house, to be absorbed by the surrounding trees which seemed to be moving closer in the darkening air.

Then finally the summons was answered.

He was looking up at the first-floor window where he'd spotted Wain watching him the night of the dinner. And suddenly there it was again, that pale narrow face in its frame of black hair, peering down at him.

He stepped forward to wave and beckon the boy down. But at the same moment something very odd happened.

The front door opened and Wain Lewis stepped outside.

It was strange how mind-blanking incredulity and panoramic revelation could come so close you could hardly say the one followed the other.

Slowed down, the sequence ran: no one can be in two places at once; it had to be Morna Lewis standing by the window and he'd mistaken her for her son because of (a) the family resemblance, and (b) he expected to see Wain there.

That was straightforward enough, but now came the visionary leap to full-frontal knowledge without benefit of clever reasoning.

Harry Herbert had made the same mistake the night he thought he saw Wain in the Mazda speeding up to Copa Cottage. And Joe should have spotted this much earlier, knowing as he did that Wain had been over at the college that night, enjoying the company of Bronwen Williams.

The boy was swaying at the top of the steps and Joe ran forward to catch him.

He looked in a bad way, but when Joe lowered him on to the topmost step, his eyes registered recognition.

'Make your money easy,' he muttered accusingly.

'Not as easy as dealing drugs,' said Joe. 'Help's on its way. You just lie there quiet while I talk to your mum.'

But that was easier said than done. Either Wain had pulled the door shut behind him or it had swung to.

Joe hauled at the bell pull with one hand and hammered at the woodwork with the other.

'Mrs Lewis, you OK?' he yelled. 'Open up, will you, please?'

No reply. He tried the letterbox again. The smell of petrol was still strong.

'Wain,' he said. 'Were you planning to torch the house?'

'Like the cottage,' mumbled the youth. 'Yeah...only fair...see what it's like...'

'But you just poured some petrol around?' said Joe, eager for reassurance. 'You didn't try to light it? Or set a fuse?'

'...poured it around...fuse...'

The boy was nearly out. Was that agreement or denial?

'Wain, don't go to sleep,' urged Joe.

He stooped and raised the boy by his shoulders.

'Wain, was that all you did?'

'...kitchen...cooker...'

Joe recalled the oven fuelled from cylinders of gas...the spare cylinders lying around the kitchen...

'Wain, you didn't do anything with the gas, did you? Wain!'

He shook the boy violently.

The result was devastating.

From the other side of the door came a sound like the exhalation of a mighty breath and the downstairs windows on the kitchen side of the house came bursting out like they'd been hit by a shell blast. Within seconds the blank, staring, still unbroken windows on the first floor were alive with a ghastly moving light.

First things first. Joe rolled the boy off the steps and half carried, half dragged him into the shelter of the nearest trees.

Then he turned back to the house, straining his eyes in search of movement upstairs. Not that he wanted to see any. What he did want to see was Morna Lewis appearing round the side of the house having escaped out the back. But somehow, the way things had gone on this trip, he didn't really expect that would happen.

And he was right. There it was, second floor now, the pale-faced figure at a window, probably her own bedroom's.

Safe there for a little while, thought Joe, straining his ears to catch the distant sound of approaching fire brigade sirens.

Nothing. God knows how far they had to come. But at least Matthias ought to be fetching help from the college any minute now.

Help to do what? Not put the fire out, that was for sure. It was eating up the old wooden-framed building like Whitey desperate to finish a stolen fish supper before he got caught.

He could hear a voice in his mind, Beryl's maybe, or Mirabelle's, or maybe Butcher's back in Luton when she heard the news, one or more of the womenfolk in his life anyway: *One rescue from a raging fire may be heroic, but two's just macho showing-off.*

Made no difference. A macho show-off's gotta do what a macho show-off's gotta do.

'Stay there,' he said redundantly to the almost comatose Wain.

Then he set off round the back of the house at a steady run.

TWENTY-SEVEN

GETTING IN THE SIDE furthest away from the fire was easy.

These windows predated toughened glass. He put a stone through a pane, reached inside, released the catch, and clambered through without damage, except that his memory banks were sending out urgent signals to reawaken the aches and pains he'd suffered last time, as if to say, *Didn't you learn anything?*

He was in the dining room. The rosewood table looked like the Mad Axeman of Llanffugiol had had his finest hour. When he opened the door into the hallway, the fire was waiting for him, licking around the lower treads of the staircase.

As last time, the answer was not to think, just to act. Like a circus dog going through a burning hoop, he leapt up to the fifth stair, felt it give beneath his weight, but managed to keep going till the stairs felt firm and the fire was just a warm breath on his neck.

Coming down this way wasn't going to be an option though, not unless his descent started in the next half-minute.

Ascent to the second floor brought a delusion of safety. The heat wasn't yet perceptible up here and apart from a little smoke which had passed with him through the upper stairway door, there was nothing to indicate the rising inferno below.

He found her where he'd seen her from the garden, still standing by the window of her simple bedroom, looking out. She didn't turn, but spoke like she was welcoming an expected visitor to her salon.

'Good evening, Mr Sixsmith,' she said. 'I would like to thank you for taking care of Owain.'

'Yeah, fine, now I've got to take care of you,' said Joe.

She turned then and gave him the Hepburn smile.

'No, I don't think so,' she said. 'You hurry along now, you shouldn't be able to get away quite easily.'

'I'm not going without you,' said Joe.

'Don't be silly,' she said briskly. 'All your friends will be terribly upset if anything happens to you. You're a much-loved man, Mr Sixsmith. It's not possible to talk with you for more than a few minutes without realizing that.'

'You too, Mrs Lewis,' he assured her. 'What will Wain do without you to protect him?'

This made her laugh.

'Owain and I have just had an interesting conversation on the subject of my protecting him,' she said. 'It seems I am now surplus to requirements. No doubt you have already worked out that it was me who set fire to Copa Cottage and killed that young woman?'

On another occasion Joe might have been pleased at this unsolicited testimonial to his detective prowess, but now he had other things on his mind.

'She's not dead,' he urged. 'She's come round and is talking.'

It was counter-productive.

'Really? Then that means it's all been for nothing, doesn't it? She threatened to testify that Owain was a drug dealer, you know. I presume that now she'll carry out her threat.'

'Maybe not,' said Joe. 'She'll have other things on her mind, I reckon.'

He hesitated, fearing the effect the news of the girl's identity and probable reason for coming to Branddreth might have on the woman, but it was a chance he had to take.

'Her name's Angela Sillcroft,' he said in a rush. 'All she's interested in is finding out what really happened to her brother. That's Simon Sillcroft. Or was. The poor kid's dead.'

His fears were groundless.

'I knew all that,' she said lightly. 'She told me when I caught her rooting around in Leon's study.'

'You caught her...?'

'Yes. It was the second time. The first time I spotted her was on the TV screen in one of the college dormitories. Owain was with her. They were being intimate' —she made a *moue* of distaste—'but of course it means nothing to a boy of that age, it's just the hormones talking. It happened once before... Anyway, once I'd spoken with them and discovered they'd only known each other a week and she wasn't even a student at the same university, I thought the matter could be easily resolved. I pointed out that the Williamses would be back from holiday the following day, to get the place ready for your choir who would be staying there during the festival. She seemed to agree very readily that yes, it was time for her to be on her travels. And when I checked the screens the following day, it appeared that she'd been as good as her word.'

'The screens...you mean the security TV screens? In the cellar? You know about them?'

She looked surprised.

'This is my house, Mr Sixsmith. Of course I know about them.'

What does she mean by *know?* wondered Joe. Were they just part of the college security system to her? Or did she have an inkling of their other vile use? She'd have to be very naive not to suspect. He found himself wanting to believe she was that naive, so he could go on liking her.

Then he recalled that this woman by her own admission had attempted to burn Angela Sillcroft to death.

'But she didn't go away?' he prompted.

'No. As I said, I caught her ransacking Leon's study. I was going to call the police. She said that if I did, I could wave goodbye to my son for several years as the police did not look kindly upon drug dealers. I said she was crazy, and then she took me up to Owain's room and showed me these boxes. They were full of tablets. I don't know what they were, but she said if I didn't believe her, all I had to do was take a couple and I'd soon find out. Then she said some awful things about Leon too.'

'What things?'

The small elfin face became closed.

'Awful things,' she repeated. 'I don't want to talk about them. I told her to go. She laughed and said she was going, but she'd be close. I followed her when she went and saw her going up the hill to Copa Cottage. Owain must have taken his father's key and let her in.'

'What did you say to Owain when you saw him?'

'About the girl? Nothing. But I said I'd found the drugs and wanted them out of my house. He didn't deny what they were, he just took them, I don't know where.'

Joe knew where. He'd hidden a strip of Decorax in the cistern no doubt for personal use, then taken the rest to the college, to Bron, whom he'd persuaded to take care of them for a while. How? Not with money, Joe guessed. But with talk of love, a lot more than just talk...the poor kid had thought they were back on track again till Joe had sown new suspicions by telling her he'd seen Wain at the hospital.

This boy might look like he'd be knocked down by the wind blast from a piccolo, but what with drug dealing and double dealing, he was a real piece of work. And his mother whom he so closely resembled...what was she?

There was a lot of noise building up outside. He went to the window and looked down. For a second he was surprised. Talking to Morna Lewis, he'd all but forgotten the fire, but now he saw by the crazy leaping light it was throwing out into the garden that it must have really got a grip on the ground floor. There were cars pulling up on the edge of that light, and people running forward, shielding their faces from the heat. He saw Lewis and Dai Bard and Mirabelle and Big Merv and Glyn Matthias. They'd found Wain and were talking to him. Probably not getting much sense back. Now they'd spotted him at the window and were waving and shouting.

He waved back and turned to the woman.

'You went up to Copa Cottage that night,' he said.

'Yes.'

'To see the girl and try and talk reason into her?'

A hesitation, then the lie. 'Yes.'

'How did you get there?'

'I drove Owain's car.'

'Why not your own? You have a car, don't you?'

'Yes, but Leon was using it. He was out at a meeting, I knew he wouldn't be back till late.'

'So you asked Owain if you could borrow his car, did you?'

Another hesitation.

'No, he was...busy elsewhere. I just took it.'

Busy. She'd probably checked the screens, seen just how busy her son was with young Bronwen somewhere in the college, cementing his arrangement to have his stock-in-trade stored in safe-keeping. What a nice safe girl Bron must have seemed all of a sudden to both mother and son.

'But why'd you need to take the risk of borrowing his car anyway, Mrs Lewis?' asked Joe. 'Not a long walk up the hill, you'd done it already when you followed Angela. OK, it was night, but you knew the road, you could have taken a torch. Why not walk?'

She didn't answer but went to the window. Her appearance caused a renewed wave of shouting from below. She didn't acknowledge it.

'I got this idea why you did it,' said Joe wearily. 'You needed transport 'cos you didn't fancy walking up there with a jerry can of petrol in one hand and a spray-can of paint in the other. You didn't go up there to talk to Angela, Mrs Lewis. You went up there all tooled up to kill her.'

She turned and gave him the full Hepburn. Only now it seemed to him like a skull smiling.

'She could have destroyed my son, Mr Sixsmith,' she said.

'Yeah? She needn't have bothered. You and his dad seem to

have done a pretty good job by yourselves. Come on, time to get out of here.'

'No,' she said. 'I don't think so. Not much point after the things Owain said to me when he came home tonight. He smashed up my furniture, did you see that? All the things I inherited from my mother, everything I valued most. He knew that and he smashed it. And now I've burned it, and soon I'll burn with it.'

'Then it was you started the fire?' said Joe.

'Oh yes. Owain threatened, but he couldn't carry it through. It takes a certain strength of character to carry something like that through and my son, I fear, doesn't possess it.'

'Maybe not,' said Joe. 'But your son will go to jail for doing it less'n you and me get out of here. Come on.'

He went to the door and flung it open.

It was a mistake. A blast of heat so strong it felt like a punch came spinning up the stairs, eager to get to grips with this new source of cold combustible air. Its source was clearly visible in the tongues of flame greedily licking round the door which led to the first-floor landing below.

'Shoot,' said Joe, slamming the door. 'We ain't going down there.'

It was his own stupid fault, letting himself get so taken up with being the great tec, spelling out the hows and whys and wheres and whens, that he'd forgotten he wasn't Hercule Poirot relaxing in the library, but good old Joe Sixsmith, perched like a November 5th Guy at the top of a house built like a bonfire.

He ran back to the window and tried to open it. It was stuck. He picked up a bedside cabinet and used it as a battering ram. The window flew apart in a shatter of glass and a crumble of rotting wood.

He looked down, saw the crowd below, heard them all screaming at him, helpful things like, 'Joe you've got to get out of there!'

'Hey, man, don't you think I know that?' he yelled back.

But there was another sound, a much more comforting sound, a bell of a fire engine. He could see its lights coming up the road from the village. He saw it pull into the college drive then turn towards the Lady House. The crowd below scattered as it arrived. From up here it looked tiny, thought Joe. Then it struck him that while he was high, he wasn't all that high, and in fact, compared with the red giants he was used to in the city streets back home, this vehicle really was small.

It must be the local fire engine, used to contain blazes till the big boys could make it from the town. Well, he wasn't proud. He was happy to be rescued by anyone and anything.

Except there was another problem. It wasn't just the engine that was small, it was its ladder too.

Trapped on the first floor they'd have been all right. But up here on the second, all Joe could do was stare in stupor at the topmost rung swaying around beneath him, well out of reach.

Now it was being withdrawn.

'Hey, fellows, don't give up so easy,' he called. 'Nobody loves a quitter!'

But they weren't giving up. They were just moving to plan B.

Second thoughts are often best, was a favourite saw of Mirabelle's.

Didn't always work out though, thought Joe, as he looked down at the circle of canvas they had unrolled below. There were about twenty men around it, hanging on to the edge and leaning back to hold it taut.

It looked about the size of a dinner plate.

'Jump, Joe! You gotta jump!'

He recognized the voice and his eyes picked out the source.

Beryl standing a little way back from the tiny circle of canvas, looking up and smiling encouragement. Now that was a real smile, a smile for a man to come home to and wake to and respond to all his life.

He yelled back, 'Will you marry me if I jump?'

She called, 'Depends on your aim. Now stop messing around, Joe Sixsmith. Jump!'

Her voice rose to a new pitch of urgency as the house gave a sudden groan and twitch as if the effort of staying upright was getting to be too much for it. Joe looked round. Morna Lewis was standing there, still smiling at him. Behind her the bedroom door was blistering.

'You'd better go, Mr Sixsmith,' said the woman. 'I should hate to think that our little local troubles had brought any lasting damage to someone as nice as you.'

Joe looked out of the window again. Those guys down there

were putting themselves at considerable personal risk. If the house collapsed they'd be in real trouble. It was showtime.

He threw back his head, yelled, *'Geronimo!'*, rushed forward, seized Morna Lewis round the waist, flung her over his shoulder like a sack of grain, turned, and as the door exploded open, he let the blast of heat and smoke carry him out of the open window into the rich and balmy star-filled night.

TWENTY-EIGHT

JOE SIXSMITH AWOKE.

He said, 'What am I?'

Dr God said, 'Don't you mean, where am I?'

'Don't be silly,' said Joe. 'I know why I am.'

Joe awoke.

He saw an angel floating over him

He said, 'Why haven't you got red hair?'

Joe awoke.

He was nowhere.

Joe awoke.

He saw Beryl Boddington's head on the pillow beside him.

He said, 'How long we been married?'

She said, 'No need to worry about that, Joe. There weren't more than a hundred witnesses.'

Joe awoke.

He said, 'Am I dying? You don't need to tell me the truth.'

Beryl said, 'You've got a busted rib, a broken wrist, twisted ankle, a lot of bruises, and a split skull and a concussion.'

He said, 'I knew I was dying.'

Joe awoke.

Dr Godsip said, 'Hello, Mr Sixsmith. Can you hear me?'

He said, 'Where's Nurse Butler?'

Dr Godsip said, 'I'm afraid Nurse Butler has left us.'

Joe awoke.

He saw Aunt Mirabelle standing on Rev. Pot's shoulders.

He said, 'How's Mrs Lewis?'

AUNT MIRABELLE SAID, 'That woman ain't got nothing worse than a bruised backside. In my gramma's day she'd have been burnt for a witch, which is no more than she deserves, things they're saying about her are true.'

Joe said, 'Believe them, Auntie, but maybe not all. She got a sweet smile and she loves her boy.'

Joe awoke.

He saw Richard Burton glaring down at him like he was an asp.

Richard Burton said, 'You awake, Sixsmith?'

Joe said, 'No.'

Joe awoke.

His arm felt like the asp had bitten it.

Prince said, 'Next time it won't be your arm I pinch. You're a hero again, Joe. Know what a hero is? It's a halfwit who smiles modestly into the camera and when he's asked questions by the press bashfully mutters, *A halfwit's gotta do what a halfwit's gotta do.* Nothing else. You follow me, Joe?'

'Don't know nothing else,' said Joe.

'Good. 'Cos we do. We know where you live.'

'Hey, where is that?' asked Joe.

Joe awoke.

Dirty Harry was sitting by his bed, cleaning his Magnum.

JOE AWOKE.

Perry Ursell was sitting by his bed, eating his grapes.

Joe said, 'Hi.'

'What am I to do with you, Joe? Turn my back for a minute and there you go again, running into burning houses.'

Joe said, 'The girl was talking, Angela. What did she say?'

'Like we thought. Her brother talked to her, pretty mixed-up stuff, but she didn't believe it was all just in his head. Something very nasty had happened to him at Branddreth. Seems Glyn Matthias had been in touch with the family...'

'I knew that,' said Joe.

'Oh yes? Didn't bother her that Matthias had been indirectly implicated, he was about the only thing at Branddreth young Simon seemed to recall with any pleasure. So when her brother died, she got in touch with him.'

'Knew that too. He told her that Wain was studying at Manchester, so she went up there to try and make contact and use him as a way into Branddreth. Found it was easy 'cos Wain was a smalltime campus dealer, got into it in the States, which was where he came across Decorax. Probably brought some back, sold it around, and when Tilly Butler said they were trialling the stuff at Caerlindys, he got into her pants, then persuaded her to help him steal the stuff.'

Ursell said, 'Joe, do you want to tell me everything while I just sit here and eat your grapes, which incidentally are beginning to taste pretty sour?'

'Sorry. Go on.'

'So Angela made contact with Wain. Told him she was bumming around for a year before going to university, fancied seeing Wales, and he said he could give her a lift and let her see the Welshest bit of Wales she was likely to see in a long day's ride. Also offer accommodation. By now they were making out.'

'She do that just to get an in on Branddreth?'

'Who knows? But from his track record, young Wain's got something the girls like, though to look at him, you'd think a good woman would crack him like a nut. Anyway, he brought her to the college, didn't want her round the Lady House, though, so he put her up in the college, which was empty, the Williamses being away on holiday.'

'But Mrs Lewis caught them at it, told her son to send her on her way, only he just sent her as far as Copa, and when Mrs L caught her again, this time searching the Lady House, there was a great row and Angela made the mistake of threatening to turn Wain in as a drug dealer.'

'You're at it again, Joe.'

'Sorry.'

'But you're right, of course. Mrs Lewis has coughed the lot to us. Not till we'd done a deal. We go easy on Owain over the drugs, she gives full cooperation on the attempted murder.'

'What'll she get?'

'The lot. She didn't go up to the cottage for a reasoned discussion, Joe. She went along with a canful of petrol to torch the place with the girl in it. It's premeditated.'

Joe sighed. That smile behind bars.

At least she wouldn't mind the food.

'She giving up Lewis at all?'

'No. Just looks blank.'

'So what's happening there?'

'Nothing, if Tom Prince and his mob have their way. To them, all he is is a possible "in" to the paedophile ring working through the Internet. They got Dai Williams in their pocket now, ready to testify that Lewis lured him up to the quarry, knocked him out and pushed his pick-up over the edge. Attempted murder seems to be that family's forte. So, Lewis has got plenty reason to cooperate and if he does, the bastard could be home and free.'

'Wife banged up, son hating him, not much of a home.'

'Better than young Simon Sillcroft's got,' said Ursell sombrely.

'So you're giving up? Prince knows where you live too?'

'He been talking to you, has he, Joe?'

'Some. Listen, what about the others round here? They gotta know something. Pantyhose. Electricity Sample.'

'Haven't you heard? Mr Sample had an accident in his workshop. Electrocuted himself. And the DCC has been taken ill, job stress, they say. He'll probably be retiring on full pension in the next few weeks.'

'My piles bleed for him,' said Joe, indignation, or hospital, making him untypically coarse. 'So that's it?'

It must have sounded like an accusation, for Ursell replied defensively, 'You know so much, Joe, you give me something. Anything.'

Suddenly Joe felt very very tired.

JOE WOKE.

Ursell was still there.

Joe said, 'Matthias was in the Lady House cellar before I was. He left the cupid's head in the cabinet. Maybe he took something out. Maybe he's looking to use it personally against the High Master. Tell him what happened to Dai. But treat him gentle. He doesn't trust the police. Talk to him like you talked to me last night, Perry. Being gay don't make him the enemy.'

Ursell nodded.

'Worth a try. Anything else?'

'No,' said Joe, thinking, here's me with a cop hanging on my every word and I'm out of words. 'Except...'

'Spit it out, Joe. I'm in the market for anything.'

'On the locker in the sickbay, where that poor kid scratched his name, remember?'

'Yes, you told me. *Simon Sillcroft, sadness.*'

'Well, there was another odd one. What was it? *Henry Loomis, sights.* Strikes me that Simon might not have been the only one that got the full nasty treatment. Maybe this Loomis kid was another. Maybe he's out there somewhere, keeping it bottled up. Some folk do, not the kind of thing they want other people to know, isn't that how these dirty bastards get away with it?'

'Yes, I know, Joe. I know,' said Ursell softly.

'Perry, I'm sorry, I didn't mean...look, maybe if someone like you talked to him...'

'It's worth a try. Joe, anyone ever tell you you're a wonder?'

'Maybe, but didn't quite pronounce it like that,' said Joe Sixsmith.

'Now I'll leave you in peace. You probably want some sleep.'

Joe consulted his wants.

'No,' he said in surprise. 'In fact, I feel quite awake. What I could do with is some grub. Like breakfast.'

'Joe, it's the middle of the afternoon.'

'Is for you,' said Joe Sixsmith. 'Me, it's any time I like it to be.'

TWENTY-NINE

JOE SIXSMITH LEFT WALES in something like Oriental splendour, lying in princely state along the backmost seat of Big Merv's coach, draped in rugs and firmly wedged in with cushions, with bunches of grapes and cans of Guinness in easy reach of his outstretched hand.

After the fire and everything, Dai Bard had felt it best to cancel the rest of the Choir Festival, which probably had them singing for joy down at the Goat and Axle. Rev. Pot had had a quiet word with some of the judges and was able to pass on to his choir an off-the-record assurance that, with the Guttenbergers gone, they were so far in the lead as to have been almost inevitably the winners.

Joe felt really proud of them till Merv, during the course of a private farewell he'd managed to arrange with his colleen, discovered that the Irish choir, and presumably all of the others taking part, had received the same confidential assurance of success.

He thought it best to keep this snippet of information to himself.

His fellow choristers, though eager to get home, refused to leave without Joe. Best medical advice was that he should stay another couple of days in hospital, but he didn't care to inconvenience his friends any further. So he announced that, fond as he'd become of many things and several persons in Wales, he had a cat back home who was pining away out of loneliness, and he discharged himself.

Before he left the hospital, he'd taken the crutch they'd given him and swung himself along the corridor to get the feel of it. A door had opened and Bronwen Williams came out. She was a pale shadow of the bright, lively girl he'd first encountered. She looked at him with a look he recognized, the expression of someone whose world has fallen apart and who longs for someone to blame.

He said, 'Bron, how are you?'

'It was all right till you came,' she said. 'Wain and me were getting it together again and Mam and Da were OK and...'

Tears, not reason, interrupted the accusations.

Joe said, 'I'm sorry.'

She said, 'Go back to England, won't you? We're better off without you.'

She walked away.

It was unfair, but Joe felt no resentment. He only wished it were true. He'd seen the end of innocence before and it never got any more bearable.

He went into the room.

Dai Williams, sitting up in bed, said. 'Oh, it's you.'

He didn't look much like Sinatra now, more like a guy in trouble who knows exactly where to lay the blame. Elsewhere.

Joe said, 'How're you doing?'

'How's it look?' he growled. Then, with an effort, 'Sorry. They tell me it was you spotted me at the quarry. Thanks.'

'My pleasure. Inspector Ursell talk to you?'

'Him!' said Williams scornfully. 'Oh yes, he was after talking me into jail till the other one came and shut him up. Never be taken in by appearances, Joe. Rank's more than what you wear on your arm. No point talking to the monkey when the organ grinder's handy.'

His attempt at worldly wisdom was unconvincing.

Joe said, 'Be careful who you do deals with, Dai.'

'Yeah? You such an expert, maybe you'd like to give me some advice about my family too? I hear you've been sticking your nose in.'

Funny how a gibe could sometimes sound like a plea, thought Joe.

He said, 'Can't help you there. Need to talk to Ella yourself...'

'Do I? So how do I do that when she won't come anywhere near me, says she's going off with that long streak of stale slops from the Goat. To think of the times I've been drinking there, and all the time...'

For a moment he was incoherent with disbelief. And desperation. At least he's not so blind he don't know what he's lost, thought Joe.

The caretaker went on, 'And all because of *this*. All because of me and the High Master...'

'Think it was more than that maybe, Dai,' said Joe.

'You think? What the hell do you know?' yelled the Welshman. 'She was here, ready to take care of me when I woke up, then bloody Ursell came along to talk to me, all this stuff about the TV system and the High Master. She caught a bit of that and after he'd gone she starts pestering me to know what it's all about, so in the end I tell her, just so's she'd know it was all for her and Bron I stuck it out in the one-hole job, building up our bank balance till I'd got enough to take them somewhere decent, see? And suddenly she's looking at me like she'd turned up a stone and out of the blue she says she didn't know what to do till I told her that, but now she's going off with John sodding Dawe! She spoke to me like I was some kind of perverted criminal. Why? You're the expert, can you tell me why?'

'Blackmail's a crime, Dai. Surely you can see that?'

'But not against someone like Lewis!' said Dai Williams earnestly. 'No one could feel any sympathy for a guy like that, could they? All right, what I was doing might be breaking the law in theory, but the sort of filthy stuff he's into, how can anyone blame me for anything I did to him?'

The worst of it was, he sounded genuinely bewildered.

Joe pivoted on his crutch and swung towards the doorway. Here he paused and glanced back. He hated sounding preachy, but some things had to be said.

'Not what you were doing to the High Master people will blame you for, Dai,' he said. 'But you knew what he was doing with those kids and you said nothing. You should have been thinking about the kids, Dai, not about lining your pocket. You should have been thinking about the kids.'

He let the door close behind him and went on his halting way. He was feeling pretty done in, but he had one more door to open before he rested.

The *Carry On* Sister was coming out as he approached. She gave him the bullet-stopping glare, but it must have been an instinctive knee-jerk reaction for suddenly she smiled and said, 'I'll give you one minute, Mr Sixsmith. You both need all the rest you can get.'

She held the door open for him and he went inside.

The Sister was better than her word for he must have sat by the bedside for well over a minute before the still figure lying there opened her eyes and looked at him.

Her lips moved, first to form a smile, then in speech. He had to lean over her to catch the slow, low, hoarse words.

'Nice to see you again.'

'You remember then?'

'Always. Thanks.'

'I'm sorry about your brother. About what happened at the college. And about the fire. His fire, I mean.'

It wasn't meant as a question but she answered it.

'Think it started by accident, but don't think he tried hard to get out. Other way round with me. But it's all right now.'

He guessed she was thinking that she'd done what she set out to do. Finding out about the deal the Prince squad was offering Lewis lay in the future. That would be a real blow. But it wouldn't be a knockout. He'd seen how this girl could fight to survive.

It struck him that probably neither Prince nor Ursell had taken her into their calculations. They had respectively an opponent and an ally here who could well tip the balance of the scales against the High Master. Plus himself. Didn't matter what threats Prince was making, anything he could do to help nail Lewis was Ursell's for the asking.

The door opened. The Sister said warningly, 'Mr Sixsmith.'

'Gotta go now,' said Joe, 'Listen, soon as you're better, you come and see me in Luton. I'm in the book.'

She smiled again and murmured, '...in my book...top of my list...' then closed her eyes.

He remembered those words now as he lay in state at the back of the coach.

He'd handed over the cheque and money he'd received from the Haggards and Wain Lewis to Ursell. Merv had thought he was mad when he'd heard.

'Man, you did the job, you earned the fee,' he insisted.

'Not how I earned it, it's how they earned it that matters,' said Joe.

'Ain't the church got enough saints?' demanded Merv. 'All that pain, all that hassle, and what do you come away with? Sweet nothing?'

He was wrong. He came away with the memory of those words...*top of my list*...and they weren't nothing, though they were certainly sweet enough to slightly mask the bitter taste of all that pain and sadness.

'And what about the Morris? How you going to haggle with Nye over that when you've got no money to haggle with?' Merv had demanded.

'I'll have to wait,' said Joe. 'Tell Nye I'll have to come back if and when any of this gets to court. Tell him we'll talk then. Anyway, I'm in no state to drive, am I?'

But, no hiding it, leaving the old car behind was a blow.

Beryl said, 'You awake?'

''Course I'm awake,' said Joe indignantly. 'Haven't closed my eyes since we left.'

'You could have fooled me,' she said lightly. 'Well, we'll soon be over the border, back in good old England.'

'We've come that far?' said Joe.

She laughed and said, 'Told you you'd been sleeping.'

'Maybe I nodded off. Say, where's Mirabelle? How come she hasn't been poking me every two minutes to make sure I'm not dead?'

'Mirabelle? Not with us. Her and Rev. Pot are travelling independently.'

'What? I know she doesn't trust Merv's driving, but I didn't think it would go that far.'

'Nothing to do with Merv. What she didn't trust was Rev. Pot's ability to get out of Wales by himself. It was a hard choice, you needing care and attention and all, but I promised I'd keep a close watch on you and signal if there was any trouble.'

'Signal?'

'Yeah. Take a look out the window.'

Joe pushed himself upright and peered through the rear window.

'You're right. I am sleeping,' he said.

Fifty or sixty feet behind the coach was the old Morris. Behind the wheel he saw the familiar face of Rev. Pot, driving with the same air of intense concentration he brought to conducting. Alongside him was Mirabelle, clutching an open map like a holy relic.

'Message from Nye Garage via Merv,' said Beryl. 'He says next time you come, pay him what you think it's worth.'

Joe blinked back a tear.

'What did I tell you?' he said. 'Country that Paul Robeson loved has to have a great heart.'

'Can't recall you telling me that, but you may be right. Talking about singing, though, message from Glyn Matthias too. He says—I think I got it right—he says he hopes your voice mends soon and next time you come, he expects to hear you singing like one of the three birds of Rhiannon, and maybe the sun this time, not the sadness. That make sense?'

'Yeah. Lots of sense,' said Joe.

From the front of the coach, Merv's voice boomed out, 'Ladies and gentlemen, get your passports ready, we are now approaching England. Next comfort stop, you'll be peeing on English soil. You people sang when we crossed the other way. Can't you raise a song now we're heading back home?'

Through Joe's mind, and he guessed through the minds of most of the choristers, scrolled a list of homecoming songs, most of them painfully patriotic or tearfully sentimental. He didn't fancy either. In particular, he didn't fancy anything tinged with sadness. A man had to face up to it, but that didn't mean he had to let it take over his soul.

Then Beryl, standing over him looking through the rear window at the odd couple in the pursuing Morris, began to sing softly, *'My old man said, "Follow the van, don't dilly dally on the way."'*

Someone else joined in.

'Off went the cart with the home packed in it. I walked behind with my old cock linnet.'

And now more and more voices were raised.

'But I dillied and dallied, dallied and dillied, lost the van and don't know where to roam.'

And finally Joe cleared his throat and added his still croaky baritone.

'You can't trust the specials like the old-time coppers.'

And though he was looking into Beryl's eyes and returning her broad fond smile and wondering whether they were engaged or not, and though the coach was crossing the border back into good old safe and prosaic England, he realized that what he had seen and heard and experienced in Wales had opened a door in his soul, the door that Ursell talked about and Dai Bard declaimed about, and he doubted if all his weight and strength could ever wholly shut it again.

'And I can't find my way home.'